The
Unquiet Dead

The Unquiet Dead

Gay Longworth

WHEELER
WINDSOR
PARAGON

This Large Print edition is published by Wheeler Publishing, Waterville, Maine USA and by BBC Audiobooks, Ltd, Bath, England.

Published in 2005 in the U.S. by arrangement with St. Martin's Press, LLC.

Published in 2005 in the U.K. by arrangement with HarperCollins Publishers Ltd.

U.S. Hardcover 1-58724-991-X (Compass)
U.K. Hardcover 1-4056-1051-4 (Windsor Large Print)
U.K. Softcover 1-4056-2042-0 (Paragon Large Print)

The text of this Large Print edition is unabridged.
Other aspects of the book may vary from the original edition.

Set in 16 pt. Plantin by Liana M. Walker.

Printed in the United States on permanent paper.

British Library Cataloguing-in-Publication Data available

Library of Congress Cataloging-in-Publication Data

Longworth, Gay.
    The unquiet dead / by Gay Longworth.
      p. cm.
    ISBN 1-58724-991-X (lg. print : hc : alk. paper)
    1. Police — England — London — Fiction. 2. London (England) — Fiction. 3. Policewomen — Fiction. 4. Exorcism — Fiction. 5. Clergy — Fiction. 6. Large type books. I. Title.
PR6112.O54U57 2005
823′.92—dc22   2005005470

To Alicia and Matt Suminski

Acknowledgments

Father Ian Hazelwood dedicated his life to the church. He was a vicar, a father, a husband and an honourable man whose effect on me was simply this — I have strived to be a little better than I was before we met. He inspired this book, but sadly never read it. He died before I finished it. Father Ian, I hope you approve. Wherever you are.

When I was nine months pregnant, Shaun Stewart showed me around the Marshall Street Baths. Magnificent even in their decay. Although I changed a few details for the sake of the story, I hope the essence of the place remains. The number of marble slabs on the pool floor is certainly accurate. Shaun counted them for me himself. Thank you for your input and expertise. I gather the developers are indeed circling and soon the old public baths will be flats and offices — but if you listen very carefully you may still be able to hear those Edwardian men and women soaping up for a shilling a time. I could.

Our daughter was born after one long struggle, the book after another. I could not have coped with either without the help of Katherine Peens and Micky Fullilove. If our daughter could speak, she would thank you too. Luckily Micky's husband is a former DI and still a biker, so thanks, Dave, for insight into the minds of policemen and petrol heads.

The other person I would like to mention is Chief Inspector Sarah Francis of Norwich police station. A real-life Jessie Driver. Except with kids and a promotion. Thank you for your time and for sharing your experiences. I salute you.

For guidance of a more spiritual nature, thanks to Jessica Adams and Amaryllis Fraser.

I appreciate those layman editors out there who gave me invaluable guidance. My sister Stephanie, my husband Adam and Anne Marie Mackay and fellow writer Imogen Edwards-Jones. To the pros, I prostrate myself humbly at your feet. Julia Wisdom and Anne O'Brien at HarperCollins, you are masters of the art. As always to my agent Stephanie Cabot, MD of William Morris Agency, I raise a glass. I know exactly how she does it. Love and wine, in equal measures. Only for you would I wear a carpet and join the family von Trapp.

In New York, busy in the Flatiron building, with a baby at home, is Kelley Ragland, editor at St Martin's Press. I doff my cap with respect and appreciation to you and Manie Baron at the WMA for allowing Jessie Driver to ride out across American soil once more.

As always I would like to thank my mother, for so many things. Finding herself in the rat-infested bowels of Marshall Street Baths and immediately thinking of me, is just one of them. On behalf of Stephanie and Greg Pavlik, Jokey and Tom Mollo, myself and Adam Spiegel, congratulations, Lord Mayor of Westminster. We are immensely proud of everything you have achieved.

To my sister Jokey, I love you for loving our daughter so much. We miss you, sand girl.

Adam, it has been quite a year. We are through it, better and stronger. I love you. Still, hugely, more.

And finally . . . a quiet dedication to my father. Because you gave me your word. I love you.

Prologue

Jessie sensed the impact before she heard it. It was the smell. The smell of hot steel, of friction, of fear. Or was it even before the smell, before she'd seen the train's headlights emerge from the gloom or heard its lugubrious rattle? She was deep underground at Oxford Circus, waiting for the Bakerloo line that would take her to Paddington and the 11.15 train to Heathrow. As she made her way to the point of impact, she knew from the look on the passengers' faces that she wasn't going to make that train and she wasn't going to be there to welcome her brother home from Africa.

A young woman, about Jessie's age, was lying on the track facing up; her eyes were open and a thin trickle of blood seeped out of the corner of her mouth. She was alive. Jessie sent for the paramedics, cleared the shocked onlookers and summoned the underground staff to shut down the power and form a barrier before she jumped down on to the track. It wasn't until she was on the filthy cement floor that she saw what she could not have seen from the height of the platform. The woman stared up at her, but the lower portion of her body was facing down. As the train had rolled her along the track, she'd been twisted around like dough.

'It's okay,' said the woman. 'I'm okay. It doesn't hurt.'

Jessie couldn't move for a moment. Was it a miracle or diabolical that the woman was still alive?

'The doctors are coming,' said Jessie finally, knowing it was futile. There was nothing anyone could do.

'I'm okay,' the woman said again. 'It doesn't hurt.'

'My name is Jessie Driver, I'm a detective with the CID. Can you tell me your name?'

'Harriet.' A blood bubble burst on her lips. Jessie wiped it away.

'Harriet, I'm not a doctor, but I think you are in serious trouble. Is there anyone I can call for you, anyone you'd like to talk to?'

Harriet closed her eyes.

'Stay with me,' said Jessie. 'The paramedics are here.'

It didn't take very long for the paramedic team to confirm what Jessie already knew. The woman lying misshapen at her feet was living on borrowed time. Her spine had twisted around itself, snapping in two. That was why there was no pain; she had no feeling at all. Her midriff had been wrung out, her insides with it.

'The weight of the train is keeping her alive, containing the damage,' said the paramedic. 'As soon as we move the train, the sudden haemorrhage from her ruptured organs will cause a massive heart attack. She is going to die. She should be dead already. She's a jumper, right?'

'I don't know,' said Jessie.

The paramedic glanced down at the tracks. 'Well, tell her to make her peace, she hasn't got very long.'

Harriet had long dark hair and startling blue eyes, but the pressure was building inside her and the whites of her eyes were now flecked with blood. Jessie stroked her hair as she delivered the paramedic's message. Jessie didn't know what response she was expecting, but it certainly wasn't a smile.

'I feel so calm.'

It's shock, Jessie wanted to say, but all she could do was smile back.

'I'm sorry to have caused so much trouble.'

'Let me call someone — your parents?'

'No.'

Something terrible had happened to this woman, something that made jettisoning herself off a platform into the path of a train easier than stepping back. Something, or someone.

'I understand,' said Jessie. 'It's okay, we don't have to call anyone.'

'I thought I'd be more afraid,' she said. 'I'm not afraid any more.'

Definitely shock, thought Jessie, struggling to find suitable words.

'Please,' said the girl who was dead already. 'I need your help.'

'Anything.'

'In my bag . . . letter . . .' She paused, her breathing was getting more laboured. 'Destroy it.'

'Are you sure?'

'It was an accident . . . I fell. Please. Tell. Them. I. Fell.'

'I . . .' Jessie sat back on her heels. It

sounded so pathetic in her head. I need to file a report. Paperwork. Take statements.

'Don't hurt them . . .' She was mumbling some of her words. 'I fell . . . The truth . . . I am calm . . . happy. Don't hurt . . . Okay, I don't hurt any more. I'm going to a much better place, it's safe and warm . . .'

'Harriet, I can't do that.'

'I'll make amends, for them,' she said, suddenly lucid. 'I've been forgiven, they need to forgive themselves.' Her eyes flickered but did not close. Jessie turned her head; she could see the bag lying a few feet away, intact. She shuddered. Unknown feet walking over her unknown grave. She looked around. In all the commotion, no one had noticed it. A dying woman's wish. Who could say for sure that she jumped? Would it really matter? To London Underground it would — better a suicide than an accident. An accident had legal implications, Health and Safety issues. They shouldn't have to take the blame.

'I'm okay,' Harriet said again, very quietly this time. 'I don't hurt any more.' Jessie squeezed her hand.

'Detective Inspector,' said a loud voice above her.

Jessie looked up quickly. 'Not now . . .'

'You can let go now. She's gone,' he said.

Jessie looked back at Harriet. 'But she just . . .' Her large eyes were fixed, her lips had parted to form the faint beginnings of a smile. If that split second had been caught by camera and not by death it would have made a beautiful photograph. The paramedic was looking quizzically at Jessie.

'Sorry, my mistake.' Jessie removed her jacket and placed it over the face of a girl called Harriet who had just died at her feet.

'It's okay now,' said Jessie quietly. 'It's over.' Death meant nothingness and nothingness couldn't hurt her any more. The pain would be absorbed by the ones left behind. That's how it worked. That was the meaning of life after death.

An officer from the transport police approached her with a cup of coffee and her leather jacket.

'Did the young lady tell you what happened?'

'Not really,' said Jessie. 'I think she was in shock.'

'She didn't tell you why she jumped?'

'You're certain she jumped then?' asked Jessie, staring into the concentric rings on the surface of her coffee.

'No. We've been through her things but didn't find a note. There may be one back at her place of residence, though it's unusual. What did she say to you?'

I'm okay. I don't hurt any more.

'Detective?'

'Sorry?'

'What did she say to you?'

Jessie handed him back the polystyrene cup and thrust her hands deep inside the pockets of her leather trousers. 'Thanks, but I'm giving up coffee for Lent.'

'Lent? Are you feeling all right, Detective Inspector?'

Jessie looked at the train, still jacked up. The body had gone. The shell. The casing. She could feel the crisp white paper that held a tormented girl's last words. But not her last wish. Finally she looked back at the policeman, his pencil poised over the pad.

'She said she fell.' A rush of wind from a neighbouring tunnel sucked at Jessie's legs as another train on another track sped off to another destination.

Chapter 1

Jessie turned into her street and saw the tell-tale desert boots sticking out from between the pillars that flanked the entrance to her flat.

'Bill!' she shouted, beginning to run. The boots retracted and moments later a tall, blond, bedraggled specimen emerged smiling through the iron gate and on to the pavement. 'I am so sorry,' she said and she hugged her brother.

'Don't tell me,' he said. 'Something came up.'

'I'm sorry, did you wait at the airport for ages? I should have got a message to you, or called the airport police —'

'Jessie, calm down, it doesn't matter.'

'I meant to be there.'

'Would you believe me if I told you I didn't even look for you in arrivals?' Bill said laughingly.

'I'd be furious, I took the fucking morning off.'

Jessie put her key in the lock.

'So, no Maggie then?'

'No, she's gone. Why? You desperate?'

'Yes, actually.'

They walked up the stairs dragging Bill's ancient canvas kitbag and a plastic carrier bag holding cartons of duty-free cigarettes. 'No stunning French female doctor to cavort with this time?'

'My colleague was a fat Scottish doctor called Rob, who, though I love, I couldn't bring myself to shag.'

'Nurses?'

'All nuns.'

Jessie winced. 'Poor Bill. Well, for a little light porn, Maggie has a late-night chat show, and I still have her number — though I fear you may not be famous enough or rich enough for her now. Then again, she might like the look of your prescription pad.'

'Bitchy.'

'Maggie taught me everything I know.' Jessie opened her front door and caught their reflections in the hall mirror. 'You are so brown,' she said, disgusted at her own pallid complexion.

Bill ran his fingers through his hair. 'Even the equator has its plus points.'

19

'I look like a ghost compared to you.'

Bill put his bag on the floor and pointed to Jessie's hair. 'You look like you've seen a ghost.'

Jessie tried to flatten it. 'Piss off! I'm growing it out and it's at a funny in-between stage.'

'You're telling me.'

Jessie took Bill to a small Italian basement restaurant that their elder brother Colin supplied wine to. As well as free wine and quick service, Jessie always got a flurry of compliments in hurried Italian that was often the perfect antidote to a bad day in CID. Today was no different once the waiters had established that Bill, six foot three and built like a rower, was family and not an overprotective boyfriend.

'So tell me everything,' said Bill after rapidly downing half a glass of red wine.

'No. You first.'

'AIDS. Death. AIDS. Poverty. AIDS. Famine and flashes of extraordinary human courage. More AIDS. Your turn.'

'Didn't you get my letter?'

'There's a glitch in the Médecins Sans Frontières' postal system — everything keeps getting stuck in Paris.'

'Well, I had my first big case. I made some good decisions and caught the guy, but I made some bad decisions too. Guess what everyone remembers?'

'Would these bad decisions have anything to do with a well-known singer who happened to be married to the first victim?'

Jessie frowned.

'Even in the wilds of the Sudan you can get your hands on a copy of a tabloid or two.'

Jessie bowed her head and groaned. 'I can't think about it, it's too embarrassing.'

'You don't see him any more, then?'

A waiter arrived with warm bread and olive oil, and Bill was temporarily side-tracked. Jessie watched him eat. P. J. Dean had been like a destructive whirlwind; he'd spun her around and sent her flying off course. He believed they had a bond. A detective and a pop star. Not very likely. She'd made her mind up that it was a bad idea for all concerned. And most of the time she was sure she'd done the right thing.

'So do you?' asked Bill, tearing apart another piece of bread.

'I try not to.'

'What does that mean, Jess?'

'It means I try not to.'

Brother and sister eyed one another knowingly. Bill backed down first.

'And how's work?'

'Good. Things are better with the other DI, Mark Ward. We finally seem to have found a common ground.' That common ground was a crypt in Woolwich cemetery where together they had watched a man bleed to death, but she wasn't ready to tell her brother that story. 'My boss is leaving. His replacement is a woman. Though I admire and like Jones enormously, I have to admit it will be a nice break to have another woman around. Better still, one who is higher ranking than me.'

'It'll take the heat off you, you mean?'

'More than that, I'll have someone on side, someone who understands what it's like to be surrounded by a bunch of pricks.'

'Literally or metaphorically?'

'Both.'

'Jessie, first signs of bitchiness and now what's this? A whiff of bitterness in the air and you cut all your hair off. Please don't become some wizened old man-hater, it's so last century.'

'I told you, I'm growing it out.' Jessie poured out more wine. They were halfway down the bottle and hadn't even looked at the menu. 'I'm not a man-hater, but it's hard, they are pricks . . . well, some of them. If they were more like my brothers —'

'A commitment-phobe who likes to play god in a very small pond, be hero-worshipped by people who have no alternative and has the occasional disturbing fantasy about a nun? I hope not.'

'One nun in particular?'

'A flock of nuns.'

Jessie nodded. 'I think we should order.'

Bill refilled their glasses, smiling conspiratorially. 'You don't really have to go back to work, do you?'

'Yes.'

'But I haven't seen you for eight months. I'm not here for very long and what's the point of being the youngest DI in the Force if you can't play hooky occasionally?'

Jessie thought about this for a second. It was true, she didn't really have that much on, she was owed masses of holiday time and many's the time she'd covered for DI Mark Ward while he was in the pub. 'I suppose I could call Mark and ask him to cover for me . . .'

'Excellent. More wine.'

The following morning Jessie walked to

work. She didn't trust herself on the bike, suspecting that she might still be over the limit. She and Bill had ordered their food finally, but not until they had finished the first bottle and drunk most of the second. They did not stop talking until after midnight. Even then they had only touched the surface. Bill had been working for MSF for six years, in places no one else would brave; he'd witnessed death on such a massive scale from disease, starvation and massacre, that the idea of a nice clean general practice somewhere in England coping with endless complaints of a sore throat and chesty cough was absurd to him. He'd been known to drive sick children through areas occupied and controlled by armed tribes with no scruples, just to see them safely to an international hospital. He'd put his life on the line time and time again, even though he knew he could only ever make a tiny difference, for the problems in Africa were so vast. It made what Jessie did seem very small. She would allocate months of her time and enormous sums of taxpayers' money to bring one person to trial, and even then it was not certain they would end up behind bars, or that bars were indeed the answer. Meanwhile thousands were dying and the culpable — corrupt leaders, multinationals, the 'first' world — would never pay. If there really was good and evil in this world, she knew her brother was all good. Even if he did fantasise about nuns.

Jessie plugged in the week's security code on the entrance door to the station and went in. PC Niaz Ahmet was waiting for her. Since Jessie had seconded him to West End Central CID during the P. J. Dean case, she had rarely seen anything but a sanguine expression on his face. Today he looked worried. Very worried.

'What is it, Niaz?'

'A sixteen-year-old girl has disappeared. Her mother has telephoned asking for you in person.'

'Me? I don't deal with missing people until . . .' She stopped herself. 'How long has she been missing?'

'Eighteen hours.'

'That's not long enough.'

'She is Anna Maria Klein. The daughter of Sarah Klein.'

'The stage actress?'

Niaz nodded, adding: 'And a close personal friend of P. J. Dean.'

'Oh God.' Jessie dropped her chin on to her chest. 'Not again. Every deranged celebrity with a security problem has been asking for me by name, I can't deal with these people any more. They're all insane.'

Niaz wobbled his head. 'I think this is serious. She went out to meet a friend for coffee in Soho and didn't come back. She hasn't phoned and she didn't take anything with her.'

'Had there been a row?'

'No.'

'Boyfriend troubles?'

'No boyfriend.'

'Well, not one that the mother knew about, anyway.' Niaz and Jessie had arrived at their floor. 'Tell me Ms Klein isn't here.'

Niaz lowered his crescent-shaped eyelids.

'Good grief!' said Jessie. 'I'm not feeling up to this so early in the morning.'

'Another hangover?' asked Niaz.

'Don't say it like that. Right, as punishment you can go and get me a large coffee from the canteen.'

'Didn't you say you were giving it up for Lent?'

'I was. Then I remembered, I don't believe in Lent. Thank God. Ask them to make it strong, sweet and milky, and tell them I'll pay them later.'

'You said that yesterday.'

Jessie growled.

'Yes, ma'am.'

Tucking a rogue piece of hair behind her ear, Jessie put on her mental body armour and pushed open the double doors that led to the Criminal Investigation Department. Someone had put up a new sign on the notice board. It read: YOU CAN ALWAYS GET ANOTHER WIFE. YOU ONLY GET ONCE CHANCE IN CID. Jessie sailed past it. It wasn't the worst she'd seen. Or the last.

She took a surreptitious peek through the window of her office door and saw two overly dressed, heavily made-up, middle-aged women sitting in front of her desk. Ageing actresses were a sight for sore eyes, and that morning she had very sore eyes. The two women were talking animatedly; one of them Jessie did not know, but she recognised Sarah Klein immediately. Over the years Jessie had seen her in numerous TV dramas and stage plays. But not so many recently.

As she pushed open the door she took in Ms Klein's appearance — the underwired bra, the unladdered stockings, the matching shoes and handbag, the repeatedly applied lipstick — and wondered how long it had taken her to dress that morning. Too long, Jessie decided, if you thought your daughter was missing.

'Good morning,' she said, interrupting the women.

'Jessie Driver!' exclaimed Sarah Klein, standing up. 'P.J. said you'd —'

Jessie stuck out her hand. 'Detective Inspector Driver,' she cut in, trying to get her point across without sounding prim. 'You must be Sarah Klein.'

'Well of course I am. P.J. said you'd —'

Jessie interrupted her again; she didn't want to hear his name for a third time. 'Please, let's deal with the problem in hand. My colleague tells me that you think your daughter is missing.'

'I know she is missing! Don't you give me that policeman crap as well. I came directly to you so that I wouldn't have to go through the usual hoops.'

'The usual hoops are there because, thankfully, most "disappearances" are nothing more sinister than simple misunderstandings.'

'She is missing, I tell you. Her phone is switched off — she never switches her phone off, she even keeps it on during the movies!'

How considerate, thought Jessie.

'P.J. is a very good friend of mine. Call him, if you don't believe me.'

'Ms Klein, it isn't a question of believing you; it's a question of dealing with this in an appropriate manner. What did she say to you when she left?'

'Bye, Mummy, I love you.' Sarah Klein spoke in a far-away, slightly childish voice. 'I remember it specifically because it was so odd.'

'It was odd that she told you she loved you?'

'No,' she replied defensively. 'It was odd because she wouldn't normally say it when she was popping out for coffee. She also told me what time she'd be back. Usually she's very vague about that sort of thing, always changing her plans, but yesterday she said she'd be back at five because there was something she wanted to watch on TV.'

'So she changed her plans often, you say?'

'Yes, but . . .' Ms Klein frowned. Jessie stared as the actress's perfectly arched brows fought against the effects of Botox. 'She would have phoned. She always phones — maybe not immediately, but she'd never stay out all night without calling me. And even if she did, she'd have phoned me by now.'

'It's only ten in the morning. Is it possible that she decided to go out with her friends, met someone and . . .' How to put this delicately? '. . . is still with them?'

'Absolutely not.' The actress slammed her hands down on the armrests for maximum effect. 'There is no way Anna Maria would go out without coming home to change first.'

There was a knock on the door and Niaz came in with a steaming mug of coffee. Jessie inhaled the aroma. Canteen coffee had never smelled so good. But she didn't get to taste it, or thank him, because Mark Ward suddenly burst through Jessie's door, slamming into Niaz and causing the coffee to spill. Her fellow DI swore under his breath.

'Sorry,' he said, backing out of the room. 'Didn't know you had company.'

Sarah Klein stood up. So royalty rises, thought Jessie, though not for women and not for people of ethnic origin. 'Don't worry,' she said, extending her hand. 'Sarah Klein.'

Ward was looking worried.

'What is it, Mark?'

'Don't worry, it can wait,' he said, retreating to the corridor with a final frantic glance at Jessie.

Jessie stood. 'Niaz, please stay with Ms Klein. Take a statement, a detailed description of what Anna Maria was wearing, her mobile number, the names of her friends and where and when she was planning to meet them. Then, Ms Klein, I suggest you go home and wait. Hopefully, Anna Maria will be back by the end of the day. If not, we'll have everything in place to act.'

'That isn't enough,' exclaimed Sarah Klein.

'With all of that we can start looking at CCTV footage. We'll be able to map her movements quite easily, provided you can give us that information.'

'And then you'll get the press involved?'

'Probably,' said Jessie, curious. 'Why do you ask?'

'It's the quickest way to get maximum coverage — for sightings and things. I hate the press myself, but I'll do whatever I have to do, for Anna Maria.'

What was it with these people? 'Let's start with the information I've requested. We'll go from there.'

'She has blonde hair and was wearing a Dolce and Gabbana dress —'

'Please,' said Jessie, taking the dripping coffee mug from Niaz. 'Tell PC Ahmet.'

Sarah Klein looked briefly at Niaz, but she was a good actress and disguised her disappointment well.

As Jessie had suspected, Mark Ward was waiting for her in the hall. She mimicked strangulation as the door closed behind her. 'I bet you a fiver the daughter has legged it,' she whispered. 'Is everything all right?'

'I don't know, how did that go?'

'A couple of ageing actresses first thing in the morning, how do you think?'

'Shit,' said Mark.

'Tell me she isn't appearing in a play that's dying a death. Can you believe how far these people will go to get good box-office receipts?'

'But that's just it —' Mark stopped but Jessie had already felt the draught. Her office door was open. She turned. Sarah Klein's clone was looking at her with a very unnerving expression on her face. Clearly she'd heard what Jessie had said. Her only option was to bluff it. But before she'd even managed to force her mouth into a smile, or utter polite platitudes, the angry woman spoke.

'That was very unimpressive.'

'I'm sorry if you think that, but in my experience —'

Mark pushed the back of his shoe into Jessie's heel. She ignored his warning. She'd had enough of the arrogance of vaguely famous people, assuming they were more important than everyone else and therefore deserving of special treatment.

'— these sort of situations —'

'How can you possibly judge the situation when you didn't ask the right questions?'

'If you have anything to add, please go ahead.'

Mark pushed her aside and stepped forward. 'Driver, perhaps you haven't met —'

'Careful,' protested Jessie.

'I think he is trying to tell *you* to be careful. Thank you, Mark, but I think we can handle this from here.'

Jessie looked from her colleague to the heavily made-up woman and back again.

'Handle what?' asked Jessie.

'That will be all, Mark. Thank you,' she said imperiously. To Jessie's astonishment, Mark nodded curtly and left. A little hole opened up beneath her feet and she looked longingly into it. But the ground was solid;

she wasn't going anywhere.

'DCI Moore,' said Jessie, offering her hand. 'I don't believe we've properly met.

'No. Seems you were unavailable to attend my induction yesterday afternoon. DI Ward said you were . . .' she paused looking Jessie up and down, 'indisposed.'

Bollocks was the only word that sprung to Jessie's mind. Bollocks. Bollocks. Bollocks.

'I wouldn't have got where I am if I didn't know the difference between indisposed and a hangover. You, DI Driver, have a hangover. I can smell it.'

Jessie opened her mouth, then closed it again. A series of other swear words were now filling the void in her head where fabulous excuses should have been.

'I am going to give you the benefit of the doubt and assume your performance in there is down to your,' she paused again, 'indisposition. However, had I been Ms Klein's lawyer — and for all you knew I might have been just that — I would have advised her to make a formal complaint against you. Don't ever treat a victim of crime like that again.'

Getting defensive wasn't going to get her out of this. 'I apologise,' said Jessie. 'I shall take over from Niaz immediately.'

'Who is this Niaz? What's a PC in uniform doing here in CID?'

'He's been seconded to CID from Putney. He shows true promise and I'm hoping he'll take the exams.'

' "True promise" in whose judgement?'

Jessie didn't reply. She wasn't going to let DCI Moore tar Niaz with the same brush. Moore turned on her high heel and walked away, leaving Jessie reeling. What bloody induction? Where was Jones? He wasn't supposed to be leaving for another week. And why didn't Mark warn her? She kicked Mark's door open. He held up his hands as if she were wielding a gun.

'She turned up about an hour after you called in.'

'Why didn't you phone me, tell me to come back?'

'I tried to, but your mobile was switched off.'

Jessie had a vague memory of listening to some messages when she and Bill got home that evening. But by then she'd been drinking for ten hours and was in a fairly shoddy condition.

'I feel like shit.'

'You look like shit. I came to find you first thing. I didn't know she was going to hide in your office like that.'

'What was she doing there, anyway?'

'I don't know. Maybe you share a common hobby.'

Hungover and slow on the uptake, Jessie just frowned.

'Star-fucking,' said Mark gleefully.

'I'm not going to dignify that with a response,' she said through gritted teeth.

'Only because you can't.'

'What is it, fuck on Jessie day? And what the hell does "indisposed" mean?'

'I don't know.'

'You told that overly made-up harridan that I was indisposed.'

Mark's eyes suddenly widened and he appeared to swell. Jessie didn't dare turn around.

'Mark,' said the cool voice of DCI Moore over Jessie's left shoulder, 'I was wondering if you would give me a tour of the premises. Jones isn't going to be able to make it in again today.'

'Yes, ma'am.' The words exploded out of him on his pent-up breath.

'Thank you.' Jessie heard the heels click away from her; she must have been tiptoeing earlier. The clicking stopped. Jessie braced herself. 'Incidentally, Driver, you should think of doing something about your hair.' Jessie turned reluctantly, imagining what it would feel like to turn into a pillar of salt. 'You may not be in uniform, but you still represent the police force. Most importantly, you reflect your superiors and that means more than getting out of bed in the morning and hoping for the best.'

Again, the doors closed behind her. She turned to Mark. 'I'm fucked.'

He shrugged.

She could have killed him.

Bill and Jessie sat on her sofa, their feet up on the coffee table, tea in hand. Neither her day nor her hangover had improved. Bill had made comforting noises when she finally fell through the door, but Jessie knew he didn't really understand. He wasn't a locker-room sort of man, whereas Jessie lived in one.

'So what have you been doing all day, while I've been having my balls busted?'

'Eating crap food and watching videos. *Malcolm X*, excellent film. I'd never got round to —'

She lifted the remote control and increased the volume. 'Shh, this is it.'

'Our main story tonight,' said the newsreader. 'Anna Maria Klein, the only child of actress Sarah Klein, is missing.

The schoolgirl was last seen in London's red-light district —'

'She won't like that,' interrupted Jessie.

'— where she was supposed to be meeting friends at a coffee shop. Amanda Hornby is there now. Amanda, what can you tell us?'

'She's foxy,' said Bill. Jessie hit him.

'Good evening. Well, the police are telling us very little at the moment. Anna Maria was reported missing by her mother this morning at West End Central police station. After initially being told to wait and see by one senior officer, the panicked mother was finally taken seriously late this afternoon.'

'Why the change in approach?'

'Sarah Klein apparently spent the day calling her daughter's friends, until she found who Anna Maria was supposed to be meeting. The friends then confirmed that Anna Maria had never arrived at the coffee shop just behind me.'

'And this had them worried?'

'No. They say that Anna Maria often changed her plans.'

'See? Flaky,' said Jessie.

'But time is very much of the essence in situations like these,' redirected the newsreader.

'That's right. Every second counts, and it's true many hours were lost before an investigation into Anna Maria's whereabouts got underway. Now the teenager is facing her second night away from home and all her mother can do is hope for her safe return. This is Amanda Hornby, Soho, in London, for Channel Five News.'

Jessie quietly shook her head.

'It sounds serious,' said Bill.

'Wait for the CCTV footage and then tell me if you think she's been abducted. They'll show it at the end of the bulletin, that way they keep the viewers glued.'

'This cynicism doesn't suit you, Jessie.'

'It isn't cynicism,' she said, looking at her brother. 'It's instinct. And if I'm wrong, Moore will have my guts for garters.'

The newsreader went on until it was time to go to a break. After the ads, as Jessie had predicted, they showed the CCTV clip. Jessie had rounded up the film from all the public cameras around Soho that covered the coffee shop and its various approaches. She had also checked the ones around the actress's house. If suspicious circumstances were ever confirmed, Jessie's next step would be to gain access to the non-public CCTV footage: the cameras outside local shops, garages and offices. Jessie didn't think it would come to that. By five that afternoon, after hours spent scanning the footage frame by frame, Anna Maria had been caught on film. The cab she had taken from her mother's house had dropped her at the beginning of Carnaby Street. She had walked through the throng to the corner of Poland Street and Broadwick Street. There, directly under the eye of a surveillance camera, Anna Maria had waited for some time before moving off towards Marshall Street. Once out of range of the camera, she simply disappeared.

Bill and Jessie watched the actress's daughter, stationary amidst the rushing crowd. She was noticeable by her stillness and her Dolce & Gabbana fur-trimmed coat and high-heeled boots.

'Obviously she's waiting for someone. Perhaps she misunderstood the plan with her friends?' said Bill.

'If she was waiting for someone she'd be looking around, glancing at her watch, maybe making a call to see where her friends are. She's doing none of those things; she's just standing there. And look at the bag.'

'It's big,' said Bill.

'Isn't it?'

'But that's fashionable.'

'Bill, you've been in the back of beyond for months, how do you know what is fashionable?'

Bill grinned. 'Didn't I tell you about the air hostess on the flight back?'

'You swapped fashion tips with an air hostess?'

'Something like that.'

'Remind me not to let you anywhere near my friends.'

'You'll have to if you're going to be burning the midnight oil on this case.'

'Bill, there isn't a case, unless it's a prosecution for wasting police time. I offer you my final piece of evidence.' She passed him a copy of the previous day's *Evening Standard*. 'You find me a programme at five o'clock that a sixteen-year-old girl would leave her friends for to return home and watch. There isn't one. Anna Maria Klein is up to something, and it's possible her mother is directing the show.'

'I don't know, Jess, she looked distraught on the news piece I saw.'

'She's an actress. It's her job to convince people.'

Chapter 2

Jessie woke early to wash her hair. Determined to rectify the situation with DCI Moore, she dressed with her new boss in mind. She wouldn't stretch to a skirt; not just because they made chasing criminals very hard, but because the piss-take she'd receive would be extreme. More extreme than normal. Instead, she opted for her black trouser suit, hoping it would endear her to the woman. If looking good was important to her new boss, well, this suit made Jessie look good, even if she said so herself. DCI Moore was obviously a hard nut. Fair enough, you had to be hard to succeed in this game. Jessie would dance to her tune. The line of command was more important than personality.

Clipping her hair off her face with slides, she put on enough make-up so that a woman would notice but a man wouldn't. If Anna Maria hadn't reappeared from wherever she was holed up, there was the possibility Jessie would be in front of the camera before the day was out. But when she saw herself in the hall mirror she nearly tore it all off. Dressing like this went against her self-imposed laws of survival. Rule number one: camouflage. You can't attack what you can't see.

Bill appeared from his bedroom in his boxer shorts, smiled at her sleepily and went to the bathroom. She envied him his fitness. The more she progressed in the police force, the more sedentary her life was becoming. She made a promise to herself that she would run home from work at the end of the day and went into the spare room to fetch her kit.

'Jesus, Bill, you should think of opening a window occasionally,' shouted Jessie. 'It stinks in here.'

'Sorry,' replied a voice as the loo flushed. 'Give me a second and I'll buy you breakfast.'

Jessie glanced at her watch as Bill entered the room.

'Come on, just a quick fry-up round the corner. It's still early.'

'Don't you want a lie-in?'

'This is a lie-in. I'm used to getting up at five.'

'Well, all right — but we'd better make it quick.'

Jessie walked down the deserted hallway of the CID unit and felt very uneasy. She sat at her desk and listened to the sound of traffic from the street below. No doors opened and closed, no radios crackled, no phones rang, so she got up again and went upstairs to Jones' recently vacated office. A group of her fellow officers were coming out of his room; perhaps she was being paranoid, but they appeared to be giving each other knowing looks.

'What's up, Fry?' she asked one of the passing detective constables.

'Best you ask the new boss,' he muttered before shouting to another group of officers about meeting them in the canteen. When Jessie got to the office door she saw Mark sitting at the former DCI's desk. He was looking out of the window, which offered a remarkable view across Mayfair to Hyde Park. In the evenings it filled with the rarely seen light of the setting sun. Jones had always had the blinds down, but Moore obviously had other decorating plans.

'Hi, Mark, you been promoted after all?'

'No,' said a now familiar voice. DCI

Moore walked into the office from the secretary's side room.

'Morning, ma'am. Have I missed something?'

'Yes,' she said.

Okay, so the woman was a hard nut and didn't mince her words. All good qualities in a commanding officer, Jessie told herself. 'What's going on?' she continued.

'Don't you think, given the circumstances, it would have been wise to get in early?'

It was only eight thirty, but Jessie didn't think it 'wise' to argue.

'Sorry.'

'I've spoken to you twice, Driver, and twice you've had to apologise. Is this going to be a running theme with you?'

'No,' said Jessie, stiffening.

'Good. DI Ward has made some rather interesting discoveries regarding the Klein case. Mark, although it's a waste of your time, would you mind telling DI Driver what you told everyone this morning?'

He tried to look humble, he even tried to look sympathetic, but neither look could hide the way his body inflated slightly. The man was enjoying this more than he should. Jessie saw months of team-building slip away from her and wondered if he had really tried as hard as he claimed to track her down. Even if her mobile didn't have any reception, she had a pager and he hadn't called that.

'Anna Maria Klein has form,' said Mark.

'At her age?'

'At her age an official warning is as close to form as you can get,' said Mark indignantly.

'I'm sorry you didn't look into this yesterday,' said Moore sternly.

Jessie wasn't going to apologise again. 'What was it for?' she asked Mark.

'Possession.'

'Dope?'

'That doesn't lessen the charge,' said Moore. 'Buying any kind of drug at fifteen is a serious concern.'

'I don't dispute that, but there are often extenuating circumstances. Buying it once to show off to your friends about how "showbiz" you are is not the same as mugging pensioners to get a crack fix.'

'Do you know Dufour's Place?' asked Moore, ignoring Jessie's observation.

'Yes, it's a cul-de-sac at the back of Marshall Street, it doesn't go anywhere.'

'It may not go anywhere, Driver, but it houses rather a historic building, as Mark has been explaining to us all this morning.'

Jessie looked to Mark for back-up and was saddened when she saw that he was busy with the papers on his knee. She waited. He didn't look up.

'I presume you're referring to the Marshall Street Baths. I believe it was built in the twenties as a communal bath house, and was still in use up to the end of the nineties as a public swimming pool. Then Health and Safety closed it down. The City of Westminster has been trying to work out what to do with it ever since. It's a listed building —'

'Used by addicts and dealers,' said Mark, cutting Jessie short.

'I thought the drug unit had cleared up that problem?'

'Drugs are a recurring problem,' said Moore, sitting on the edge of Jones' old desk.

'Normally the baths are patrolled and checked by a caretaker called —' Mark checked his pad — 'Don Firth. But he's been off sick for three weeks.'

'We have reliable information that the addicts are back,' said DCI Moore.

This was all getting a little chummy for Jessie's liking. 'So what are you thinking, Mark?'

'Anna Maria makes a prearranged rendezvous with her new dealer. He doesn't show, so she goes to Marshall Street Baths where she knows she can score.'

'It's all chained up,' said Jessie disagreeing.

'If the addicts and dealers can get in, so can anyone.'

Jessie didn't think so, not in those heels.

'We think something happened to her inside the building,' said Moore.

'I see,' said Jessie. And she did. 'What do you want me to do?' she asked. Knowing the answer. It was in those knowing looks.

'Nothing. It's DI Ward's case. It's a high-profile assignment, Driver, so it's probably better handled by Mark until last year's debacle is forgotten about.' Jessie tried to remain passive. 'Aren't you pleased? You didn't seem very interested in it yesterday.'

She wasn't pleased. Being uninterested and being uninvolved are two different things. She'd messed it up with Moore, she admitted, and it was her own fault, but she couldn't understand why Mark was so happy to put the boot in. Just in case she was being paranoid, she tried a final litmus test. Principles of reason.

'Ma'am, there was nothing in Anna Maria's body language to indicate that she was waiting for anyone,' said Jessie. 'The poor creatures in Marshall Street Baths aren't going to attack anyone. They're there because they've got the money, they've scored, and the only thing they can think about is the fix, which once administered renders them impotent.'

'That does not apply to the dealers,' contradicted Mark. 'And Anna Maria stood out like a sore thumb.'

'Exactly. You don't buy drugs in broad daylight in a fake-fur coat and six-inch heels.'

'You didn't see what she was wearing when she got busted last time,' Moore interjected.

Jessie knew when she was outnumbered. 'So what are you going to do?'

'Search Marshall Street Baths,' said Moore. 'As soon as possible.'

'And you really expect to find her in there?'

This question was followed by an exchange of glances between Ward and Moore. 'We just hope it's not too late and she's still alive.'

They'd failed the test. She wasn't being paranoid.

A thousand arguments and counter-arguments revolved around Jessie's head as she returned to her office. *We* think something happened to her? *We* hope she's still alive? *We?* Moore had only been in the building twenty-four hours and already they were a 'we'. Where the hell was Jones? Surely he wouldn't leave her like this, surely he'd have given her a heads up, some warning that DCI Moore was one of those women who pulled the ladder up behind them. Obviously Jessie wasn't going to appreciate Moore's legs folded provocatively over her desk, so of course Mark should get the case. It stood to reason, thought Jessie as she unconsciously pulled the slides out of her hair and let her fringe fall across her eyes. She would have been willing to dance to Moore's tune, but not if she was the only one dancing. Jessie slumped into her chair, deflated and a little scared. Jones had made the differences between Mark and herself work. Under his guidance, Ward and Driver were quite a good balancing act. Not good cop, bad cop, but old cop, new cop. With Moore and Ward in bed together, it would turn what had been complementary back to being contrary. A horrendous thought passed through Jessie's head. Mark and Moore in bed together, actually in bed together.

'If that happens, I'm putting myself in for a transfer,' she said aloud.

'If what happens?'

Jessie looked up. Mark had pushed the door open with his foot. He was holding a box of files.

'Gee, thanks for the support back there, Mark.'

'What did you want me to do, climb up on the gallows next to you?'

'No. Just act like a reasonable human being and take your nose out of Moore's arse.'

'Oh dear, are you a little worried because you're not the teacher's pet any more.'

'Mark, listen to yourself.'

'You'll put yourself in for a transfer if *what* happens?'

She tried to defuse the tension by smiling. 'Don't get all excited, I'm not going anywhere.'

But Mark didn't want it defusing. 'If what happens?'

'If you find Anna Maria's body in Marshall Street Baths,' she replied coolly.

'Would you be willing to make that into an official wager?'

'What is wrong with you? You've been bolshie for days,' said Jessie.

'It isn't rocket science. If we find her body at the baths, you get your arse transferred out of here.'

'And if you don't?'

'Name it,' he said confidently.

It dawned on Jessie then what Mark was doing with the box of files. They were his files, from his office. His old office: the matching shoebox across the hall from hers.

'I get your office.' He looked back over his shoulder and smiled. 'No, Mark. Your *new* office. Upstairs.'

'Who told you?'

Jessie smiled sadly to herself. Was his professional opinion of her really so low? The fact she'd seen him sitting at Jones' desk in the presence of the new DCI, the fact that he was now carrying a packing box, these giveaways were obviously not enough. 'A white rabbit,' she said. 'Okay. Deal: my transfer for your office.' Jessie stood up.

'Are you prepared to shake on it?' demanded Mark.

'Is this for real, Mark?'

Mark set the box down on Jessie's desk.

'Yes,' he said, putting out his hand. Somewhat dazed, Jessie shook his hand. As she did so, he laughed. 'And by the way,

Jessie, this isn't a transfer out of CID, this is a transfer out of West End Central. That way I can get you out of my hair once and for all.'

'Mark, you haven't got any hair.'

Mark glared at her. It was her turn to shrug. 'What? You started this. Remember that, won't you?'

Mark had officers stationed around the perimeter of the building, up on the roof and on the top storey of the Poland Street car park. The drug squad had sent a team and they now joined Mark's men outside the chained double doors of the old public baths. Everyone was wearing body armour. The handcuffs glinted against the black flak jackets, radios crackled with expectation. A SOCO team waited by their van. The street was cordoned off, which gained the attention of workers in the adjacent offices. Everyone was waiting for the whistle.

Jessie sat in the surveillance room and watched it all live via a video link. She was tuned in and ready to go. A slightly stooped man with a thick moustache inserted a key from a large selection into the padlock that held the chains in place. He turned the key and pulled; the chain slithered to the ground like a boa constrictor dropping from a tree. The team entered in twos. Jessie watched as the video camera followed them in. The first room was a foyer complete with a wood-and-glass kiosk. One of the doors hung haphazardly from its rusting hinge. The floor was laid with intricate diamond-shaped tiles worked into a graphic design, the type you see in the entrances of elegant Victorian terrace housing. Peppermint. Cobalt. Burnt sienna. Black and white. The once majestic windows were coated in grime and protected by a thick wire mesh. The camera automatically adjusted to the reduction in light. They'd gone through the portal of a time machine and entered a long-forgotten era. Victorian bath houses, where the great unwashed came to bathe en masse. The team moved further into the building. The screen went fuzzy, then a new image came into focus.

'Jesus Christ —' Jessie heard Fry mutter — 'it's a bit fucking spooky.' Jessie saw what he was looking at. The pool was enormous, a marble-tiled gaping wound in the ground, the swimming lanes neatly delineated by black tiles. What must once have been a majestic pool was now empty except for the green sludge that filled the deepest part of the deep end. The high glass-domed ceiling was mottled with moss and grime. Lines of empty spectator benches flanked each side of the drained pool; it looked like the whole structure was sitting dormant, waiting for people to return. Waiting for life.

Men in waders began to walk a slow line along the bottom of the pool until they reached the dark green water. On the count of three, they all took a step forward. Jessie grimaced as she watched the water level rise up their boots while they poked at the water with sticks. There was a shout. Jessie's heart leapt. The line stopped. Someone dragged up a sodden, rotting piece of cloth. It was a blanket. There was a tremor of excitement. It was well known among the police that bodies often came wrapped in blankets. The search increased in intensity but they reached the end having found nothing more. Mark ordered them to retrace their steps. Still nothing. Jessie watched as the camera followed them to the second, smaller pool. This pool was in much worse condition. Jessie could hear the trickle of water before the camera turned towards the sound. Water was falling from the ceiling to the floor along the wall on the left-hand side. The building must have been leaking for some considerable time, for the tiled wall was coated in a slick of green slime. A similar puddle of brackish water had accumulated in the deepest part of the swimming pool. The men in their waders jumped down into the empty pool and walked to the water's edge. The search began again.

Elsewhere the drug squad must have been having some success, because people, or shapes that resembled people, were being taken, dragged or carried out. There were ambulances waiting outside, along with specialist care workers who would deal with these sorry few. The camera ran its critical eye over them, searching for Anna Maria. They were Dickensian in their ghostliness: milk-white skin flecked with scabs and sores, stretched over malnourished features. None of them were Anna Maria. Half a mile away, Jessie shuddered. If few had the strength to walk, then none had it in them to summon the enormous amount of energy required to kill.

The team moved upwards floor by floor. There was one smallish circular room with a domed glass ceiling that became a temporary focus of attention. One of the glass panels had been smashed and was letting in the rain that had steadily begun to fall. Desperation had forced the addicts over the rooftops and through the glass panel. But not Anna Maria. Jessie was sure of it. There was one long room where many of the homeless people had been huddled together. The lino floor was badly soiled with human faeces, but what the camera zoomed in on was the rat's droppings. Jessie could only imagine the smell. Moore had been right in one respect: drug addiction was a recurring problem.

There was a sense among the search team that the raid was over. They had been to the top of the building and found it empty. None of the addicts had had the energy to mount the extra flight of stairs; they had fallen on the floor that they'd arrived at. The general level of chat increased as the team made their way back down to the lobby, but silence fell when a call summoned them to the boiler room, the beating heart of Marshall Street Baths. Jessie wasn't out of danger yet.

When the person holding the camera walked into the engine room, Jessie's spirits rose. It was like returning to modern times. The lighting was bright, the tanks were new and painted in shiny red Hammerite, the flumes looked like concertinaed silver foil, while the network of water pipes resembled Willy Wonka's chocolate factory. It was immediately obvious that the water tanks had not been tampered with. It was a closed-loop water system and the bolts had not been removed since installation; the original paint still covered the joins. No one had used this scalding water to make evidence broil away.

Jessie was beginning to envisage the view from her new office. A good sunset was like a religion to her. In fact it was a religion. She believed in the cosmos. In the structure of the world around her. In what she could see and feel. The sea. The air. The stars. The moon. The sun. And watching it set gave her a feeling of peace; she felt united with the vastness of their universe on one hand and infinitesimally small on the other. It was another remedy for a bad day in CID. Having the high office would mean that she'd no longer need to make detours to the elevated section of the Westway in order to get a look at a mammoth red sun drop below West London's skyline. Now she would have it for her delectation and delight at the end of every day.

'There is another boiler room,' said a voice over the radio. 'The original one,

58

built in 1910. They stopped using it in 1953, but you can still get down there.' Jessie snapped out of her reverie. It was the man with the moustache. The man with the bunch of keys. He must be the caretaker, thought Jessie, back from his sickbed for this sickly spectacle. 'It's one floor below. I don't go down there unless I absolutely have to.'

'Why not?' Jessie heard Mark Ward ask, but she didn't hear an answer. Everybody else had; they had all gone quiet. Jessie followed the camera out of the brightly lit boiler room and through a set of double doors. Suddenly the screen was plunged into darkness.

'Hang on,' said a voice. 'We need the generator for this bit.' For a few quiet, dark moments everybody waited. Then a hiss, and a faint glow that increased until a struggling light filled the gloom. The low-ceilinged corridor in which the men stood looked like a concrete trench. Their boots echoed like hammers as they proceeded along it. Jessie leant forward to get a better look. A small knot of anxiety had tightened in her stomach. At the end of the corridor was a set of steep concrete steps leading down to a rusty steel door that swung on its hinges. The man with the moustache tutted. 'It's supposed to be locked,' he said. Unaware, Jessie had put her hand over her mouth. The camera shook as it went unsteadily down the steps. No one was talking now. Someone pushed the door open. It was obviously heavy, because whoever was opening it was using two hands. The interior was pitch black.

'Just a minute,' said the disembodied voice of the caretaker. 'The light switch is through here.' Jessie heard the heavy sound of rattling chains and jangling keys. It was so deliberate that she wondered whether he was doing it for effect. If he was, it was working. Still no one spoke. There was no other sound except the familiar hiss of electricity.

A murky image appeared on the screen: DO NOT ENTER. The cameraman ignored the sign and went in. Jessie found herself transported to the bottom of the Atlantic. In the pale light the ancient redundant machinery reminded her of a documentary about the *Titanic*. She'd been inside the engine room via a submersible eye. She was inside it again. Placed between a grid of square wooden pillars that looked like the underside of a disused pier were four huge round boilers, each covered in a thick skin of rust. She could see the breath of the men, huddled in a pack at the edge of the room. It was cold down there. Something was making the policemen wrinkle their faces and grimace. Jessie hoped it was the musty odour of age, not death.

In front of each tank was a rill. The first two disappeared into black holes; the two furthest away from the door ended at what looked like a large manhole cover. Beyond them were brick archways that led to recesses in the back wall. Above them was a series of steel girders held up by wooden beams. Rotten wooden beams.

'Careful,' said Jessie, but the men on the screen couldn't hear her.

'What are those?' Mark asked. Jessie couldn't see what he was pointing to.

'Coal was used to fire 'em up.' The caretaker patted the belly of the boiler affectionately. 'Men would shovel it out of the coal stores to the bottom of the Archimedes screw. That way the fires were always stoked.' Four steel posts rose up from the ground. ' 'Course, the screws have long gone. Nicked and picked at over the years, like everything else. Got no respect.'

'Yes, but what are those?'

Jessie knew Mark was talking about the two open pits in the ground. It would have been the first place she would have looked, too. The man with the moustache hadn't let go of the boiler, and it occurred to Jessie that he was hanging on to it.

'The ash would fall out the bottom and be taken away by running water, along these narrow channels into the pits to cool.' The camera pointed down into the pit.

'Where do they go?'

'Hell,' said the caretaker.

'What?' said Mark and Jessie in unison.

'Smell,' he said. 'Then tell me where you think they go?'

'Sewers,' replied Jessie to the electronic image. That was why all the men were pulling faces.

'Get the torches down there!' shouted Mark.

'Careful, the ground isn't stable,' said the caretaker.

'What do you mean?'

'You don't know when the ground is going to give way and swallow you up.'

Jessie felt a chill up the back of her neck. This guy was freaking her out. She watched as four police officers pointed torches into the pupil of the pit. One of them beckoned for the boat hook and a few seconds later he fished out a shoe.

'They should all have been covered,' said the caretaker.

The old shoe was discarded. They moved on to the next pit, wading through filth. Once again the search was fruitless.

'What about the other two?'

'There's nothing down there.'

'Get those lids up,' shouted Mark. His voice trembled as much as the caretaker's, whether with excitement or fear, Jessie couldn't tell.

The elderly man was still hanging on to the boiler when the crowbar arrived. 'I wouldn't do that if I were you,' he said.

Jessie didn't want to know why not.

They prised open the first lid. The camera gave her a bird's-eye view of a dry, lead-lined pit with a grate at the bottom. It was empty. One more to go.

'Mind your heads, boys, the ceiling gets lower.'

Jessie was out of her seat and pacing. The crowbar was inserted into the dusty ground. The men heaved with exertion. A corner came up.

She heard a voice. The caretaker's voice: 'We shouldn't really be down here. They don't like it when people come down here.'

The screen started to flicker like mad.

Jessie could make out Mark as he knelt down and stuck a torch into the gap.

The screen went fuzzy. And then nothing. Jessie hit the television screen. The radio clicked.

'I can see someone!' shouted Mark.

'Alive?'

'Can't tell — they're not moving!'

There was a terrible crack.

'Move!' shouted a voice over the rumble of falling masonry. The radio clicked again and Jessie lost contact with the boiler room.

Chapter 3

For a few seconds Jessie continued to stare at the blank screen. Then she pulled on her leather jacket and ran down the stairs to the exit. Outside, the rain had stopped and the sun had come out. Her bike was parked in its normal place; it only took a minute before she was in her helmet and off the stand. It wouldn't have taken long to walk to Marshall Street, but she didn't want to waste any time. Something serious had happened in that boiler room. Why did she feel as if she had known it would?

Up ahead she saw the blue-and-white police tape spinning in the wind. The search crew were just beginning to spill out of the monolithic building as she pulled up. She dismounted, flashed her badge and joined the constable on guard.

'What happened?'

'Roof caved in. One man down. They're

bringing him out now.'

'Came from nowhere,' said a young man covered in dust.

'I knew something was up with that place,' said another. 'You could just feel it.'

Jessie followed paramedics through the labyrinth that was the underbelly of the baths until she reached the cement corridor. The clattering wheels of the medics' trolley stopped; they snapped up the undercarriage, lifted it and carried it down the flight of steeply cut steps. DCI Moore was standing at the bottom. She looked Jessie up and down but said nothing. Jessie's high-heeled boots and trouser suit looked ridiculous now.

'Is it Anna Maria?'

'Too early to say,' said the DCI. 'A beam came down on the lid, sealing it shut. Now the fucking structural engineers won't let anyone in until they've given us the all clear. Meanwhile, she may be down there, suffocating, and we've got an officer with serious concussion after being hit by a falling brick.'

'Where's Mark?'

'They're patching him up. He nearly had his arm sliced off by that lid.'

'Four people and they still couldn't lift it,' said Jessie.

'What's your point?'

'I don't know. Pulling something like this off would have taken planning, people.'

'Maybe all that was required was a victim.' DCI Moore suddenly pushed herself away from the wall. 'I can't just wait around gossiping. I'm going to talk to that bloody engineer again. Call me if anything happens.'

Jessie felt the insult keenly, but did not respond. She sat on the bottom step and waited, her bad mood deepening with every minute she sat there. How could she have been so stupid as to bet on something as unpredictable as other people's lives? The paramedics returned with their trolley. The injured officer's head and neck were encased in a thick padded yellow brace. He was fastened to the stretcher. What they couldn't strap down were his eyes, which were rolling in his head like a mad mare's. He was singing nursery rhymes. When he passed Jessie, his eyes fixed on her for a long moment that left her feeling as if she'd just seen something she shouldn't.

'Go away,' he said. Then his eyes started rolling again.

The medic made a sign and the trolley was again lifted into the air and Jessie was alone once more. Soon the damp had seeped through her trousers, leaving her skin cold and itchy. Men with measuring instruments came and went; she took no notice of them. The cold air chilled her to the bone, but she did not leave. The voice behind her made her jump.

'I was thinking Reading — lots of petty crime that creates an avalanche of paperwork and no results,' he said, walking heavy-footed down the steps towards her. 'Or maybe Birmingham, where the men really know how to treat a woman.' In the poorest areas of Birmingham rates of domestic violence were extremely high. 'And don't get on your high horse, Driver. You know they often ask for it.'

The black mist turned red. Jessie felt the fury whip through her like the wind as she turned on Mark. 'Did you ask for it when your mother abused you?' she said in a mean whisper.

'You bitch,' spat Mark.

Jessie stood. 'And when you said, "No, don't lock me in this cupboard," you really meant, "Yes, leave me here in the dark for hours."'

Mark didn't respond immediately. Finally he said, 'I've been waiting, wondering how long it would take you to throw that back at me. All that bullshit about how I could trust you — what a load of shit. Mum had no choice and you know it.'

'Trust! You don't know the meaning of the word. Moore has been here two seconds and you turn on me in an instant. And as far as choice is concerned, there is always a choice.'

He flew down the stairs towards her. 'Sanctimonious cunt.'

It was reflex. A spasmodic response to his ugly words. To his descending mass. A bent elbow, fast and hard, into the solar plexus. Mark fell forward, letting out a high-pitched wheeze, landing on his knees on the hard floor. Jessie reeled from the shock of the words, from the shock of her own actions. Mark coughed. Jessie stood motionless.

'You all right, Mark?' asked Moore from the top of the stairs.

'It's the damp,' he croaked.

Jessie bent down to his level. 'Don't ever speak to me like that again,' she whispered.

He turned to face her, a look of real hatred in his eyes. 'I'm going to see to it that you end up in fucking Dundee.'

Jessie stayed low, talking low. 'Don't count on it, Mark. That lid hasn't been moved for years. You've just stumbled across some old skeleton, that's all.'

'What are you two whispering about?' They both ignored Moore.

'I saw hair. I saw flesh. I saw clothes. You're wrong, and that's something you can't stand. Go away,' he seethed, echoing the words of another delirious man.

Jessie backed off, but only because she was so frightened of her own feelings. She had already hit him, but still she wanted to grind her nails into his face and pull the flesh off. She wanted to hurt him, destroy him.

'We've been given clearance,' said Moore as she passed. Jessie didn't care. She wanted to get out. She ran up the steps, back along the corridor, through more doors and up more steps until eventually she found herself bursting out on to the street. A dozen cameras flashed. The news was already out. Behind the barrier, men and women jabbed microphones and shouted questions. Jessie took gulps of air as the name Anna Maria filled the cul-de-sac. The dead end. There were only two ways to go. Through the pack on the street or back into Marshall Street Baths. For the first time ever, she preferred the press pack to her fellow police officers. Nothing would induce her to return to that place. She may have been at loggerheads with

Mark on many previous occasions, but nothing like that had ever happened. She had been taught unarmed combat in order to be able to disarm a person, defend herself, break up a fight. She never thought she'd use the skill to start one. A small corner of her brain had to applaud Mark for not hitting her back. He must have wanted to, but he didn't. She'd lost control. He hadn't. Now she'd have to apologise to him. Violence was never the answer. Wasn't that what she was always telling the schoolkids, the young men banged up time and time again?

'DI Driver,' called a woman's voice as she walked to the car. Jessie turned. It was Amanda Hornby, the Channel Five crime reporter. 'Have they found a body?'

'No comment.'

'They've sent SOCO in there, so they've found something.'

'No comment.'

'Come on, Detective, give me a break.'

'Leave me alone,' Jessie hissed, pushing on past her and out into the gathering crowd. Dazed, she walked on as the pavement grew thick with onlookers, some staring without shame, some shuffling past and smiling into mobile phones, trying to pretend they weren't really interested, while others stood away from the gossipmongers, watching and waiting for the body-bag. She had to elbow her way through the crowd. 'Excuse me —'

'They've found a body,' Jessie heard one woman say.

'All cut up,' spoke another.

'I'm trying to get through —'

'That poor girl,' said a third. 'Her dad buggered off, her mother's always away . . .'

An old man blocked her way. 'Will you please move!'

The man turned, tipped his hat and stepped aside.

'Thank you,' said Jessie, escaping at last.

The man nodded. 'Check the date,' said a voice. Jessie turned back, but the man in the hat had already merged into the crowd.

Jessie moved on, turning down streets in no particular order, fuelled only by a desire to lose herself. She looked down at her hand and saw that she was shaking; the fight had caused adrenaline to rush around her system. Wanting Bill, she phoned the flat but there was no answer. She cursed herself for not making an arrangement with him, she should have hired him a phone. Where would he be? Where was she, for that matter? Jessie's phone buzzed in her hand. It was a local number she didn't recognise.

'Hey, Jess, fancy a drink?'

'How did you know?' she said, smiling with relief.

'Because you're terribly bad at hiding your alcohol dependency,' he replied.

'Where are you?'

'In a phone box, outside, hang on . . .'

Jessie saw the glass door rotate towards her. Bill emerged, looking skyward.

'It's okay,' said Jessie. 'I know exactly where you are.'

'You do?'

She put her phone away and called his name. He waved, astonished. She hugged him tightly.

'That's weird,' said Bill.

'That's magic.'

He took her arm. 'I always thought you were a bit of a white witch.'

Jessie took the seat opposite her brother. Before picking up the tumbler of neat whisky, no ice, she slid Bill's packet of fags towards her, pulled one out and lit it. Bill said nothing. She inhaled deeply, took a sip of whisky, inhaled again, then stubbed out the cigarette. Bill winced. 'I've got some fairly serious codeine at the flat,' he said.

'Thanks, but I like to annihilate myself the old-fashioned way.'

'I thought you didn't smoke.'

'I don't.' The alcohol hit her empty stomach and the nicotine rushed to her head. Her heart beat a little faster for a while and then settled back down again. She finished her drink.

'Feel like a new woman?' said Bill.

Jessie nodded. 'Yeah, and that new woman's thirsty.' She stood up. 'Same again?' Bill passed his glass over. 'You'd better grab a menu — they do food and you look like you need some.'

'Liquid lunch today.'

'What's happened?'

'I'll tell you when I get back.'

Jessie ordered another round, picked up a menu for Bill and returned with the drinks in hand.

'I hit Mark Ward,' she said, once a good amount of the second drink had hit her stomach. 'Don't worry, no one saw.'

'You *hit* him? Why? Where?'

'In the solar plexus.'

'No, I mean where were you?'

'In this horrible place around the corner. I'm feeling a bit better now, but as soon as I walked in there, I don't know . . .' She frowned, trying to remember where the feeling had come from. 'I can't explain it. He's called me names before. Big deal, right; don't dignify it with a response, all that crap . . . So why today? I could have killed him. I'm not joking. I have never felt so angry in my life. Except . . . no, not even then.'

'Except when?'

Jessie paused for a moment. No one really touched on this subject. It was taboo. 'When Mum died, and the doctor told us she'd known for months. I was furious, still am. But not like today. I didn't want to kill the doctor.'

'But you wanted to kill Mum?'

'Yeah, well, the cancer had done that for me.'

They sat in silence for a while.

'Do you miss her?'

'That's a stupid question, Bill.'

'Sorry.'

'We never talk about her,' said Jessie quietly. There was another pause.

'It's been five years, what more can we say about it?'

'Nothing. But we should still talk about her.'

Her mother had energy enough for all of them. A husband, three sons and a daughter. That it was not inexhaustible, as Jessie had been led to believe, was something she still could not comprehend.

Bill lit a cigarette. He offered the packet to Jessie. She refused. The moment had passed.

'I dream about her,' said Bill, halfway down his cigarette. 'She's always laughing.'

'I don't,' Jessie admitted. 'You know the thing that terrifies me the most? I can't remember what she sounded like. I can't hear her voice.'

'I've got tapes she sent me when I first went to Africa. I'll send them to you, if you like.'

She looked away from her brother crossly. 'I don't want tapes, Bill. I want her.'

This statement was followed by the awkward silence that Jessie was used to getting from her brothers when she tried to talk about their mother. Her father was the same. None of them would talk to her about it.

'I feel cheated,' she said to the windowpane. 'I want to go shopping with her for my wedding dress.'

'Christ, Jess, I thought you said it was over with that guy.'

'It is.'

'Who are you getting married to then?'

'I'm not getting married to anyone.' Bill looked more perplexed than ever. 'Oh, never mind,' said Jessie, finishing her drink. 'I don't know what's wrong with me.'

'Boss?' said a voice behind her. It was Burrows. 'They need you at Marshall Street Baths.'

'Is it Anna Maria?'

'They wouldn't tell me.'

Burrows looked over at Bill, nodded curtly then returned to the door, which he held open for Jessie. She kissed her brother on the cheek; he held her hand.

'You'll be all right, Jess,' he said.

She pulled her hand away. Sometimes she wasn't so sure.

The media frenzy had doubled in the short time Jessie had been in the pub. White vans with satellite dishes and company logos were stretched back into Broadwick Street. She and Burrows made slow progress through the crowd. No one took much notice of them, they blended in with all the other hacks and hawks. As they pushed to the edge of the pack, in a quieter place further away Jessie saw Amanda Hornby. She was standing in front of a camera, a small microphone clipped on to her lapel. She glanced nervously at the spiral-bound pad she held in her hand. Jessie looked at her watch. A special bulletin. Live from the scene. There must have been some development or else there wouldn't be this frenetic activity. Amanda looked up and caught her staring. Jessie tried to look away but it was too late, the news reporter had clocked her and she was coming over.

'Oi, get back here!' the cameraman shouted.

'I'd do as he says,' said Jessie.

'Why are you back, Detective Inspector? What's going on? Is Sarah Klein here to identify her daughter?'

Sarah Klein? Here? 'Three minutes to air,' said the cameraman, sounding exasperated.

'It's not my case.'

'But you're here.'

Jessie couldn't argue with that.

'Why?'

A car pulled up to the barrier and Jessie inadvertently looked around. She saw the familiar red hair emerge.

'Sally Grimes — isn't she the pathologist who helped you with the celebrity murders?' said the reporter. Jessie ignored her. 'So you've definitely got a body then?'

Jessie turned back to Amanda Hornby. 'You know too much.'

'That's my job.'

'Amanda!' shouted the cameraman. Amanda put a finger to her ear then glanced down at her watch. She started walking slowly backwards. 'I know nothing. Just one thing, give me one fact, that's all I'm after.'

Jessie watched her retreat.

'One fact, that's all,' she pleaded again.

'My brother fancies you,' said Jessie flippantly. 'And that's a fact.'

Amanda swore silently, turned to the camera and nodded once. 'That's right, Sarah Klein the mother of the missing girl arrived here ten minutes ago, creating quite a scene. She was driving her car, turned into Marshall Street just behind me and was blocked from continuing any further by the growing number of photographers and journalists who have congregated here. Eventually she got out of the car and forced her way through the crowd, refusing to answer any questions. It was only when the extent of her distress became evident that they allowed her to pass.'

Jessie listened in horror.

'That's correct. The actress was due to

appear in a West End production of *Who's Afraid of Virginia Woolf* in a month's time. The much-revered director, Timothy Powell, isn't saying anything at present as to whether this is still the case, though it is assumed she will not carry on with a play the subject of which is a couple with an imaginary child. Things are looking less hopeful here. Just a few moments ago the pathologist Sally Grimes arrived and was rushed inside. Although the police are saying nothing at this stage, I think it is safe to assume that rumours regarding the discovery of a body are true. The exact cause of death is unknown, but it is being treated as suspicious. Sally Grimes became a fully qualified Home Office pathologist just a few weeks ago.' Jessie watched the reporter's face go taut with concentration as she listened to the next question from the studio. Amanda nodded. 'That's right, it means that Ms Grimes' evidence can be used by prosecutors, in this case the Crown Prosecution Service, in a court of law. However, the police are refusing to confirm that Anna Maria Klein's body has been found, so for the moment —' she glanced briefly at Jessie — 'nothing is fact.'

Jessie fell in behind Burrows, and they made their way slowly to the front where

Jessie showed her badge once more. Waiting at the door was Sally Grimes. Burrows raised the crime-scene tape for Jessie to duck under and she went to join Sally.

'What are you doing here?' Jessie whispered.

'Carolyn Moore paged me.'

'You know her?'

Sally nodded. 'In a manner of speaking.'

'What did she want?'

'They've found something they've never seen before. They want me to have a look at it.'

' "It"?'

'That's what the message said.'

'How well do you know her?'

'She's a ball breaker.'

'Any advice?'

'Give her a wide berth,' said the red-headed pathologist. 'She wasn't always like that.'

The officers who had performed the search that morning milled around the foyer in silence. Somewhere a radio was on.

'. . . Clinical psychologist Dr Martin Rommelt is here in the studio discussing the disappearance of Anna Maria Klein. Dr Rommelt, what effect do you think being rejected from *Celebrity Big Brother, Jnr* would have had on Anna Maria?'

Jessie looked at Sally for explanation.

'I heard this on the radio coming down here. Some journo found out that she'd put her name up for the Big Brother house, but was turned down because she wasn't famous enough.'

'And they think what exactly?'

'They don't think anything. All they can do is speculate until you lot make an announcement. Before the Big Brother story broke they were discussing what effect having an absent father and famous mother would have on a teenager.'

Sally and Jessie walked back through the increasingly familiar network of subterranean passageways and doors. Outside the new boiler room another group of people stood listening to another radio.

'. . . Friends are saying that Anna Maria was depressed recently. Normally a gregarious girl, she had become a little withdrawn, secretive. One schoolfriend who wishes to remain anonymous said that Anna Maria had been fighting with her mother more than usual. When asked what was usual, the friend replied, "Most days there was something . . ."'

'I hope the poor woman isn't listening to any of this,' said Sally.

Jessie experienced the same feeling of

apprehension as they left the bright light of the boiler room behind them and approached the final set of doors. Sally pushed them open and they both felt a rush of cold air. It was Sally's turn to shudder. The long narrow walkway came to an abrupt end where it fell away to darkness. Jessie could hear someone crying. A woman. They walked towards the sound. Sarah Klein was sitting at the bottom of the stone steps, her head in her hands. Jessie immediately changed her mind about the actress. She'd heard too many women cry not to know the difference between crocodile tears and the real thing. When she heard them approach, Sarah Klein looked up, startled.

'Sorry,' said Jessie. 'We didn't mean to frighten you.'

The woman started sobbing again. Sally carried on without stopping, but Jessie held back. Sarah Klein shouldn't be on her own. There should have been a family liaison officer with her. Where was the tea, the hanky, the gentle arm on the shoulder, the offer to call someone, drive her somewhere? Why wasn't she being looked after? Sally called her from inside the ancient boiler room. Jessie didn't respond.

'Jessie —' it was Sally again, this time

more insistent — 'I think you'd better come in here.'

Reluctantly, Jessie left the sobbing woman and walked into the dank and dimly lit room. Curled up on a piece of tarpaulin, on the dry earth between the tanks and the coal stores, was the body of a perfectly preserved middle-aged man.

Chapter 4

His skin was yellow and pulled taut over the bones. His eyelids sunk over the empty sockets. His lips were stretched back over his blackened teeth. His dark hair was slicked back and held in a ponytail. It was a terrifying death mask. His clothes had stiffened as hard as armour; each crease in the jacket, each fold in the shirt as unyielding as bronze. He was not a man any more, he was a mummy. The sleeves of his jacket were rolled up to the elbow, revealing more yellowing flesh that bore the signs of a vicious attack. Worse still, the tip of each preserved finger was missing. His thumbs were nothing but stumps.

'What is it?' asked DCI Moore. 'And how the hell did it get here?'

'It's the corpse of a Caucasian male, approximately forty years of age.'

'Is it real?'

'Yes.' Sally pulled on a pair of synthetic gloves and began to feel around the body.

'Are you sure? It looks plastic.'

'The corpse is showing visible signs of preservation. The body has been drying out, not decomposing. The skin takes on a leathery consistency, like biltong.'

'How long has it been here?' asked DCI Moore.

'Check the date,' interrupted Jessie, peering over Sally Grimes' shoulder. 'On the watch.'

Sally leant over so that she could get a better look. 'That's strange.'

'What is?' asked DCI Moore.

'It's today's date.' Sally put her ear to the timepiece. 'It's stopped.'

Mark Ward was pacing the perimeter of the room like a caged beast. One of the lights flickered on and off, making his actions look jerky and disconnected. He stopped and barked at Sally: 'What does that mean, if he didn't die today?'

'I don't know, but he definitely didn't die today.'

'What the hell can you tell me?' DCI Moore's red lips were outlined by a faint trace of blue. She'd been standing in the cold room for some time.

'I'd say he's been here since the eighties,'

said Jessie, jumping to Sally's rescue.

'Don't be ridiculous,' said Mark. 'A watch battery doesn't last that long.'

'Look at the clothes. My elder brothers used to dress like that — winklepickers, baggy trousers. Look how the jacket sleeves are folded and pushed up the arm. It's the New Romantics: Depeche Mode, Nick Kershaw. Madness — remember?'

He clearly didn't.

Sally bent down to get a better look. She carefully slipped her fingers into the back pocket of the jeans. She pulled. Nothing happened. After a few more attempts she took a pair of scissors and began to cut off the pocket. The square of stiff material came away in her hands. Sally turned it over. Stuck to the material was a canvas wallet of indeterminate colour. It was the type that folded over itself and fastened along a Velcro strip. She pulled the Velcro apart. The inside was orange. Bright orange with black edging.

'I remember those,' said Jessie. 'They were very trendy. They came in all the fluorescent colours.'

'So this man took his eighties retro look very seriously,' concluded DCI Moore.

'Not retro,' said Sally. 'This is genuine. Look at these —' she held up some flimsy rectangles of paper — 'one-pound notes.' In the side zip pocket there was a collection of change. Sally ran her fingers over the coins. 'I'd forgotten how big they were.' The ten-pence pieces looked like giant money, filling her dwarf palm; the five-pence pieces were twice the size of the new ones, and there was something that Jessie had almost forgotten existed: a halfpenny.

'Anything useful like ID in there?' asked the DCI.

'No.'

'Are you telling me this man has been down there since the eighties?'

'Not necessarily, but it looks as though he's been dead since the eighties. He should have decomposed by now. Where did you find him?'

Moore pointed to the cleared site of the fourth open pit. 'It's an old ash pit — lead-lined and sealed.'

Sally touched the wall. 'It's very cold, but it would have to be dry, too.'

'It was when we prised it open, but all four pits used to be connected to the sewers.'

'And they're not any more?'

'We won't know until the contractors have been down here. Something still is, you can smell it.'

'What I can tell you is that he's been in this foetal position for a long time. Either here, or a large domestic refrigerator. Because of his immaculate condition, the day he died, and therefore the way he died, is set in stone. I'll get him to the lab and —'

'No,' said DCI Moore.

'What? Why did you call me down here?'

'As a favour.'

'I don't mind doing favours, Carolyn —'

'DCI Moore.'

'I don't mind doing favours, *DCI Moore,* but I like to know when I'm granting them.'

'I have to think about our budget,' Moore replied tartly.

Jessie stepped forward. 'But, boss, this is a suspicious death. Look at his hands — someone cut his fingers off. No fingers, no ID.'

'That may be, DI Driver, but according to you he could have died twenty years ago. Hardly the sort of case we want to blow a lot of money on.'

'Unlike Anna Maria Klein, you mean, who guarantees the police much more press?'

DCI Moore pulled herself up. 'If you care so much about this, it's yours. I'm putting you in charge. Identify him, find a match in Missing Persons and if any of his family are still alive you can let them know. But you don't get Sally. Now that she's a fully qualified Home Office pathologist she's become far too expensive. Bad luck,' she told Sally. 'You've priced yourself right out of the market.'

Jessie turned to the scenes of crime officers. 'Can we get a sample of —'

'Hold your horses, Driver,' said Mark, suddenly bounding forward. 'This is my crime scene, my search party, my lads from SOCO. Off you go, boys — time for a break.'

'Don't go anywhere. I don't mean to state the obvious, but Anna Maria isn't here,' said Jessie. 'You heard the boss, this is my crime scene now.'

'You don't know that this is a crime scene,' said Mark. 'And we haven't finished the search yet. You may not have noticed, but there are four old coal stores we haven't investigated and below this level are the foundations of the workhouse that was originally built on this site. We haven't even started this search.'

'You think this guy mutilated his own hands and dropped himself in a hole and pulled the lid over his head? Come on, of course this is a crime scene. I can't have you lot trampling all over it — you'll contaminate it.'

'That is quite enough melodrama, DI Driver.' DCI Moore moved towards the exit. 'Mark has a point. This place may still be unsafe. Let's keep going with what is essential: finding Anna Maria Klein. When Mark is finished, you can continue with your investigation. But, please, don't move the body until the hyenas have moved on. Sarah Klein and I are going to make a statement.'

'I bet you are,' whispered Jessie under her breath.

DCI Moore shot her a look, then left. Sally took out a card and quickly scribbled a name and number on it.

'He's a doctor, but he's studying forensic pathology. He's got great potential and passion, and he'll relish a challenge like this. Send him the body. That way we'll get it examined without the cost of a coroner, and if he finds anything we'll go down the normal channels.'

DCI Moore reappeared as Jessie pocketed the card. 'Sally, would you accompany me back up to ground level? There is something I'd like to discuss with you.'

'It's not balls this woman is after,' whispered Jessie as Sally made to leave.

As soon as they were out of the door Mark moved in. He started by picking up one corner of the tarpaulin and dragging it across the floor. The stiff shifted.

'Wait,' shouted Jessie. 'Let's at least take a photo of it.' She reached out to the police photographer hovering by the rusty boiler tanks.

'No,' said Mark. 'I need you upstairs, where they found that blanket. Quick, before we lose this light.'

'She isn't here and you know it.'

He raised his heavy lids to meet her eyes then slowly rubbed his chest.

'Fine,' she retorted. Placing herself between the body and the hole in the ground, she pulled her backpack off her shoulder. 'I have my own camera. So go to hell.'

The flickering light stopped flickering, popped and then went out, taking all the other lights out with it. A soupy darkness wrapped itself around them.

'Shit,' said Mark. Jessie heard a thud. The corpse of an unknown man being unceremoniously dropped.

'No one move,' shouted Jessie. 'Torches, anyone?'

'Someone go and find out what's going on!' shouted Mark.

'No, don't move. You don't know where you're walking. Burrows, you're nearest the door, you go.'

Jessie heard a rustle.

'No one else move, the pits are open!'

'We're not,' came the chorus.

'Someone is moving!'

'Jesus Christ,' said Mark. 'Fucking pussies, the lot of you.' Jessie heard the strike of a flint. Mark was holding up a lighter. Two more strikes. Two more lighters. Then another, then another.

Mark started waving his lighter in the air. 'It's like a fucking Barry Manilow concert.' There were a few laughs.

'What can we conclude from this?' asked Mark.

'That the place is spooked?' said a voice from the darkness that Jessie recognised as Fry.

'No, lad. That coppers smoke too much.' More laughter. 'Now, let's get the fuck out of here and have a break and a smoke, like I suggested.'

All the lighters moved at once.

'Not all of you,' exclaimed Jessie. But the lighters kept on moving until there were none left. Jessie felt warm air on the back of her neck. Finally she found her torch. She swung round with it, illuminating

Mark's face. He stood a few feet away.

'Very funny,' she said, with no trace of humour in her voice.

'What? Get that light out of my face.'

'Stop pissing about.' She could feel little hairs bristle as she rubbed the nape of her neck. She shone the beam of light towards the floor. Open, empty eye sockets gaped back at her. Startled, she nearly let go of the torch. 'Now look what you've done, Mark!'

'What? I didn't do anything.'

'You dropped him.'

She passed the light over the body again.

'I didn't.'

Jessie frowned. The lids lay closed as before. Hiding the holes that lay beneath. 'Sorry,' she said, 'it must have been a trick of the light.'

'Trick of your mind, maybe,' said Mark. 'Don't tell me this place is getting to you. Not the fearless, indomitable Jessie Driver.' He took two steps towards her, snatched the torch from her hand and switched it off.

'Mark, don't!'

She could hear him moving about in the darkness.

'This is so childish. You could fall.'

He didn't reply. She imagined the infantile grin on his pasty face.

'Turn the light back on before you do yourself an injury,' said Jessie, following the sound of him feeling his way through the dark. Still he didn't reply. He was mistaken if he thought she'd fall to her knees and sob like a baby. That was his speciality.

'I thought you didn't like the dark?'

Silence.

'Remember? In the dark, alone, scared.' A cold blast of air came from nowhere, wrapped itself around her legs and made her shiver. She could still hear Mark. His shuffling was getting closer. She braced herself for whatever was coming. Blinding light in her eyes. More warm air on her neck. A soft moan. Rattling chains. What? What was it going to be?

'I can hear your elf-like footsteps, arsehole.'

There was a bang. The sound of something heavy being dropped.

'Stop messing around and put the fucking light back on!' she shouted.

A pale blue bulb popped and glowed, then another. They got brighter as the power seeped through the circuit, gradually illuminating the long-forgotten boiler room. Jessie looked around. She was all alone.

Curled around her feet lay the lifeless body.

Jessie sat high up on one of the spectators' benches. She'd watched the last of the police officers leave and was just waiting for Moore to phone her with the all-clear to move the body. She looked up at the sound of approaching footsteps. It was Sarah Klein.

'I didn't know anyone was still here,' said Jessie.

Sarah Klein sat down on the thin wooden seat next to her. 'I can't go out there.' She looked at Jessie with red-rimmed eyes. 'Just look at me.'

'Ms Klein, did P. J. Dean really recommend me to you?'

She looked sideways at Jessie. 'No,' she admitted. 'I thought — hell, what does it matter what I thought?'

'What statement did you make?'

'I told you, I couldn't go out there. Your boss did it.'

They fell into an awkward silence. Jessie stared down at the empty pool and imagined what it must have looked like in its heyday. Line upon line of Italian marble tiles. Chlorine and laughter rising off the warm water. Sunshine streaming through the now filthy domed glass.

'It's a work of art,' said a voice above them. Jessie and Sarah Klein jumped. 'Do you know, that pool never leaked a fluid ounce of water since the day it was built? Not one. That's real craftsmanship. Something to be proud of. Seeing it reduced to this . . . Well, it isn't right, is it?' He moved down the terraces. 'Give me a shout when you want to go, and I'll lock up.'

'Thanks,' said Jessie.

'Who is that?' whispered Sarah Klein.

'The caretaker,' Jessie replied quietly.

'She isn't here, you know,' said the moustached man, looking back at them.

'No, I don't think she is either,' said Jessie. Anna Maria didn't look so lacking in streetwise that she would climb into a drug hovel for some spliff. In all likelihood she'd never been here. She was probably unaware such a place existed. In an area where space cost £60 per square foot, a disused building of this magnitude was unimaginable.

'How do you know?' asked the missing girl's mother.

'I'd have heard her.' Jessie and the actress exchanged mystified glances. The caretaker looked back at the heavy set of keys in his hand. 'Let me know when you want to leave.'

He climbed down the benches and disappeared through the double doors that led to the foyer.

'What a strange man,' said Sarah Klein.

'Eccentric but harmless, I think.'

'All mad people are harmless until they slash you with a razor,' the actress said dramatically. 'Maybe he did it.'

'Did what?'

'Killed my daughter.'

'I don't think so. The truth is, I don't think your daughter's dead,' said Jessie. 'And I'm not sure you do, either.'

The actress didn't say anything.

'I don't even think you believe she's been abducted,' said Jessie, pushing a little further.

Sarah stared straight ahead. Finally she spoke, very quietly. 'I did at first.'

'But not now?'

She shrugged again. 'I don't know. According to your colleague, she hasn't spent any money. That isn't good, is it?'

'Not necessarily. She might be staying with someone — a boyfriend . . . ?'

'I've rung everyone.'

'Everyone you know.'

Jessie watched the actress swill the thought around in her head, then dismiss it. 'There is too much coverage of her disappearance. Even if someone had lent her a large sum, surely they'd come forward?'

'Has anything been stolen recently, any money missing?'

'What? No! Are you suggesting my own daughter would . . .' Her voice trailed off. 'There was . . .' She stopped herself. 'No. Absolutely not.'

'There was what?'

'It's nothing to do with Anna Maria.'

'Try me. Another person's perspective may shed some light.'

Sarah Klein brushed the hair back off her face. 'It was months ago, I had to sack a cleaner because a few things went missing. She was new.'

'What did she take?'

'Nothing much. A few knick-knacks, clothes, little items of jewellery and some foreign currency. Every time she came, something disappeared.' Out of her handbag she began to apply a fresh face to her ravaged one.

'Did she admit to it?'

'Don't be ridiculous! Of course she didn't. But who else would it have been?'

Jessie let the question hang in the air. Then she changed tack. 'Why were you crying before, on the steps?'

Sarah Klein's face turned sour. 'You

don't know what it's like.'

'Because I don't have children?'

'I don't mean that!' she said, snapping the compact closed. 'The director was all over me until I said yes to doing the part. Now he's shagging someone else. Guess who — the fucking understudy. Christ, you couldn't buy publicity like this and still the vultures are circling. "You're under too much stress to come in to rehearsal," he says, "let the little tart cover while you get through this." As if I don't know what's happening, the bastard!'

'Sarah, do you know where your daughter is?'

'No,' she said emphatically. 'Of course not.' She stood up. 'I need to get out of this godawful place. How do I look?'

Like Aunt Sally. 'Much better,' said Jessie.

Jessie followed her down the spectators' benches and over the tiled floor where bare feet once reigned. Together they crossed the foyer. She opened the main door a crack. 'I'm afraid they're still here. Let me find the caretaker — there must be another way out of here.'

'It's fine,' said Sarah Klein, removing a headscarf from the pocket of her coat and a large pair of tinted glasses from her bag.

It was dusk outside. 'I've got to face them eventually.'

'One more question: is it true that there were the arguments between yourself and Anna Maria?'

'She's always pushing me to the limit,' Sarah Klein replied defensively. 'Anything for a bit of attention. I've no idea where she gets it from.'

'Ms Klein, do me a favour, tell DI Ward about the thefts, I think it might be useful.'

'Anna Maria didn't steal from me, Detective. She may be lying in a ditch somewhere and you're worried about a little problem with my domestic staff!'

'You didn't report it, did you?'

'I didn't want her to get into trouble.'

'The cleaner?'

'Of course the cleaner. Now, do you mind? I have to go.' She put her hand up in front of her face before the first flashbulb popped.

Chapter 5

Jessie put a call through to the council. She was sure that the caretaker was a harmless eccentric, but before she spent any more hours alone with him in an empty building, she wanted to make sure. What they told her was both alarming and reassuring. Though the man suffered from bouts of 'unspecific' mental illness, his alibi was watertight. He'd been discharged from the Gordon Hospital psychiatric unit that morning after a three-week stay. Was he better? The lady on the phone couldn't say.

As the more persistent of the journalists began to trickle away, Jessie made arrangements to have the body removed. For some reason, Moore wanted this one kept under wraps, so the mortuary van had been ordered to wait out of sight until given the all-clear. It would transport the body to Sally Grimes' friend, who was waiting to receive it at St Mary's. The same hospital where the concussed officer had been sent. Jessie hoped they wouldn't be sending any more.

'It has a life of its own,' said the caretaker, joining her by the abandoned pool. 'Especially when it rains. Can't you hear it?'

Jessie had been listening to the sound of the wind in the ancient pipes and the rain pelting the glass roof. With such a cacophony of ghostly sounds even a rational mind could get jumpy. She couldn't imagine the effect on an irrational mind.

'Is that why the lights keep going out — because of leaks?'

The caretaker didn't reply. She wasn't going to push it.

'We can go now. Everything has been, um, taken away.'

'He's gone, then?'

'Yes.'

'You sure?'

Jessie had seen the body-bag into the car. 'Yes.'

'Don't you want the tour before you go? They're going to pull it down soon. Tragedy.'

'Pull it down, when?'

'Soon as they can find out what's wrong with the place.'

'What is wrong with the place?'

The caretaker changed the subject. 'You got a name?'

'Call me Jessie.'

'Jessie — that's a boy's name, isn't it?'

'There aren't many people who can say that to my face and survive.'

The caretaker chuckled. 'Follow me. There's no one who knows this place better than I do. The name's Don.'

'You've worked here a long time then, Don?'

'All my life.'

She pointed halfway up the wall over towards the deep end of the pool where two rusting brackets stuck out of the wall like miniature gallows, the type you draw when playing hangman. 'So can you tell me what those are for?'

'It was a platform. Had a wooden seat, see?'

'What for?'

'Why all these questions?' he suddenly snapped.

'Sorry,' said Jessie. 'Just curious. Occupational hazard.'

'I expect you'd like to see where the slipper baths were. People used to wash there because they didn't have no bathrooms at home.'

Jessie looked at her watch; it was late.

'It won't take long.'

Jessie followed him out through the foyer and into an impressive Art Deco stairwell. 'They aren't there any more, of course. It's all exercise rooms now. I've seen everything: keep-fit, Jane Fonda workout, step, karate, judo, Callanetics . . . The best was the karate. I liked the teacher. He said I had special powers.'

'Really?' said Jessie, running her hand along the wooden banister as they mounted the central stairway. From a small landing Don pushed open a carved wooden door to a circular room she now recognised as the one the junkies had broken into. 'They got in here via the roof,' he said, pointing to the broken glass in the domed ceiling. It was a beautiful wood-panelled room with benches all the way round.

'This was the first-class bathers' waiting room. They'd pay their two and sixpence and that gave them unlimited hot water. When a tub became free, they'd come on in here —' he led her through to where most of the addicts had congregated. It was longer than Jessie remembered from the video that morning. 'On either side were baths, each sectioned off by more wood panelling. In they'd go for their weekly soak. Can't even imagine it now, can you — public bathing? Sometimes,' he said, 'when I turn my back, I can still hear them, singing away, soaping up, shaving, the doors slamming, the steam . . .' He looked at Jessie for confirmation. All she saw and smelt was human detritus. She wanted to go home.

'Yes,' she said.

'Upstairs was where the second-class bathers went. No refills for their shilling. Sometimes you can't concentrate for all their chattering.'

Jessie heard footsteps above her.

'Just the pipes,' he said quickly.

Didn't sound like pipes to her. 'Are you sure?' she asked.

'There's no one there, Jessie. There never is.'

'I'd still like to see for myself.'

The long narrow room above matched the one before. It had old rubber flooring in a lurid shade of green. As Don had said, it was empty. But even in this deserted exercise room there was something strange. Preserved buildings were like preserved people, their very refusal to decay, their obstinacy, could teach you something. Something of the past. If you were prepared to read the signs.

'He doesn't come up here.'

'Who?'

'What?'

'Are you feeling all right, Don?' He'd only just come out of hospital and this had been no ordinary day.

'They said it wasn't my fault.'

'Of course not. People with drug addictions are desperate, they'll go wherever they can,' said Jessie. 'It wasn't your fault you got ill.'

'I'm not ill,' said the caretaker defensively.

'Sorry, my mistake.'

'I get the wobblies sometimes, that's all.' He put his finger in his ear and rubbed it as if he were clearing some wax.

'It's been a long day,' said Jessie. 'It's time to go home.'

He stared at her. Her phone rang, making her jump. It was a number she didn't recognise.

'Best stay up here,' said Don, quickening his step as he made it back to the stairwell. 'Only place you'll get reception on those things. I'll go and start the locking up. You stay up here where you . . .' He'd gone down the stairs so fast, she didn't hear the rest.

'Hello? Is anyone there?'

'DI Driver,' said Jessie into the phone.

'Hi, my name is Dominic Rivers. I just wanted to tell you I've had a quick look at your body — sorry, that didn't come out right. The stiff, um, the —'

'The mummy?'

'Yeah, the mummy, right. Thanks for sending it my way — it's fascinating. I've never seen anything like it. It's perfectly preserved. Didn't find it in a peat bog, did you?'

'No. A lead-lined ash pit.'

'He's very clean.'

'It was empty and sealed.'

'Well, I won't know why he is this beautifully preserved until I've done some tests, so why don't you come by in the morning? By then I should be able to tell you a little more about this bloke.'

'How he died?'

'And if I'm doing my job correctly, how he lived.'

'Damn!'

'Sorry, isn't that what you wanted?'

'No, it's not you — there's been another power cut. Don!' Jessie heard someone moving about on the floor below.

'Where was he found?'

'Marshall Street Baths,' said Jessie,

feeling for the banisters. 'Sorry, I can't see anything, I'll have to call you back.'

'No worries, just come by in the morning. About nine.'

'Nine it is.'

'That's a date. Have a good one.'

Yeah right, thought Jessie, feeling her way back down the stairs in the darkness. She cursed the fact she'd left her bag in the foyer.

'Don!' She called out. 'The lights have gone again!' The yellow streetlights oozed through the windows, reflected and re-peated a million times by the raindrops that clung to the dirty panes. She looked down the central well.

'Oh, you're there,' said Jessie. The figure looked up. It wasn't Don.

'Detective Inspector Driver.' It was a statement rather than a question.

'Who are you?'

'My name is Father Forrester. Anglican. Good and high,' he said with a smile. He removed a brown felt trilby from his head and performed a small bow. A shock of white hair hovered around his crown in wisps as thin as clouds. 'At your service,' he said, his face dissected by laughter lines. Even in the dim light, Jessie could see his eyes sparkle.

'What are you doing here? You're not supposed to be in here.'

'I was hoping I might be able to help you.'

'How did you get in here?'

'The door was open.'

'Don!' shouted Jessie again. It was a ruse, to let the man know they weren't alone. 'Well, it wasn't supposed to be. I'm afraid I'm going to have to escort you out. This building is closed to the public. It's unsafe.'

He looked around the small atrium. 'Unsafe. Indeed, especially to those who remain here. I expect you can feel it.'

'Feel what?' Jessie walked slowly down the last couple of steps, stopping a few feet away from him when she reached ground level.

'The heavy atmosphere, a terrible feeling of regret.'

'No,' she said. Actually, now you come to mention it . . . 'No,' she said again. The strange old man stared over her left shoulder.

'Have we met before?' asked Jessie, resisting the temptation to check behind her.

'I don't think so.'

'You look familiar to me. Have you been in trouble with the law, Father Forrester?'

He chuckled. It sounded like someone shaking a bag of marbles. 'Not since leaving Oxford University when there was an embarrassing moment with some underpants and a flagpole. You could say I am a reformed character.'

She moved round him to the door that led to the entrance. Never let the unknown entity stand between you and the exit. Especially in a dark, derelict building. 'Are you sure? You aren't wearing a dog collar.'

'I am now retired, but not redundant. I think I can help you.'

'And how is it that you can help me, Father Forrester?'

'Someone in here needs forgiveness. As it happens, I am in the forgiving business.'

'Don't you normally knock on the door with leaflets?'

His faint smile didn't falter. 'Does the name Ann mean anything to you?'

Oh dear, thought Jessie. One of those. It was extraordinary what human peculiarities crime scenes conjured up. From nowhere gypsies with crystals would arrive; wailing women, pagans, hippies, spiritualists offering to talk to the dead, housewives who'd had vivid dreams. Body-bags brought out the supernatural in everyone, it seemed. Personally, Jessie liked to stick to the facts.

'Nearly right, Father. Her name is Anna. Anna Maria. And she isn't here. Now I know a lot has been on the news, and that rumours of a body rushed through the press, but it isn't her. Anna Maria isn't here. Now, I insist you leave.' She opened the door. Don was standing just the other side of it.

'Sorry, didn't mean to scare you,' said the caretaker.

'You didn't,' she said, removing her hand from where it had jumped to her chest. 'I need to escort this gentleman off the premises.'

The vicar looked at Don. 'It is often the guilty who cannot move on,' he said.

Don shrank from the vicar. 'Go away,' he said in a strained voice.

'It's all right, Don, he's going.' Jessie turned to the white-haired man. 'Right now.'

But the retired priest was not listening to her. 'An earthbound spirit can make a place feel unsafe. They make themselves heard in a number of ways.'

'I can hear them,' said Don.

'What?' said Jessie, turning back to Don. 'Who?'

'The voices.'

'Everyone, just stop,' said Jessie. 'This conversation is over.'

'He drowned. It was an accident,' said Don.

'What was an accident?' Jessie looked at him sharply. 'Who drowned?'

The caretaker began to quiver slightly; he looked around the room nervously.

'Do you know anything about the body downstairs?' Jessie persisted.

'Questions, questions, questions — I don't like questions. They give me the wobblies.' Jessie didn't want the caretaker getting the wobblies. Whatever the wobblies were, a psychiatric ward meant they were probably more harmful than the name suggested.

'It's all right, Don. Let's sit you down. We don't have to talk about this.' She walked him back through to the foyer. 'Don't you go anywhere,' Jessie shot back over her shoulder to the priest.

'An infested location will often attack the human element within it,' he called after her. 'Especially if the human —'

Jessie held up her hand. She helped Don on to an upturned box. The quivering stopped as suddenly as it had begun, and when he looked up at Jessie, he seemed quite unaware of what had happened.

'Did you know they used two hundred and eighty-six marble tiles for the big swimming pool? Each one three foot by four foot, put there by hand.'

'No,' said Jessie. 'I didn't know that.'

'I've worked here all my life,' said Don.

'Yes,' said Jessie, 'I know. But now it's definitely time to go home.'

'It's about money,' said Father Forrester, walking through the double doors towards them. 'Old money.'

'Who have you been talking to?' she asked, then immediately regretted the question. He smiled benignly. If he was expecting enlightenment, he was talking to the wrong girl.

'That is a complicated question, Detective, and one that I should like to answer in the fullness of time. Until then, perhaps it is better to simply pass over my details. It will become increasingly evident when and why you'll be needing me.' He handed her a piece of paper. 'I'm staying with some very good friends of mine: Sister Beatrice and Mary at the Rectory, Mill Lane, Wapping. I took the liberty of writing the details down. Call me when you want to talk. I'll be ready.'

'Ready for what, exactly?'

'For whatever is needed of me.' He bid

her goodnight, replaced the trilby on his head and walked out into the rain. There was something about him that made Jessie feel uneasy. She was about to call after him when she felt a hand on her shoulder. She turned abruptly.

'Sorry, didn't mean to startle you again.'

'Again, you didn't.' Again, she lied.

They watched as the elderly man was swallowed up by crowds of commuters battling with the steady downpour.

'If you're ready . . .'

Jessie nodded. 'Are you feeling better?'

'I'm not sick, you know, I just get the wobblies sometimes.'

Jessie was suddenly very tired. 'Goodnight, Don,' she said. 'I'll see you tomorrow.' She stepped out into the rain. Behind her the caretaker pulled the thick metal chain through the door handles and began the lengthy ritual of locking up his keep.

Jessie was walking towards her bike when she remembered she'd left her helmet in the foyer. Unable to face going back, she pulled the collar of her leather jacket up and thought about hailing a cab and going home. It had been quite a day and she felt emotionally drained. Her relationship with Mark had never been easy to navigate, but today the velocity of the storm that Marshall Street Baths had thrown in their faces had been overpowering. She'd never felt the antagonism quite so intensely as she had standing on the threshold of that bizarre old boiler room. Since the fry-up at breakfast, her only sustenance had been two whiskys — no wonder she was feeling low. Two whiskys and a fry-up, thought Jessie ironically; whatever Mark might think, she was becoming a card-carrying copper despite herself.

She stood on Regent Street long enough to get bored, wet and cold. Welcome orange taxi-lights were evading her. The queues at the bus stops stretched back to the shop doors. Oxford Circus tube station was closed due to a security alert and the rain was now falling in a relentless stream. Even returning to work seemed more appealing than attempting public transport, so she crossed the busy road and headed down Maddox Street. Rain had brought its usual effect on the commuter traffic and the customary crawl was now stationary. Horns blared to no effect except to increase the blood pressure of all who heard them. The pavements were slick with grease and rainwater, but at least off Regent Street, they were empty. Each step made a small splash. She stopped to wipe water from her eyes and thought she heard someone stop behind her. She listened through the falling rain then started walking again, stepping carefully and precisely, changing momentum. Now she was almost sure she could hear someone walking in the rain behind her. She stopped again and turned. Her ears were playing tricks on her. Ears and eyes, all in one day. Marshall Street Baths was getting to her.

Up ahead, Jessie could see the panda cars and the IRV drivers waiting for instructions and, although it was silly, she felt relieved. Behind her, a phone played a ring-tone she recognised. Jessie turned involuntarily and looked around. The street was still empty. The P. J. Dean song started revolving in her head. That was something she was haunted by.

The Klein incident room was empty. All the boys were probably in the pub. She didn't blame them. It was a good night for a Guinness or two. Or three. She sat down at the computer terminal and inserted the CD-ROM that the CCTV tapes had been transferred on to. If she could prove that Anna Maria was not in the Marshall Street Baths she could make sure Mark had no excuse to disrupt her investigation again. The two of them couldn't be in that building without fighting. One location, two crime scenes and two investigating officers was a recipe for disaster as today had already proved. Mark was going to do everything in his power to remain in Marshall Street Baths, even if it meant prising up every floorboard, every tile. What really saddened Jessie was that the girl's disappearance clearly meant half as much to him as getting Jessie out of CID — which came as a real shock to her because she had genuinely thought things had improved between the two of them. Well, she wasn't leaving CID, and she wasn't going to rest until she had handed Anna Maria Klein to him on a plate.

Jessie began as the sixteen-year-old moved out of range from her position on the corner. Green high-heel boots, a fur-trimmed coat under which peeked a long, floating skirt. She looked stockier in the CCTV images than she did in the 'professional' photographs her mother had shown them. Had the photos been touched up, like so many were, stretching her to seem longer and leaner? Or was the photo accurate and something else accounted for Anna Maria's bulky appearance on the CCTV. Not the dress. That was made of very thin material. Too thin to be worn in February, surely? Jessie carried on watching frame by frame for the next fifteen minutes until something finally caught her eye. A girl walking quickly through the CCTV's range. She had long dark hair and wore a stripy woolly hat. She wore a thick, oversized jumper and jeans, and carried a large duffel bag over her shoulder. A perfectly normal-looking girl. Jessie had watched hundreds come in and out of the frame. Runners. Shop assistants. Secretaries. Models. Schoolkids. Language students. Tourists. They all looked the same, except this one. This one was wearing green six-inch heels. Jessie froze the image and saved it. Next she brought up the clearest still of Anna Maria standing on the corner. She enlarged the picture to get a more detailed image of the boots she was wearing. They were high. The shape of the heels matched. The colour matched. A lawyer could argue that boots like this were sold in their thousands, and they were probably right, but these weren't the clodhoppers with thick robust heels that most people wore. These had thin soles and spiky heels, and that made them expensive. Expensive and green reduced the likelihood of a sixteen-year-old girl wearing them. The build and height of the two girls were the same. The hair colour and the clothes were different. Jessie tried to remember what was up Marshall Street that would allow a girl to change her wardrobe with no one noticing. There was a café, but it was very small, some doorways in which to hide maybe, a telephone booth, a car park. Jessie smiled to herself. A car park would have security surveillance of its own. She picked up the phone and made the request.

'Hello, Jessie,' said a voice from the door. Jessie looked up. It was Jones. The person who'd given her the job in CID.

'Sir!' Jessie leapt to her feet and bounded towards him, then checked herself. 'It's great to see you.'

'So great that you can't even make time for my leaving party?'

Jessie put her hand to her mouth. 'No. I could have sworn Mark told me it was . . .' Her voice trailed off.

'I think it was, then it got changed,' said Jones, ever the diplomat.

'I thought it was a surprise. You're not

supposed to know,' said Jessie, seeing right through him.

'Trudi keeps me in the loop.' Trudi had been Jones' assistant for years. Jessie had seen her moping about the corridors since Jones announced his retirement.

'Has she told you about your replacement?' she asked hopefully. Jessie believed she and Trudi had always had a certain understanding.

'Trudi only told me that they hadn't had time to get acquainted yet.'

Which Jessie interpreted as, Stupid cow hasn't bothered talking to me yet because I'm a woman and only a secretary.

Jones shook his head. 'No, Jessie, it wasn't anything like that at all. Give Carolyn a chance. She appears a little frosty, but she'll thaw. She's just nervous.'

'As nervous as a panther.'

'Come on, Jessie. Usually you have very good intuition for people in pain. It's what makes you a good police officer, seeing in people what they are trying to hide from themselves.'

Jessie relented. It was as much the power of the compliment as the word 'pain'. 'What happened? Her husband run off with a thirty-three-year-old DI with dark hair who drives a bike?'

'Drop the bike, and you're pretty much there.'

'There's no hope for me,' said Jessie, lowering her head.

'You'll win her over in the end.'

'Great,' said Jessie. 'By which time I'll be in an institution. Honestly, guv, why should I be punished? It wasn't me.'

'No. You're just lower down the food chain, that's all. Now, are you coming to my party or not?'

'Course I am. I wouldn't miss it for the world.'

Jones smiled. 'You nearly did.'

They'd taken over a room above a local pub. There were barrels of beer, bottles of whisky and endless sausage rolls. The three ingredients to make a perfect policeman's party. There was a huge roar of respect and admiration as Jones entered the room. DCI Moore turned and looked at Jessie and Jones. Jessie smiled and moved straight for the whisky.

'Is it true?' asked Niaz.

'Is what true?' Jessie accepted a tumbler from the PC behind the table and took a sip.

'What the SOCOs are saying.'

'What are the SOCOs saying?'

Niaz lowered his head to one side.

Something he did when he was concentrating or confused. Tonight he was confused. 'Boss, why are you angry? This is a party. DCI Jones has had many years in the service. You should respect that by making sure he has a very good party. And good parties require happy people.'

'Sorry, Niaz, I fear I'm losing my only ally. I'm suddenly quite afraid,' she said, speaking honestly before she had the good sense to stop herself.

'Please, ma'am, don't speak of such things. I am your ally. I will always be your ally. And before you respond, remember this: it is just as important to have support from below. A general is nothing without the respect of his foot soldiers. Her foot soldiers.'

Jessie patted Niaz on the back. 'We're a small army,' she said.

'I grant you that.' He clasped his hands together. 'But a strong one.'

A young man approached them. He introduced himself to them both, though they knew exactly who he was: Ed from SOCO. 'We met in Richmond Park when they found the body of that artist.'

'Eve Wirrel,' said Niaz. 'PC Niaz Ahmet, at your service.'

'Hello, Ed,' said Jessie.

'Hello, Detective Inspector Driver. How's it going?'

'Fine, thanks.'

'Really? I heard you'd unearthed a ghost.'

Jessie frowned.

'Yeah, rumour has it that place in Soho is haunted. The lads tell me the lights kept flickering on and off.'

'That's called a problem with the electrics. Nothing more.'

'Don't be so sure. There was a house in our village that was haunted. The light in the top bedroom went on and off for no reason. Story was that a woman gave birth to an illegitimate child. The child was suffocated and it's the woman who keeps coming back to look for her kid.'

'That's nonsense, Ed.'

'My mate here says there was definitely a bad air in the place. And what about the roof falling in just as the body was found?' Ed nudged his friend, who nodded in collusion. They were joined by others, some of whom Jessie recognised from the Marshall Street Baths search that day. All agreed that the place had a strange feeling about it.

'It's a derelict swimming pool in the middle of Soho. Of course it feels weird,' said Jessie. 'It is weird. Empty swimming pools always are, even without the slime effect, the echo and, of course, the dead body.'

'What about those lights?'

'The caretaker told me the electrics never work properly when it's raining. And as you are all demonstrating by your damp hair and sodden collars, it is raining at the moment — harder than usual.'

There was sniggering as some of the men picked up a double entendre from nowhere.

'My aunt lived in this old house in the middle of nowhere, right,' said a voice from the crowd. 'One day her daughter — she was seven or eight at the time — said to my aunt at breakfast, "Mum, who is the old lady who comes and sits on my bed every night?" God's honest truth.'

'You shivered,' said Ed, pointing to Jessie.

'I did not,' she replied.

'You've got goosebumps.'

'I'm soaking, what do you expect?'

'A friend of a friend of mine once . . .'

Jessie walked away from the group as they began telling each other increasingly far-fetched tales of ghouls and ghosts. Niaz caught up with her halfway across the room.

'Don't you believe in spirits?' he asked.

'No,' she said.

'So you don't believe in God?'

'Mine or yours?'

'Either. They are one and same, it's just the semantics that are different.'

'If only that were the case — there would be a lot less murdered people in the world.'

'Religion isn't to blame,' said Niaz.

'It's killed more people than any disease.'

'No. Men have killed in the *name* of religion; that is not the same thing.'

'I don't believe that.'

'What do you believe, then?'

'That's a very personal question, Constable.'

'I think it is a universal question, Inspector,' said Niaz.

'All right. I believe in upholding the law. I believe that killing is wrong, as is beating someone to a pulp, stealing a car and killing a baby through reckless driving, strapping a child to a radiator, injecting someone with the AIDS virus, robbing a house and raping the daughter while forcing the parents to watch . . . Shall I go on?'

'You didn't answer the question,' said Niaz.

'I thought I just did. And don't give me

that crap about God giving us freedom of choice, because I just don't buy it. If he's around, he isn't listening.'

'So you do talk to him.'

'No, Niaz. Trust me, I don't.'

'Who do you go to for guidance?'

My mother. 'Myself.'

'I concur on one point,' said Niaz solemnly. 'No one knows for sure whether we survive death. This is true. But belief in some kind of life after death provides the basis of religions that stretch far back into antiquity. Surely you are too intelligent to dismiss such overwhelming evidence?'

'It was merely a way to suppress the poor and uneducated and scare them into submission.'

'You are wrong. God is hope. Their belief is deeper because they have more to hope for.'

'Please, God,' said Jessie sarcastically, 'I hope you will save me from this conversation with Niaz.'

Niaz looked over Jessie's shoulder.

'What?' asked Jessie, knowing a self-satisfied look when she saw one.

'God works in mysterious ways, but rarely this quickly,' said Niaz softly, before moving aside. Jessie turned. It was DCI

Moore. She was being punished for her sarcasm.

'DI Driver, you must be terribly sad that Jones is retiring.'

A cunning question. One that required dexterity of mind. To agree meant insulting Moore and to disagree meant insulting Jones. 'Surprised, more than anything. I thought he'd be commander of the Met one day. It is a great loss to the entire police force that he is going.'

'Indeed,' said DCI Moore. Jessie noticed that she had dressed up even more than usual for the occasion and applied a new coat of lipstick: red. Her hair, dyed and coiffed, had been pinned up in a chignon, and she wore a tight pencil skirt with a silk shirt. Her stockings and high heels were black.

Jessie fiddled with her hair. Now her smart trouser suit felt dowdy. She couldn't win with this woman.

'I'm glad to see that the leather trousers you were wearing yesterday have been discarded. Not very officer-like.'

'Sorry to disappoint, but I wear them more often than not.'

'Really? That's fashionable, is it?' she said as if she were talking to a sixth-form student.

'No. But it's safer.'

'Safer for whom?'

'Me. I ride a bike to work.'

'Really. And you wear leather for a bicycle?'

Jessie laughed. 'It's not a bicycle.'

'Oh, I see, a moped —'.

'No, ma'am, it's a motorbike. A Virago 750cc-41 horsepower, 0–60 in 3.2 seconds,' she said, unintentionally puffing out her chest.

DCI Moore eyed Jessie up and down. 'You're a biker,' she said incredulously. Then she seemed to relax, looked at Jessie's hair and nodded to herself. 'OK, I see,' she laughed. 'They always say you shouldn't believe everything you read in the papers. My mistake. I should have known — the hair sort of gives it away.'

Jessie was momentarily confused. 'Gives what away?'

DCI Moore didn't respond.

Then it washed over her, the horrible creeping feeling that she knew what Moore was referring to. But she couldn't believe it. She repeated the question. 'Gives what away — that I ride a bike? Is that what you mean, boss?'

'It's all right, Driver, settle down. Whatever your persuasion may be is none of my business. However, I think you should move away from the . . .' She paused, seemingly unable to find the appropriate words for what was an entirely inappropriate comment. 'No need to wear it on your sleeve. From now on I expect to see you in skirts. You can leave the leathers for the weekends when you're out with your . . .' she paused again, '. . . friends.'

Jessie couldn't believe it. As she watched the departing back of her new boss, she caught Jones watching her. Jessie shook her head very, very slightly. He mouthed the words, 'You'll be fine.' He was wrong, thought Jessie, sneaking out of the room. Jones was wrong for the first time since she'd met him. She was now working with two bigots, and one of them was a woman. Worse, she was her boss. Her life at CID was about to become intolerable, she thought as she left the party, and intolerable wasn't how she planned to live her life. She walked angrily down the deserted street. As she clicked open her phone to call Bill, it rang.

'DI Driver.'

'Jessie?'

The line was unclear.

'Bill, is that you?'

'Who the hell is Bill?'

It was P.J. Jessie was stunned into silence. Her heart did a decisive round in her chest.

'Don't put the phone down, please. Jessie, are you still there?'

'Yes,' she said meekly.

'I'm back in London and I was wondering, I know it's late, but how do you fancy dim sum and champagne? I know what you're like about being seen in public with someone as sleazy as me, so I thought I'd pick up the food, pick up the booze, pick you up and we could order the driver to cruise around a bit. Before you turn me down, it's a limo. Lots of leg room, the glass is tinted and the driver can't see anything. What do you think?'

No. No. No. No. No. 'I'm tired, P.J.' She was struggling to get the words out.

'Well, I'd offer you a fat line of coke, but somehow I don't think you'd be interested.'

'Ha. Ha.'

'Come on, Jessie. I've been surrounded by sycophants for weeks, no one to put me on the spot, insult me, tell me how it is. I'm in withdrawal.'

If only. 'You mean everyone thinks it's a good idea you getting rich on the back of your murdered wife.'

'Rich*er*.'

This was a really bad idea. 'I'm busy.'

'Come on, I was only joking.'

'Well, I'm not. Sorry, P.J., but I am busy.'

'No you're not.'

'I am.'

'Don't be so petulant. You're walking down a dark street, alone, with no one to go home to since that flatmate of yours got famous on the back of *her* brush with death.' Jessie turned around instinctively. A set of headlights flashed at her.

The P. J. Dean ring-tone. 'It was you!'

'Me what?'

'You've been following me.'

'Sorry, wrong stalker. Must be another spurned lover. Who is Bill, by the way?'

Jessie ignored the last question. She didn't mind too much if he thought there was someone else. 'How the hell did you find me then?'

'The desk sergeant is a fan. I had to give her my T-shirt though. Come on, Detective. One dough ball and I'll let you go.'

'I really don't like you,' she said, melting faster than an ice-cream cone on a hot day.

The door of the limo swung open. 'Yes, I know, but it's raining and you look like you need a ride.'

P.J. emerged from the car, his phone still

pressed to his ear. The streetlamp provided the international rock star with his own private spotlight. Typical, thought Jessie, resisting the temptation to start walking towards him. Very quickly his hair got wet and stuck in tendrils to his forehead; his worked-on, model-worthy chest glistened in the rain and his jeans hung loosely off his hips. Jessie smiled to herself. Even a lesbian would be hard pushed to resist. She took a step towards the car. Behind him a previously elusive orange light appeared. Jessie didn't believe in signs, but she recognised good sense when she saw it. She stuck out her hand. The taxi pulled over.

'Sorry, P.J., you'll have to find someone else to suck on your dumplings.' She flipped her phone closed and climbed in. This time no one followed her. This time, she didn't look back.

Chapter 6

Dominic Rivers was a doctor with a penchant for cadavers. Aged twenty-nine, he found his calling late in life. His first calling had been football. Then he broke seventeen bones in his foot, was admitted to hospital and caught a bug that no amounts of antibiotics could cure. The medicine bug. The desire to heal. He never played football again and still walked with a slight limp. He was limping now, as he made his way towards Jessie. She introduced herself. They studied each other. His tanned skin belied his ghoulish pastime and would not have looked out of place on a surfboard. He had large hazel eyes and fawn-coloured hair worn long around his ears. The limp was a curiosity on someone as fit as he was.

'You look like you were expecting someone else,' said the young doctor, catching her staring.

'Sorry, it's just that you don't look like your average pathologist.'

'You don't look like your average DI.'

'Compliment accepted,' said Jessie.

He smiled. 'I've been pawing over your body all night.'

'Not mine. Legally, I believe he belongs to the country. So it's the Queen's body you've been pawing over — or, if you're more of a republican, Blair's.'

'I think I'll go for the former, I like the regal ring of that. Any idea who Betty has on ice down here?'

Behind him were a number of bodies laid out. Only one was uncovered: the man with the leathery skin and hollow eyes. Jessie shivered. Morgues were always too cold.

'I was hoping you would be able to tell me.'

'There was no form of identification on his person. No bank card, driver's licence — nothing. The only thing I did find was a ticket to the pools. Not so much the ticket, but the imprint of its ink on his shirt pocket. However, I can tell you how he died.'

The trainee forensic pathologist pulled the sheet back as far as the dead man's waist. The skin on his torso was patched with black Dalmatian spots.

He drowned. It was an accident. 'It looks like he was beaten to death.'

'Does, doesn't it? But this man drowned.'

'Are you sure?'

'The ink from the ticket would only have transferred if it had at one point been wet, so I had a look at the guy's lungs. I found evidence of waterlogging. The bruises could be the marks of an amateur attempt at resuscitation. Now, look at this —' He pointed to the wrist. The withered skin had been cut away to reveal the preserved muscle below. 'This tissue damage implies that the man was tied up at one point, or strung up. Either way, the wrists must have taken a lot of weight to cause this. Were there any chains found with the body?'

'Chains?'

'Rope would leave a more regular mark. This is sporadic, something that went in and out. My guess is that these are the imprints of chain links. His feet, however, were tied by rope.' He ran his finger over the blue skin around the cadaver's ankles. 'I take it you didn't find any rope either?'

'No.'

'I think these injuries occurred before he drowned, not as he drowned.'

'Well, it makes more sense than someone tying him up, throwing him in a pool, then attempting to resuscitate him.'

The doctor shrugged. 'Unless it was an accident that someone was trying to cover up. When resuscitation failed, whoever was responsible panicked and threw this guy in a hole . . .'

'And what about the scratches?' asked Jessie.

'That could have happened as the man was drowning, flailing in the water, scratching himself against something or someone. To be honest, the scratches are a mystery. As is the damage to the fingertips, but I'll do some more work on them. What I can tell you is that you should have found nothing but a skeleton. This man has been dead for about fifteen years.'

'So why isn't he a skeleton?'

The doctor smiled and from beneath the bench produced a jar of brown jelly. Jessie swallowed nervously. 'Contents of his stomach?' she hazarded.

'Very interesting they are too. The preservation of this man was much assisted by what he ate.' Dominic held up the jar and jiggled it around. 'Pot Noodle. This man lived off E-numbers and additives. He's eaten so many preservatives he'd have taken an age to decompose wherever he'd ended up buried.'

Jessie found this more disgusting than the jar.

'He's not alone either. We're all taking longer to decompose these days. Preservatives are toxins that the body cannot always break down, so it stores them in our fat reserves — ergo, we are preserving ourselves. Human pickles, if you like.'

Jessie grimaced. She did not like.

'But this man was particularly unhealthy, eating processed and tinned food at a time when checks on quality and content were not as rigorous as today. I doubt a fresh vegetable passed his lips. That and the conditions of his impromptu burial resulted in mummification.'

'The lead pit acting as a sarcophagus?' said Jessie.

'I presume the temperature in the room was even?'

'Evenly cold, yes.'

'And dry, it would have to be dry. Even then,' said Dominic, looking back at the relic on the bench, 'it's very freaky.'

'And you've found nothing that can help me ID him?'

'Well, you can forget about trying to track him through dental records. This man took as much care of his teeth as he did his diet. I doubt he visited a dentist in his life.'

'Not a rich man, then?'

'No, not a rich man. I'd guess the clothes are second hand; they have a confusion of fibres on them.'

'So what would a man who cared little about what he ate, and nothing about dental hygiene, be doing in a public swimming pool? Not taking exercise,' said Jessie.

'No. Muscle quality very poor.'

'What then?'

'Perhaps he was taken there to be drowned,' guessed the young medic.

'You can drown someone in a bucket, you don't need to pay to go to the swimming pool.'

'It doesn't make sense, does it?' said Dominic. 'All the more strange when you think this guy should be long gone.'

Jessie shivered again.

'You get used to the cold eventually,' said Dominic. 'It's preferable to the smell, I can tell you.'

Jessie excused herself and turned to leave.

'How do you feel about meeting me at the end of the day?'

Jessie turned. 'I'm sorry, I don't mix work and —'

'I meant work. I can't do anything else now, but I could get you some DNA that you could run through the system. I'll see what I can find in those scratches. I have to squeeze it in between patients, but if you don't mind burning the midnight oil, you're welcome to come back and keep us company.'

Jessie smiled, embarrassed. 'Sorry.'

'Don't be, I'm sure you get asked out all the time.'

'No, I don't.'

'Oh,' said Dominic sympathetically.

'I mean, I do sometimes.'

He shrugged. 'So, it's just me then?'

'No, of course not.'

'Then you would go out for a drink with me if I asked?'

Checkmate. Jessie smiled.

'Great! It will be nice to talk to someone who isn't a patient or dead.' Dominic looked at his watch. 'Shit, I've got to go. I'll let you know when I'm off duty and we'll take a closer look at Betty's body.' He moved past her and opened the door. He extended his hand to Jessie. 'Great to meet you,' he said. Jessie took his hand.

'What is it that you do, when you're not down here with these guys?'

'Gynaecologist,' he said.

'Oh.' Jessie unconsciously retrieved her hand.

'But I'm thinking of changing.'

'Really? Why?'

'It's a great career, but it's ruining my love life.'

'Funny that,' said Jessie. 'My love life is ruining my career.'

'Well, you know what they say about opposites?' He flashed her a smile.

'Don't go anywhere near them, they'll make your life hell?'

He nodded. 'But being good isn't fun.'

'You're right about that, Doctor.'

Jessie walked into a muted police station. There was a faint whiff of alcohol on the air. She could hear the odd groan from behind closed doors; officers regretting the inevitable lock-in. Others were laughing, dissecting the night before.

Burrows was coming out of her office as she approached. He was very tall, and had a lean but well-exercised figure. He carried himself like an athlete: sure-footed and consistent. There was something of the gentle giant about Burrows. He never raised his voice, he never told filthy sexist jokes, he didn't swear at people and he treated everyone fairly. He wore his brown hair at a standard army length. His cropped hair could make him appear scary to someone who didn't know him. He wasn't at all scary to Jessie.

'Hey, boss,' he said. 'Where did you disappear off to last night?'

'Home.'

'Oh, right.'

'You sound relieved.'

'I thought you might have got a lead.'

'Don't be daft, if I'd had a lead I would have informed you, you know that. I was just knackered, that's all.'

'Right. I got your message this morning. PC Ahmet has been going over back issues of newspapers to see if he can find any story relating to a drowning incident. I haven't heard from him yet. Unfortunately DI Ward can't spare any manpower because of the Klein case, so I think the poor lad is going to be at it for some time. What do you want me to do? Go and help?'

Jessie beckoned him into her office. She inserted a CD-ROM into her computer and selected an image of a dark-haired girl wearing high-heeled boots and trousers, covered up by a large jumper. She was carrying a duffel bag.

'Who's that?' asked Burrows.

'You're probably going to think I'm mad, but I reckon that is Anna Maria Klein.'

Burrows set the image in motion again. 'Boss, she's a brunette and she's wearing cheap clothes.'

'She looks like a brunette, I agree.'

'You can't see her face — she's wearing huge glasses, a hat and she's looking at the pavement.'

The girl disappeared from the screen. 'But look at the boots! I've ordered footage from all the cameras in the NCP car park and I'd like you to go down there and question the waiters in that little café near the baths. Those are the only two places she could have changed without being noticed.'

Burrows looked at her in disbelief.

Jessie played with the computer and located the footage of Anna Maria Klein standing at the crossroads. 'Let's see how long it took her to change.' Together they watched Anna Maria move away, and then waited in real time for the brunette to reappear.

'You think that Anna Maria ran into a smelly, grotty car park, stripped off her clothes, put on a wig, threw everything into a duffel bag she spirited from nowhere, and then marched back out again and disappeared into the ether?'

'I think she was wearing some of the gear under her dress and coat — that's why she appeared bigger that usual. The rest she was carrying in that big bag. All she would have had to do was throw them off, put on the wig and shove everything into the duffel that she'd hidden inside her other bag. Hey Presto, new identity. Quick sprint back to Carnaby Street and young Anna Maria Klein has disappeared. We have a missing teenage girl on our hands and all the hysteria that ensues. For once, all focus is on the daughter of the star.'

'You think she's doing this for attention?'

'Why not? Young girls run away all the time. This is just a trifle more theatrical.'

'You know what DI Ward would say.'

Jessie raised an eyebrow. 'Bollocks.'

'Exactly.'

'Which is why I need proof from the car park or café. Come on, it won't take long.'

'What about the case we're supposed to be working on — or the GBH, or any of the other stuff that has been piling up on your desk for weeks?'

'We don't have another case while all this is going on. You said so yourself, all the manpower is tied up on the Klein case.'

Burrows didn't answer her. He crossed

his arms in front of his chest and pretended to watch the screen.

'Don't blame me, blame Moore and her band of merry men.'

'Do you know what I think?' he said finally.

'By the look on your face, I'm not sure I want to,' she replied petulantly.

'I think it would be easier for all of us if you and Mark just left each other alone. I don't know what has got into the two of you all of a sudden.'

'He's been winding me up.'

'So? Rise above it.'

'Hey, normally you're on my side — by my side,' she said quickly, seeing Burrows' expression. 'I meant "by".'

He wasn't convinced. 'This is a wild-goose chase, and it's not even your wild goose to chase.'

'You don't think it's her then?' Jessie pointed to the brunette who now crossed the screen. 'Seventeen minutes — more than enough time to change her appearance.'

'Even if it is — which I think is highly unlikely — what does it matter? This isn't your case.'

'So you can just sit back and watch thousands of pounds being wasted on this circus?'

'But it isn't about the circus, is it? It's about you and —'

'Shh!' exclaimed Jessie, staring at the screen. 'Quick, stop the disk!'

Burrows leant over and hit a button. The screen went blank.

'Get it back.'

'You said stop —'

'I meant pause, pause the bloody thing. Just before the brunette leaves the picture.'

Burrows fiddled with the mouse and the disk resumed playing. He reviewed the image several frames and then stood back to watch as the brunette walked across the screen frame by frame. Just as she was about to exit, he paused the image. Jessie leant in. Then she pointed to the left of the screen where a man in a trilby stood frozen in time. 'There —'

Burrows looked.

'She's being followed.'

Burrows frowned. 'By whom?'

'By Father Forrester.' Jessie pulled out a notebook from her back pocket and flicked over several scribbled pages. 'He turned up at the baths late last night and was wittering on about Anna, about how she needed forgiveness. Told me the place was infested or something.' She found the page she was looking for. 'Here it is — he said it was something to do with old money. That was a great circus act.'

'You didn't question him properly?'

'I thought he was a nutter,' she said defensively. 'I wasn't really paying attention. The caretaker didn't seem very well and I didn't want him ending up back in hospital.'

'Are you sure he's following her?'

'Go back.' Burrows played the scene again. 'Definitely. It's the hat, I've seen it before. He was outside the baths on the morning the roof caved in.' *Check the date.* 'I think he tried to speak to me.'

'What did he say?'

Jessie shrugged. 'I was in a hurry.'

'You want me to tell Mark?'

'Just to be insulted? No thanks.'

'What are you going to do?'

'Go visit some nuns,' said Jessie.

'Then I'm coming too.'

Jessie smiled. 'You and my brother.'

'What?'

'Bill, he likes nuns . . . You met him the other day in the pub. He's staying with me at the moment.'

'That was your *brother?*'

Jessie looked at him quizzically. 'Who did you think he was?'

'I . . .' Burrows shrugged. 'Well, he did

look a bit dishevelled.'

'I'll tell him you mistook him for a perp. So, how about it? Will you go with me on this one?'

Burrows turned back to the screen. 'And if it's nothing . . . ?'

'I'll drop the whole thing.'

'And keep out of Mark's way?'

'And keep out of Mark's way,' she promised.

'You didn't introduce me, by the way.'

'What?'

'To your brother.'

'Oh,' she said, grabbing her jacket. 'Sorry.'

Jessie checked the A–Z and directed Burrows down a narrow cul-de-sac off Wapping High Street. The mottled city tarmac gave way to the smoothed humped backs of old cobbles. The car juddered along the narrow street as it snaked around to the left. On either side of them garage doors were chained or boarded up. They drove as far as they were able until Burrows halted the car outside the only building that looked remotely habitable. Tucked away in the middle of this industrial wasteland was a two-storey redbrick house with an arched door, stone windows complete with grimy glass and several chimney stacks.

Jessie checked the map. 'Maybe he gave me a false address.'

'I don't think so,' said Burrows. Jessie looked up.

'Either not many visitors come down here or you're expected, boss.'

The door was pulled back to reveal a gloomy hallway. Thin bony fingers clasped the peeling paint. It was all they could see of their welcoming party.

'What do you think now?' asked Jessie as she opened the car door.

'Never mess with an intuitive woman,' said Burrows, simultaneously easing open the door on his side of the car. As they approached the building a dog barked ferociously from inside. Jessie jumped. The fingers disappeared. The door started to close. Burrows caught it just before it shut on them and slowly pushed it open again. Inside, a tiny woman stood holding on to a dog that stood level with her shoulders. The dog snarled and barked again.

'So sorry,' said the tiny woman in a high-pitched voice. 'It's only Deuteronomy. He's a sweetie, really, just looks a little frightening.' The dog barked again. Her small hand rubbed his nose affectionately.

'Daft old thing. Settle down now, we don't like to bark at friends.' She looked up to Jessie and Burrows. 'You must be the police officers. We thought you were coming yesterday. Deut was locked up yesterday.' The giant German shepherd growled again; clearly he hadn't enjoyed being locked up.

'Is Father Forrester here?'

'Absolutely. He's in the study. Would you mind waiting while I put Deut in the kitchen?'

Jessie shook her head. 'Not at all.'

'Come on, Deut, biscuits.' The woman and her enormous dog turned away from them. She trotted after the animal as they disappeared around a corner. Jessie looked briefly at Burrows, shook her head as if she was trying to clear her vision, then looked back up the hall. The tiny woman was back. All four feet four of her.

'So rude of me,' she said, extending her hand. 'I am Sister Beatrice, a fond and faithful friend of Father Eric. Welcome to our little rectory.'

'I didn't see a church,' said Jessie.

'No,' said the nun. 'It burnt down eighty-two years ago. Terrible, terrible. Would you like some tea? The kettle is on.'

'Thank you, no, but if you could just tell

Father Forrester that we are here to see him, I'd appreciate it.'

She smiled at Jessie. 'He knows. He won't keep you long, in fact . . . yes, I think that'll be him just now.'

The white-haired man Jessie had encountered at the baths now emerged from the gloom and walked along the black-and-white diamond tiles towards them. He wore grey trousers, a blue shirt that had worn thin at the elbows, a burgundy sleeveless cardigan and brown shoes. His white hair glowed like a halo in the dark. He removed his spectacles as he approached them, smiled widely and extended his hand. Burrows nodded curtly, took the offered hand and introduced himself. Jessie was about to speak when Burrows addressed the vicar himself.

'Sorry to intrude on you, Father,' he said. 'But we need to speak with you on a delicate matter.'

'Is it still Father?' asked Jessie. 'Even though you've retired?'

Burrows looked at her sharply. Father Forrester seemed unperturbed. 'I gave up my day job, not my life's work. But if it makes you feel more comfortable, you could call me Eric.'

'Well, *Eric,* I'd like to talk to you about Anna Maria Klein.'

'Who?'

'The girl who disappeared, Father,' the diminutive nun chipped in. 'We watched it on the news. Such an attractive newsreader.' She turned back to Jessie and Burrows. 'Short-term memory isn't what it was,' she said quietly, giving a nod in Father Forrester's direction.

'Oh, I think the Father remembers only too well,' said Jessie.

The nun looked searchingly at Jessie, then at Burrows, then back to Jessie. She tilted her head gently to one side, smiled, turned away and left in the same direction she had taken the dog. 'I'll make some tea anyhow.'

'You'd better follow me,' said the elderly man. 'This way.'

He moved quickly for an old man, and was soon lost in the darkness. Burrows grabbed Jessie's arm.

'You should show these people some respect,' he whispered.

'We don't even know if he *is* a retired vicar.'

'Of course he is,' said Burrows. 'You think the church gives out these properties to anyone? You think Sister Beatrice is wearing a habit for fun?'

'It wouldn't be the first time some nasty little man has hidden behind a cassock and a cross, Burrows. Mostly with the church's blessing, I seem to remember. So forgive me if I don't seem quite so reverential as you.'

'You're making a mistake, boss.'

'Don't tell me you've suddenly found religion,' said Jessie before following the retreating footsteps up the dimly lit corridor.

Of the seven doors leading off the hallway, only one was open. Jessie knocked briefly and, without waiting for an answer, walked in. The man sat behind a desk, dwarfed by bookshelves plump with reading material. He slipped his glasses back up his nose.

'Sister Beatrice is right, my memory does get a little fuddled now and then. Reprehensible in a parish priest, I'm afraid. Does the Church no good if the doddering old vicar can't remember his eulogies from his Eucharist. Is your colleague going to join us?'

Jessie slipped a colour printout of the brunette over the blotting pad that lay ink-stained between them. 'Do you recognise this girl?'

'No.'

'How can you be so sure, if you have problems remembering things?'

'Things maybe; names often; but never faces. No, never faces.'

'How about this face?' Jessie passed over a picture of Anna Maria as she usually looked.

'It's the same face.' He looked up at Jessie. 'You haven't really come here to talk about this girl, have you?'

'Why, are there others?' asked Jessie.

Father Forrester leant back in his chair. He folded his hands across his chest.

Jessie pulled up a chair and sat down. 'You came to Marshall Street Baths and you told me that this girl needed help. You said that Anna needs help.'

'Did I say Anna? I thought I said —'

Jessie interrupted him. Her temper rose a notch. 'Yes. You did. You also said something about old money and forgiveness.'

He nodded. 'I believe you need my help in that place.'

'I need your help in locating Anna Maria Klein. The girl who you followed out of Marshall Street.'

'Is she dead?'

'I don't know — you tell me.'

'I don't think so,' said the white-haired man. 'Someone is, though. They're stuck there, one of a number of unfortunate spirits who cannot cross over. I felt it very strongly at that place, and I am not the only one.'

'Why did you follow that girl?'

'Terrible feeling of regret, the moment you step inside — did you feel it?'

'Had you met her before?'

'Strange things have been happening there for some time.'

'What were you doing there?'

He looked straight at Jessie, then his focus wandered just to the left of her. 'I'm sorry, we seem to be going round in circles. Perhaps I haven't explained properly what it is that I do.' He looked straight at her again.

'You told me you were a vicar.'

'Indeed, but even vicars specialise in something these days.'

'And what do you specialise in?' asked Jessie.

'Deliverance,' said the old man.

'Had Anna Maria Klein been bad?' she asked.

He chuckled to himself. 'No, no . . . I mean I do soul rescue work.'

'Excuse me?'

'Exorcism, boss. Father Forrester is an exorcist.'

She turned around crossly. Behind her, Burrows filled the door frame, holding a tray full of tea things. He looked ridiculous. 'Don't be ridiculous,' she snapped.

'As a matter of fact, your sergeant is right,' said Father Forrester. 'Except we don't like to use that term any more, it has too many negative connotations. That film undermined the integrity of our entire profession. You see, very few infestations are actually demonic, though it is always wise to keep the devil in your sights, just in case he is plotting some nasty surprises. Usually it's simply a matter of some poor soul who has lost his way and is causing a little trouble until someone notices they are there and helps them move on. The trick to my work is finding out why they got stuck in the first place and then releasing them from their earthbound locality. See? Deliverance, as I said. It's all very simple really.'

Jessie listened to the sound of clattering porcelain as the nun poured the steaming brew into a mismatched collection of chipped cups. She wanted to say something, but all her words had evaporated. Sister Beatrice passed Jessie a cup of hot sweet tea. She was about to refuse, but the nun pressed it on her so forcefully that she took a sip and was surprised to find that hot sweet tea was exactly what she wanted.

'You've told her about Mary?' said the nun.

'No,' replied the vicar.

'Oh.'

He nodded knowingly.

'Oh,' she said again, this time holding the word until it stretched out like gum. She passed Burrows a mug with a picture of St Christopher on it. 'Whom did you lose, Detective?'

Jessie slammed her cup down on the desk. 'I'm sorry to break up this happy tea party, but we are talking about the disappearance of a girl and you haven't answered any of my questions yet.'

'This may seem far-fetched . . .' said the priest.

'Try me.'

'Marshall Street Baths houses a stubborn spirit who will not move on. The name An—'

'Yes, yes, you've already told me that bit, but it doesn't explain what you were doing there,' said Jessie.

'Before a priest can enable a soul to leave a place, they must first find out who they are and why they are stuck. Although I have heightened psychic awareness,' he said, 'for the tough ones I require help.'

'Mary,' said Sister Beatrice. 'She's what you might call a medium.'

'Someone who talks to the dead,' said Jessie with as much sarcasm as she could muster.

'Not dead. In limbo.'

'Right.'

'Boss,' warned Burrows. Even Jessie was taken aback by the force of the sneer in her voice. She inhaled slowly and sat back.

'The ones that get stuck often have a message they need passing on. Mary gets those messages, she can tie up the loose ends, help with the unanswered questions.'

The white-haired vicar with the smiling eyes leant forward over his desk. 'There are many reasons why a spirit would remain here. A horrific act, for example, an injustice — this is often the case in unsolved murders. An inability to accept one's death, when death has come too quickly and the person hasn't had enough time to examine their life. Sometimes they are obstinate and won't move on, and sometimes they are confused and can't.'

'Gee, Heaven must be really empty.'

'Oh, there are many more. Some simply haven't been commemorated as they should have been. Even an unborn life is a little soul. Others are guilty. "Forgive us our trespasses, as we forgive those who trespass against us" — it is as important to forgive as to be forgiven. An entity often remains due to an inability to do either. We get them there in the end.'

'All this is very interesting,' said Jessie, trying not to be drawn in, 'but it doesn't tell me what you were doing in Marshall Street.'

'I know most of the infested places in this city. As a Christian Sensitive and an expert in deliverance, it's my job to know. So, when news of the girl's disappearance hit the headlines, naturally I thought I could help.'

'The same girl you couldn't remember or recognise a few moments ago.'

'Yes, sorry about that.' He smiled, picked up a plate from the tea tray. 'Ginger nut?'

'Marshall Street,' Jessie prompted.

'Oh, yes. So I went down there.'

'To the baths?'

'Yes. Strangely enough it had been in my dreams lately. I awoke with terrible feelings of regret.'

'What do you have to regret, Father?'

'These weren't *my* feelings, though I suppose one is always wondering if one could not have lived a better life.'

'You're telling me that you saw Marshall Street Baths on the news and went down there because you'd been dreaming about it?'

'Right.'

'Wrong. You were there before Anna Maria disappeared. You were there before the story even broke — we have you on CCTV. You appear to be following her through the crowd.'

'I wasn't following anyone. But you're right about being there before the news story. It is an amazing thing, though I shouldn't be amazed any more. I was in town attending a two-day seminar at St Martin-in-the-Fields. I took a stroll through Carnaby Street on the first afternoon and returned there when I saw the news piece the following day. Obviously, I knew where it was. Luckily, the door had been left open for me, so I went in and found you. Why attend a seminar on those days, of all days, at that place, you may well ask. But ours is not to reason why, now, is it? Would you believe how many spiritualists found themselves in New York on September 11th. Some spent days channelling confused spirits to the other side, but I am afraid even so many got left behind and much more work needs to be done there if the pall is ever to be lifted.'

Jessie stood up.

'I'm not sure the detective is really taking this in,' said Sister Beatrice softly.

'I'm not taken in, if that's what you mean.'

'Boss . . .'

'What! People died. You should not mock it!'

'Perhaps you'd like to speak to Mary?'

'Mary the medium?'

The nun nodded. 'My sister.'

'Another nun?'

'No. My twin.' Sister Beatrice laughed. 'It's a good joke though, isn't it? My sister the sister!' She laughed again. 'Yes, very good joke.' She looked up at Jessie, suddenly serious. 'She may convince you where we cannot. She has worked with the police before, though they don't like to admit it.'

'I don't need to talk to your sister. That can wait until I return with a warrant to search these premises.'

'What on earth for?' asked the woman, startled.

'For Anna Maria Klein,' said Jessie.

'This hasn't got anything to do with

Anna Maria Klein. This is about the man in the baths,' said Father Forrester calmly.

'What man?'

'The man whose body you found.'

Jessie felt suddenly queasy. No one knew they'd pulled a man out of the baths. DCI Moore had made sure of that.

'I thought we were talking about Anna Maria Klein.'

'No. You were,' said Father Forrester.

'No. You were.'

'Listen to yourself, Detective.'

Played for a fool, one thing; patronised, another. 'Burrows, we're out of here.'

'But, ma'am, you should hear —'

'Now.' Jessie signalled to the door and Burrows reluctantly left. She turned back to the vicar and the nun. 'You may find my behaviour shocking. I do not apologise, I have been in this business too long and seen too much to take anything at face value. I have arrested child protection officers for molesting children. I can arrest a priest for any number of broken commandments —'

The vicar looked right through her. 'I understand your pain. Loss is a great challenge to one's belief.'

Tears unexpectedly pricked her eyelids.

'I don't know where you're getting this information from, but I will find out.'

Burrows was waiting for her in the dark corridor. They left the rectory in silence, but as soon as they were outside, he turned to her.

'You shouldn't dismiss what they were saying so quickly. I've heard of mediums helping investigations.'

'Bollocks,' said Jessie.

'That is an interesting argument — well constructed. Just the sort of thing I'd expect from your fellow DI.'

'What is it? You want me to go along with all that mumbo-jumbo crap?'

'That mumbo-jumbo crap happens to be what I believe in.'

'Jesus, Burrows, you telling me you're a Christian?'

'Why do you have to say it like that, like it's some kind of disease?'

Jessie stopped walking. Her sergeant looked at her, she could see in his eyes how serious he was.

'You'd bend over backwards if I wore a turban and a dagger hanging from my neck. You wouldn't bat an eyelid if I left work early every Friday for Shiva, but Christian — oooh, scary Jesus creepers and jamborees. I believe in God. There, I said it.'

'Good for you.'

'Don't be so bloody patronising.'

'Burrows, don't swear at me.'

'Then don't disrespect me,' he replied firmly. 'I've never disrespected you.' It was true, even during her previous murder inquiry, when all about her were rejoicing in her demise, Burrows had stood up for her, redirected her and advised her. But she wasn't really angry with him.

'I don't believe in Heaven,' said Jessie.

'That is your prerogative.'

'You do?'

'Yes.'

'Lucky you,' said Jessie, walking towards the car.

'Luck has nothing to do with it, ma'am. Belief in the scriptures requires a leap of faith. That's what people like you can't get your head around. Throw all the science and reasoning you like at me, a leap of faith cannot be challenged.'

'I'm not challenging you, Burrows.'

'Yes you are.'

Jessie put her hand out to open the car door and saw that it was shaking again. For a moment she stared back down the cobbled road to where it bent out of sight. Burrows got in behind the wheel and started the engine.

'Just because you can't see her, it doesn't mean she's not there.'

'What?' said Jessie.

'Doesn't matter,' said Burrows.

Jessie looked back to the rectory. Father Forrester was standing in the door frame watching her, smiling.

Jessie climbed into the car. 'Take me to the library,' she said.

'What about getting a warrant to search for Anna Maria Klein?'

'I'm not going to give them the satisfaction. These people are just touting for business. When he turned up at the baths he said he was there to help Anna. When she wasn't there, it suddenly became old money and a dead guy. He probably overheard my conversation with Don the caretaker. Either way, it's bollocks. I bet they're nothing to do with the Church. Loads of people live in old rectories — they were sold off to pay for all those child-abuse cases.'

'If dismissing them makes it easier for you, go ahead.'

Jessie couldn't cope with any more religious debate. She simply ignored him. 'Anna Maria is where I thought she was.'

'And where is that if it isn't under the

rectory floorboards?'

'Holed up in a hotel, watching her own little drama unfold on the TV.'

'In which case she could be anywhere.'

'Not in those heels.' Jessie looked at the rectory in her wing mirror. They drove along in silence for a while. Jessie wanted to apologise. She never wanted to make Burrows feel the way Mark Ward made her feel. Belittled. Not taken seriously.

'Talk about goose chases! I'm sorry, Burrows; you were right, as usual. I should leave well alone. And I'm sorry if I seemed disrespectful. I admire you enormously, I hope you know that.'

He looked at her briefly. 'Admire,' he said.

'Yes,' reitcrated Jessie. 'And need.'

Burrows cleared his throat. 'So what do you want me to do now?'

Jessie thought for a moment. 'What I asked you to do in the first place. Get the CCTV from the car parks, ask at the café —'

'You said —' Jessie shot him a look. He closed his mouth, indicated right and drove away from the cul-de-sac. Jessie turned on the radio and let music fill the gulf between them. By the time they were halfway down the high street, Jessie laughed.

'You've got to admit it, that was a bit like falling into a David Lynch film. Please — a midget medium and her twin sister the nun.'

Burrows didn't say anything, but she saw the right side of his mouth quiver before he turned away to look out for oncoming traffic. She hoped she'd witnessed the beginning of a smile.

Chapter 7

Niaz stood up from his position at the microfiche as soon as he saw Jessie enter the library research room. When she got closer, he offered her his seat.

'You sit,' said Jessie. 'Any luck?'

'Well, I decided to search through the local paper first. Any incident relating to Marshall Street Baths would automatically be covered by the local press, but not necessarily by the national papers. Unless it turns out to be a big story. You said in your message that the pathologist had estimated approximately fifteen years had passed since the man was killed. To be safe I began searching from 1980, in keeping with the dead man's clothes. So far Marshall Street Baths has appeared twenty-one times in a single year, predominantly for fund-raising events. Marathon swims for a children's trust, celebrity races, and of course local school competition days. The safety record seems to be exemplary. I think I may be here all night.' He pointed to a pile of photocopied articles. Jessie picked up the top one; a group of disabled swimmers and volunteer helpers smiled back at her.

'We are looking for a drowning on February 23rd, year unknown — but start with 1987.'

'You think the date is significant?'

'His watch stopped on February 23rd because it wasn't waterproof. Ergo, we know the date he drowned.'

'The same date he was discovered. Isn't that strange?'

'Compared to the lottery, odds of 1 in 365 sound pretty good.'

'But, ma'am, it wouldn't have made the news if the body was hidden.'

Listen to yourself. 'Just check the date, Niaz. Was there a drowning or not?'

'I beg your patience while I change the sheet.' He fiddled with the machine for a while, flicking through local history in the blink of an eye. 'No.'

'Okay, try 1988 . . .'

Jessie waited.

'No.'

'Go to 1989.'

'Yes.' It was the headline. The main event.

'Can we get a hard copy?'

'Better than that, we can get the original. I'll take the reference number to the desk, it won't take long.'

Jessie took Niaz's place at the machine and while waiting began to read:

LIFEGUARD LETS
LOCAL BOY DROWN

Tragedy struck Marshall Street Baths last Tuesday, February 23rd. Schoolboy Jonny Romano drowned in the pool after suffering a seizure halfway through completion of a length. It is not clear why the lifeguard on duty, Michael Firth, failed to respond to the sixteen-year-old's cry for help. The staff of St Barnaby's Secondary School have claimed that the boy had been particularly boisterous during that afternoon's lesson and perhaps the lifeguard was under the illusion that Jonny was simply messing around with his friends. It wasn't until his body slipped under the surface and went still that anyone realised the situation was serious. Finally the lifeguard dived in to rescue

Jonny and brought him to the side of the pool where mouth-to-mouth resuscitation was performed.

Sadly, the boy never regained consciousness. Despite prolonged efforts to revive him, he was pronounced dead on arrival at hospital. A full inquiry is expected to take place into his death. Meanwhile, Marshall Street Baths has been closed and the lifeguard has been taken in for questioning. At present no charges have been made, though there were angry scenes outside the police station as parents of the drowned boy's friends gathered outside. 'It could have been my boy,' said one mother. 'This was no accident. We want answers.' The school released the following statement:

'Everyone is devastated by Jonny's death. He was a talented and bright student who had no history of seizures or fits of any description.'

The results of the postmortem will be released later today. Meanwhile a vigil outside the baths continues.

Niaz arrived holding the original newspaper and a photocopy of the article.

'What have you got?'

'The article, but I don't think it is anything to do with your man in the morgue.'

'Don't be so sure, Niaz. Look at the headline the following week, after the PM —'

Niaz leant over her shoulder. 'Lifeguard exonerated — drugs blamed.'

'A routine autopsy revealed the lad was on speed at the time. That means this boy's death wasn't an accident. It was manslaughter. Or murder, depending on whose angle you're looking at it from. If this boy drowned because of the drugs he was taking, I want to know who sold him the drugs. There will be a police file. Find it. Our man in the morgue may not have died on that day, but the date meant something to someone.'

'You think he might have supplied the boy?'

Jessie thought about the dead man's teeth and stomach contents. His 'trendy' second-hand clothes, his slicked-back hair, the cash in his wallet, the lack of identification.

'Either he didn't want to be ID'd or someone else didn't want him being ID'd. He wasn't an upstanding member of the community and he had no reason to be in a public swimming pool.' Then she thought of the scratches. Scratches made by a furious woman — a bereaved mother, perhaps. Then drowned by a grief-stricken father. After he was dead, perhaps they panicked. Killing a person was not an easy thing to do. Desperate, they might have tried to empty his lungs, pounding on his chest to force out the water and force in the air. But it failed, just as it had in their son's case. The bruised man died. Mistake or not, it was still murder.

'Boss,' said Niaz, 'look at this —' The following week's paper featured a police sketch artist's impression of a man's face. 'They were looking for a man seen frequently on the premises and known to some of the children as Ian.'

'Ian.' Jessie peered at the rudimentary drawing. 'He looks like those men in "wanted" posters in cartoons.'

'Look at the hair.'

The artist had used a soft lead pencil to indicate thick black hair. It appeared to be slicked back. 'Every fashion-conscious man with enough hair on his head would have been wearing his hair like that. Look at the picture of Jonny Romano, it's almost identical. A hairstyle doesn't mean anything.'

'But this man went missing,' said Niaz.

'Let's pull up the broadsheets and see if

they've got a clearer image of him.'

'We can do better than that,' said Niaz. 'The librarian will show us the originals. I took the liberty of asking her to locate them for me.' Jessie followed her constable along the polished floorboards of the research room. 'She didn't seem to think the request was excessive. Look, there she is.'

A slim Asian girl was spreading papers across a vast table. On each pile was a plain piece of A4 with the name of the paper written neatly in black ink: *The Times*, *Daily Telegraph*, *Guardian*, *London Evening Standard*. She looked up and smiled shyly as Niaz approached. Jessie was about to nudge Niaz knowingly, but seeing the strict way in which he held himself, she thought better of it. Niaz was not really the teasing type. Jessie noticed how his large hand tapped the side of his leg. The unflappable PC Ahmet was nervous.

'I have used the post-it notes to indicate where the story appears,' said the young woman.

Jessie put out her hand and introduced herself.

'Asma,' said the girl quietly. She returned to the piles of paper. 'It was a big story at the time. Many of the papers were calling for the lifeguard's head until news of the drugs broke. Then they changed tack and the *Daily Telegraph* offered a reward for any information relating to the missing man.'

'The man in the picture?'

'Yes. According to these articles his name was Ian Doyle. He lived in a squat, but by the time police raided the address all evidence of the mysterious man had been subsumed by the vagrant population. The turnover of squatters was high. No one knew, or no one admitted they knew the man in question. He had no job, no paper record, no National Insurance, nothing. It was as if he didn't exist.'

Which meant he probably didn't, thought Jessie. Not as Ian Doyle anyway. There were several reasons a man would change his name. None of them good. 'You've done all this very quickly,' she said, impressed.

Asma looked worried for a moment.

'I could see that the police officer had a big job on his hands. I know my way around these papers. As soon as he gave me the local piece, I knew where to look for the rest. I was only trying to help. It is my job.'

'Don't get me wrong, I'm delighted,'

said Jessie. 'Ever thought about becoming a police officer?'

Asma shook her head nervously, but she smiled as she did so.

'Pity, we don't have enough resourceful people on the Force.'

'I like the library,' said Asma. Jessie didn't blame her. Quiet intellects were usually not racist, bullying misogynists. She opened a copy of the *Guardian* where Asma had earmarked the page. The paper had turned the sketch into a photofit image. The face of the unknown man stared back at her from a mismatch of other people's features. Wolverine eyes, a large nose, a sneering mouth, stubble. Every schoolchild's image of a bad man. A description of his clothes was more helpful. The paper claimed he was last seen on the day of Jonny Romano's death by many of the boy's friends. He had been wearing baggy trousers and winklepickers. She pointed the paragraph out to Niaz, who nodded solemnly. 'So he did die that day.'

'Not necessarily. He was on the run, he was homeless, he had no possessions therefore no change of clothes. And don't forget, like the hair, everyone else was wearing similar-styled clothes. It doesn't mean Ian Doyle is our body in the baths.'

'But it is getting more likely.'

Jessie nodded in agreement.

'Would you like me to copy each relevant article and place it in a folder? It would be ready in, say, three-quarters of an hour,' said the librarian.

'That would be great.'

'If you give me a bit longer, I can cross-reference the story.'

'Sorry, I don't quite understand,' said Jessie.

'It is a way of discovering whether the story spawned other articles. Editorials. Other revelations of, let's say, the dead boy's family. And at what point the story went cold, and whether it was ever picked up again, years later, following a new discovery.'

'Look at this, boss —' Niaz held up an article from the *Evening Standard* and began to quote from it: ' "I don't care where he is, he can't hide forever, I'll find him and, when I do, God help me, I'll kill him." ' Niaz looked up. 'The words of an enraged father.'

'Or a very clever double bluff. What is the date of the article?'

'March 1st.'

'If you're right, the man we're calling Ian Doyle was dead by then. It is possible he never left Marshall Street Baths.'

Asma's eyes widened. Jessie withdrew with Niaz. 'When you are through with this, dig up everything you can about Jonny Romano and his family. Let's find out if the father was a violent man and where he lives now. Somewhere in that lot will be the name of the police officer in charge. If he's still alive, I want to talk to him. If not, get me someone who served under him.'

'What are you going to do?' asked Niaz.

'If Doyle was killed on the premises — which is fairly likely, considering he drowned — whoever killed him would have had no option but to hide his body then and there. Did the killer stumble upon the boiler room by accident, or had someone shown them to the disused slurry pits?' A scenario played itself in Jessie's head. A boy slowly sinks to the bottom of the pool and suddenly everyone panics, alarm bells ring, children run screaming from the baths; emergency services are quick to respond, but the boy dies. Ian Doyle lurks somewhere in the building. Hearing the rising commotion, he plans a quick exit but is foiled by the swarm of people down the central stairwell. He's slippery, he knows the back passages and the back stairs. Unable to leave unnoticed, he disappears into the basement to hide until everyone has gone. Perhaps he chooses the boiler room . . . No, the lights would have been too bright. So he goes down one more floor to the old boiler room. What a perfect place to hide. An old coal store. Now all he has to do is wait it out. But someone finds him. Someone with access to chains strong enough to hold him in place.

I've worked here all my life.

Jessie suddenly turned towards the door.

He drowned. It was an accident.

'Where are you going?' Niaz asked worriedly.

'The caretaker at Marshall Street Baths — he knows all about this.'

'Be careful,' said Niaz.

'He's an old man.'

'He doesn't worry me.'

'What does?'

'The rain.'

'Don't worry, Niaz, I had an electrician go down there first thing with a back-up generator, and I've got a torch. That place isn't going to catch me again.' She smiled at him. He didn't smile back. 'All right, all right, I'll get Burrows to meet me there. He's in the area.'

'That would quieten my beating heart,' said Niaz, fanning his dark fingers over his crisp white shirt. Jessie looked over to Asma, busy sorting through the complex filing system. 'I don't think my safety is the reason for your beating heart.'

Niaz slowly put a finger to his lips.

'Your secret is safe with me,' said Jessie, winking, before hurrying out of the library.

Jessie expected to find the doors to Marshall Street Baths unlocked, but not unguarded. The rain had driven the press away. Old bones, old story. She stepped inside.

'Hello?'

Her voice rang out in the empty foyer.

'Mark? Fry?'

Jessie opened the door to the pool-room. Water gushed down the wall. The stagnant pool had deepened.

'Don!'

No answer came except the faint echo of her own voice off the stone walls.

'Godamnit! Anyone could walk in here.' She turned back to the foyer, closed the main door, then pushed through the doors that led to the underground levels until she again found herself standing at the end of the corridor that led to the top of the stone steps. Once more she experienced a strange desire to turn and run. The lights were on but she wasn't taking any chances. She removed her torch from her bag and set the bag down on the top step. A strange and musty smell rose up the stairs to greet her. A damp, fetid smell. Jessie peered down the stairwell. The doors moved open and closed in a dull, repetitive motion. Every time they opened, dirty brown water flushed through the gap. The boiler room was flooding. Jessie heard a strange high-pitched screech from inside.

'Is anyone in there?'

She pushed the door open and turned right into the narrow passageway that opened quickly into the main room. Flotsam floated around her legs. That put an end to the battle between herself and Mark. No one could use this crime scene now. Dirty water lapped at the base of each rotting wooden pillar. She could have been standing beneath the old pier in Brighton. The smell that she hadn't been able to put her finger on before was now stronger than ever. It was a strong acrid odour that stuck in the back of her throat. In amongst the pillars were the four rusty tanks. Jessie heard another screech. This wasn't wind in the pipes or the noise of a distant tube train. It was an animal. And it sounded in distress. She looked at the beams, trying to make out their faint outline against the dark space above her head. They were moving.

Jessie blinked. Her eyes were playing tricks on her again. She pulled the torch out of her pocket, switched it on and pointed the beam upwards. The movement stopped. Then the screeching started again and suddenly, from nowhere, the whole room began to move. From unseen holes in the wall they poured out at the double, scrabbling over themselves to stay above the rising water. They spiralled up the pillars, fanning outwards along the beams. Within moments the water was thick with them, screeching and clawing for something more solid than another rat. Jessie felt something brush past her. She looked down. A rat was climbing up her leg. She screamed, kicked out and dropped the torch. As the slim tube hit the water, the central lights went out. For a brief moment the water around her feet glowed a pallid yellow, then the water seeped inside the torch and killed the light. Once again, Jessie was sucked into complete darkness.

For a second she stood absolutely still, then the wave of vermin that had spilled out from behind the wall hit her. She was surrounded by screeching, clambering rats that began to claw up her legs. She forced herself to swipe madly at them, shuddering in disgust each time her hand brushed against the coarse fur. She felt something sharp slice across her skin and snatched her arm back in pain. She couldn't have gone more than two steps into the room. The door was just behind her. She wiped down both her legs, turned and jumped through the water, her arms outstretched, desperately searching for the metal door. She hit a wall. A brick wall. Behind and above her the rats still screeched. Jessie screamed. Madly she searched the brick wall for the door. Brick. Brick. More bricks, and more and more rats. Overwhelmed, she screamed again:

'HELP ME!'

She hit a corner. A dead end. They were everywhere: on her, above her, below her. And more were coming. She could hear them scrabbling for a way out of the stinking, cold water. She was trapped. The door had vanished. She could feel their claws through her cotton shirt, their teeth biting. 'Help me,' she pleaded.

Suddenly a shaft of white light shone into the room.

'Help me,' she said again, her voice just a croak. There was a sudden clatter of metal on metal.

'Get out of it!' shouted an old gravelly voice. The beam moved round to where Jessie stood pressed against the wall. The door was pushed open wider. The door that she'd missed. The door that hadn't been there seconds before. The door that she'd just walked straight past and felt nothing but brick. She saw a chain swing high and wide, the rats retreated.

'Who's there?' shouted the voice on the end of the torch.

'Me,' said Jessie, shaky and quiet.

'Bloody vermin!' he shouted, swinging the chain again. 'Quick, take my hand.'

He pointed the light in Jessie's face. She put her hand up to shield her eyes and noticed immediately that her hands were bleeding.

'What the hell are you doing down here in this weather? I told you, I told you this place floods when it rains.'

'Don?'

'Yes. Who did you think it was?'

'I can't see your face,' said Jessie.

'Don't matter,' he said. 'Take my hand,

I'll see you get out of here all right.' A thick, calloused hand appeared in the funnel of light. 'Come on, Jessie, the water level is rising. After a certain level, this door will close for good.'

She lunged forward and grabbed the man's hand. He pulled her towards him and in an instant she was back at the bottom of the stone staircase. Jessie shivered. They were both knee-deep in filthy water. The rats did not follow them. Jessie's lower lip was quivering.

'Let's get you to the new boiler room, it's warm in there.'

Jessie didn't trust herself to speak. It wasn't the cold that was making her shake.

'You'll need a tetanus injection for them,' he said, pointing to the bloody patches on her arm. 'Keep your hands away from your mouth till we've got you cleaned up.'

She followed him up the steps until they were once again standing in the concrete corridor. Dry ground. Below them the dark, swirling water held the doors tightly shut. How could she have missed those doors? How?

'Follow me, Jessie. You're safe now.' He swept the corridor with light then pointed the torch at their wet feet. Up ahead was more darkness. Jessie hesitated.

'Don't let them get to you,' said the caretaker. 'Remember, they're more scared of you than you are of them.'

'What?'

'The rats.' He put a hand on her back and coaxed her gently down the corridor. 'You shouldn't have been down there. Not even the junkies go down there.' As soon as they reached the door at the far end, the lights returned.

'And I told you about those lights,' he said, putting away his torch. 'I told you to install a back-up.'

Jessie stared at her bleeding arms. 'I thought we had.' She was still shaking, but less and less with every step away from the basement. 'Don, I have to ask you a question.'

He nodded as though he'd been expecting it. 'I should have told you about them. We've developed a sort of respect for each other. I let them know when I'm coming down by rattling the keys and making a loud noise. They don't like it when you creep up on them. Basically, I leave them alone, they leave me alone, and I never go down there when it's raining.'

'What are you talking about?'

186

'The rats. Weren't you going to ask me about the rats?'

'No, I wanted to ask you about Jonny Romano.'

The caretaker stopped dead in his tracks. 'I rescued you, didn't I?'

'Of course. And thank you. But this is about something else.'

'That happened a long time ago,' he said, staring at his feet. He kicked at the ground, agitated.

'What exactly happened a long time ago?'

He looked up sharply. Like Niaz, the man was nervous. He kept tapping his hand against his leg, the weighty chain rattling with the movement. Jessie tried to step back but the passageway was narrow, one swing of the chain and she would be unconscious. Or worse.

'It's the sewage,' said Don. 'It backs up with all the rain. Used to take hours, but these days it floods in a tick. One minute you're standing on dry land, the next you're up to your middle in shit. It comes up like a geyser through the drains at the bottom of those pits. Typical that the two with no lids are the ones that were never closed off.'

'So it has always flooded?'

'As long as I can remember —'

Jessie tried to push open the door at the end of the corridor, but the warden grabbed her wrist. 'You're not going to tell, are you?'

'No,' said Jessie as calmly as she could. 'I just thought you were the one to talk to, being such an expert on the baths.'

He accepted the compliment with a nod. 'I've been here the longest.'

'Perhaps a cup of tea would be nice,' said Jessie, 'if you can spare one.' She smiled with false bravado.

'You're all the same. Friendly at first, then questions, questions, questions.' He let go of her wrist and abruptly turned away. 'I have to go now. My overall will be ruined if I don't get it to the laundrette.' He moved quickly through the doors and along a pipe-lined passageway to the boiler room. Jessie's arms were hurting; she was torn between following him and escaping to the nearest pub. Then the lights flickered, making the decision for her. She had no intention of being caught in the dark again.

When Jessie reached the modern boiler room, Don was already filling the kettle, humming softly to himself. On the wall were newspaper clippings of proud moments in the history of Marshall Street Baths. Jessie recognised many of them from the articles Niaz and Asma had put together in the library that morning. What the country did in civic duty, it did well. There were sponsored swims for the disabled, volunteer lifeguards teaching children and adults to swim, fancy-dress lifesaving classes . . . Happy, smiling, decent people — all giving back to the place they had been given. Jessie could understand how such a place and the people within it could become a man's life. She could also see how its slow decay and his dissolving circle of friends might depress him.

'Let's see what we've got for your arms,' said Don, as calm and charming as when she'd first heard him speak. 'I've got some Dettol in the first-aid box. This place may be closed, but we are still a stickler for Health and Safety regulations.' The man reached inside a small cupboard on the floor. On the top shelf was the kettle, a box of PG Tips, two cups and a teaspoon.

'That wasn't the case the day Jonny Romano died, was it?'

Don, already on his knees, lowered his head as if in prayer. He sighed heavily.

Jessie pressed on. 'I'm sure it's difficult

to talk about it, but you are the one person who has the facts. You were here.'

'The Marshall Street Baths' staff were ex . . . exor . . .' He paused.

'Exonerated?' ventured Jessie.

'Yes. Ex-on-er-a-ted.' He sighed again. 'They decided that in a court of law.' Don turned his torso and looked at Jessie from over his shoulder. 'It seems I don't have any antiseptic after all. Sorry.'

'That's okay. Where were you when Jonny drowned?'

'Didn't you hear me? A court of law. That makes it final, right?'

Jessie nodded. 'It doesn't hurt to talk about it, though.'

He stared at her for a moment with a look of incomprehension on his face. 'You'll get a bad infection if you're not careful.' He turned back round. Jessie could hear him fiddling with something, but she couldn't see over his hunched back.

Her arms were beginning to throb. 'I'll go to casualty later,' she said.

'I'm not supposed to talk about it.'

'Says who?'

'I don't like questions. No more questions.'

'No more questions,' repeated Jessie.

'That's what they all say.' He stood up and turned around. In his hands were a large pair of rusty scissors and a roll of bandage. He started to walk towards her. Jessie stepped back. 'It's okay,' he said quietly. 'I've done lots of first aid.'

Chapter 8

Niaz knocked on Jessie's door and heard a grunt from inside. He walked in to see Burrows lifting his head off Driver's desk. Burrows had a long red welt along his cheek. It matched the edge of the notepad that the sergeant had been sleeping on.

'Do you know the whereabouts of DI Driver?' asked Niaz.

Burrows blinked, looked at his watch, then blinked again. He rubbed his face with both his hands and tried to focus on Niaz.

'What?'

'I saw her bike. Perhaps I was mistaken, but I made the presumption that she was here.'

'I must have dozed off, I've not seen her yet.'

'She is probably in the canteen. Yes, I should have gone straight there.'

'When you find her, will you give her a

message? Tell her she was right about Anna Maria Klein. The girl went into the car park and changed unseen behind a Range Rover.'

Niaz smiled graciously. 'She is a truly remarkable detective. She was also right about February 23rd.'

'What about February 23rd?'

'The date the watch stopped. The date Jonny Romano died.'

'Who?' asked a sleep-deprived Burrows.

'Jonny Romano, the boy who drowned.' Burrows frowned more deeply. 'Didn't you go with DI Driver yesterday?'

'Yes. To the vicarage.'

'The vicarage?' Now it was Niaz's turn to look confused.

'Then I dropped her off at the library, where I thought she was meeting you.'

'Correct. At the library we ascertained that on February 23rd, 1989, a boy called Jonny Romano drowned as a consequence of a fit, most probably induced by a reaction to amphetamines.'

Burrows shook his head. 'You've lost me.'

'The drugs were sold by a middle-aged man called Ian Doyle, who subsequently disappeared.'

Burrows shrugged.

'The man in the morgue.'

'Ah,' said Burrows, finally enlightened. 'Great, so we know who he is.'

'Indeed. DI Driver returned to Marshall Street Baths to question the caretaker, but obviously discovered nothing. However, there is good news: I have the address of the dead boy's father.'

'Why did Driver want to talk to that old man?'

'He would have known all about the incident. He had access to the basement and possibly chains. Doyle was tied up by a chain before he drowned. I thought you were meeting her there?'

The words hung like icicles in the air: still, sharp and dangerous. Niaz waited hopefully for his senior officer's confirmation. Instead, Burrows ran his hand nervously through his hair.

'And you haven't heard from her since?' asked Burrows.

'No fear,' said Niaz confidently. 'She is most likely to be found in the canteen at this time of the morning. Caffeine. She cannot start the morning . . .' His voice trailed off. Burrows was already halfway down the corridor. Niaz waited patiently for his return. His boss had left no clues to her whereabouts on the desk. Her computer showed that she had messages waiting. Niaz clicked the mouse. The first e-mail awaiting her attention had been received from Dominic Rivers at 10.28 a.m. the previous morning. Niaz started to tap his foot. Then, on a whim, he picked up the phone and dialled Driver's mobile from memory. It rang. And rang. And rang. He left a short message. A few moments later he heard footsteps hurry back down the passageway. Burrows pushed open the door. Niaz had only to look at him to know DI Driver was missing. The phone rang, making them both jump. Burrows got to the receiver first.

'DI Driver's phone.'

'Hi, is she there?'

'Who's calling, please?'

'Bill Driver — her brother. It's not important.'

'She hasn't arrived in the office yet,' said Burrows, playing for time.

'Oh,' said Bill. 'Could you tell her I rang?'

'Certainly. I believe we nearly met the other day, in the pub.'

'Oh yes, um . . .'

'DS Burrows, I work under DI Driver's command.'

'You poor sod,' said Bill. 'Sorry, I didn't mean —'

'You're staying with the DI, aren't you?'

'Yup.'

'May I ask whether you saw her this morning?'

'Actually, no, I was just calling to explain my whereabouts last night — out with mates, got a little out of hand . . .' Burrows looked up at Niaz who was almost leaning over him as he listened. 'She'd gone by the time I got home.'

'Okay,' said Burrows, trying to sound light-hearted. 'Thanks.' He mouthed three words to Niaz. Marshall. Street. Baths.

'Anything the matter?' asked Bill.

'No, no,' said Burrows, wanting to end the call as quickly as possible.

'But she isn't there yet?'

'I'll let her know you called as soon as she gets in.'

'Hang on a sec.' Burrows heard Bill Driver's heavy footsteps on bare wooden boards. A door hinge squeaked. 'The bed doesn't look slept in,' said Bill, returning to the phone. 'Now do you want to tell me what's going on?'

'I'm afraid I really have to go. I'll get her to call you as soon as I see her.'

Jessie's brother didn't respond immediately. Burrows paused for a second too long.

'Don't dick me about here,' said Bill. 'She's my sister and I'm no fool.'

Niaz arched his long neck and pointed to the door. Burrows swallowed. 'DI Driver may have gone to question a suspect alone yesterday. She hasn't been back to her office and, according to you, she hasn't been home. There is probably a perfectly logical explanation to this . . .' he faltered slightly.

'But you can't think of one at the moment?'

'No. And the longer you keep me on the phone, the longer I am from getting to where she went.'

'Well, goodbye then.'

The phone went dead. Burrows and Niaz ran down the hallway, down the stairwell and out on to the street. Burrows hailed an IRV driver, told him to drive first and ask questions second. They pulled up outside Marshall Street Baths three and a half minutes later. Burrows pushed the door, expecting to find it locked, but it swung open. He half fell, half ran into the foyer of the decaying building.

'DRIVER! DI DRIVER!' What the bloody hell was she thinking?

Niaz walked solemnly past him and

pushed open the double doors that led to the giant crater of the empty pool. A man was walking along the middle lane. Slowly and methodically, swinging his arms, one by one over his head. He reached the stagnant pool, turned and began his return length.

Burrows' call rang through the cavernous room. 'DRIVER!'

'Excuse me,' said Niaz. The man stopped and appeared to tread water. 'Do you mind stepping out of the pool so that I can ask you some questions?'

'More questions?' said the caretaker.

'Sorry, but yes, more questions.'

Niaz watched as the slightly stooped, moustached man walked back up the swimming lane. Once at the shallow end, he cut across to the ladder, climbed out, smoothed his hair back and walked towards Niaz.

'I like to do my lengths,' he said. 'It's important to keep fit.'

The door opened behind them. Burrows looked angrily towards the caretaker. Niaz placed himself between his colleague and the much smaller, frailer man.

'We were wondering where our boss, DI Driver, was. Do you have any idea?'

'She went to casualty,' said the man

quickly. 'The rats got her. I told her, you'll need an injection for those. Get a nasty infection, she will. I tried to help her — you see, I've done a lot of first aid.'

'When was this?'

'About sixish, I think. It was still raining. The water level had come up, see.'

Burrows took a step forward. 'Perhaps my colleague didn't make himself clear. DI Driver is missing. You were the last person she was with.'

'She went to casualty,' repeated the caretaker, his eyes darting nervously between the two policemen.

'Are you sure about that?'

'Yes, well, no, not sure . . .'

'What do you mean, not sure?'

The man was beginning to stutter. 'M-m-maybe she didn't go.'

'Where is she then?'

'I don't know, you s-s-said —'

Niaz placed his hand on the caretaker's shoulder. 'Perhaps DS Burrows can go and have a look around, just in case.'

Don nodded. Burrows didn't like it, but he knew when to back off.

'I've been reading a lot of old newspapers about this place,' said Niaz.

The caretaker looked at Niaz suspiciously.

'All those sponsored swims.'

'And I had the best view for every race.'

'So you weren't caretaker back then?' asked Niaz.

He shuffled nervously. 'My shift starts soon. Need to get changed. Big responsibility. Excuse me.'

'What did you do, Don, before they closed the pool?'

'Questions, questions, she was asking me all those questions.'

Niaz took a piece of folded paper out of his jacket pocket. He opened it up carefully and passed it to Don. The caretaker looked at the article and the photograph above it. The page began to shake.

'It's you, isn't it?' said Niaz.

'Red,' said Don. He looked back up at Niaz. 'You can't tell in this photo that the shorts were red. You should see my scrapbook.'

'You worked as a lifeguard at the pool for nearly twenty years.'

He nodded. 'I still do my lengths. It's important to keep fit.'

'What happened when Jonny Romano died, Don?'

'I could always hold my breath longer than any of the other cadets.'

'What happened?'

'They told me he was messing around. It was their fault, they should have let me do my job, but they said he'd soon get bored if we didn't pay him any attention. I shouldn't have listened. All those years and when I am finally tested, I fail. It was my fault, whatever the judge said, it was my fault. They all know.' He looked around the empty pews. 'They won't let me forget.' Don's eyes travelled upwards to the set of rungs embedded in the crumbling wall. Two rusty brackets remained bolted in place. 'What good is a pair of red swimming shorts and a whistle if you can't save a young boy's life?'

'Did you tell DI Driver all of this?'

He continued to stare at the brackets. 'She guessed.'

'Where is she now?'

'I'm not supposed to talk about it. It rattles me. The doctors say I shouldn't be rattled.'

'What happens when you're rattled?' asked Niaz.

'It all goes black,' he said quietly. 'She promised she wouldn't tell, you see. But here you are already, making noise. I don't like noise.'

The double doors opened again. Burrows held up a black rucksack. 'I found it on the steps leading to the basement. Tell me what you've done to DI Driver.'

'It wasn't my fault.'

'Where is she?'

'Don't push him, he's confused,' said Niaz.

Burrows threw down the rucksack, ignored Niaz and strode up to the shrinking man. 'What have you done? I swear to God, I'll —'

'All right, all right, I killed him,' cried the caretaker.

'He thinks you're talking about the boy who drowned,' said Niaz, more loudly.

'Where is she?'

'He doesn't know.'

'I killed him, by doing nothing I killed him. You see, they know, they've always known. I may as well have chained him up and thrown him in the pool myself. I sat there, I did nothing, I killed him. They know, they all know —'

'What the hell is going on?'

The three men turned. Jessie stood in the doorway.

'A millions praises,' exclaimed Niaz. 'You are safe.'

Don sobbed. 'You said you wouldn't tell. I don't like to be rattled. It isn't good, the doctor said.'

Jessie walked towards the uneasy care-taker and put an arm around his shoulders. 'It's okay, Don, it's still our secret.' She looked at Burrows, who was staring angrily at her. 'There must be some sort of misunderstanding here.'

'Where have you been?' asked Burrows.

'A & E.'

'You didn't go home last night,' continued Burrows.

Horrified, Jessie turned her back on him. 'Come on, Don, let's go and get you a nice cup of tea. I brought you a tin of biscuits to say thank you for rescuing me last night.' He dropped his shoulders a little. 'I don't know what would have happened if you hadn't come along and saved the day.'

'Seems you don't need red shorts or a whistle to be a lifeguard,' said Niaz.

'Well said, PC Ahmet,' said Jessie, still rubbing Don's shoulders.

'I don't like to be rattled,' the old man said again, sounding tired but less strained.

'I know. It's over now. The police officers are leaving.'

'Look, boss —'

'Now. I will see you back at the station in half an hour.'

There was the clatter of a door slamming from the foyer.

'Hello?' called out a man's voice.

Jessie recognised the voice immediately, pulled nervously at her shirtsleeves and then called out her brother's name. He had stubble, bloodshot eyes and smelt of stale beer, but he smiled broadly at Jessie.

'What are you doing here, Bill?'

'Checking to see if I still had a sister. Seems I do. Very good. Now I can go back to bed.'

Jessie looked angrily at Burrows.

'Your brother didn't think you'd been home. We hadn't heard from you,' pleaded Burrows.

'You weren't answering your phone,' said Niaz, coming to Burrows' defence.

'I left my bag here by mistake.'

'And your bed didn't seem slept in,' offered Bill helpfully.

'I make my bed in the morning, Bill.'

'But I didn't —'

Jessie glared at him. 'I don't want to have this conversation right now. We have disturbed Don enough —' As she said the words a phone rang. Everyone looked towards Jessie's bag lying on the floor by the double doors. Jessie knew immediately it wasn't her phone. She wouldn't have a personal ring-tone that played a P. J. Dean song if her life depended on it. From behind the double doors she heard a woman swear quietly to herself just as the ringing stopped. Jessie pulled back the doors. The news reporter Amanda Hornby stood in the foyer.

'Oh, hello,' she said, nervously looking over Jessie's shoulder. 'I was wondering if you had any information on the body you pulled out of here?'

Jessie crossed her arms slowly in front of her chest. 'Nice little ring-tone that,' she said. 'Immediately identifiable.'

'Yes, well, it helps in the newsroom when all the phones are going at once.'

'You should remember to put it on silent when you're stalking people,' said Jessie.

'I don't know what —'

Jessie cut her off. 'You've been following me.' She was about to deny it. 'I heard your phone.'

'I was interested in the story, that's all.'

'Really? Funny that, everyone else is still stuck on the Klein case.'

'I like to be a bit different.'

'You could have just come to the station, or called me like an ordinary reporter does, rather than skulking around in the dark.'

Amanda suddenly stood up straight. 'Your boss was denying you'd even found a body, so I suggest you get off the moral high ground.'

Bill put his hand on Jessie's shoulder. 'Hey, I know who you are —'

'Not now, Bill —' said Jessie.

'— Amanda Hornby,' he said, grinning. 'You look even better in the flesh.'

The news reporter purred like a cat. 'Your sister has told me all about you.'

'Jess, you didn't tell me you *knew* Amanda.'

'I don't. And she's leaving.'

'What a coincidence,' said Bill, 'so am I. Fancy a coffee or something?'

Jessie watched in horror as Bill offered Amanda Hornby his arm and she took it with a gloat visible only to other women. There was nothing Jessie could do without appearing like a crazed incestuous freak. Instead she turned back to the pool. 'Don, help — I need rescuing again.'

Chapter 9

Niaz, Burrows and Jessie drove to the Romanos' flat on the Lisson Grove Estate in silence. Even Niaz's diplomatic skills couldn't break the stand-off between his two senior officers. Jessie was furious with Burrows for reporting her missing to her brother and wading in with two left feet at the Marshall Street Baths, and he in turn was furious with her for putting herself in danger and ignoring police procedure. She hadn't been in danger, she insisted over and over again. But she could have been, he retaliated. Jessie felt like Burrows had pried into her personal life, had overstepped the boundary. What she did at night was her own business. She certainly didn't want him knowing whether she'd slept in her own bed or not. Too much information. Too close. Too personal. Jessie stared out of the window. Was she really angry with Burrows for prying, or angry with herself for straying? Bill was right, she hadn't made it home, but she wasn't going to tell him or anyone else that. To be truthful, she was glad to have something else to think about.

Jessie had not left the baths until she had made sure Don was calm. It had taken three cups of tea and a look through his scrapbook. Don — or Michael 'Donnie' Firth, as he was known back then — had had an exemplary record as a lifeguard. For twenty years he had perched on that seat, twenty feet above the water, in his red shorts. In all that time, no one had drowned, no one had even come close to drowning. The man was married to the job. He was Marshall Street Baths. All the children knew him as Donnie and treated him as one of their own. All the parents and teachers trusted him and treated him as one of their own.

On that fateful Tuesday, the class of teenage boys had been getting steadily out of control. They were boisterous, rowdy and aggressive. Don was told by the teachers to ignore their increasingly far-fetched cries for help. It was a decision that would steal his sanity. Jonny Romano cried wolf three times; on the fourth he was dead. It wasn't until the boy sank below the surface and lay like a stone on a riverbed, that Don realised this drowning had not been an act. He performed mouth-to-mouth resuscitation for forty-five minutes, but the boy never regained consciousness. Michael 'Donnie' Firth had to be physically removed by the paramedics. He went with the boy to the hospital. From there he was taken directly to the police station. The questioning had been intense and relentless, they needed someone to blame. The press clawed over his professional and personal life, the mob shouted insults outside his cell for three days and three nights until the drug story broke. By then it was too late. The lifeguard had a massive nervous breakdown from which he never recovered. Two years later, management agreed to give him a job as caretaker. He had been working the boiler room ever since. According to his doctors he heard voices, saw people when there was no one there and told tall tales to anyone who would listen. When this happened too frequently, they upped his medication and the voices died down.

The lifeguard had had nothing to do with the death of Ian Doyle. Police records confirmed that he left the baths in the same ambulance as Jonny Romano and did not return for two years. He was nervous about people knowing his secret, certainly; he was tormented by guilt over the boy's death, but he wasn't a murderer. Don's trouble was that he hadn't accepted Jonny's role in his own death, nor that of the man who sold him the amphetamines. As far as Don was concerned, all the accusations stuck, and the boy's death lay entirely at his feet. Fourteen years on, he could still see the blurred shape of a boy's body lying twenty feet below him at the bottom of a pool. *He drowned. It was an accident.* These were hollow words. An ineffectual mantra which meant as little as *exonerate.* Don would always believe it was his fault, whatever the doctors, psychiatrists and lawyers told him.

A car door slammed.

'I said we're here.' Burrows held open her door, but they didn't look each other in the eye as she passed him.

It was a typical London housing estate, built in the thirties with rust-coloured bricks and covered walkways running the length of every floor. Door. Kitchen window. Door. Kitchen window. Door. Kitchen window. As far as the eye could see. Of all the estates in London, Jessie particularly loathed Lisson Grove. If hatred had a smell it would be of rotting rubbish, beer-bottle dregs and cat spray. Here children weren't children, they were an enemy to be feared.

The three of them hurried into a stinking stairwell and up the concrete steps to the fourth floor. The usual paraphernalia lined their route: used condoms, scraps of foil, syringes, crack pipes, beer cans, Burger King boxes, dog shit. They continued along the walkway, past the flat doors, the sound of a TV or stereo blasting out from almost every flat. Few had been gentrified. Right-to-buy had not applied to Lisson Grove. Niaz knocked on Flat G and within seconds the door was opened by a thickset man with olive skin and oiled black hair, wearing a thin white shirt and black jeans pulled high around his middle. Mr Romano.

'Welcome, welcome,' he said. 'Please come in.' They dutifully obliged. 'Three of you!' he said, expressing what sounded like delight. 'Why the uniform?'

'PC Ahmet is part of CID,' explained Burrows.

'CID, CID. Excellent, excellent. Are you in charge?'

'I am,' said Jessie. 'DI Driver. I know it happened a long time ago, but may I express my deepest sympathies. No parent should bury a child.'

'Seems like yesterday,' said Mr Romano dropping his head. 'Sometimes I think he'll still walk through the door, kick off his shoes and demand his spaghetti al funghi. For an English woman, his mother was an excellent cook.' His expression changed suddenly, his face contorted into a snarl. 'He'd be blown away not to see his mama in the kitchen. But I make do.' He offered them coffee and biscuits. Accepting, Jessie made a silent promise to herself to eat a plate of fresh vegetables when she got home that evening.

'I'm sorry, I didn't know you'd divorced.'

'The bereavement counsellor said it is not unusual.' He stared at Jessie with wide black eyes. 'Grief eats away at you until there is nothing left.'

Jessie held his gaze uncomfortably. She could recognise grief; she just wasn't sure it was grief she was looking at.

'Mr Romano, we'd like to talk to you about Ian —'

'Have you found the murdering bastard?'

'Would you be surprised if we had?'

'Well, I haven't been able to find him.'

'Where have you looked?' asked Jessie.

Mr Romano stood up. 'It would be easier to tell you where I haven't looked, that's how hard I've been looking.' He walked over to a pine dresser and began opening drawers and cupboards. Where glasses and plates should have been displayed, there were notebooks and files. 'It is all documented here. A life's work, you might say. It certainly gave me reason to get out of bed in the morning. Ian Doyle was a nobody, a vagrant; he lived in a squat in Soho and, according to another of the squatters, he'd been there a good many years. But they wouldn't talk to the police, only me. Selling the drugs was his idea of getting a job. It's disgusting what people will do for money. His greed killed my son.' He looked the dresser over. 'Everything you want to know is in there,' he said proudly before turning back to his three visitors. 'He was a very bright boy, my son. God knows where he got it from, came from nowhere, but he was bright, says so in all his reports.' He opened another drawer. 'I've got them all here. His mother wanted them, but no way, she wasn't leaving with those.'

'When did your wife leave, Mr Romano?'

'Two years after Jonny was killed. She

wanted to move on. "Move on?" I said. "How can you move on from something like that?" She said I was caught in the past, I had to choose between Jonny and her — daft cow. He was dead, wasn't he. I think she had some psychological problems.' He twirled a thick finger around by his temple. 'She wanted me to stop searching. How could I stop? I wouldn't do that to Jonny. One day I came home and she'd tidied out his room. Can you imagine? Not been dead two full years and she throws all his stuff out. Thank God I came home early that day from the search. I saw his stuff on the landing out there. I went ballistic, I can tell you.' He shook his head. 'I put it all back, don't worry. I knew exactly where everything went.' He beckoned to Jessie. 'You can come and have a look if you like, get more of a feel of him.' Mr Romano pushed open one of the doors off the central hallway to reveal a museum to the eighties. A shrine to his son. The bed was unmade, there were shoes and socks spread on the floor. A poster of Duran Duran curled off the wall. Mr Romano patiently pushed the corner back up. 'The Blue Tack has lost a bit of its stick.' He stood back. 'It's exactly like when he left for school. Lucky I've got a photographic memory,' said Mr Romano. 'So maybe he did get his brains from my side of the family.'

'Mr Romano, did you ever see Ian Doyle?'

'No,' he said quickly. 'He disappeared fast.'

'So how did you know who you were searching for?'

'Description from Jonny's friends. Friends — ha! I blame that black kid, Pete Boateng. Bad family, the Boatengs, you could tell. So called best friend, didn't do anything to stop Jonny taking those drugs, did he?'

Jessie smelled the pungent air of racism.

'The kids said Doyle hung around the pool a lot, and they weren't the only ones who remembered him. I asked everyone who left the pool that day. Everyone. And I kept notes.'

'May I see?' said Jessie.

'Of course. It's nice to have someone take an interest after all these years.'

Jessie flicked through a blue schoolbook. It had Jonny's name and his class number on the front. Inside was a long list of names and descriptions of people, the time they left the baths and what answers they gave to Mr Romano's questions.

'What did you ask them?'

'Had they seen the devil who killed my son? A lot of people had.'

Jessie glanced back at the book. *15.19: Swimming teacher in tears, no. 15.25: Woman in white coat, ponytail, no English. 15.40: Fat lady, too upset to talk. 15.42: Spotty girl, hook nose, yes — frightening man, black hair . . .* Jessie placed the book down. The notes were nonsense but they told her one interesting thing.

' 'Course it's much easier now with the internet. It has done a lot to help my cause. I've even been to Spain after a tipoff. Wasn't him, though. But it will be one day. He can't run from me forever. The police may have forgotten about it, but he knows he won't escape me. I bet he thinks about where I am every night before he falls asleep. I'm waiting for him to show his face. This time I'll be ready.'

Jessie could sense that Burrows wanted to tell him about the body, put him out of his misery, but she wasn't yet convinced that Mr Romano hadn't concocted a great alibi in his unrelenting search for a man he knew would never be found.

'This time?' asked Jessie.

'I saw him once,' said Mr Romano. 'He stood right outside the kitchen window. I don't know what made me pull back the blind. Some sixth sense, I think. There he was, just the other side of the glass, staring back at me. He gave me the slip during the chase.'

'Mr Romano, it says in your report that you were at the baths before Jonny's body was removed. How did you get there so quickly?'

'I worked for a company in Soho very close to the baths — Vision Inc. Italians make good security men. Jonny had come over with his friends before. The lad was still wet when he reached me.'

'And how soon did you know to look for Ian Doyle?'

'One of the girls squealed about the speed there and then. She said she'd even seen Jonny take it. If that man hadn't forced his drugs on my boy . . .' He mumbled the rest of the sentence.

'But, according to the paper, it wasn't known that he had taken anything until the autopsy three days later.'

'No. I didn't believe her, I didn't believe my son would do something that stupid. He was leaving that dump of a school, he'd got a scholarship. He was getting out.'

'But you *did* believe it. You started

searching for Doyle that day. It's all here, neatly logged.'

Mr Romano's eyes flitted to each of them in turn. 'What do you think she is getting at?' he asked Burrows.

'Just trying to establish the facts. If you had told the authorities about the drugs and Ian Doyle that day, they might have been able to catch him.'

'Please, the police do the "I-ties" a favour? Don't be fucking ridiculous. Back then they didn't bother answering calls in this area.'

'So you didn't trust them to find him?'

'I know what you are doing — you're trying to pin this on me. You're saying it's my fault he got away, just like it was my poor boy's fault he drowned. Oh yeah, you're all the same.'

'So you went looking for Doyle?'

'Yes.'

'And you found him?'

'No.'

'Are you sure?'

Mr Romano laughed.

'Well, someone did.'

Mr Romano stopped laughing.

'Doyle never left Marshall Street Baths. He's been buried in a boiler room for fourteen years.'

Mr Romano stopped breathing.

'The man you've been searching for died the same day your son did, and the only person who knew he'd had anything to do with it was you. Everyone else blamed the lifeguard.'

Jessie felt the buzz of the job race through her as she drove her bike through Central London. The traffic was thin; she and the other petrol heads around her were the new kings of the road. She parked the bike outside St Mary's Hospital and went in. The morgue was three floors below ground; she took the lift down and eventually emerged into the cool quiet corridor. As she pushed through the swing door, she saw Dominic Rivers bent over a corpse. He looked up and smiled.

'Finally. Where have you been?'

'Sorry, temporarily lost my phone and I haven't been to the office to check my e-mails. What have you got?'

'You've obviously been busy. So, let's see — science versus slog. You first.'

Jessie wasn't going to miss this opportunity to show off. When she had last seen Dominic all they'd had was a stiff, no ID, no cause of death, no nothing.

'Well, he went by the name Ian Doyle.

He was a vagrant, living in Soho, selling drugs to kids. On February 23rd, he sold some speed to a sixteen-year-old called Jonny Romano at Marshall Street Baths. The boy subsequently drowned after having some sort of epileptic reaction to the drug. I believe he was taken to the boiler room, or was found hiding in the boiler room by someone who sought quick retribution. He was chained up and dropped into a narrow, deep pit, which at the time was full of rainwater. He drowned, yes, but not in the pool. When he was dead, whoever killed him moved him from the flooded pit to the dry pit, which could be sealed with a lid. And there he has remained, slowly drying out, ever since. Am I right?'

'You're right in that he didn't drown in the pool. I found no traces of chlorine in his lungs. What I found was not as innocuous as London rainwater.'

'Human faeces?'

Dominic grimaced. 'That couldn't be a random guess.'

'No. High rainfall causes the sewage system below the boiler room to back up, filling two of the four pits with sewage.'

'And that explains the scratches . . .'

Jessie nodded. 'Rats.'

'They didn't just get him on the arms; the scratches go all the way up his body.' Dominic pulled the covering sheet off the corpse. 'The material of the trousers protected him at first, when the water level was low and the rats were not particularly active.'

'So the pit wasn't full of water when he went in?'

'No. As the water level began to rise, the rats reacted more aggressively. Which is why the scratches get more intense as you get nearer to the head.'

'Hang on — you think he was alive when the room was flooding?'

'Yes. The wounds bled significantly.'

Jessie knew how it worked. Dead people didn't bleed. 'I can double check with the Met Office. If it rained before February 23rd, then the room would already be under water. If it started raining afterwards, then it flooded after he was chained up.'

'The injuries to his wrists are consistent with the room flooding after he was chained up. He was twisting and turning right up to his last breath.'

'Wouldn't he twist and turn anyway?'

'Not that frenetically. He'd have to have been a very frightened man to cause such a high level of injury to himself.'

The scene materialised against the back-drop of her closed eyelids. 'He's trying to fight off the rats,' she said quietly. 'The water level is rising, it's pitch black and no one can hear him screaming because the baths are closed. When the water is up to his neck, the rats swarm him. He's their last island.' Jessie opened her eyes and looked at Dominic. 'He drowns slowly, overrun by vermin, in other people's waste.'

The doctor nodded. 'His fingers weren't cut off by anything manmade.'

Jessie put her hands together and raised them above her head. 'The water stopped rising, and all that was left sticking above the surface was his fingers.'

'Rats are carrion-eaters. Beggars can't be choosers.'

Jessie lowered her arms slowly and tried to rid her mind of the image.

Dominic pulled the sheet back over the dead man's chewed body. 'You got caught down there, didn't you?'

She pulled up her sleeves. Blood had seeped through the cotton bandages in a few places. 'I got stuck in the boiler room during a rainstorm. Suddenly the lights went out and water was pouring in. They were everywhere. Hundreds of them. I couldn't get them off me.'

'You poor thing,' said Dominic, instinctively walking up to Jessie and putting his arm around her. 'Are you all right?'

Jessie shook her head. 'Not really,' she said honestly.

He turned her bandaged arms over. 'What did you do?'

'Well, I meant to go to casualty, but there were so many people and I wasn't really top priority. I waited for hours and when the scratches started hurting I decided that only one form of medication would suffice.'

Dominic had been slowly unravelling the bandage. 'Tell me you stayed long enough to get a tetanus injection.'

Slowly she shook her head, then grimaced as he pulled the sticky cloth away from the now oozing scratches.

'And the medication?'

'Whisky.'

'Detective, whisky is not an antiseptic.'

'This I now know.'

'Okay, I'm going to give you a tetanus injection right now. Wait here; don't touch anything, and don't go anywhere. I'll be back in a moment.'

'I should be going —'

He cut her off. 'Have you ever heard of the Black Death?'

'Don't be daft, that doesn't exist any more.'

He looked at her very seriously. 'You want to take that chance? The rat population is out of control in this city. You know what they say: you're never more than ten feet away from a Starbucks or six feet away from a rat — and who knows what strains of disease either are carrying. Now wait here.'

Jessie unwound the bandage on the other arm while she waited. She was glad he hadn't seen her first attempt at a field dressing. Three o'clock in the morning, after a lot of neat whisky, she and the one person she'd promised herself she wouldn't call, had tried to dress her wounds. Sluicing TCP on to her arms had not done the trick. She could see from the yellowing flesh that they were already infected. Of course she hadn't felt a thing at the time. It was only in the morning, when she realised what she'd done, that it began to hurt.

'I'm never drinking again,' she promised quietly to herself. What had she been thinking? After so many months of resisting the temptation to call. She'd even managed to turn him down to his face.

Jessie stared forlornly at her arms. She could have blamed it on the shock or the booze, but the truth was, secretly, tucked away in the recesses of her mind, she knew, she still liked P. J. Dean. The rats, the fear and the whisky were merely the excuse she'd been waiting for. Weak and delirious, she'd run to him; weak and delirious she'd stayed; weak and delirious, she'd crept away at dawn.

The door opened again and Dominic walked in holding a packaged syringe and a glass vial of clear liquid.

'Bet you're feeling stupid now,' he said, looking at her arms.

'You have no idea,' said Jessie.

'Right. Bend over,' he ordered, peeling back the plastic. 'Got to put the anus in tetanus.'

'Excuse me?'

'You heard me.' He stuck the needle through the top of the vial and pulled back the plunger. 'Bend over, Detective, or go wait in line at A & E. Either way, someone is going to stick a needle in your arse.'

'Are you qualified to do this?'

He winked at her.

'Oh my God,' she grimaced.

'Consider it punishment for behaving so foolishly.'

Jessie undid the buttons on her leather trousers and peeled them down. The humiliation was made worse by the fact that she was wearing a rather unattractive thong that had been through too many wrong washes to boast any identifiable colour.

'Okay,' said Dominic, 'bend over, hold on to your knees and try to relax. This is going to —'

'FUCK!'

'— hurt.'

Tears sprang to her eyes as he massaged the serum into her bottom. 'Sorry, but you'll thank me for this tomorrow when you can sit down rather than can't.'

Jessie exhaled loudly. 'You're all sadists.'

'Right,' he said. 'Pants up, you're done. Come here,' he added, beckoning her across the room. 'I'll dress them for you. And if you're very good, I'll re-dress them in a couple of days.'

'Thanks, Dominic. I owe you.'

'Well, don't get too gushy. I might be about to put a spanner in the works.' He squeezed out some antiseptic cream on to his finger and began rubbing it gently into the cuts. 'When you get home, take the bandages off, have a long soak in a salty bath, then put more of this cream on. Is there anyone who can put fresh bandages on?'

'My brother. Actually he's a doctor.'

'And he didn't force you to go to the hospital?'

'I haven't shown them to him.'

He was shaking his head, but there was no anger in his eyes.

'He was out,' she claimed. Which was mostly true. 'So what's this spanner, Doctor?'

Dominic finished wrapping up the bandages then moved back a few paces from her.

'I want you to come here and feel my thigh.'

Jessie laughed nervously.

'All for science.' He beckoned her over. 'Right.' She squeezed his right thigh. 'Now left.' She squeezed again. 'Feel the difference?'

'Your left is rock solid.'

Dominic nodded. 'Very good.'

'And the point is?'

'Tell me, in any of the descriptions of this dealer, Ian Doyle, was there mention of a limp?'

'A limp?' she echoed.

'I missed it at first because the drying out of the flesh has caused the fascia and muscle tissue to shrink. Also, to begin with the baggy trousers made the legs look bulkier, so it was harder to notice.'

'Notice what?'

'Just like me, he had a left leg that was stronger than his right. It bore the brunt of his weight. In fact, his right leg was almost entirely wasted. My guess is polio as a child. Knowing what we do about his lifestyle and eating habits, it's pretty safe to assume he was born into a poor family. Back then, vaccination wasn't nationwide; he'd have eaten a poor diet, had a low immune system as a result and contracted polio.'

'How severe would this limp have been?'

'Much worse than mine. You couldn't miss it.'

But everyone had. None of the police paperwork she'd seen listing the descriptions and sightings of Doyle, none of the countless articles that had been written, had mentioned a limp.

'Any chance he could have disguised it?'

Dominic shook his head. 'Only by staying still.'

'There was a nationwide search for this man, rewards were offered, he was known in the area . . .' Her voice trailed off.

'There was a search for someone, but not this guy.'

'Are you absolutely —'

'Certain? Yes. But you can get Sally Grimes down here if you don't believe me.'

'No, I trust you. It's just disappointing.'

'Who first described this Ian Doyle?'

'According to Mr Romano, a friend of his son's.'

'Can you find him?'

'We can find anyone.'

'Well,' said Dominic, 'that's your answer. But if Ian Doyle didn't have a limp, then this is not Ian Doyle.'

Chapter 10

Jessie threw the file across her desk. 'Damn it!' She swore loudly enough for Burrows, now ensconced in Mark's old office across the hall, to look up. 'Sorry,' she said quickly.

'For what?'

'Swearing.'

He looked away, disappointed.

'Now what?' asked Jessie.

He didn't reply. Normally in synch with one another, she and Burrows were missing the target in every conversation.

'I was trying to be polite,' she protested.

'No you weren't, you were walking on eggshells around me. You've been doing it ever since I told you about my faith. And to be honest, boss, it's getting very wearing.'

'I'm not.'

'Then stop trying to curb your language in front of me. I'm not going to start saying Hail Marys.'

'So I can say "Fuck it"?'

'You can say fuck, shit, wank, cunt, if you want. Just don't ask me to.'

Jessie smiled for the first time since she had begun her search for a missing limp. 'So cocksuckingmotherfuckersonofabitch doesn't bother you?'

'You're like that petulant child in *Malcolm in the Middle*.'

'I don't watch TV, but I have a feeling I've just been insulted.'

'You have.'

'Touché.'

Niaz put his head around Jessie's door, noticed the relaxed atmosphere, and relaxed himself.

'I can't sit here all day bantering, let's get a search going on NIB 74c.'

'Please remind me, what is this NIB 74c?' asked Niaz.

'Burrows, you explain.'

'It's the form you fill out after an arrest, describing the perp. Hair colour, height, weight, distinguishing features, like scars, tattoos —'

'Limps,' added Jessie.

'All that information gets fed into the National Identification Bureau database, which is supposed to assist us in catching persistent criminals. Trouble is, it's subjective, and therefore open to enormous variance.'

'A limp isn't subjective,' protested Jessie.

'What makes you believe this man was a criminal?' asked Niaz.

Someone in here needs forgiveness. 'Because it requires an extreme level of hatred to chain up another human being, dump them in a pit and leave them to be eaten alive by rats. If you ask me, this has all the hallmarks of a revenge killing.'

'What about the IRA? They were active in the eighties.'

'Good idea, Burrows — run it past the anti-terrorist unit.'

'It could have been an accident,' said Niaz.

'How do you accidentally chain a man up and suspend him over a hole in the ground?'

Niaz did not answer, but Jessie knew that didn't mean he had nothing to say.

'Let's start with the search, if only to cross it off the list. Stick to what we know: limp and dark hair. Less room for error that way.'

Niaz suddenly looked over his shoulder, then back to Jessie. 'Take cover,' he whispered. 'Incoming missile.'

Jessie knew what that meant and rose to

her feet. She'd had enough of being talked down to. 'Take a seat, Driver,' said DCI Moore sharply. 'This isn't a social call. Is it true that you ordered CCTV footage from the NCP adjacent to the baths?'

Jessie glanced over DCI Moore's shoulder at Burrows, who sat quietly at his desk. He was the only person she had shown the CD-ROM to. He met her look with an impenetrable stare. DCI Moore glanced back at Burrows. 'I take it from your silence that my information is correct. I would be fascinated to discover what possible link exists between that footage and the body DI Ward discovered.'

Nifty little spin that, thought Jessie. She made it sound as if Mark had gone out of his way to locate the missing man's corpse.

'I was looking for a man who claimed he had information that would help me. He'd approached me in the baths while I was there alone, and seemed to know more about the case than he should.'

This answer obviously took DCI Moore by surprise.

'Bollocks,' said Mark, stepping into the doorway.

'Hello, Mark, I didn't see you there.'

'You've been tampering with my case.'

'Why would I do that? I want your men

clear of Marshall Street Baths, not extending their stay.'

'We'll be back there as soon as the flood water has subsided,' he challenged.

'There's no point, Mark. Anna Maria is not there. She took herself off as far as her six-inch heels would carry —'

'Did you find this man, Driver?' Moore cut in, manoeuvring herself slightly so that she stood between her two DIs. Jessie found this interesting. Moore may have sided with Mark Ward, but she obviously knew he was a danger to himself when he felt threatened, challenged or made to feel stupid. If he was a danger to himself, he was a danger to her, so it was in her interest to control the situation. Knowing this made Jessie even angrier. Deep down, DCI Moore knew that Mark was shit-stirring, but still she wouldn't disarm him. Jessie recalled what she'd said to Jones: it wasn't fair that she was being punished for another person's wrong doings.

Life isn't fair, said her mother.

'What?'

'I said, did you find this man?'

Jessie's brows knitted in confusion.

'Are you feeling unwell, DI Driver?' asked DCI Moore, leaning closer to her with a concerned expression.

'Good stalling tactics,' said Mark.

'Mark, enough now. She doesn't look well.'

Jessie cleared her mind and focused on DCI Moore's red mouth. 'I did find him. His name is Father Forrester. He was at Marshall Street Baths the day Anna Maria went missing, he was there the day the body was found and he was there the day after. I did of course ask him if he knew anything about the missing girl, but he claims to have been attending a seminar at St Martin-in-the-Fields. The seminar organisers have confirmed this. He is a slightly old and forgetful man who fancies himself to be an exorcist. The news of a body piqued his interest and he came to offer his services. I may be missing something and the place *is* haunted, but I didn't believe the budget would stretch to a full exorcism. Don the caretaker doesn't seem to mind the voices, so I let Father Forrester go on his merry way.' Jessie looked at Mark. 'If you're easily scared, you could always take a cross with you. Or Burrows,' she said spitefully.

Burrows stood up and walked to the door. 'Excuse me,' he said, pushing it shut, 'I have some phone calls to make.'

Moore started to laugh. 'Do you mean

Father Eric Forrester?'

'Yes,' Jessie grumbled, instantly regretting having brought Burrows into the fray.

'Jessie, Father Forrester is one of the most respected men in the clergy — you thought *he* was a suspect? You must be losing your touch.'

Mark laughed hard at that.

'You've used him then, in investigations?'

Mark stopped laughing.

'Not personally, no, but he is an exceptional man, Driver. Exceptional. You could do worse than to listen to what he has to say. Old souls are his speciality, I believe. Now, tell me what you know about the dead man.'

Mark jumped in. 'You must have ID'd him by now, surely.'

Jessie gave her boss a breakdown of the situation.

'So, it isn't Ian Doyle?' said DCI Moore finally.

'But he looks like him in every other way; he's a dead ringer for the photofit. I've also discovered that the deceased boy's father got to the scene very quickly and talked to the kids before the police did. He knew about the drugs but didn't say anything to the authorities — that strikes me as pretty odd behaviour.'

'This Mr Romano lost his son, he should be forgiven for not acting normally.'

'But —'

'You don't have children, Driver, you couldn't possibly understand.'

'No, I don't, but I have nieces, I can empathise. I know what it's like to lose someone, I know what it feels like to behave irrationally, I know what it's like to want to lash out at everyone. I do understand, DCI Moore.'

For a moment there was an impasse. DCI Moore stared at Jessie and Jessie stared back. But just as she sensed the trace of a thaw, Mark bulldozed his way in.

'Shouldn't we be concentrating our efforts on finding the missing teenager?'

Jessie had her neck in front for the first time, she didn't want to lose her lead. 'I've already found her, Mark. She went into the NCP car park, changed her clothes and tottered off in disguise — wig and everything. She staged this. I suggest you ask her mother why.'

'You're having me on, right?'

Jessie shook her head. 'It's all on the NCP security footage. The silly girl didn't even check for CCTV cameras. I've got the tape.'

'Very good, Driver. That's very good. I didn't want a dead girl in my first week.

Well done. Perhaps Jessie is right, Mark, and you should start checking out hotels in the area. You can do that, can't you?'

Mark was too much of a self-preservationist to react the way he wanted to. He simply nodded.

'Good.' Moore glanced at her watch. 'I've got a meeting with the Chief Constable. Let's get him some more results soon.' She turned back to Jessie. 'Look, I'm sorry to have to bring this up again, but the trousers, Jessie . . . Please, I'd rather not make this official.'

It took a second or two before Jessie realised that DCI Moore had not turned back to congratulate her. She saw the smirk on Mark's face. Sometimes she hated her job. She hated her colleagues. She hated the line of command and the required subordination that came with it. She wondered what the hell she was doing there. Her friends had chosen such different paths to her. From university they had gone on to banking, TV, film, PR; most of them were grossing fat salaries and large expense accounts. They had perks. What were hers? Getting through the day without being insulted, hit, shot at, run down, bawled out. True, they all had problems; true there were politics in companies the world over, but nothing that compared to the Force.

A tense silence remained until the double doors at the end of the corridor clattered shut. The fight had barely started.

'You're a back-stabbing bitch, Driver,' said Mark.

'Ditto.'

'Will you please get over that? I did try and call you, it wasn't my fault you were out getting bladdered. You're fucked because you can't work your special brand of magic on her.' Mark looked at Niaz. 'Surrounded by too many yes men, that's your trouble.'

'Niaz, I think you'd better go.'

He hovered.

'Please,' said Jessie firmly. She did not want to give Mark the opportunity to say something to Niaz that she would not be able to ignore. He left them.

'Let's end this now, Mark, before it gets really out of hand.'

'You think I'm going to give you my office?'

'I don't care about the fucking office. I can't stand this animosity. It's creating a barrier between everybody — and you should apologise to Niaz, too.'

'Fuck off.'

Burrows opened the door, looked at Jessie, then followed Niaz out of CID.

'You had a little tiff with lover boy?'

It was a stab in the dark, thought Jessie. No one knew she'd seen P.J. 'What is wrong with you at the moment, Mark? Is there anything you want to talk about?'

'I really thought a boy like that would have had more taste.'

'Mark, if you aren't capable of having an adult conversation, then just go away.'

'Huffing and puffing and pouty lips. Did you forget his birthday or something?'

'What are you talking about?'

'Doe-eyed Detective Sergeant Burrows, of course. Your little lover boy.'

She stared at him, speechless.

'You don't deny it then?' he said, chuckling.

Jessie squinted at him. 'Have you been drinking cappuccino?'

'What?'

'The chocolate seems to have come off on your nose.'

Mark rubbed it instinctively.

'Oh,' said Jessie. 'Must be something else — can't imagine what. And by the way, a bet's a bet. That office is mine and

240

I'll let everyone know you're a welch if you're not out of there by the end of the day.'

Her mobile phone rang. She quickly answered it before Mark could retaliate.

'Hello, you,' said P. J. Dean. 'Can I tempt you away from whatever you're doing? The press junket is over, I'm all alone at the Ritz and I was hoping I could play field nurse again. You must need fresh bandages by now.'

Jessie looked up at Mark. He mouthed something at her, which she didn't catch but might have been something as infantile as 'I'll get you.'

'I'm on my way,' said Jessie.

'Really? Great! It's the St James's Suite. You're not fobbing me off, are you? You really are coming over?'

'Yes,' said Jessie, leaving Mark gawping behind her. 'I really am.'

'Well hallefuckinglulya! My first aid must have been good. I'm ordering champagne.'

Jessie climbed on to her bike and revved away from the police station. At that moment in time, she would have been happy never to return.

A well-girthed man in a long green coat

opened the door for her as she approached. It seemed only the police force discriminated against leather trousers. The Ritz welcomed them with a slight bow and a smile. She didn't ask for directions, she simply walked to the lift and pressed the button to take her to the top floor. A brass plaque helpfully pointed out the way. The St James's Suite was somewhere off to the right. She walked along the corridor; hotel-like in every way, except that the doors did not line the route like soldiers on parade. Here they were widely spaced and intermittent. She found the St James's Suite and knocked on the door. There was a bell, but she felt daft ringing it. After waiting more than a minute, however, she tried it. Could a suite really be that large? P.J. opened the door wearing his signature faded jeans and white T-shirt. He had bare feet. They were brown. Jessie knew he was brown all over. He leant forward, his face edging closer. Jessie leant closer. He sniffed loudly.

'Well, well, well, no booze on the breath. For once you've agreed to see me without being so pissed that you can barely stand.'

Jessie turned to go.

P.J. grabbed her arm.

'Hey, I'm only kidding.' Jessie looked at him seriously. 'I guess you're not in a kidding mood?' he ventured. 'Don't tell me — the pigs are after you, and you need a bolt hole? Well, you'll be at home here. World's best criminals only on this floor.'

'It's criminal you get paid so much to sing the crap that you do,' she retorted.

'Oh,' said P.J. 'So we are in a kidding mood.'

'Can I come in?'

P.J. moved aside. 'I thought you'd never ask.'

She was wrong about the suite. 'It's huge,' she gasped.

'Why, thank you.'

Jessie hit the rock star playfully and walked to the window. She could see across St James's Park, over the wall of Buckingham Palace and into the grounds. A lake twinkled in the sunlight.

'I've been trying to catch a glimpse of the Queen in tennis whites, but to no avail,' said P.J. behind her. She turned around. He popped a cork. She jumped.

'Drink?'

Jessie nodded gratefully.

'How are the cuts?'

'Oozing with pus.'

'Nice.'

'I had to have an injection in my bottom.'

'Ouch! You know how to make a man jealous.'

He passed her a glass of champagne. 'Thanks,' said Jessie, beginning to relax.

'I'm glad you came over last night,' he said. 'Don't shoot the messenger, but I've missed you. Then I started missing you again, the moment you staggered out of my house at dawn. God knows why. Every time I see you, you tell me I'm a sub-species, barely worthy of sharing the same oxygen with you.'

'You're being typically masochistic for a person in your position. Lots of famous people are like you. I guess I'm cheaper than paying a visit to the House of Pain.'

'And there was I thinking I was unique and special.'

'God no. It's because you've reached the pinnacle of your career,' she continued. 'You've done it all, seen it all, tasted it all.' She shrugged. 'You like the challenge of trying to date a copper. It could just as easily be clandestine meetings on Clapham Common.'

'I thought I *was* dating a copper,' he said, taking a step towards her. Jessie turned away. She didn't know how long she could keep this up.

P.J. laughed resignedly. 'There was a time when girls seemed to like the idea of dating me.'

'Must have been a long time ago,' said Jessie, still facing the window. 'You're pushing forty.'

He put his arm round her waist. 'I can't tell you how nice it is to have my tigress home.'

Jessie couldn't help it, she started crying. It wasn't because only P. J. Dean, in his virtual life, could call a hotel suite home and make it sound normal. It wasn't because DCI Moore was a bitch who might just be able to succeed where Mark had failed and run her to ground. It wasn't because Father Forrester was making her ask herself questions she thought she'd escaped from. And it wasn't because she'd been caught in a pitch-black vortex and lost her bearings so badly that she'd frightened herself to the core . . .

'What's happened?' P.J. asked softly, holding her against his chest while stroking her hair. 'Come on, sweetheart. Shh, don't cry.'

She sobbed again. 'Sorry,' she tried to splutter.

He put his hands on her cheeks and lifted her face up to him. 'What is it, Jessie? Tell me.'

'I can't.'

'You can. Tell me.'

'You'll think I'm an idiot.'

'I won't. Please.' He kissed her cheek as tears ran down her face. More came as the feeling overwhelmed her again.

'I miss my mother,' said Jessie, so quietly that P.J. stopped breathing in order to hear her better. 'And I want her back.'

P.J. said nothing. He stared into her face, slowly brushing tears away with his thumb. P.J. might have his weaknesses, but he knew about familial loss. His sister had drowned herself when she couldn't take the sexual abuse their father forced on her, and P.J. had never forgiven himself for not being brave enough to save her.

'I'm so fucking angry with her,' said Jessie suddenly. 'She could have told me. She should have told me, I was busy, you know, there was always something to do, something that stopped me from getting home. Stupid things: parties, boyfriends, too much work, too little time, too tired, too fucking lazy — and all the time she was dying and she didn't say anything! Why didn't she say, "Jessie, come home"?

That's all she needed to say. I would have known, I would have come home.'

'That's why she didn't tell you. You were living your life. The life she had worked so hard for you to have.'

Jessie blinked at him through stinging eyes. 'You don't know that.'

'I love my stepsons like my own. All I want is for them to be brave enough and confident enough to take on this world. If you've achieved that, you've done well as a parent. Your mother would have loved your busy schedule, your friends, your parties, your boyfriends.' He kissed her gently on the lips, 'Though of course I'd have to take umbrage with her over that.'

Jessie laughed quietly, then sniffed. 'They weren't so bad.'

'Your mum wouldn't have wanted any of that to stop. Not for her.'

'But I could have just hung out with her for a little while.'

'You wouldn't have, though. You'd have watched her and waited, and that's no way to live.'

Jessie sighed heavily.

'Don't be angry with her, Jessie, be proud of her.'

She rubbed her eyes with the tips of her fingers and sniffed again. 'Sorry,' she said.

'Don't be sorry. And don't worry, your secret is safe with me. Though I never bought the indomitable Jessie Driver bit in the first place.'

'Is that so? I seem to remember you were pretty scared of me.'

He pulled her closer. 'Still am, sugar, don't you worry about that.' He wrapped his arms round her and she could feel his biceps hold her. 'So, what do you want to do? We could order lobster and foie gras or burgers and chips, watch old classics on DVD, or take a swim in the tub, or —'

'Go to bed,' said Jessie.

He took her hand. 'Call me old-fashioned, but I'm not waiting to hear you say that twice.' He looked up. 'Now which of these fucking doors leads to the bedroom?'

By the time she emerged from the bedroom it was dusk outside and all of London lay below them like a flashing electronics board. Jessie was enveloped in a robe that draped to the floor. She was dishevelled, happy and hungry.

'I'm running a bath,' called P.J. from the adjoining room. 'It may take a week.'

'Steak and string fries, maybe a little mustard sauce — what do you think?'

'I think you're gorgeous,' he said,

standing on the threshold of the room.

Jessie turned around. 'Aren't you supposed to throw me out of here and call up the next groupie?'

'Hey, I'm not your average rock star.'

'Yes you are,' said Jessie. 'But you're making a supreme effort to hide it from me. I bet you throw terrible tantrums when your press department serve up the wrong mineral water during interviews.'

'Did you read that on Popbitch? It wasn't true. Everyone knows Badoit tastes of sperm. It was perfectly reasonable of me to throw it across the room and fire everyone on the payroll. Badoit! Good God! Who do they think I am — Boy George?'

'See, that's a little too convincing, and I don't even want to know why or how you know what sperm tastes like.'

'Casting couch ain't reserved for the ladies these days. Bath oil or bubbles?'

'Oil.'

'Good choice, madam,' said P.J., retreating to the bathroom.

Jessie joined him after ordering food. She found him standing naked in the middle of a bathroom that was bigger than her living room at home.

'Wow,' said Jessie. 'Hotel bathrooms, my

new rescue remedy.'

'You could have this all the time.'

'Right.'

'You could. I'm going on tour, you could come with me.' P. J. Dean had a perfect body. It was lean and toned, enough muscle to hang on to, not too much to look waxy. She would have crawled along the floor to get a feel of his stomach, but he would never know that.

'I can't. I have a job.'

'Not one that you enjoy.'

She sidled up to him. 'What did you have in mind — some kind of personal service?'

'Actually, I need someone to head up our new security unit. A lot of police officers do that.'

'Only the ones who've been farmed out because the Force can't cover their alcohol dependencies.'

'Perfect. I'll put you down for the job.'

'Not funny,' said Jessie.

'I wasn't joking — about the job, anyway.' P.J. leant over and turned off the taps.

'Thanks, but I think I'll pass.'

'How about coming with me anyway, just not on the payroll?'

Jessie looked at him. Life as a pop phenomenon's girlfriend, she suspected, would be a more perilous job than the one she was in.

'And what about all those leggy models?'

'I don't want any more leggy models.'

'Wrong answer.'

'Serves you right for asking trick questions. So, how about it?'

This was getting dangerous. She had to nip it in the bud. 'P.J., I'm a detective inspector with CID. I earn a pittance compared to you, and I work all hours of the day and night. CID has broken up some of the best marriages. The music business must have had its fair share too.'

'Who said anything about marriage?'

Just like Bill. Why, when you mentioned the word marriage, did men come out in hives? 'You're focusing on the wrong thing here.'

He grabbed a towel. 'Don't spoil this, Jessie. Just give yourself five minutes off, one night. We'll re-engage tomorrow. For now, the battle is shelved, all skirmishes are cancelled. Everyone has been given a pink ticket, R'n'R is compulsory, as decreed by the super major general in command — me. Now, strip off and give me fifty.' He grinned to himself. 'I've always wanted to say that.'

'I could as well.'

'No you couldn't.'

'I could.'

'Go on then.'

'What's it worth?'

'Jesus, woman, there's no let up with you! Everything has to be a deal.'

'So, what's it worth?'

'I'll write you a song.'

'Don't you dare.'

'I'll buy you a bike.'

'Now you're talking.'

'A Harley.'

'Triumph Bonneville — pink.'

'Done.' They shook hands.

Jessie started getting into position.

'Hey, hey, hey, what do you think you're doing?'

'Fifty press-ups.'

'Yep, but in the nude.'

'What?'

'That was the deal.'

'Deal's off.'

'Can't — you shook on it. Now, strip off and give me fifty. Great, I got to say it again.'

'All right, a deal's a deal. But you tell anyone about this and I'll let everyone know you don't write your own songs.'

P.J. shrugged. 'Everyone already knows.'

★ ★ ★

Jessie let the dressing gown fall to the floor. She did fifty press-ups to his count. And then she did fifty more. Because she couldn't help herself. Inside, she wanted P.J. to be impressed.

Much later, after their bath, food, a movie — well, half a movie — another bath and breakfast, Jessie started to dress quietly. She felt better than she had in a long time. At some critical point, the battle she waged with herself to stop her seeing P.J. had become more damaging than seeing him. Would it be better to live a whole life for a short while, or half a life indefinitely?

'Does that mean I have to buy you two bikes?' said P.J., emerging once again from the bedroom.

'You're supposed to be asleep.'

'While you sneak out on me? Sorry, I'm sneaking with you.' He read her mind. 'It's five o'clock in the morning. No one will see.'

'My bike is downstairs.'

'So, I'll escort you to the bike. You are not sneaking out of here like a high-class hooker.'

'I hadn't actually considered that, but thanks.'

'Trust me, you don't look like one. And yes, that is a compliment.'

'P.J.,' said Jessie, picking up her bag, 'you don't really have to buy me a bike.'

'A deal is a deal. Even if I was hustled.'

'I could have done two hundred.'

'You couldn't.'

'I could.'

'Go on then.'

'Do you really want to do this again?'

'I'd pay for four bikes to see you naked again.' He held out his hand. 'But I'm hoping I don't have to.'

For a second she tried to resist. 'I have to go.'

'It's five in the morning — no one has to be anywhere at five in the morning. What difference will an hour make?'

Jessie dropped her bag. 'No difference at all.'

An hour later, at two minutes past six, several police cars pulled up outside the Ritz to reunite a hysterical Sarah Klein with her daughter. As Jessie had predicted, the sixteen-year-old had spent a week racking up a terrifying bill, hidden away in her room ordering room service. No one had forced her, kidnapped her or cajoled her.

At five minutes past six, just as Sarah Klein, with her salon-sharpened nails, took a swipe at the concierge and the first camera went off, P. J. Dean stepped into the lobby holding Jessie's hand. Instinctively, P.J. took flight from the flashes, jumping between the closing lift doors and leaving Jessie standing alone in the midst of the pandemonium.

'How could you give her a room!' screamed the actress, unaware another drama was mingling with her own. 'She's only a *child!*'

'As I told you, Ms Klein, she didn't look like a child when she checked in. She looked . . .' he stumbled over the words, 'well, she looked like . . .' The concierge's eyes flashed over the furious woman in front of him. 'Like you.'

At six o'clock in the morning Sarah Klein was expertly made-up and dressed in a flattering, fashionable outfit. Yet another flash went off as the missing teenager joined the fray.

'Get these vultures away from us!' the actress screamed again. It was quite a scene, or a very good act. Everyone was watching it except Mark Ward and Burrows. They were both staring at Jessie.

Chapter 11

Jessie caught up with Burrows halfway down Piccadilly. He was walking alone. She put her hand lightly on his arm. He turned, took in the sight of her, then carried on walking. The look on his face told Jessie that what Mark Ward had inferred was true. In that extra hour, she had shattered Burrows' dream and her own reputation.

'You must be very pleased with yourself,' he said.

'Why?' She couldn't have been less pleased with herself.

'You were right.'

Jessie didn't understand.

'About Anna Maria Klein.'

'Oh. That.'

'Apparently she had five grand in cash on her.'

'That's a lot of money for a little girl.'

'Do you think her mother gave it to her?'

'That would be difficult to prove. I'm fairly sure she tipped off the press this morning,' said Jessie. 'We could try and find out if Anna Maria made any calls during her stay.'

'It's not your case. It never was. You shouldn't have gone looking for her.'

She fell into an embarrassed silence.

'I don't mean last night,' said Burrows stiffly. 'I mean from before.'

They walked along in silence while Jessie struggled to find a way to explain something that she shouldn't have to.

'You might want to know,' Burrows allowed grudgingly, 'we got nothing concrete out of the NIB 74c so I've widened the search. I also did some background work on Father Forrester: he's the official exorcist for his diocese and very well respected. Perhaps it's worth listening to what he has to say, as a qualified expert.'

Jessie snorted.

'What is your problem with priests? What do you think they do?'

'Drink tea,' said Jessie scornfully. 'At least, that's what our vicar in Somerset did.'

'Then you were unlucky. A good priest is someone who can not only sense a soul in distress but is in a position to help. Apparently, Father Forrester does a lot of work

with the mentally ill and the bereaved —
he's well placed to answer those difficult
questions that death always brings.'

'Really? He can sort it out just like that?
"It was God's will." "Oh, thank you, I feel
so much better now." '

Jessie spotted an Italian coffee shop setting out its tables in one of the side streets.

'Why don't we have some coffee?' she
said. 'I'm absolutely knackered.'

Burrows looked at her. She realised what
she had said and squirmed.

'I know what you're thinking,' said Burrows.

Her embarrassment increased. She
busied herself with ordering coffee and
pretended not to hear him.

'You think I told Moore about the car-
park CCTV. I didn't. Perhaps I should
have. I could see from the moment Ward
and Moore paid you a visit yesterday, you
put my name on the charge sheet. That
hurt — I'm not the type to go sneaking
around behind your back. I thought you
knew that.'

Relieved by the change of subject, she
apologised. 'I'm sorry. I shouldn't have
jumped to conclusions. Worse still, I
shouldn't have dangled the threat of revealing your beliefs like that. I promise

you, I will never do that again.'

Burrows sighed heavily. 'You won't have a chance to.'

Jessie grabbed his arm. 'You're not thinking of leaving?'

He turned to face her. 'Would you ask me to stay?'

'Burrows, I —'

'I can't deny it any longer.'

'Please, don't say anything that is going to make this any more difficult.'

'It will be difficult, but that's the point. I can't go on pretending any more that I don't love —'

Jessie put her hands to her face. 'No, Burrows —'

'— the Lord Jesus.'

Jessie stood ready to catch the words as they came tumbling out of Burrows' mouth, hoping to bundle them up and throw them back so quickly it would be as if they'd never been said. *You don't love me, you just think you do because we spend so much bloody time together. It's a common mistake made by co-workers everywhere . . .* She hadn't been expecting to hear the name Jesus. A relieved laugh escaped her lips.

'Is it really that bad?' asked Burrows. 'Does the word freak you out so much?'

'No. Sorry, it's just weird hearing you

say it like that, with such conviction,' she said, recovering herself.

'I'm as bad as Peter if I go on denying him. You have made me realise that. So I suppose I should thank you.'

'Don't thank me — you're facing certain persecution.'

'I'm ready. And if it gets really bad I will take the matter to the courts. An officer should not be treated differently because of the colour of his skin, nor for his beliefs. It's true what I said: the Force would bend over backwards to accommodate me if I was a Sikh, well it shouldn't be any different being a Christian.'

Jessie jumped gratefully on to the soapbox. 'It shouldn't be any different being a woman, but it is. You ask officers what they think is worse, racism or sexism, and they'll give you the same answer every time: racism. Equality on all levels is what we should be aiming for, but the government has decreed that racism is the ugly word of the day, so now we have papers and memoranda and away-days to defeat it. All the while sexism continues unchecked and filters through to all levels of policework. Prostitutes had it coming and battered wives probably deserved it.'

'I'm sorry,' said Burrows. 'I thought we

were talking about me.'

Jessie relaxed and put her arm playfully on Burrows' arm. 'Sorry. What I meant to say was that, as your superior officer, I will give you my full support.'

'But only as my superior officer,' he said, looking at her.

Jessie removed her hand. 'And as your friend.'

'Don't look so nervous,' he said. 'I'm not in the converting business. I don't go to that sort of church.'

'You would have had your work cut out for you,' said Jessie, hiding her confusion. Mark had placed a poisonous seed in her brain.

'I know, you don't believe in all that mumbo-jumbo crap.'

'That's right, I don't.'

'It's interesting, though,' said Burrows as two small espresso cups were placed on the table.

'What is?'

'That you could be so angry with someone you don't believe in.'

They drank their coffee in silence.

Jonny Romano had indeed been a smart boy. According to school records, he and his friend Pete Boateng had been smart enough to gain scholarships to a nearby

Catholic school that gave away sixth-form places to gifted children from poor backgrounds. A few months more and Jonny would have been on a completely different path, away from the estate kids and the downward spiral of drugs and petty crime. A few months more and Jonny would have benefited from a private education and probably university. Possibly Oxford, like Pete Boateng. It was Pete who had first 'confessed' to the police about the speed; it was Pete who had first described the dealer to the police artist, and it was Pete who had first named the man 'Ian'.

Jessie thought about the newspaper article as she crossed Lincoln's Inn. The kids had been particularly rowdy that day. They had been described by onlookers as unruly, boisterous, disobedient and aggressive. Pete had been a bad boy saved by the Catholic Church. The other boys in the group of swimmers had not been so fortunate. One was inside for drug-related theft; it was his twelfth time in the nick. One had been shot dead by his girlfriend. Another had been paralysed in a joy-riding incident and died a few years later of kidney failure. Jessie would get on to the man in prison as soon as she'd had all her questions answered by — Jessie looked at the brass plaque — Peter Boateng, Barrister at Law.

At thirty-two Peter Boateng had to be one of the youngest partners on record of any chambers within the revered Inner Temple. He was already earmarked for silk. All he had to do was complete twenty years service and remain as successful and pro-establishment as he had been thus far. His chambers — Edmonds, Travis, Sloane & Boateng — ranked among the best criminal barristers in the country. In a very short time, Peter Boateng had swum a long way from Marshall Street Baths.

Jessie and Niaz were shown into an office, and a few seconds later the lawyer appeared through a side door, wiping his hands on a crisp white linen hand towel. It was monogrammed. Peter Boateng had grown from a scrawny youth with a large afro into a tall, slender, self-possessed man with closely cropped hair. The years 'Ian' had been buried beneath the baths, unmissed, unreported and unclaimed, had been good to the boy who had named him.

Having introduced herself and Niaz, Jessie took her seat. Peter Boateng professed himself to be confused as to the purpose of their visit.

'I'd like to talk to you about a case you were involved in.'

'The clerk could probably have answered your questions. He knows the cases as well as I.'

'This was before you were qualified.'

He leant back in his chair. 'Back to the terrifying days of running the gauntlet that is articles?'

Jessie noticed his immaculate diction, his perfect pronunciation. His suit was Savile Row or smarter, his shoes were shined; the flash of sock Jessie saw as he crossed his leg was pulled up taut around his ankle. Peter Boateng had worked very hard to iron out all the creases.

'Back even further than that I'm afraid,' said Jessie. 'Back to the terrifying days of Lisson Grove Estate.'

Peter Boateng did not bristle. He was a pro. 'My, my,' he said, 'that is a long time ago.' He managed a small smile. Relaxation personified.

'And I bet it seems a long way away, too,' said Jessie, looking around the immaculate office.

He shook his head slightly. 'It is never that far away. The old adage of keeping one's friends close and enemies closer applies just as well to places. I have kept Lisson Grove in my sights, if only to remind myself what it is I've been striving to get away from. What case can I help you with? As far as I can remember, I wasn't involved in any criminal matters.'

'No, sir,' said Jessie amiably. 'But you were a witness to a drowning — your friend Jonny Romano.'

Peter Boateng lowered his head as if the mention of his dead schoolfriend still brought back painful memories. Jessie couldn't help wondering if it was genuine.

'He was a very clever boy,' he said, looking up.

'Not clever enough to leave drugs alone though?'

'No. Not that clever.'

'Were you that clever?'

'Clever enough to get out.'

'Impressively so. I salute you.'

'Thank you.'

'Mr Boateng, I know this may seem a strange question, but do you think that the man you said you saw supplying drugs to Jonny could possibly have had a limp?'

He paused for a few seconds before answering. 'I can no longer picture the man I thought I saw give drugs to Jonny. When I think of it, all I can see is that police artist's drawing.'

Jessie looked from the barrister to the

notes lying open on her lap, then back to the barrister. She had expected surprise at her question, a quick dismissal, perhaps derision; she hadn't expected to be side-stepped. 'I'm sorry, Mr Boateng, but according to my records you were pretty certain at the time that you had seen the drugs being passed to Jonny.'

'Why are you asking me about this now?' he asked lightly.

'Why aren't you answering my question?'

'It was a long time ago.'

'True, but all I'm asking for is what you must have repeated a hundred times when you were seventeen. A description of the man you saw giving drugs to Jonny Romano on the day he died.'

'I can't remember.'

'Can you recall if he had a limp?'

'No.'

'Can you recall if he didn't have a limp?'

'I told you, I cannot clearly remember the man I saw that day.'

'Mr Boateng, would you accept that as an answer from a witness?' Jessie stood up. 'I don't think so. Perhaps I should go and ask the other witnesses, they may have less to lose.'

'They have nothing to lose. Tony, Michael and Vincent are all dead.'

Jessie had assumed the barrister would know nothing about his old schoolmates. Clearly he'd kept a close eye. 'I think you'll find that Vincent is still alive,' said Jessie.

'No he isn't. The drugs finally got him — bad batch. His heart stopped. They found him dead in his cell.'

Jessie was genuinely taken aback. Peter Boateng saw it in her face.

'What a surprise, a long-term convict dies of an overdose in the slammer and they sit on the story. A statement will trickle its way into his file in a few months' time, that's the usual practise when this sort of thing happens.'

Jessie needed to recover some ground. 'You seem to have taken a keen interest in your fellow witnesses' lives.'

'As I said, I have kept the estate in my sights.'

'Mr Romano sends his regards,' said Jessie, watching him closely.

'Does he?'

'Yes.'

'Have you found his wife yet?'

Jessie wasn't to be deflected. 'I have a body in the morgue that I would like to identify, a body that fits your description of Ian Doyle perfectly. Would you be willing to do that for me?'

'No.'

'Why not?'

'Because I am neither his GP nor his next of kin, nor was I his boyfriend, girlfriend or significant other.'

'Off the record then, while we are tracking down any of the above?'

'He would have aged. I wouldn't recognise him as the man I saw in the baths,' said the barrister.

'Ah, but he didn't age. Though he died the same day as Jonny, his body was so well preserved that he will look the same as he did the last time you saw him.'

'That's impossible,' said Peter Boateng.

'Freakish, I know, but not impossible. Unless of course by impossible you mean you didn't see him?'

'I meant about the preservation.' Peter Boateng rubbed his chin. Now Jessie had the upper hand.

'How did he die?' he asked eventually.

'Someone chained him up and drowned him.'

'Murdered?'

'Definitely. I gather you are going for silk,' said Jessie, closing her file. 'You have to have a spotless record for that, don't you?'

'My record is spotless,' he said, refusing to appear threatened.

Jessie ran her eyes over the room. 'Are you sure about that, Mr Boateng?'

The lawyer stood up.

'Yes, I know,' said Jessie. 'You have an appointment. Don't worry, we're going.' As Jessie placed her hand on the door handle she heard the lawyer return heavily to his seat. He'd relaxed just a fraction of a moment too soon. She turned. Peter Boateng straightened up.

'You know what I think?' she said, slowly turning the polished chrome handle. 'I think that Jonny Romano wasn't the only boy on speed that day. The lifeguard described you lot as out of control; all the papers backed up that claim with independent witnesses. There was no girl who sneaked to Mr Romano — he talked to you, Mr Boateng. He talked to you rather than accompany his dead son to hospital. That means he had something very important to say, or something very important to hear. And immediately after that conversation took place he started searching for a man called Ian. He asked every single person as they left the baths whether they'd seen him. In fact the only people he didn't mention Ian to were the police. When you remember the details of that conversation, perhaps you would give me a call. Save me the trouble of returning to your chambers again, and again, and again.'

Jessie and Niaz made their way out through the aged buildings of the Inner Temple to Fleet Street. She had assumed that a visit to Peter Boateng would be the quickest way to determine whether or not Doyle had a limp, but it seemed that nothing about the Romano case was straightforward. Like Mr Romano, Peter Boateng had reacted with genuine disbelief and confusion at the news of Doyle's death. That should have laid to rest any suspicions about their involvement, but Jessie was still uneasy. There was something strange about Mr Romano that she couldn't put her finger on, and not for a moment did she believe someone as meticulous as Peter Boateng would have forgotten the man responsible for his best friend's death. She turned to Niaz.

'If Peter Boateng knew about the deaths of his old peers, it's fair to assume he'd have kept an eye on Mr Romano and his search for Jonny's murderer, right?'

'Right,' said Niaz.

'And yet, when the solution to the mystery of Doyle's whereabouts is finally revealed, neither of them seemed . . .'

'Enlightened?' offered Niaz.

'Exactly. At last they understand why Mr Romano's years of searching got nowhere — because Doyle was dead all along —and yet it doesn't seem to make any impression on them. Why?'

'Perhaps they had their own explanation for why he couldn't be found. For example, if he never existed . . .—'

'You're saying Peter Boateng made Doyle up?'

Niaz nodded.

Jessie thought for a while. 'I suppose that would explain why he doesn't want to go over the details now. He has taken an oath to uphold the law. Lying as a seventeen-year-old schoolboy isn't the same as lying as a qualified barrister, but damaging nonetheless. And Mr Romano, was he in on it?'

'Why would Mr Romano spend his life searching for a man he knew never existed?'

'Haven't you ever told a lie so many times that you actually start to believe it?'

Niaz looked horrified.

'No, of course you haven't.'

'With respect, ma'am, isn't it more likely that Mr Romano doesn't know that Peter Boateng lied? It seems to me that Burrows was correct: searching for Doyle has given the man a reason to live,' said Niaz.

Jessie could see the strength in Niaz's argument.

'So it was Peter and his friends who claimed they saw Doyle sell Jonny the drugs, and in doing so exonerated themselves.'

'Why would they want to exonerate themselves?'

'Because they gave Jonny the drugs. They were kids, their friend had just died; they would have been terrified. Peter Boateng especially; he was about to go to public school on a scholarship and couldn't risk the scandal ruining his chances of a better life. So he concocted an evil drug pusher and got his less intelligent friends to back him up. That would explain why Peter Boateng kept such a close eye on the others. Now they're all dead, there's no one to contest Boateng's version of events. He can afford to be relaxed.'

'Except, he wasn't relaxed, was he?'

'No. He had more to tell.'

'So, ma'am, if Ian Doyle the evil drug-pusher never existed, who is the man in the morgue, the man with the limp?'

'I have no idea, and neither does Mr Romano or Peter Boateng.'

Jessie closed her eyes in concentration. Peter Boateng was an intelligent man, trained to ask questions and give nothing away. A man who spoke and acted by design.

'What was the most interesting thing Peter Boateng said in there?' she asked.

'That it was impossible Doyle's remains had been preserved?'

'No. When we were talking about Mr Romano he said, "Have you found his wife yet?" *Found,* Niaz. Why would we need to find her?'

'I thought he was just changing the course of your questioning.'

'So did I. But he could have said any number of things about Mrs Romano's departure from Lisson Grove. Instead he asks, have you found her? He chooses his words very carefully, by "find" he meant to tell me that she was missing — and missing is very different to divorced and living elsewhere.'

'What do you want me to do?'

'Find Mrs Romano.'

Jessie expected nudging and whispering,

sniggering and pointing, but there was nothing. The usual greetings from the usual people: the staff on the front desk nodded hello, the beat officers stood smartly to attention as she walked past. Mostly she was ignored as her fellow officers waded through another hectic day. Mark Ward could not have returned from the Ritz, thought Jessie, pushing open the door to the canteen. But there he sat, surrounded by his usual cronies, eating gammon and pineapple. He waved a curt hello to her. Where were the P. J. Dean posters? The humiliating chants? The crippling comments? Jessie wandered nervously to the lunch queue and picked up a sandwich. Talk was of the spoilt little rich kid who'd run away to the Ritz. No one mentioned Jessie's presence there. This was very strange. Had Mark kept his mouth shut? She took her sandwich and headed back to the door. Mark joined her on the staircase.

'So Anna Maria was found safe and well,' he said. 'What a relief for her poor mother.'

Jessie wasn't sure where Mark was going with this one, so she remained silent.

'Lucky for me, you're unlikely to feel in a gloating mood, having been found in such a compromising position yourself.'

Focusing on the metal treads, Jessie took one step at a time.

'Gold-digger,' he whispered.

Jessie turned.

Mark held up his hand. 'Now, now, settle down. We wouldn't want anyone hearing about your little indiscretion. DCI Moore was quite taken aback — she'd begun to think there was nothing in the Dean rumours and that you were a dyke. Imagine how surprised she was to discover that you're actually a whore.' He held on to her arm. 'What, you can't take a little teasing? That's a pity, because you're going to be getting a lot more, and worse besides. But then you should have thought about that before banging a suspect. Jesus, I thought you might have learnt by now, but he obviously has something that keeps all those women coming back for more. I guess it's his sparkling personality.'

Jessie prised his fingers off her arm.

'Of course, we could keep your dirty little secret quiet, I suppose . . .'

She backed away from him.

'. . . come to some sort of agreement. Let's say I get to keep my nice new office and you get to keep some sliver of respect among your peers.'

Mark stepped closer until Jessie had her back against the wall.

'I wouldn't have thought it was a difficult choice. But I know how slowly a woman's brain works, so I'll give you until the end of the day. You should know that I've come to like my new office a lot, and I would be very sore to lose it. Catch my drift?'

He left her standing on the stairwell. Jessie hated to think what Mark Ward had done to suspects over the years he'd hidden his anger behind the protection of a badge. She wandered to her shoebox of an office and sat in her slightly wobbly chair.

Across the hallway, Burrows' door was open but his office was empty. On his desk was a small cross. By not taking on Mark, she was like the empty-worded fisherman, she was like the battered wives who walked into doors. If Burrows was brave enough, she was brave enough. Mark Ward wouldn't get his office and she wouldn't allow him to degrade her any more. Jessie picked up the phone.

Niaz knocked on Jessie's door.

'Hang on a sec.' She blew her nose and quickly straightened her hair, then shouted, 'Come in.'

'There is someone here to see you. I've put her in the conference room.'

'Who is it?'

'She says her name is Mary Adams — she is the medium who works with Father Forrester.'

'She doesn't have an appointment and I don't have time for that kind of thing right now.'

'I think you should see her,' Niaz said calmly. 'What harm can it do?'

A lot, thought Jessie.

'For your information,' said Niaz, 'the structural engineers have finished checking the Marshall Street Baths. They couldn't find anything wrong with the electricity.'

'I don't care what any of you think, I refuse to believe in anything I can't see,' she said as she stood up and stalked off in the direction of the conference room.

Mary was sitting by the window in an electric wheelchair. She wore a frumpy blue nylon trouser suit and jaunty red trainers. Her hair was pulled back in a bun and Nana Mouskouri-style glasses hung from a chain around her neck, entangled in an amber pendant.

'Can I help you?' asked Jessie.

'I was hoping to be able to help you,'

said Mary in a voice that stroked the soul. This was how it began, thought Jessie angrily.

'That's where you are *all* wrong. I don't need your help, or Father Forrester's, and I certainly didn't ask you to come here.'

'Well, now that I am here, perhaps you will give me a few minutes to explain why I thought it was important to come all this way.'

Jessie winced as she involuntarily looked down at the wheels. Mary laughed and said, 'Yes, they are a great help in the art of manipulation.'

'All of it is manipulation,' replied Jessie, suddenly feeling too tired to stand. Too tired to fight.

'I agree that certain elements of institutionalised religion depend upon manipulation. A big clue is if they start taking donations by direct debit. Those churches are definitely to be avoided.'

'You're not religious then?' asked Jessie.

'I spend a lot of time with religious people, but I'm a heathen compared to them. Luckily, Father Forrester and Beatrice are not the type of fundamentalists who deny the right to Heaven to anybody outside their particular sect. Those churches, too, are best avoided — though they usually go hand in hand.'

'How come your sister went that way?'

'I'm fairly sure I scared my sister Beatrice into Holy Orders,' Mary replied. 'When we were kids we used to play this game of guessing what colour car would come round the corner next. At first it was funny because I always won, and then it got plain weird. Beatrice obviously thought I was a witch and we needed some top-of-the-range divine influence on our side to counteract the demons. Hence the habit.'

'Why are you telling me all this?' said Jessie, folding her arms.

'I know you're struggling with this, but it isn't about you, Detective,' said Mary. 'Something happened at Marshall Street Baths that falls outside your remit.'

'Murder is my remit.'

'And what happens after they're dead is mine,' Mary stated. 'I receive messages from people who are no longer physical entities. Whether they are floating around us or carried within the heart of another person, I don't know. What I do know is that, since my accident, I have been able to hear what previously I could only sense.'

'You couldn't throw me a name, could you?' said Jessie. 'It would save me an awful lot of time.'

'Sorry,' said Mary. 'It doesn't work like that.'

'No, I don't suppose it does.'

'Let me tell you how it does work. I believe in the redemption of scarred souls and that people can try to make amends for past wrongs, either before or after they've passed over. You should know that you are looking for someone filled with regret for all the bad decisions they chose to make in their life. They are stuck here until an act of forgiveness releases them.'

'Aren't you contradicting yourself? If it's all mapped out for us, if you know what colour car is coming round the corner, how can our decisions effect us — we have no choice.'

'It is true that psychics can see into the future and receive concrete messages and evidence for their claims — like the colour of the cars,' said Mary. 'But that doesn't mean everything you do is predestined. Think of life as a tube map — your life begins in Wimbledon and will end in Potters Bar. How you get there is up to you. We are all given guides who try to direct us on the best journey, but you need to acknowledge the possibility of their existence and be prepared to listen to their messages. Ever noticed electrical appliances or lights doing funny things?'

'I'm a bit deaf when it comes to extra-sensory babble,' said Jessie.

'No you're not. You're listening all the time, you just call it intuition. In fact, Jung described intuition as communication by means of the unconscious.'

'Meaning?'

'Intuition is simply how we communicate psychically. In other words, how we get in touch with sources of the past and future that are beyond rational knowledge.'

Jessie was shaking her head.

'You are receiving messages from your guides all the time, Jessie. Things you think of as "coincidence" —'

'Actually, I don't believe in coincidence.'

'Well, there you are then. You think of a friend out of the blue, the friend calls. You're trying to make a decision and you'll find pointers in strange places. Posters, adverts, songs on the radio. Those are messages from your guides. Trust me, you are more psychic than you think. It's what makes you a great detective.'

I can't hear her. 'You're wrong. Your psychic powers must be letting you down.'

'Actually, I'm a *sensitive*. That's a psychic, healer and medium all in one.'

'Busy lady,' said Jessie, standing. 'I

wouldn't want to take up any more of your time.'

'It certainly gets noisy sometimes,' Mary laughed. 'And before you jump down my throat, I don't do any of this for money. I don't agree with that. Mostly, I help Father Forrester with his soul-rescue work. I channel the spirits and try to understand why they are stuck, and then Father Forrester can set them free.'

'Yup, Father Forrester told me why they get stuck and all the absolution bit. Truly, it was very enlightening.'

Mary leant forward. 'Tell me honestly that you didn't feel a sense of foreboding at Marshall Street Baths?'

Jessie shivered as she remembered the mist surrounding her in the basement and the effect it had had on her mood, the unreasonable level of anger she'd felt towards Mark, hitting him — an act so out of character, and the lessening of all those feelings as she moved away from the boiler room. She stopped and stared out of the window. 'You really believe that the Marshall Street Baths are haunted?'

'Haunted is your word, but, yes, I think there is a great deal of unsettlement there. You're right to search for the logical explanation to all this, but you will not always be able to find one. Wouldn't you prefer this world to have just a little bit of mystery, a little bit of magic?'

'Of course, and our need for mystery explains why we have religion. We need to believe in something greater than ourselves. Call it faith, call it Christianity, call it astrology, magic — I don't mind. Without it, what is the point? Why continue? Belief is simply an adaptive Darwinian trait. By keeping our spirits, even in the face of overwhelming scientific evidence to the contrary, we keep ourselves alive. It gives us a sense of purpose, a reason to continue. The uneducated and the poor are the most willing believers. Why? Because they have more need than most to believe that further down the line they'll be rewarded for surviving their shitty lives.'

'That's a little patronising don't you think? If that were really the case, there would be no animals, no birds, no fish or fowl, for they do not have gods. And yet they manage well enough to survive.'

Jessie would not back down. 'They don't have the brainpower to question what we question.'

'Maybe not to question, but they can sense things that we cannot,' continued

Mary. 'While the caretaker was in hospital, the council hired a security guard with a dog to patrol Marshall Street Baths. But the dog wouldn't go in there. In fact, every potential developer has encountered problems in the basement. Why do you think that a prime site in the middle of London has stood empty for so long? Father Forrester was approached by the developers a long time before the schoolgirl disappeared.'

'First I've heard of it, and I'm in regular contact with the council over this case.'

'Then they are not telling you for a reason.'

Jessie continued to stare out of the window into the courtyard below. She heard Mary's chair edge towards her, but she wouldn't turn round. 'Tell me what car is going to pull into the street and I might start believing you,' she said before she could stop herself. 'Sorry, I didn't mean to say that.'

'But you were thinking it.' Mary leant over the sill and looked down.

'I wasn't being serious, honestly,' said Jessie, moving away from the window.

'Yes you were.' Mary watched the road. She frowned. Jessie studied her closely. 'A pink motorbike,' she said finally.

Jessie swung round so fast she heard her neck crick. She bore a hole staring at the street below. A few seconds later a white van pulled in and parked.

Mary's frown deepened. 'Sorry, pink motorbike didn't sound right to me either. I must have been picking it up from somewhere else.' She turned to face Jessie. 'Wishful thinking, maybe.'

Jessie scowled.

'Look, I know that there are many charlatans out there ready to exploit the newly bereaved, and I don't agree with any of them. Please, don't let your experience colour your judgement of us all.'

'That's just what a charlatan would say,' said Jessie, turning her back on the woman. She listened until she could no longer hear the hum of the mechanical chair pulling away. For a long time she stayed in the conference room, staring out of the window at the roof of a dirty white van. The silence was rudely broken by a radio bursting into life from another office. She marched down the hallway towards the noise, ready to tear a strip off whichever police officer was messing around, but the Klein incident room was empty. Everyone had gone home for the weekend.

'. . . that was the Malcolm McLaren hit "Buffalo Gals" on Magic 105.4 FM . . .'

Furious, she hit the off button and stormed away.

Chapter 12

Jessie slipped into the seat next to her former boss, the grey-eyed Jones. Already he looked older. More tired. How, wondered Jessie, could retirement leave you more tired? In front of him stood an untouched pint of beer.

'How are you, sir?'

He ignored the question. 'Tell me about the case,' he said instead. 'It feels like I haven't talked shop for a while.'

'We're still trying to identify the corpse. The NIB 74c search threw up a few names; we're trying to establish whether anyone on the list can be linked to the Marshall Street Baths. Burrows is working on it. You probably heard we found Anna Maria Klein. She made one phone call from the Ritz. We're trying to trace the number. And that's about it. What have you been up to?'

'You didn't come here to talk about my life, did you?'

'No, sir, I didn't.'

'Thank God for that. It's dull living it, torture retelling it.'

He smiled, so Jessie smiled with him, though she wasn't sure what they were smiling about.

'What's on your mind, Detective?'

Jessie let it tumble out. All through her vitriolic outburst about Mark Ward's behaviour towards her, Jones sat quietly staring into his pint. When she was finished he nodded once. Jessie waited. Finally he spoke.

'This is a big step you're proposing to take. A harassment case is no picnic, you know. They'll go over every case, every interview, every decision . . .'

'I can't just go on taking it.'

'You joined a boy's club, Jessie. Don't tell me you're surprised by what you found.'

'I'm surprised by the relentlessness of it. Mark Ward has not given me a moment, sir. He called me a whore — surely there's a line?'

'Have you entertained the idea that he may be the scared one?'

'Scared of what?'

'You and Moore. The boy's club becoming a girl's club.'

'Well, there's no chance of that, sir. She doesn't like me. And so far the feeling is mutual. I don't know how she got to be a great detective. She wants me to use a frigging ghost buster on the case!'

'What?'

'Some guy called Father Forrester. He sees dead people, or some shit like that.'

'Jessie, have you noticed that your language worsens whenever you're feeling threatened or upset?'

'I am threatened. I am upset.'

'Not by Father Forrester, I hope.'

By all of them. She counted to three. 'No,' she said. 'I'm sure he's a good man, if a little misdirected.'

'As a matter of fact, I know Father Eric, and he's a great man with powerful friends.'

'Not you as well, sir!'

'If you go through with this harassment case, Jessie, you could use a man like Father Eric in your corner. It gets very dirty, very personal. All your colleagues will be questioned; they will be asked to choose sides. How can you be so sure that they will choose yours?'

Jessie leant back against the upholstered

bench. 'He thinks that I'm too afraid to fight him. I can't exist like that.'

'You could just go.'

Jessie was horrified. Go? Retreat? Lose?

'It isn't always about winning, Jessie. At some point you have to decide on your quality of life. Maybe it would be easier to move on.'

'I never thought I would hear you say that.'

'You have to decide, Jessie: CID or life.'

'No, I do not have to choose, I should be able to have both. But that won't be possible while I'm terrified that Mark Ward is going to perform a public ritual of humiliation every time I get close to someone.' Jessie stood up. 'I know you like him, sir, and I know he's an old colleague, but if I was your daughter you would be incensed by what he puts me through. Well, you should be incensed. I like being teased as little as the next person, but I can handle it — I grew up with three brothers. This isn't about being teased. This is about being torn apart, and it shouldn't happen.'

'You and he have been getting on so much better. Have you asked yourself why he should start behaving like this now?'

'Because he's an arsehole.'

Jones wasn't going to agree or disagree.

He remained silent. It annoyed her that he could go on defending Mark when, like Moore, he knew what the guy was capable of. 'You should talk to Mark,' said Jones, 'rather than be angry with me.'

'I am angry with you. At some point inertia becomes collusion — isn't that what we tell the women who stand back and watch their partners kill their children?'

'That isn't comparable.'

'No, it isn't. They at least have the excuse of being terrified.'

'Well, I am terrified.'

'What?'

'They've come back to haunt me,' said Jones.

Jessie was not sure she'd heard him correctly. Slowly she sat back down again. 'Did you say —'

'All those dead people, all the bodies we drag up, dig up, peer over, discuss and debate. Those photographs pinned up on the baize board, all the faces, the limbs, the lacerations, strangulations — just your normal, everyday image at CID. It was all so matter of fact at the time. Didn't matter what age it was, or sex, whether it had been sexually assaulted or stabbed, we'd discuss it quite normally over tea and biscuits, like we were chatting about the weather. You'll be doing it now — staring over those preserved limbs and wondering, wondering . . . How did they get there? Who did this? Why? There isn't time to really absorb the person, the person is a problem and remains a problem until the case is solved, then he or she is filed away, buried under the next problem. Well, finally, when there are no more problems to think about, the people come back. The names, the voices, the home videos, the terrible pain they suffered in the days, hours or seconds before their death, they come back. There is so much anger. So much pain.'

Jones had been speaking over the rim of his pint, his breath creating tiny waves and oscillations over the surface of the beer. A little had spilt; it ran down the glass and over his bent fingers. Suddenly he turned to Jessie.

'Do you really want to finish this race with no one but ghosts for company?'

The man was clearly not well. Hadn't Moore alluded to it? Hadn't she said that Mark was doing the job Jones felt he was unable to do. No wonder he hadn't been into the station, no wonder he hadn't gone through the motions with the new DCI. He was depressed.

'I'm not depressed, Jessie,' he said, echoing her thoughts. 'I'm tired because I'm not sleeping very well. I'm not sleeping because I have such terrible dreams, dreams that I didn't think were possible to have. I wake up screaming. I can picture them now.'

'Have you thought about seeing a counsellor?'

'I don't need a shrink, I need a priest.'

'Sir, are you being serious?' she asked.

He placed his drink down untouched. 'Do I look like I'm joking? Jessie, I wouldn't have told you, but you're young and intelligent and the truth is you could do anything in the world. Why fight an ugly battle just to end up in so gruesome a field as this?'

'I've always wanted —'

'Yes, but why?'

. . . There was a woman, she was found with no head. She wore a Marks and Spencer's nightie, of which thousands were sold. No one reported her missing, no one reclaimed her body, no one was brought to justice over her murder. Jessie had been very young when they found the woman near their home in Somerset. Not so young that she hadn't felt a deep-seated empathy for that abandoned woman. They spoke to her. The unquiet dead . . .

'You have brothers —' said Jones.

'It's got nothing to do with them, sir.'

'Really?'

Jessie wanted to change the subject. 'If you're serious about needing to see a priest, what about Father Forrester?'

'He's got more important things to worry about.' Jones' forehead creased in anguish. 'I pray for silence. I haven't been granted it yet.' He finally took a long sip of his drink. 'I'll back you up, DI Driver, whatever you decide to do.'

Jessie returned to work after an all too brief weekend, sat at her desk and thought about her former superior officer. She wanted to tell herself that it was the shock of retirement. She would have liked to think that in a few weeks, when Jones was acclimatised, he'd feel differently about his life's work. But she had seen the look in his eyes, she had seen the newly acquired nervousness in him; a two-week break wasn't going to make a difference. Soldiers suffered the same anxiety. On the front line, during battle, they withdrew into the safety of siege mentality. It was only when they got home — back to their comfortable beds, TV, hot water — that what they'd seen returned to haunt them. Well, Jones had been on the front line for forty years. The onslaught of CID had become his life-support mechanism and someone had just switched it off. What had Father Forrester said to her? *I'll be ready . . . for whatever is needed of me.* Perhaps she had just identified what was needed of him: to be Jones' new life-support system.

Her mobile rang. She quickly went round her desk to close the door, then took the call.

'Can you talk?'

'Finally! Where the hell have you been?' she said.

'Sorry, I had a record company shindig to attend,' said P.J.

'All weekend?'

'It was in Germany — are you all right?'

'No. Mark is threatening to tell everybody if I don't give him back his office.' *Gold-digger. Whore.* 'Don't ask, it makes me too angry just thinking about it.'

'I suppose proudly acknowledging me to everyone is out of the question?'

Gold-digger. Whore. 'Utterly,' said Jessie.

'Well, it may be out of your hands.'

'What do you mean?'

'The *News of the World* have a picture of us coming out of the lift. They've been asking me to comment on who the mystery brunette is. It won't take long for them to work out who you are.'

She sank into her chair, lowered the phone to her lap, and covered her face with her hands. Why had she stayed that extra hour? Who was she trying to kid? She should never have been there in the first place. This was all her fault, she had only herself to blame.

'Are you still there?'

Reluctantly, she put the phone back to her ear.

'Look, Jessie, don't worry. I've been in these situations before,' said P.J. conciliatorily. 'We'll go into crisis management. I'll disappear and it'll all blow over. You'll see.'

'It's all right for you, you don't have to go into an office every day.'

'I'm going to be so low key your colleagues will forget I ever existed.'

'P.J., you can't be low key — you're on *Top of the Pops*, for God's sake!'

P.J. sounded pleased. 'So you *do* take an interest in my career.'

'This isn't funny.'

'I know it's not funny, I'm not an

arsehole. I don't go treating people like shit, I don't shag everything that moves. I'm not such a bad choice. I won't embarrass you, I promise.'

'Look, the truth is, it isn't about what you do or don't do. The problem is how we met — I was investigating your wife's murder.'

'I'm sorry Verity died, but our marriage was a sham. Don't ask me to mourn that.'

'It's a matter of *my* ethics, not yours. I took you away to my brother's house in the middle of the investigation. I lost serious ground because I felt sorry for your stepsons —'

'Oh, so you did all this for the boys.'

'You know what I mean.'

'Not really,' said P.J.

'Please, I'm trying to explain something.'

'Oh, I understand perfectly what you're trying to explain.'

'Do you?'

'What you do is really important, I know that. Much more important than what I do, in fact.'

'Once again, this isn't about who you are or what you do,' said Jessie.

'Right. So if I'd been some builder boyfriend of a murdered hooker, dating me would be fine?'

'No, not then either.'

'But if I was the builder boyfriend of a murdered hooker, I don't suppose I'd have been whisked off to your brother's house, would I? Like you said, Jessie, this has nothing to do with who I am or what I do.'

Jessie felt the ice creep into her voice. 'And so you show your true colours.'

'Before you get all moralistic on me, let's remember, you turned up at my house in a backless dress on a police matter. If all your suspects get the same hands-on treatment, it's no wonder you're so *fucking* busy.'

Jessie tried to shake out the insult, but it wouldn't stop ringing in her ears. 'I can't do this,' she said to herself.

'Jessie, please, I didn't mean that.'

'Yes you did. Deep down, that's what you think. What chance have I against Mark Ward?'

'Come on, you know I don't really think that.'

'You've got a strange way of showing it.'

'Jessie, please, I'm sorry.'

'I've got to go.'

All conciliation left his voice. 'You decided all this the moment the lift doors opened. It wasn't what I said. I could beg your forgiveness, but it wouldn't be granted. You gave up the fight before the fight even started. Well, thanks for that vote of confidence, it sure is sweet.'

'You're the one who left me standing in the lobby.'

'To protect you.'

'Sure.'

'You know what? It isn't worth the fucking hassle.' He sounded exhausted. As exhausted as she felt. 'I've tried, you know I've tried, I know I've tried. The problem is you can't get beyond my public persona. You, Jessie, not me. Despite your protestations to the contrary. And the sad thing is, I really thought you were above all that.'

'Don't try and turn this round, I'm not as easily manipulated as your late wife.'

'I was trying to help her.'

'Save it for the press corps.'

'Fuck it.'

The phone went quiet. She looked at the display. *End call?* She leant back in her chair and closed her eyes. A car horn blared from the street below.

Niaz put his head round the door. 'Are you all right?'

She nodded unconvincingly.

He closed the door behind him. 'You didn't tell me how it went with the medium.'

'She couldn't tell me who it is in the morgue or where Mrs Romano is. I'm hoping your more scientific approach can.'

'Not exactly. There is no death certificate registered under her name. No new marriage certificate either. She has contributed nothing to National Insurance and has taken not one penny from the state since she left her husband.'

'So Peter Boateng was right, she's missing or hiding.'

'Why would she hide? If Doyle didn't exist, then what could the dead man have meant to her.'

'Doyle may not have existed, but she thought he did at the time and the dead man matched the description. Because of the limp, he would have been easy to overpower. He would have protested his innocence but she'd have been expecting that. We know that Peter Boateng doesn't throw away words carelessly, well he said something else in that interview, he said that he couldn't recall the man he saw in the baths that day. That means he saw *someone*. Someone he described as a drug dealer, but who may just have happened to be on the premises; someone who stuck in the boy's memory. Someone who looked like your archetypal "bad guy".'

'Looked like a criminal or was a criminal?' asked Niaz.

'We don't know yet. The National Identification Bureau database threw up five possible candidates. None completely fit the bill, but they do all have limps. So far we've narrowed it down to three likelies. The first, Glen Thorpe, is from Newcastle. Eighteen years ago he nicked a couple of thousand from his employer, did maximum time, and nothing's been heard of him since.'

'Maximum time? No probation then?'

'Exactly. So something must have happened in the nick, and now he's disappeared. His ex-wife assures me he is alive and well and living on the Costa Brava, but I want proof. The second guy, David Peart, was done for ram-raiding in Leeds. No record of him ever being anywhere near Marshall Street Baths. Also quiet for the last fifteen years. If he's dead, I want to see a death certificate.'

'Isn't it more likely that, after getting caught, getting his fingers burnt, he went straight?'

'Since when did the justice system work like that? At least the third guy, Malcolm Hoare, was from London. He has a form sheet as long as your arm. Only trouble is, he stopped breaking the law twenty-seven years ago, and our guy has only been dead for fourteen.'

'What was his last recorded crime?' said Niaz.

'Abduction. He kidnapped a ten-year-old girl in 1976.'

'That is interesting, for it was a suspected kidnapping that led us to Marshall Street Baths in the first place.'

Jessie chose to ignore him.

'What was the girl's name?' asked Niaz.

'Not Ann, Anna or Annie — if that's where you're going with this.'

'A paedophile?'

'The motive was more likely money. The girl came from a very wealthy family. Anyway, he was acquitted.'

'Didn't Father Forrester say something about "old money"?'

'He was talking about Anna Maria Klein.'

'Why don't I go back to the library and check the 1976 papers?' suggested Niaz. 'See if this kidnap took place on February 23rd, 1976.'

'What would it prove if it did?'

'It wouldn't prove anything, ma'am, but it would be a strong indicator —'

'Malcolm Hoare weighed the same as a

Sumo wrestler and had blond hair. Our dead guy is skinny with black hair. It isn't him.'

'A man with form would have plenty to regret,' insisted Niaz.

'This man didn't die of regret. He died because of something he'd done. Think of the exceptionally hateful way he was killed. Who in all of this has the most reason to hate? Mr and Mrs Romano. I'm not certain of Mr Romano, and Mrs Romano is a mystery. What if she wanted her husband to stop the search because she knew exactly where it would end?'

Two years spent looking over her shoulder, terrified that the corpse would be found. That kind of pressure would have been difficult to live under, thought Jessie. That kind of pressure would easily ruin a marriage. Paranoia is a far harsher jail sentence than anything Her Majesty's Prison Service could impose. 'Perhaps she ran to save her sanity, perhaps she ran to save herself. Perhaps Mr Romano is covering for her. You want to be a detective, Niaz, what do you think?'

'I think you should listen to yourself.'

Jessie frowned.

'By that I mean you've always suspected Mr Romano was hiding something,

303

ma'am, so we should continue to follow your instincts — it's got us all this far.'

Instinct, she liked that word. Jung could go to hell. 'Call Burrows, tell him to meet us at Lisson Grove.'

Jessie peered through the plain pane of glass and saw a kettle softly exhale a curling line of steam. The sink was full of dirty plates; on the sideboard were half-eaten tins of beans and congealing Pot Noodles. Mr Romano was at home. Jessie looked at her watch.

'He'll be here,' said Niaz.

She waited until Burrows came into view before knocking on the door. The man who opened it bore no resemblance to the well-groomed individual they'd questioned a couple of days earlier. Without saying a word, Mr Romano retreated to the sitting room.

A quick glance through one of the open doors revealed his bedroom to be in a similar state to the kitchen.

Burrows whispered, 'Doesn't look as though he's ventured out since we were last here.'

'Couldn't be a guilty conscience, could it?'

'Boss, he's spent years looking for a man

who's been dead all that time. So long as he was searching, he never had to come to terms with the death of his son. He's had to do fourteen years of mourning in a matter of days. Go easy on him, okay?'

Mr Romano was seated on the edge of the sofa. At his feet were strewn empty beer cans. He did not look up when they entered the room.

'Mr Romano, do the names Glen Thorpe, David Peart or Malcolm Hoare mean anything to you?'

Nothing in his body language changed. 'Huh?'

Niaz shook his head.

'What about Peter Boateng?'

With a jolt, he straightened up. 'Toe-rag. Always getting into trouble. Always getting my boy into trouble.'

'Was that why you went to talk to him at the baths?'

His eyes looked around the room nervously. 'He had to have something to do with it. Jonny loved Pete. He would have done anything that Pete told him. I don't know how that boy had such a hold on my son. Those African types, they do voodoo and stuff, you know.'

'Mr Romano, did you have any specific reason not to like Peter Boateng, other than the colour of his skin?'

'They're all the same.'

'Who are all the same?'

He looked to Burrows for support and found none. He slumped back down.

'Jonny would never have taken drugs if it hadn't been for that —' he rubbed his forehead with the heel of his hand — 'Bastard.' The last word was whispered under his breath.

'Peter Boateng says he doesn't remember Ian Doyle now.'

'I cannot forget him so easily.' He tapped his temple. 'He is always here!'

'But you never saw him there, did you?'

'I've seen him,' said Mr Romano. 'I've seen him. He comes back to taunt me, because he knows he got away with it. Read my notebooks — you'll see, you'll see where he's been.'

'Perhaps you're right, Mr Romano. I know I told you that Ian Doyle was dead, but I believe the body we found is not Doyle,' said Jessie, treading cautiously.

'I told you!' he said triumphantly. 'He's not dead. Not yet. I'll kill him. It's him or me.'

'You think he killed your son because of what Peter Boateng told you?'

'The Boatengs were a foul-smelling —'

'Mr Romano,' warned Jessie. 'I think that Peter Boateng was a scared boy. He was in trouble, so he made the drug dealer up.'

The man on the sofa winced. 'No. I saw him, they were talking.'

'When?' asked Jessie, surprised.

'You can't trust him,' said Mr Romano, frowning. 'He'll twist things. Confuse you.'

'When did you see them talking?' She placed herself in front of him.

'It's a bit of a muddle now. It's all in the notebooks.' He turned to the dresser. Once again Jessie declined the offer; she couldn't face wading through the ramblings of an increasingly deranged mind. She was more interested in this new piece of information.

'Why didn't you mention this before?' Jessie felt a hand on her arm. Burrows signalled to her to back off. The man had started to shake.

'Okay, Mr Romano. What about your wife? When did you tell *her* about Ian Doyle?'

'She knew straight away. She was mad with rage. She wanted to kill him, but I talked her out of it. At that time we didn't know for sure that he'd done it.'

Niaz and Jessie exchanged looks. 'That

he'd given Jonny the drugs?'

Mr Romano nodded.

'But what if he didn't give your son the drugs?'

'But he did!' he shouted.

'Okay, Mr Romano, let's concentrate on your wife.'

'Ex-wife.' Tears sprang to his eyes. 'She left us a fridge full of food and a note. Everything I've eaten since has tasted bad . . . except my tomatoes. They remind me of her.'

'Us? Who's "us"?'

'Me and Jonny — I know he's dead, but sometimes I can feel him right here, sitting next to me. How could I leave here, how could I leave him here alone?'

'Why did she walk out on you?'

'She said she wanted to escape the memories. But you can't escape the memories, can you?'

'Where did she go?'

'I don't know. But I'd have her back. I still love her. There hasn't been anyone else. No room for anyone else.' He put his hand to his heart.

'Do you ever hear from your ex-wife?'

'No.'

'Do you know where she went?'

'No.'

'Have you still got her note?'

'No.'

'She's never been back?'

Pause. 'No.' He was sobbing now. 'I try to think of her in Spain,' said Mr Romano, his shoulders heaving. 'She always liked Spain. She liked to feel the sun on her bones. She liked tomatoes, too.'

Jessie moved away. It was never easy to see a grown man cry. Burrows went to comfort him, but Jessie had her doubts.

'One last question, Mr Romano. You said your wife wanted to kill Doyle. Is it possible she did?'

'No,' said Mr Romano.

'How can you be sure of that?'

He tapped his chest. 'Because he's still alive. I can feel it.'

Chapter 13

The following morning Burrows drove Jessie and Niaz down the cobbled road towards the rectory for the second time. Sister Beatrice opened the door and welcomed them before they'd had a chance to ring the bell.

'Don't worry,' she smiled, 'the dog's in the back. And the kettle's on.'

Tentatively Jessie pushed open the door to Father Forrester's office. He was precariously balanced on a ladder, reaching for a book on the top shelf.

'Let me do that,' said Burrows, rushing forward, ever the decent one.

Jessie held him back. 'No, Burrows, let me. Perhaps you should offer Sister Beatrice your help in the kitchen.'

'Niaz is —'

'Please.'

Jessie helped Father Forrester down the

ladder. She took his hand and was surprised to find a feeling of calm sweep over her as she settled him into the chair.

'I'd like to accept your offer of help, Father Forrester.'

'Yes,' he said. 'I gather Mary went to visit you.'

'Actually, this isn't about that. I was hoping you could talk to a colleague of mine. I believe you know him — DCI Jones. He isn't handling retirement well. Says he's haunted by the victims of the murders he investigated.'

'Of course I can go and see him. He's a fine man.'

'Funny, he said the same about you.'

'You didn't have to come all this way to ask me to do that, Detective. Is there anything else on your mind?'

So many things, she didn't know where to begin. 'Marshall Street Baths,' she said finally. 'Mary tells me you've been approached by prospective developers.'

'A whole series of developers,' said Father Forrester. 'They've been experiencing troubles in that place for some time.'

'What kind of troubles?'

'Well, often it's just a sense of foreboding, as we have discussed. In the case of Marshall Street Baths, one poor builder

311

was chased down the corridor by an empty gas cylinder.'

Jessie laughed nervously.

'That's just one of a number of unexplained phenomena to have occurred on that site. Unfortunately the developers keep changing. I hadn't actually been in until the day I met you, and that wasn't long enough.'

'I spoke to the council, they were unable to recall enlisting your help.'

'They wouldn't, would they? Calling in a Christian Sensitive to perform a ritual that was nearly banned by Parliament until the Bishop of Canterbury stepped in is a political hot potato in this multi-ethnic society. Sometimes I am asked to go into a place without my dog collar and robes in order to draw less attention to what is taking place. I refuse point blank. Would you go into battle with your enemy unarmed? Of course not. Nor would I.'

'What happens when you do go in?'

'It is the atmosphere of a place that often defines the nature of the psychic entity; that would be the first thing to concentrate on.' He rubbed his hand over his chin. 'You could take me back there, see what we could discover . . .'

'I don't think so. I can't do that.'

'Well then, tell me what has happened to you while you've been there.'

'What makes you think something has happened to me?'

He gave her a penetrating look then his focus wandered to over her left shoulder.

'Well, okay, like what?' asked Jessie, unnerved.

'Maybe there's been a bad smell. Or a particular smell that doesn't suit the surroundings.'

'Yes, a bad smell,' said Burrows, returning from the kitchen with Niaz.

'Hmm,' said the vicar.

'The sewage backs up when it rains,' said Jessie. 'Of course it smells. And it's cold too, just in case that's another sign.'

'Temperature rarely drops when a place is infested with an earthbound spirit. That is one of the most common mistakes made by those dreadful movie people. Occasionally you may feel as if you're standing in cement and are rooted to the spot, but rarely would you get cold or shivery.'

'Good to know,' said Jessie.

'The best way to gauge the presence of a psychic entity, however, is the effect on the mood of people within the place. Have there been any arguments, a combative mood while in the building?'

'No more than usual,' said Burrows, laughing.

Jessie didn't reply. Burrows hadn't seen her hit Mark. No one had.

'Detective Inspector?'

It was hard to lie to a man of God, whatever her beliefs. Jessie tried to look thoughtful.

'It can often leave a lasting impression, even though you've moved away from the source. I certainly got the impression that the caretaker was feeling oppressed.'

'He's mentally unstable,' said Jessie, on safer ground. 'He had a terrible breakdown and has been on medication for years.'

'So the drugs aren't working,' said Father Forrester knowingly. 'There is a strong parallel between psychic infestation and mental illness. A maligned spirit will usually contaminate a weak person. By weak, I mean already depressed, someone who is guilty of some misdemeanour, or simply a person who has fallen away from their faith.'

'He hears voices,' said Niaz.

'Aren't you two supposed to be helping Sister Beatrice?'

Niaz grinned.

'Don hears voices for a very good reason,' said Jessie. 'A boy drowned under his care.'

'And you think *that* was what he meant when he said those strange words in the baths?'

He drowned. It was an accident. 'Yes.'

'I have seen cases of schizophrenia where psychiatric assistance has offered no reprieve. Spiritual guidance, however, has borne some relief. These are the few cases where the tormented man or woman is suffering from genuine psychic attacks.'

'He's mentally ill,' said Jessie. 'Brought on by stress — which, as I'm sure you're aware, is as responsible for mental breakdowns as biochemical disturbances of the brain.'

Father Forrester leant back in his chair. 'So you haven't felt it then, this feeling of oppression?'

She blamed it on the increasing pressure between her and Mark. She blamed it on the insult. She blamed it on the proverbial last straw. She blamed it on P.J. She blamed it on herself. She would not blame it on an angry ghost. She shook her head.

'Very well, what about problems with the

water supply, or the electrics?' asked Father Forrester.

'Yes on both counts —' said Burrows.

'No,' said Jessie, cutting him off. 'We've had a problem with water *in* the electrics when it rains, but the whole building leaks, so it really isn't surprising.'

'But the engineers —'

'*Thank you*, Niaz. I checked with the engineers, and there isn't a problem with the electrics until it rains. What they haven't yet discovered is why, but they're still working on it.'

'Perhaps it was raining when the man was murdered,' said the vicar. 'Perhaps rain is the trigger.'

Jessie knew for a fact it had rained because the Met Office had confirmed that the rain started at 14.32 on the afternoon of February 23rd and had barely let up for three days. But that was hardly surprising. 'It was January, in England — of course it was raining. Father Forrester, you've not yet convinced me that dark forces are at work here.'

'Who said anything about dark forces? These earthbound spirits are not necessarily evil; most of them are just misplaced. As for convincing you, I don't have to. Marshall Street Baths will do that all by itself.' Again his eyes shifted a fraction, over her left shoulder. 'That is, if it hasn't already done so.'

Jessie left Burrows and Niaz at the station and walked the short distance to the baths. After what Father Forrester had said, maybe it was worth checking up on Don again. Maybe he knew more than he realised. Not because there were spirits whispering in his ears, but because he'd spent his life watching what went on at Marshall Street Baths. He'd had a bird's-eye view.

Jessie hammered on the door for five minutes before Don heard her. Standing in the old foyer she felt again the sheer weight of human traffic that had passed through the doors during the building's lifetime. Staring at the sad, empty pool, she felt sorry for the place. Of course it made her feel miserable, it was a miserable place. A broken promise in brick.

'I'm here all the time now,' said the caretaker. 'It's my fault those druggies came back, I mustn't let it happen again.'

'Don, do you mind if I ask you some more questions?'

'More questions,' he said sadly.

'Not about Jonny,' said Jessie quickly.

'About the building, about the other people who used the baths.'

His face lit up.

'I like talking about the building. It was built in the twenties. God, we Brits were a bunch of wimps, not fit for the front line. They needed to beef us up, so they started building pools and everyone was encouraged to swim. Fat lot of good it did them, they got slaughtered second time round just the same. Still, we benefited, I suppose. As for me, I always wanted to be a lifeguard.'

'The man we found in the boiler room, he must have used the pools.'

'I suppose so.'

'Do you remember a man with a limp? It would have been very pronounced.'

He scratched his head.

'Easy to notice,' she said, simplifying things for him.

'It's a long time ago now,' he said, still looking perplexed.

'I know. Take your time.'

' 'Course there were special lessons for the handicapped and such. They weren't allowed in my pool. They had to go to the baby pool.'

'Who looked after them?'

'The council. People who had no arms

and legs came sometimes. That was weird, seeing them trying to swim. We did sponsored swims for people like that. Some of the regulars became friends.'

'Anyone with a limp?'

'Not the . . . you know, them. Their helpers, though, they were always nice. Bloody saints, if you ask me. They were always making funny noises. There've been so many people, so many faces, so much noise. It could drive a man crazy.'

'That's okay, Don. What about the boiler room? Did anyone go down there other than you?'

The elderly man suddenly reached out for Jessie's arm. 'Will they be opening up the other pits down there?'

'They looked in all the pits, Don. You know that.'

'And the coal stores?'

'Yes. Why do you ask?'

'Well, I thought it would all stop when they took him away, but it hasn't.'

'What would stop, Don?'

He looked at her for a second with such frightened eyes that Jessie took a step back. He put a hand to his head. 'Questions, questions, questions. No more questions.'

Jessie took his arm gently. 'I'm sorry. How about you show me your scrapbook?

You could tell me who your friends were.'

'Danny was my friend, and Rose, then there was Tim and . . .' He went on listing names as Jessie led the way out of the empty pool-room and descended to the lower level. She switched on the light and waited for all the bulbs to glow before walking down the corridor that led to the modern boiler room. '. . . it's been a long time since I've had friends like those.'

'Don, the voices that you hear — the medication does help, doesn't it?'

He looked around shiftily. 'If I tell you, you won't tell the doctors, will you?'

'No.'

'I pretend he goes away, but he never does.'

'Who?'

'Jonny Romano.'

'You didn't kill Jonny Romano. He took drugs, he had a seizure, he drowned.'

'I could have saved him. I know that, you know that, and he knows that. He won't let me forget. We're both trapped here.'

'It was an accident. You said so yourself.'

'It was NOT an accident. Do you think I'm stupid?'

Don's confusion was genuine.

Jessie thought about what Father Forrester had said, that a bad place could seep into a person's mind and contaminate their spirit. 'Perhaps you shouldn't be here all the time. It isn't your sole responsibility to keep the drug addicts out. Your only responsibility here is to check the boiler room. You don't have to be here all the time.'

'Boiler room,' he said.

'It's just an empty building,' said Jessie.

'He's waiting for me,' said Don. 'He's very close now.'

Finally all the lights came on and they proceeded to the entrance of the boiler room. 'See — there's nothing to be frightened of in here —'

It came from nowhere. Just as Don peered into the room a blue ball of flame ignited in front of them. They were sent tumbling backwards. Jessie put her hands to her cheek and felt where the flame had licked her face. Her skin felt hot and crinkly, but she couldn't feel any pain. The explosion burnt itself out as quickly as it had ignited. She rolled over and pushed herself up off the floor. 'Don, are you all right?'

He lay beside her, curled up in a ball. He wasn't moving.

'Don,' she said again softly. Cautiously,

she turned him over. She knew at once that he was dead.

'You bastard!' she cried out, her voice echoing through the empty corridor. She didn't know who she was shouting at or why she was shouting or whether she expected an answer. She looked down at Don.

This was not happening. He couldn't be dead. It wasn't his time. Jessie rolled him flat on to his back and without further thought performed emergency CPR. She pressed the pads of her palms into his chest, five jerks, followed by a long slow breath. Five jerks. One slow breath. Five jerks. One slow breath. 'Please don't die, please don't die, please don't die,' she repeated quietly. Five jerks. One long breath. Something moved. His eyelid fluttered. She pressed her ear to his chest and listened. It was faint, but it was there: a very weak heartbeat.

Niaz, Burrows and Jessie sat round a small table in the hospital cafeteria. An announcement blared out over the Tannoy system:

'. . . Will Mr Malcolm Edwards please report to neonatal immediately . . .'

News of the explosion had quickly

reached CID and Burrows and Niaz had rushed over to make sure Jessie was okay. She was. The burns on her face were superficial. Don had borne the brunt of the blaze.

'What did the gas company say?' asked Jessie.

'That there hasn't been any gas piped into the building for years.'

'What do the boilers run off, then?'

'Oil,' replied Burrows.

'It was in the air, it had to be gas.'

'There hasn't been any —'

'Then it must have been trapped. We've been traipsing all over the place, someone could have knocked a pipe and released it somehow.'

'I asked them. They said that was highly unlikely.'

'Highly unlikely means it's possible, right?'

Burrows and Niaz exchanged looks. 'Father Forrester did say —' ventured Burrows.

'Don't,' warned Jessie. 'A man nearly died. Please do him the respect of sticking to fact.'

'The fact is, ma'am,' said Niaz, 'we may never be able to explain it.'

'Don't you start, Niaz.'

'He said "unexplained phenomenon",' continued Burrows.

'Unlikely isn't unexplained. I was there: the flames were blue. Blue means gas. However unlikely that may sound, it was gas.'

'But it isn't the first time something strange has happened there,' said Burrows.

Jessie was furious with both of them for leaping on the spiritualist bandwagon and leaving her and common sense behind.

'I can understand why people want to believe in exorcists. If the result is a clearing of the air, then all the better. It's the placebo effect. It happens time and time again in clinical trials. Fifty per cent of the time the sugar pill works, so why not in the case of the supernatural? A robed man turns up with the Bible, Holy water and a bit of incense, says a few prayers and, Hey Presto, the spirits have moved on.'

'What about the gas cylinder?'

'It's cylindrical; cylindrical things roll, and from watching the flood water it's clear the ground isn't level. Next.'

'The explosion?'

'Trapped gas, Burrows.'

'The electricity cutting out?'

'If you want it to be ghosts, then fine. Personally, I put it down to a leaky building and dodgy wiring. Everything can be explained your way, but equally, everything can be explained my way.'

Check the date. He drowned. It was an accident. Listen to yourself. In fact the only thing she couldn't explain was what went on in her own head.

The three sat in silence watching the activity in the cafeteria as patients and their families clustered round their formica tables, sipping lukewarm tea, full of forced jollity and inane conversation, all the while avoiding any discussion of death.

Burrows asked Jessie, 'What were you doing down there anyway?'

'We were going to look at his scrapbook.'

'It's as if someone wanted to stop you getting it.'

Jessie reached down into her bag. 'Well, they didn't succeed.'

She made room on their table for the worn journal and opened it at random. Placing her hand on a yellowed newspaper clipping, she turned to them.

'Burrows, I want you to talk to the archives department at the council. They must have some sort of record of the disabled swimming groups that Don talked about. I want names, details of their disabilities and the dates they occurred. Niaz,

see if your friend Asma can find out anything about Mrs Romano. Do that cross-
pollinating thing, see if her disappearance
raised any eyebrows.'

'She's not my friend,' said Niaz very quietly.

'Whatever. We have to find Mrs
Romano. Begin a nationwide search.'

She looked down at the photograph
under her hand. Michael D. Firth, the
proud lifeguard, was staring back at her
from the midst of a group posing in the
foyer of the baths. Danny, Rose, Tim . . .
They'd raised money for a minibus. Everyone was smiling; the sense of pride radi-
ated off the yellowing page.

The door of the canteen opened and a
physician approached their table. Jessie,
Burrows and Niaz stood.

'Which one is DI Driver?'

Jessie stepped forward.

'Congratulations. You saved a man's life
today. Not many people get to know what
that feels like.' Jessie wasn't sure whether
he was congratulating her or himself.

'Why did he just die like that?'

'He had a heart attack. You got it going
again. Physically, he is a fit man, and that
helped. I cannot venture what triggered the
attack. His heart looks healthy. Did some-

thing happen to frighten him?'

'There was an explosion, right in front of us. He took the full impact.'

'I thought that was what the nurse said, but I dismissed it.'

'Why?'

'He has no burns. Not even a hair of his moustache was singed.'

'But he was in front of me,' said Jessie. 'And look at me.'

'You should see someone about that,' said the doctor. 'Now, if you'll excuse me —' With that he turned and made his way out. But Jessie wasn't satisfied. Moments later she chased him down the corridor.

'No, hold on! We've been waiting for hours — is that all you can tell me? What about the medication he's on?'

'Well, he's been on a lot of different drugs over the years.'

'Might that have contributed?'

'I couldn't say. Is this part of an investigation?'

'He told me the pills didn't work. He said he lied to his doctors.'

'Schizophrenics always lie to their doctors. We expect it and up the dosage.'

'What if he were telling the truth?'

The doctor snorted. Enraged by his arrogance, she turned back towards the cafeteria, now more confused than ever.

Dominic Rivers was standing by Niaz and Burrows.

'I heard you were casing the joint,' he said. 'What have you done to yourself this time?'

'Never mind,' said Jessie sternly. Dominic looked at her arms.

'Do you want me to check — ?'

Seeing the quizzical glances Niaz and Burrows were exchanging, she cut in: 'Nope, I'm fine.'

'Right. Can't stop, but I thought you'd like to know: your dead geezer, he'd attempted suicide on two, possibly three occasions. None were successful, as we know.'

'How?'

'Wrists. The rat scratches hid the scars. Might have been some serious self-harm, I suppose. Either way, I don't think the man was particularly happy. Does that help?'

They could add scars to the identification form. 'Thanks, it might narrow it down.' Though Jessie didn't think so.

'Would it help if I told you he used to be much larger?'

'Possibly,' said Niaz, adding scars and weight to his notes.

'How much larger?' asked Jessie.

'Not easy to say, but significantly larger. Maybe as much as eighteen stone. He has stretch-marks, and the wear and tear on the weight-bearing joints doesn't make sense in a man that slim, unless he was an athlete — which is highly unlikely, considering his limp.'

'So, he used to be a big, unhappy man who lost a lot of weight and changed his appearance.'

'Yes. Intentionally, would be my guess,' said Dominic.

'Why intentionally?'

'When I examined the hair, I noticed that the roots were fairer. As I'm sure you know, hair continues to grow for some time after death. I've sent some off to the lab, but I'm pretty sure they will confirm what I suspect . . .'

'He dyed his hair.'

'That's right. He was a natural blond.'

Jessie, Burrows and Niaz turned to each other.

'Malcolm Hoare' they said in unison. Once again the Tannoy crackled:

'. . . Will Mr Malcolm Edwards report to neonatal immediately . . .'

By the time the next shift came on it was

dark outside. Jessie sat alongside Don's bed in intensive care. He was still unconscious. The nurse tapped her on the shoulder and motioned for her to leave. She stood up and stretched. Her face and arms were sore, her clothes were crumpled, her eyes were itchy and the constant bleeping of the machines had given her a headache. She leant over Don's bed and gently kissed him on the forehead.

'He drowned,' he mumbled. 'It was an accident.'

'Who drowned?' she whispered. But he didn't speak again and she felt foolish for asking. After a few minutes Jessie squeezed his hand and walked out. Don slept on.

Chapter 14

Jessie woke early, immediately glanced at her mobile phone, saw that she had no new messages and walked stiffly to the kitchen. It was over. It should never have started again. She switched on the kettle, grabbed a couple of eggs out of the fridge and filled a saucepan of water. It was because she was so busy, she told herself, that P.J. kept a strange hold over her. She never got a chance to meet other men. There were plenty more out there, just as good-looking, fit, funny, rich . . . Jessie filled the cafetiere and watched the coffee granules eddy in the darkening water. Who was she trying to convince? There was only one P. J. Dean. Was it true, had she only taken him and his two stepsons up north because of who he was? Was Mark Ward right, was she just a star-fucker, no better than the busty blondes who soaked up a celebrity through their naked skin? P.J. could go back to his shiny life with all the other warped celebrities. Meanwhile, Jessie would shelve the episode under fantasy and stop imagining the happy ending that would never arrive.

There was a noise behind her. Bill emerged from Maggie's old room wearing boxer shorts and looking more dishevelled than usual.

'Hey, Jess,' he said quietly, closing the door behind him. 'Another late night.'

'For me or you?'

'Both.'

'Looks like it. Do you want some breakfast?'

'Sure. I've got to take a pee. I'll be through in a minute.'

Jessie put in more eggs, toast, got the coffee cups out and laid breakfast on the tiny table in the kitchen. This was more like it. Normal breakfast, with her brother, where nothing was served from under a silver dome. She was cutting the toast into soldiers when Bill came through, pulling an old sweatshirt over his head. He peered at her face.

'It wasn't particularly sunny yesterday, was it?'

Jessie touched her cheek. 'Got a little too close to a candle,' she said.

'Big candle,' he replied.

She broke the top of her egg. 'There was

a small explosion at the baths. I got in the way.'

'Is that where you hurt yourself?'

Jessie pulled at her shirtsleeve. She thought she'd been hiding the bandages well.

'I saw the discarded ones in the bathroom bin. What happened?'

Jessie hadn't meant to tell her brother anything, but as soon as she started describing what had taken place in the boiler room, the memory overwhelmed her and she found herself telling him everything. Being trapped in the dark, the rats, the rising water, the sound of footsteps, the caretaker who heard voices, the explosion, the heart attack, the preserved body, the limp, the drowned boy, the dwarf nun, the exorcist, Burrows, Ward, Moore — everything except P. J. Dean.

'If you want me to tell you it adds up to nothing,' said her brother, 'you're asking the wrong person. There's so much black magic and voodoo in Africa, you dismiss it at your peril.'

'I didn't say it adds up to anything,' she said, falling back against the chair, exhausted. 'It's been a bit weird, that's all. I shouldn't have told you.'

'I won't tell anyone.'

Jessie picked out some cold egg white from the shell and put it in her mouth.

'I don't think it means anything,' she said again. 'But I obviously needed to get it off my chest.'

'Don't be so sure, Jessie.'

'Don't tell me you believe in ghosts. You're a surgeon!'

'Not ghosts, necessarily, but something. Do I believe that we all go and sit on a fluffy white cloud and prune our wings? No. Do I believe in the force of energy that each human being has? Yes. And if you follow physics, then you'll know that energy cannot be created or destroyed, it just changes its form. Potential to kinetic, kinetic back to potential, and all that jazz.'

'Very scientific, bro. Amazing you're allowed to cut people up.'

'I'm going to tell you a story.'

'If it's a ghost story, I'm leaving.'

'It isn't. A young girl was given a heart transplant. After the operation she had such terrible dreams and her behaviour became so erratic that she was sent to a shrink. The shrink was so fascinated by what she was being told that she researched the providence of the donated heart. It came from a child who had been murdered. The recipient had been having dreams about that murder. The shrink passed on the information and a man was arrested, tried and convicted. The Chinese believe that every muscle has its own memory — a theory backed up by sports therapists and psychiatry. Or maybe your Father Forrester is right. Justice was being sought by the victim's soul, unable to rest, and the person she chose as her messenger happened to be the recipient of her donated heart.'

Jessie stood up suddenly. She ran to the loo and, to her total surprise, was violently sick. Bill tried to follow her into the bathroom, but she kicked the door shut in his face. There was only one thing worse than being sick and that was being sick in front of someone. Finally her stomach stopped heaving, she brushed her teeth and doused her head under a cold stream of water. She scooped some gel on to her fingers and swept her hair back, then studied the face in the mirror. Of all the children, she was the one who looked most like their mother. Jessie had seen her the day she died; her grey skin was mottled with patches of red caused by all the toxins in her blood. Her liver had begun to fail a few days before death finally rescued her. Her dark eyes stared blankly back, her wide mouth was cracked and dry from dehydration, her dirty hair scraped off her face . . . Jessie pulled the mirrored cupboard door open and focused on the collection of medicines inside. She picked up a sachet of Diorylite and left the bathroom without closing the cupboard. The image of her dead mother's face revisited her enough times, without wanting to see it in the bathroom mirror. Bill was waiting for her in the kitchen.

'Are you all right?'

She blew her nose. 'Bad egg,' she said. 'I've got to go to work.'

'Hey, I didn't mean to freak you out.'

She turned back to him. 'You didn't.' She emptied the remainder of her food into the bin. 'I should have checked the dates.'

There was a click as the kettle turned itself back on. Jessie ignored it.

Bill lifted his plate. 'Mine seems fine.'

'There was a mixture,' Jessie offered by way of explanation. 'Being the loving sister that I am, I gave you the fresher ones. I won't kiss you goodbye.'

'Thanks.'

Jessie walked down the corridor, reached the door, and turned back to face Bill. She was about to say something, thought better of it, and left. A few minutes after she left the flat, the telephone rang. Bill picked it up.

'Who was this girl then, and what was the name of the man who was put away?' asked Jessie over the sound of the bike's engine.

'I don't know the names. A doctor friend told me about the case — it happened in America.'

'*America*,' laughed Jessie. 'Well, that explains it.'

'He knew the man who performed the transplant. It's a true story.'

'What a load of bollocks. I'll talk to you later.'

Bill looked up at the sound of his bedroom door opening and put his finger to his lips.

'Yeah, have a good day.'

He replaced the receiver and went back to the bin.

'I've heard of reading tea leaves,' said Amanda Hornby. 'But eggshells?'

He spread them out over his hand. 'You want to know what they say?' he asked.

'You've got to be somewhere and you'll call me later?' she ventured.

'No.' He stared at his hands. 'I see coffee, toast, maybe some sausages . . .'

Amanda looked at her watch. 'Well,

they're wrong, I've got to go to the office and file a story. It won't take more than a couple of hours — how about we pick up the eggs at lunch?'

'I thought you said you had the day off?'

'It's just come up,' she said hurriedly.

'What's the story?' asked Bill.

'Nothing very interesting,' said the news reporter, 'but the sooner I go, the sooner we can meet up. Okay?'

'Okay,' said Bill, letting the eggshells fall back in the bin. Amanda returned to the bedroom to dress while Bill opened the fridge. There were no old eggs in there either.

The first sign that battle had begun was on the dartboard in the canteen. Usually it featured a Page Three model. But today the perforated face of P. J. Dean stared back at her. It hadn't taken long for him to slip back into the realm of fantasy, the place he rightly belonged. A place that he should have never left. Thousands of little ink dots on a dirty page. Owned by the great unknown. A parallel universe to which the likes of her did not belong. 'I knew him once,' she imagined saying to her future children, and they would smile sympathetically at their deranged mother and laugh about it behind her back.

'I knew him once,' she whispered quietly to herself, turned and made her way to CID. She checked her e-mails; there was nothing. She quickly turned to her in-tray and mechanically went through the motions of her daily routine. Thankfully, Burrows soon walked through the door.

'Morning, boss. Anna Maria did make a call from her room, just one, in the early hours of the third night of her stay. Unfortunately, we can't trace it. It's an over-the-counter pay-as-you-go mobile phone.' He handed her a slip of paper with the number on it. Jessie looked at it. The Kleins and their theatrics seemed to have taken place in a different lifetime. Jessie screwed up the piece of paper. Sarah Klein had called the press to the hotel, that was why she was so dolled up at such an early hour. It was her fault the cameras had been there that morning. Jessie knew from experience that it was a trick they all used. P.J. probably did it himself. He could have done it himself.

Jessie must have shaken her head, for Burrows went on: 'I agree. Total waste of police time. But I don't think they'll press charges. She's too young.'

She unravelled the crumpled piece of paper. 'Unless this number belonged to Sarah Klein.'

'We've got her mobile — it's a different number.'

'It would be, wouldn't it.'

Jessie put the number in her pocket. 'Let's get on with the more serious matter of Malcolm Hoare.'

'Wasn't it weird that, just when we said his name, it was announced over the Tannoy?'

. . . *Malcolm X, Malcolm in the Middle, Malcolm McLaren, Malcolm Edwards* . . .

. . . *be prepared to listen to their messages.*

. . . listen to yourself.

'It wasn't his name, Burrows. Come on, let's put it in the system and see what it comes up with.'

Within a few moments Jessie's password had been accepted and she was completing an application by RIC to Scotland Yard. She knew it would take a little while for the information to come through, so she took Burrows out for a quick bite to eat. Her empty stomach was growling. When they returned to the office, nothing had arrived. She picked up the phone and called through to the admin department. After holding a few minutes she was told that the details had been sent. Jessie checked the fax number. Her heart sank as she realised the information had been sent to Mark's office by mistake. It was the office she was supposed to be in. Was that a sign to fight? Was everything a sign? Flustered, she quickly replaced the phone and went upstairs. Mark was not in his office. There was nothing on his fax machine either.

'Shit,' muttered Jessie. She peered over the machine, checked it for paper, but it was working fine. She was halfway towards the canteen when she saw DC Fry. He was holding a stack of paper.

'Oh, DI Driver, I was looking for you. This just came —'

Fry was one of those officers whom Jessie wasn't sure of. Friend or foe?

'I've just come that way, I didn't see you.'

'Needed a waz, sorry.' He passed over the pages without glancing at them. 'Thought you'd be in the penthouse by now.'

Her grunt was noncommittal.

Fry shrugged. 'You should be. A bet's a bet, right?'

'He told you?' said Jessie surprised.

'Oh yeah, right pissed off he was too, but you know Ward — his bark's worse than his bite. Once he's necked a few pints, he'll forget what it was he was getting pissed about.'

'So I don't need to watch my back?' she said.

'I wouldn't go as far as that, ma'am.' He bounded off with a smile. She didn't know whether to feel queasy or relieved. It depended, as always, on how you looked at it. Gas explosion or psychic intervention? Instinct or intuition? Goodwill or trap? Jessie took the pages back to her office, acknowledging that although half of her felt the excitement of picking up a new scent, the other half was wary of where it would lead.

Jessie and Burrows looked into the face of a podgy twenty-year-old. He had wavy blond hair, ruddy cheeks and terrible skin. The words of Dominic Rivers echoed in her mind. Fresh fruit or vegetables had never passed this man's lips. He had the complexion of a white bread, tinned beans and Pot Noodle eater. But he looked nothing like the scrawny, dark-haired corpse they'd pulled out of the ash pit.

They began to flick through his rap sheet. Malcolm Hoare was seven years old when he first went into care. Within a few months he had been caught stealing. At sixteen he was locked up. He was accused of raping a fourteen-year-old girl who he claimed was his girlfriend. The rape charge did not stick, but sex with a minor did. It was a slur that he could never escape from. Further charges were made with alarming regularity and a decade of playing cat and mouse with the police began. Aggravated assault. Grievous bodily harm. He nicked cars, radios, videos, handbags — anything he could get his hands on. There was no mention of drugs. He wasn't an addict, he was a thief. Prison did what prison often does: it locked him up for the required time, during which he honed his skills and expanded his network, then it spat him back out again to practise what he'd learnt. In the twenty-two subsequent arrests, he was never caught with another 'perp'. He was a loner, a drummer. On March 10th, 1976 he was arrested in the port of Felixstowe on charges of abduction and extortion. Nine months later he was found not guilty and released. He had not committed another crime since.

No other details were available except one: the arresting officer was DI Paul Cook, West End Central. Jessie looked at Burrows. They both knew what that meant. The case file would be right here on the premises.

'Arrested in March — chances are the kidnapping took place in February,' said Burrows.

'February 23rd means the case was wrapped up in under a week. If it was that cut-and-dry, how come he was found not guilty?'

'The justice system isn't infallible, boss,' said Burrows. 'Perhaps his punishment was to come later.'

Jessie returned to the photograph. She stared into a wayward young man's eyes. Nothing stared back. His eyes were empty. No guilt. No pity. No remorse. No embarrassment. No guile and no regret. More than that, in them she'd found no sign of what she'd been searching for. A reason to eliminate Malcolm Hoare.

She put another call through. This time to the West End Central CID Administration Department. She gave them the crime number and case reference number and the year of the arrest, and asked the woman on the phone to check whether the files were there. Half an hour later, the admin department rang back. Yes, they were. All three sections of the DPP file.

'Do you want to check it out?'

'Can I?'

'Sure. It's a dead file. No one has been interested in this for years.'

Jessie stared back at the young man's eyes. She wanted the answer to be, no, put it back on the dusty shelf, it's a dead file, no one's been interested in it for —

Check the date.

'Yes,' she said. 'I just want to check one thing.'

Jessie and Burrows walked quickly, so quickly that by the end of the hallway, they were running. All this time, they'd been so close. Burrows called the lift, but it was a single-shaft archaic contraption that could not be relied on for speed.

'Let's take the stairs,' said Jessie. She was off lifts.

'I think I can hear it,' said Burrows. 'The lift will be quicker.'

She hesitated at the top of the stairs. She shouldn't have. The lift doors opened and DCI Moore appeared, holding the door open with her manicured hand.

'I need you now,' she snapped.

Jessie hoped she was barking at Burrows.

'Now, Driver.'

Thwarted, she moved towards her boss.

'What's happened?'

'Gun siege on Mount Street. Get in the lift. I'll tell you en route.'

Burrows stood back to let her pass. Jessie silently communed her message to her sergeant with a single look. If she had psychic powers, and he had the ear of God, then maybe Burrows would receive her message: *Check the date.*

The lift doors closed. Jessie turned to Moore.

'Sarah Klein is taking pot shots at the windows. The owner is trapped inside; he's barricaded himself in his bathroom. He rang us from his mobile.'

'Who is it she's shooting at?'

'Timothy Powell.'

'The director?'

'The very same.' The lift shook to a stop and the doors winched open.

'Where's Mark?'

'On personal leave.'

'Really?'

'His mother died last night. It's been on the cards for weeks now.' Jessie felt her conscience grind. 'You may have noticed he hasn't been particularly happy recently, but he didn't want to tell anyone. Come on, I've got a car waiting.'

When weren't there extenuating circumstances? thought Jessie. *Never.* When weren't you responsible for your own actions? *Never.* When did life get less complicated?

'I get the feeling their relationship was complex,' said Moore as their driver took them round Berkeley Square at high speed. 'Do you know anything about it?'

Mark's mother locked him in a cupboard while she went to work, leaving him with a morbid fear of the dark and a conflicting mistrust of any woman he liked.

'No,' replied Jessie. 'Why is Klein shooting at Powell?'

'He sacked her from the show. It was supposed to relaunch her flagging career, but the part went to her understudy.'

'A younger woman. Sarah thought that might happen.'

'It invariably does,' said DCI Moore.

'Where's Anna Maria?'

'We don't know. She's not at home, we've tried all her friends — luckily we still had the numbers.'

Jessie pulled the piece of paper out of her pocket. 'Was this one on the list?'

DCI Moore paled. 'Where did you get this?'

'The Ritz. Anna Maria made one call.'

'To Powell. This is the number we are

communicating with him on. Why would Anna Maria have been calling him?'

Jessie looked at her boss. 'Because the girls keep getting younger.'

'Goddammit — she's only sixteen.'

'Actually, she only just turned sixteen. A few days before her disappearance she was only fifteen.'

'A schoolgirl crush,' said Moore. 'Timothy Powell is a very well-respected — oh, fuck it! Who am I kidding? You think she's in there?'

The car pulled up at the police line and the two women got out. The whole of Mount Street was barricaded off. It was a gently curving street with wide pavements and glass-fronted restaurants. The residential buildings stood five storeys high in burnt sienna brick and stone window surrounds. This was old-establishment money.

Sarah Klein stood alone in the middle of the road; armed police were stationed either side. A single catch in a large net. Her car was parked across the road, the driver's door still open, the engine running. Jessie had seen Anna Maria Klein at the Ritz, and she'd seen the photographs in the papers. If Sarah Klein had been expecting the press, then her daughter had not. Her eyes were red from crying and ringed by dark circles from lack of sleep. She'd kept quiet since her discovery, though the papers must have been offering her enormous sums of money for her story. Jessie stared at the car. If Sarah Klein had found out that her beloved director was sleeping with her daughter, who would she blame? Jessie looked sideways at Moore. She'd blame who they always blamed. The other woman. Any other woman.

Moore spoke to a man in a Kevlar vest. 'Break in at the back. Find out if he's alone and get everyone out of there.'

'She's not in there,' said Jessie.

'How do you know?'

'If their affair was still on, he would have gone to the hotel. But he didn't. I bet she rang him a million times on her mobile before resorting to the landline. Perhaps she resorted to the landline so that someone would check. A final act of revenge. Timothy Powell two-timed her mother with Anna Maria and then two-timed them both with the understudy.'

'So where is she?'

Jessie stared at the boot of the car. 'Let me go over there and talk to Sarah Klein,' she said.

'No. I'll do it,' said Moore. 'I'm less of a

threat than you.' There was no malicious edge to her voice. Were they finally beginning to understand each other?

'First thing you must do,' insisted Jessie, 'is turn the engine off.'

'I was going to get the gun.'

'Don't worry, she won't shoot you,' said Jessie. 'Killing a person isn't as easy as it looks.'

'Your confidence is not exactly reassuring, Detective.'

Moore handled Sarah Klein brilliantly. Jessie watched from behind the barrier, protected by her own bullet-proof jacket. What passed between the two women remained between the two women. But the first thing Moore did was turn the engine off. Jessie could breathe a little easier after that.

Getting the gun proved more difficult. Two long hours passed in negotiation while everyone waited on tenterhooks. The press arrived. The paramedics arrived. More police arrived. Eventually, Sarah Klein handed over her weapon and collapsed on to the ground. Timothy Powell had long since been whisked out of harm's way. Pity really, thought Jessie, watching the paramedics pull a semi-conscious

Anna Maria Klein out of the boot of the car. Jessie turned away to answer her phone.

'So what was the date of the kidnap, Burrows?'

'February 23rd, 1976.'

'I knew it: revenge! We're getting closer,' said Jessie, triumphant.

'Closer than you think.'

'Go on . . .'

'You're standing outside the Scott-Somers' family house — number eleven Mount Street.'

'How do you know where I'm standing?'

'You're on telly again, boss.'

Jessie tucked her chin into her chest. 'Shit.'

Before climbing into a patrol car with Sarah Klein, Moore called out to Jessie. 'Go house to house and let everyone know the situation is under control.'

'I'd call that divine intervention, boss,' said Burrows.

'I call it good police work. Now get your arse down here and start on the other houses.'

Jessie stared up at the multimillion-pound house. 'What do I need to know before I go in there?'

'Nancy Scott-Somers was ten when she

was snatched off the street. The abduction was reported by her younger sister, Charlotte, who told her parents that the nanny had lost them and a man had taken Nancy. No one took her seriously until a ransom call came in. Three days later instructions were posted through the letterbox. In total, Nancy was held captive for seven days. Mr Scott-Somers made the drop alone — his insistence, according to the notes — and brought her home. DI Cook let him go alone because he'd had a tracking device sewn into the lining of the bag of money. That's about as far as I got. I'll leave the box files on your desk and come on over.'

'So Malcolm Hoare was definitely guilty?'

'Well, he didn't get bail, so I assume the evidence was stacked against him.'

'Then why was he acquitted?'

'I don't know.'

'You said her name was Nancy?'

'Nancy Valeria Eugenie Rose Scott-Somers.'

Jessie nodded to herself. Not even an A among the initials. Father Forrester had got his lines crossed.

Bracing herself, she rang the doorbell. After a few seconds a relieved voice came over the intercom. A member of the domestic staff appeared and politely examined Jessie's identification before inviting her into the vestibule. Vast gilded mirrors bore down on her from both sides. Marble-topped side tables held silver vases jammed with irises. The smell was overpowering. Ahead of her were glass doors through which the hall opened up into a space big enough for a large round table displaying more expensive bits and pieces than a Harrods display window. A very fine-looking gentleman in a pale grey suit, white shirt and black tie appeared through one of the many doors. His patent leather shoes clipped the marble slabs as he speedily crossed the hall.

'Detective Inspector Driver — luckily none of the family are at home at present, but thank you very much for showing them such concern. I assume we can all return to our daily business?'

Jessie must have looked a little confused because he quickly apologised and introduced himself. His name was Terence Vane and he was, to all extent and purposes, the butler. Of course he didn't call himself the butler. He called himself personal valet to Mrs Scott-Somers, mistress of the house. It was only then that Jessie recalled the death of Mr Scott-Somers about a year previously. Mrs Scott-Somers had become a very rich widow indeed.

'Mr Vane, I wonder if you can help me. I'm trying to locate Mrs Scott-Somers' daughter. Am I right in thinking that she lives here?'

'Quite. Though, as I said, she is not at home at this moment. May I leave her a message?' He smiled like a TV host.

'And she still goes by the name Scott-Somers?'

'Yes,' he clipped. 'Charlotte Scott-Somers.'

'Oh,' said Jessie. 'You misunderstood me. I meant Nancy.'

Terence Vane made a small fish movement with his lips, recovered himself quickly, then apologised again. 'My mistake, I should have enquired which of Mrs Scott-Somers' daughters you sought. With Charlotte being in residence, I naturally assumed you were seeking her.'

'Naturally,' said Jessie, matching the butler's forced smile.

There was a pause.

'So where is she — Nancy?'

'Oh, um, I believe she is skiing at present. Yes.'

'In Europe?'

'Oh, no. America. Possibly Canada — you'll have to ask Mrs Scott-Somers.'

'And when will Mrs Scott-Somers be home?'

Jessie watched the man tick his boss's schedule silently off on his fingers. 'She is out for the evening. Perhaps I can pass on the message to her, she usually answers all her mail and phone messages in the morning.'

'Yes, if she could call me at —' Jessie was interrupted by the sound of the doorbell.

'Would you excuse me?' said Terence Vane, clicking his heels and bowing slightly. He made the same hasty beeline for the front door. All Jessie could see was the butler being passed heavily embossed shopping bags and a slim hand wrap itself around his pressed jacket sleeve.

'Can you believe it? Sarah Klein tried to kill Timothy. I watched the whole thing from the street, it's mayhem out there —'

'Miss Charlotte, a pol—'

'— She locked her daughter in the boot of her car! Terence, what is wrong with people? I bet Timothy has something to do with it, he can't keep his hands to himself. It's probably why the poor thing ran away. Do you remember when he came over for Christmas and tried to fondle —'

'There is a police woman here to see you,' said the butler more firmly.

'There is?'

The door opened wider. A pin-thin young woman stood on the threshold. She had long blonde hair, worn tousled and free, and large dark-brown eyes. Her face looked scrubbed and clean, a look that required work over the age of twenty-one. Jessie knew that Charlotte Scott-Somers had to be at least thirty. Her clothes accentuated the adolescent image. A V-neck pink cashmere cardigan revealed a flat chest and her wide, swirling skirt was drawn in tight round her tiny waist. On her feet were flat court shoes. She reminded Jessie of a child dressed up for a tea party.

'I didn't mean that — about Timothy.'

Yes you did, thought Jessie, and you were right too.

'Is everybody in the house all right?'

Jessie nodded. 'Everyone's fine. I'm looking for your sister.'

'I informed the detective that I believe Miss Nancy to be skiing,' said the butler hurriedly, and a little too helpfully, in Jessie's opinion.

'Yes. Skiing. Lucky cow.'

The butler and Charlotte Scott-Somers

stood side by side, smiles fixed, staring at Jessie.

'Where is she skiing?'

'I'm not sure. Canada, I think. Possibly the States.'

Terence nodded in agreement.

'That doesn't really narrow the field. Perhaps she has a mobile number I could call her on?'

'Not Nancy — far too modern for her.'

Jessie felt the presence of an invisible brick wall rise before her.

'When will she be back?'

'Goodness,' said Charlotte with a forced laugh, 'we have so many houses, she may never be back. Isn't that right, Terence?'

'Yes, Ma'am. Many houses.'

'I really do need to speak to Nancy,' said Jessie, in a low voice intended to convey the seriousness of the situation. But Charlotte wasn't listening, or didn't want to hear.

'Why don't you leave your details with Terence and I'll get my mother to call if she can help.'

'I'd appreciate it if your mother called anyway.'

'Fine, fine — whatever. I'll tell her to call you. Now I really have to go. I'm very late, you see — it was being caught up in the blockade outside. Must go!' For all her persistence, Charlotte remained rooted to the floor.

'Fine,' Jessie replied.

A few more seconds passed before the blonde scooped up her shopping bags. Only three per cent of the British population were true blondes. Jessie didn't think Charlotte Scott-Somers was one of them.

'Fine,' Charlotte repeated, then streaked through the hall and disappeared behind a set of double doors. As Jessie handed her card to the butler she thought she heard the sound of clinking glass from the next room. She hadn't expected the staff to ask why the police were looking for Nancy Scott-Somers, that would be too indiscreet; but for her sister not to enquire could mean only one thing. Her nonchalance was as forced as her laugh. The sound Jessie had heard from the other side of those doors was the top coming off of a heavy crystal decanter. Whatever it was about Nancy that forced her sibling to turn to drink, it wasn't 'fine'.

Chapter 15

Early the following morning, Jessie plugged in the security code to the station and went upstairs to her office. She placed a paper cup of take-away coffee down and looked at the five unread box files on the desk. Hearing the door swing closed behind her, she turned.

'DCI Moore? Good morning.'

'Sorry to startle you. I wanted to congratulate you on your handling of the situation yesterday.'

'You're the one who got the gun.'

'But I would have left the engine running if it hadn't been for your uncanny reading of the situation.'

'What did Sarah say?'

'That Timothy Powell had seduced her daughter while he was in the house waiting for her to get ready. Anna Maria is in pieces. She thought Powell loved her.'

'Well,' said Jessie, 'at that age you've no reason not to believe them.'

'You were right, she was only fifteen when they met.'

'Poor girl. How old is he? Fifty?'

'More like sixty. They're animals,' said Moore angrily. 'The fucking lot of them.'

'Did they have sex?'

'Yes. It only went on for a few weeks, then he moved on to other pastures, leaving Anna Maria desperate. That was why she planned her own abduction: to get his attention. She thought he'd come running.'

But he hadn't.

'Why did Sarah lock her daughter in the car?'

'She says she was too scared to leave her on her own. That it was for her own safety.'

Jessie didn't have to point out the contradiction of that statement.

'Two nights ago Anna Maria Klein was rushed to a private clinic to have her stomach pumped. Vodka and her mother's Diazepam. Sarah Klein managed to keep the story out of the press.'

Probably because for once she didn't leak it, thought Jessie.

Moore continued, 'I believe her when she says she didn't realise the engine was running.'

Jessie wasn't quite so sure. 'What's going to happen now?'

'Sarah is trying to convince Anna Maria to press charges against Powell. Legally, Sarah cannot do that without her daughter's consent. Anna Maria doesn't want to, she says she loves him.'

'What a mess.'

'And it'll get messier when Sarah's case comes to trial. Anyway, I would have brought you a drink last night, but you didn't come to the pub with everyone else.'

'Sorry about that; my brother is only in town for a few more days and we had a dinner planned.'

Moore looked over at Jessie's desk. 'So you weren't here, burning the midnight oil?'

'I'm afraid not.'

'Good. Don't want you working too hard. Burn-out is high among ambitious young detectives.'

Jessie offered Moore a drink, Moore declined. Jessie offered her a seat, Moore declined. Jessie began to wonder if this was the friendly chat it was being dressed up to be.

'Anything else I can help you with?' she asked.

'There is, actually. I think you and I may

have got off to a bad start. I would like to apologise for that.' Jessie was so taken aback by these unexpected words that she was totally disarmed. It was only later, when the full purpose of the conversation revealed itself, that Jessie realised total disarmament had been DCI Moore's intention. Jessie not only took full responsibility for the bad start, she thanked Moore for the 'unnecessary' apology. Hours later she was still smarting. *Unnecessary!* The woman had over-ruled her, belittled her, offended her *and* told her what to wear. At the time, however, she had apologised and her apology was accepted.

Moore fiddled with the only photo frame on Jessie's desk. 'Who's that in the photograph?' she asked, picking it up.

'My mother.'

'She's very beautiful.'

'Thank you.'

'You look a lot like her.'

'Not as beautiful.'

'In your own way, Jessie, you are.'

'Is that a compliment?'

'Take it, I don't give them out very often.'

Jessie laughed at that. 'Not so you'd notice.'

'Sarcasm is not ladylike,' said DCI

Moore, though Jessie detected a hint of humour.

'I gather you went to see Jones the other day.'

Jessie's guard rose a couple of notches. 'Yes.'

'I hope it wasn't because you don't feel able to talk to me about things.'

'I just wanted to know how he was.'

'And how was he?'

Friend or foe? Goodwill or trap? 'It takes a while to adjust to the change. I guess he's adjusting.'

'I'm not sure that he is,' said Moore. 'You probably don't know this, but he and I go back a long way. Mutual friends inform me that he isn't sleeping. Insomnia and depression are linked, you know.'

'I think all his friends need to rally round him. I've asked Father Forrester to go and see him.'

'Excellent idea. Jones is lucky to have your support. You and he were always close.'

'Yes,' said Jessie, refusing to find a hidden meaning in Moore's words. 'And we still are. He's my mentor. I know every case he worked on, I've studied them all and I respect him enormously. I would hate to see this end badly.'

'We won't let that happen.'

Moore turned as if to leave. 'One last thing: any formal ID on the body in the baths?'

'Nothing concrete,' Jessie replied.

'And Mrs Romano, have you found her yet?'

'No, she's still missing. A definite suspect, though I haven't ruled out her husband either.'

'They certainly had a very good reason to want this man dead if they believed him to be responsible for their son's death.'

'Yes, they did.'

'In which case you won't need to return to the Scott-Somers' house, will you?'

Jessie couldn't hide her surprise. 'How do you know about that?'

'The answer I need from you is no.'

'I'm not sure I understand,' said Jessie.

'It's important that you do understand. You cannot go anywhere near the Scott-Somers family. That is an order.'

'From who?'

'From people far higher than me, Jessie. Do not pursue that line of inquiry, or you may give DI Ward what he lost in that bet.' Jessie frowned. 'Yes, I know about that too. His office is yours when he returns to work — as long as you don't do anything stupid, that is.' She laid a hand on the un-read case notes. The name Scott-Somers stood out boldly on the label. 'Are these all of the files?' she asked.

Jessie nodded.

'Luckily for you, I'm on my way down to CID admin now.'

Jessie pushed the files over. 'My, that is convenient,' she replied.

It took a while to track him down but eventually she did. According to personnel records, Paul Cook was living off a nom-inal police pension on the outskirts of South London. He'd spent the rest of his time in the Force as a DI, which told Jessie quite a lot, but not enough. She jotted down the address. A ride to the south coast would be good for her. She'd abide by DCI Moore's rules. For now.

It started raining before Jessie even got to the river. It was going to be a long, cold, wet ride through the eternal high streets of South London before she reached the motorway. Something had gone wrong with the Scott-Somers case that had blighted his previously unblemished ca-reer. Maybe he just wasn't as pro establish-ment as higher-ranking positions required. If so, Jessie hoped he wasn't the type to be frightened off by a warning from on high.

Deep grey clouds moved east over the Thames basin as Jessie steered her way south, rising higher up the foothills of the South Downs until sunshine broke through and she sped on to the sea. Finally she turned the bike into a street of modern terrace housing on the outskirts of Hove and edged forward, trying to read the small brass numbers on the brightly coloured doors. It was a sweet, cherry-tree-lined street and Jessie felt a strange gladness seep through her that this retirement had had a happy end. She was coming up to the address. Of course she meant ending, not end. Paul Cook was alive and . . . Jessie stopped the bike. A young woman was coming out of number 42 carrying a packing box. Two small children trailed behind her. Jessie noticed three things in quick succession. The children were playing cops and robbers, the girl was playing the part of the copper, and their mother had been crying. A beaten-up Volvo estate was parked outside the house. The boot was open and inside were more boxes. Jessie's excitement was rapidly replaced by apprehension. Just as she was deliberating on whether to turn the bike round, the woman looked up. She had short brown curly hair and a figure that came of being constantly on the move. She smiled naturally at Jessie. Jessie kicked the stand out and leant the bike carefully on to it. The kids stopped playing and ran forward to admire the machine. Jessie removed her helmet.

'Kids! Don't pester the lady.'

'It's okay,' said Jessie.

'Can I help you?'

'I'm not sure. I was trying to find Paul Cook.'

The woman bowed her head briefly, then looked up with a brave face. 'I'm afraid you've missed him,' she said.

'He's gone to heaven,' piped up the smaller of the two children — a boy about her niece Ellie's age. What would seven days' captivity do to a child as young as this?

'I'm very sorry to hear that,' said Jessie sincerely.

'Why?' asked the older girl. 'Heaven's a nice place.'

'I wouldn't know,' said Jessie. 'I've never been.'

'I've never been to Paris,' said the girl. 'But I know it's very nice. That's where French fries come from. That's a chip, by the way.'

Jessie resisted the urge to smile.

'Come on, you two,' said the children's mother. 'You're supposed to be helping. There are still all the gnomes in the garden.' She looked up at Jessie. 'Cookie loved gnomes,' she explained. 'He said they kept him company when he couldn't sleep.'

Another copper who couldn't sleep. Not such a happy ending then.

'Cookie being your — ?'

'Father. Their grandfather. I'm afraid they won't remember him.' She stared at the empty space where her children had recently filled.

'When did he die?'

The woman sighed heavily. 'Tuesday. It was expected, but . . .'

Jessie couldn't believe it.

'Does this seem mad, clearing out the house so soon? I needed something else to think about. He'd been ill for some time. Everyone says it's a relief, but . . . He wasn't very old . . .' Her voice croaked under the strain of holding back her emotions. 'I'm sorry, you don't need to hear this.'

'When my mother died they said it would be a relief, but it wasn't.' Jessie stared at the woman whom she hadn't even introduced herself to. 'I'm sorry,' she said.

'I have no idea why I just said that.'

The curly-haired lady smiled sadly and stretched out her hand. 'Emma. Pleased to meet you.'

'Detective Inspector Jessie Driver. Likewise.' The boy and girl appeared clutching brightly coloured garden gnomes. Gaiety in resin. 'You have lovely kids,' she ventured.

'You have a lovely career, Detective Inspector.'

'Sometimes,' said Jessie.

The children jostled her for attention. 'Likewise,' she replied, collecting the offered gnomes and thanking them both profusely. Happy, they ran back for more. 'What am I going to do with all these? I never understood the fascination in them, myself. A few months after he took early retirement, they started to appear. He was forever talking to his gnomes. They all have names,' she said, showing Jessie the underside of one of the gnomes in her hand. 'This one's called Nancy — poor old gnome, not a very good name for a boy. I don't suppose you're in the market, are you?'

It felt like someone had placed a heavy hand on her solar plexus.

'Are you all right?'

'I'm sorry I missed him,' said Jessie, walking backwards to her bike. 'I should leave you in peace.'

The dead man's daughter frowned for a moment. 'What did you come here for?'

'It doesn't matter now.'

'Try me. We were very close. I was in the Force myself.'

'Why did you leave?'

The kids made a timely appearance. 'I was a child protection officer,' said Emma, looking at her offspring. 'I'd seen too much to leave my kids with anyone. Know what I mean?'

Jessie had seen the footage, listened to the tapes, studied the photographs. 'Only too well.'

'My husband earned more than me,' she shrugged. 'So that was that. Cookie was the only one who didn't give me a hard time.'

'Because he knew,' said Jessie, comprehending the situation.

'Only too well,' said Emma, echoing her again.

'Maybe I will have one of those gnomes,' said Jessie, 'if you're serious about trying to off-load them.'

'I am. I have sleepless nights, but not for the same reasons, and my husband isn't really a gnome kinda guy.'

'It takes a special kind of man to love a gnome,' said Jessie smiling. 'And I think I know just such a man.'

Emma put her hand to her heart. 'He was special.'

If Jessie was supposed to offer warm words about her father being in a better place, she couldn't. Instead she picked her helmet off the seat of the bike and pushed it over her head. The mother of two touched her lightly on the shoulder. 'Detective Inspector, don't think I'm mad, but you didn't come here to ask Cookie about the kidnapping, did you?'

Jessie peeled the helmet back off.

'You did?' Emma smiled. 'I thought so. It was your reaction to the name Nancy. That is so weird.'

You're telling me, thought Jessie.

'Has Malcolm Hoare been found? Are you reopening the case? It haunted him, you know, I think it may even have killed him.'

So, definitely not a happy ending. 'Why?'

'He never forgave himself for not putting Malcolm Hoare behind bars. Mr Scott-Somers never wanted Cookie to go after him; he just wanted Nancy back. He certainly didn't give a shit about the money.

But once a policeman . . . In Cookie's defence, the evidence against Hoare was concrete. They caught him trying to leave the country with half the money.'

'The tracking device?' offered Jessie.

'No, Hoare was too smart for that. He dumped the bag immediately. It was the shoe-mould that got him. Cookie matched a shoe-print from near the drop point to one they had on record. Malcolm Hoare had a limp, you see. The tread of his shoe was as individual as a fingerprint. It's a statistical fact that most thieves only have one pair of shoes — their lucky shoes. It was a brilliant bit of detection and Cookie was right to be proud of himself. But then, as you know, it all went wrong in court.'

'I knew about the limp,' she said truthfully.

'That poor little girl survived seven days trussed up like a chicken in a disused well, only to be dragged through hell by Malcolm Hoare's lawyer.'

Jessie had heard enough. *Trussed-up . . . disused well.* But Emma had more to say.

'Children were tried like adults in those days, remember. And after all that, he walks on a technicality. I became a child protection officer because of the Nancy Scott-Somers case. Between her parents,

372

the police, Malcolm Hoare and that lawyer, they pulled her apart. They absolutely destroyed that little girl. Cookie played his part, that's why he feels, I mean felt, so guilty. Right up to the end he was still talking about Nancy Scott-Somers.'

'What was she like?'

'I never met her, of course, but Cookie always said she was angelic. The most beautiful child you ever saw. Her personality matched her face too. When they brought her back, she didn't speak for five days. Cookie and the family doctor stayed with them round the clock. When she did finally talk it was to ask whether Charlotte was okay.'

'What about her parents?'

'Couldn't say. They didn't really feature much.'

'I don't suppose you remember what the doctor was called?'

'Turnball, Christopher Turnball. Isn't it on the record?'

'He wasn't a witness,' said Jessie, taking a punt.

'No, silly me, of course he wasn't. Cookie liked him. I think he was the only one connected to that household who showed them equal affection; everyone else preferred Nancy. You see, Charlotte was fat with frizzy dark hair and a sleepy eye, or something like that. Not attractive like Nancy, but definitely the spirited one, always in trouble, always running away from the nanny. Even so, imagine blaming a nine-year-old. I don't suppose you recover from that.'

Jessie was struggling to fit the description to the Charlotte she'd met. She was certainly not unattractive, she didn't have a sleepy eye, or dark frizzy hair, and she wasn't fat. Whether Emma was also wrong about her recovery, however, Jessie wasn't so sure.

'Honestly, it's enough to make you believe in the Scott-Somers curse.'

'Sorry, did you say "curse"?'

'I know — nonsense. But a lot of bad things did happen to that family. Crashes, early deaths, accidents, childhood illnesses, family rifts. Personally, I think the reason bad luck seems to beset very wealthy families is because they're the ones skiing and flying and boating and generally living a fast life. Still, they blamed it on the "curse". God forbid they should take responsibility for their own lives.'

'I know the sort,' agreed Jessie. 'Listen, thank you for talking to me. My condolences about your father, I know words don't mean an awful lot right now, but I am sorry.'

'I'm sorry he died before he met you. I'm sorry it was before Malcolm Hoare was found and brought to justice. I think Dad's death wouldn't have been such a struggle, if he'd been able to . . . I don't know, forgive himself.'

Someone in here needs forgiveness. 'I don't suppose he kept anything that I could look at? Any personal angle on the case that I wouldn't find in the police file?'

Emma shook her head. 'He kept a book of cuttings, but nothing about the Scott-Somers case. It never made the papers.'

'Isn't that odd? It ought to have been newsworthy at the time?' Jessie knew that Niaz had returned from the library empty-handed.

'The whole thing was kept out of the press. Mr Scott-Somers wanted to protect the girls.'

Jessie wasn't so sure about that either.

Jessie pulled over in a lay-by and called Burrows and Niaz. She had already told them what had happened with Moore. Suspecting they were being squeezed, she asked them to find everything they could about the Scott-Somers using extreme caution. Now she added a name to that checklist: Dr Christopher Turnball. They were to communicate only by mobile and she wanted any information dropped off at her flat at the end of the day. There was a spare key in her desk. The name Scott-Somers could not be mentioned anywhere in the station.

'DCI Moore came looking for you this afternoon,' said Burrows.

'What did you tell her?'

'That you were chasing up the Romano case by re-interviewing Peter Boateng.'

'I'm sorry you had to lie for me, but thanks.'

'Actually, it's true.'

'It is?'

'He called here for you. I said you wouldn't be back until this evening. You'll find him in the Boudin Blanc in Shepherd's Market. He said he'd be there till closing time if necessary.'

Jessie looked at her watch. 'I hope he's paying,' she said, ending the call.

By the time Jessie reached the pedestrianised turning into Shepherd's Market, it was past seven. Drinkers battled with the cold on the crowded corners, late workers rushed through the narrow streets towards

Hyde Park Corner and home. She approached the restaurant and peered through the condensation-streaked window. Peter Boateng was nursing a bottle of wine. Gone was the air of self-possession, so too the relaxed gait and the untroubled smile. Peter Boateng had come unravelled. And it wasn't just the wine. Jessie pushed open the door; he turned as the cold air billowed into the bustling restaurant.

'I hope you're hungry?' he asked as she sat down. 'They keep telling me they're not a wine bar.' Jessie nodded. Once again, she hadn't eaten all day. 'Good. Menu is on the board.'

This she knew. She had often come to the Boudin Blanc for important work meetings and more importantly girly dinners. It was a noisy, busy restaurant, where the waiters threw down wine and bread and never loitered long enough to derail a conversation.

'You should eat,' said Jessie.

Peter Boateng shook his head.

'Clear your conscience and your appetite might return,' said Jessie.

He cleared his throat. 'I hope so.' He emptied his glass, then poured two hefty measures of viscous claret before looking

Jessie directly in the eye. She watched him summon his inner strength.

'I made the man up,' he finally blurted out.

'I know,' said Jessie calmly.

'You know!'

'There was no dealer, no one pushing drugs on you innocent young boys. You were all in it up to your necks. That's why the teachers couldn't control you that day: you and Jonny, Michael, Tony and Vincent were all off your heads on speed.'

'You've put me through hell this week.'

'No, Mr Boateng, you did that to yourself by taking drugs on the eve of a once-in-a-lifetime opportunity.'

He bowed his head. 'You're right. I was a fucking idiot. We both were,' said Peter Boateng. 'I had a full scholarship — not like Jonny, he was only awarded half a scholarship — a real chance and I so nearly blew it. Those teachers should have been pleased Jonny and I had got into the private school, but you could see the envy in their eyes. They would have stopped either of us going, given half a chance. The black kid and the spic — seems we didn't deserve saving. They'd been watching our every move for weeks. We'd been scruti-nised, picked on, shown up wherever possible . . . I had to do it. I had to pass the blame or lose my chance.'

'If you'd been under that amount of scrutiny, why risk it by taking drugs?'

'Maybe that was why, because we'd been put under so much extra pressure. I don't know, Detective. We were being idiots. Maybe Jonny knew he was never going to get to that school, maybe secretly he wanted us to get caught.'

'Why?'

'Half a scholarship isn't very useful to a boy who can't afford the other half.'

'I see that,' said Jessie. No one likes to be left behind.

'I didn't know what I was risking. It's only with hindsight that I can see those six months were the most crucial of my life. Had I fucked up then, I wouldn't be here now.'

'But you did fuck up, Mr Boateng,' said Jessie. 'That seventeen-year-old boy may still have jeopardised everything.'

He shuddered as the door to the restaurant opened and another blast of cold air hit them. Jessie turned involuntarily. The door clicked shut. The figure of a man walked quickly away. Something about his hurried stride caused Jessie to frown. The unfamiliar dining companions sat in silence for a while. From the outside it may have looked like a comfortable stillness, but there was nothing comfortable about coming face to face with your own demons. Jessie read the blackboard with one eye, observing the young lawyer with the other. He must have been imagining this moment since the day he was called to the bar.

'So who was he, the man you described?'

Even unravelling, there was nothing sloppy about Peter Boateng's attire. When he shrugged, his sharp suit moved with him. 'I'd seen this creepy bloke around the place. I found myself describing him before I'd even realised that was what I was doing.'

'So you left out the one defining trait that would identify him?'

'Yes. I left out the limp.'

'Was he there often?' asked Jessie.

'Every Tuesday. Sometimes he'd sit and watch us — which is pretty odd in itself, right?' Jessie wasn't going to demonise Malcolm Hoare so readily. 'No one talked about that sort of thing — you didn't in those days — but I suppose my description ignited something in the kids' imaginations. The next thing I knew, everyone had seen him. Everyone knew the scary drug dealer with the black ponytail; he'd approached us all, one by one, with his terrible wares.'

'And yet no one mentioned the limp.'

'Well, it wasn't really him we were talking about. You know what it's like when a drama unfolds: people want to be involved in it, they want to have played their part. That's what happened. I knew they were all making it up, they probably knew they were making it up, but there was credence in numbers — and you should have heard the conviction in their voices. It was just like *The Crucible*. Everyone pointed their finger at the evil drug dealer. I don't even know when he got a name.'

'So the man with the limp wasn't called Ian?'

The lawyer looked at her. 'I don't know what his name was, but I very much doubt it was Ian, and I've no idea who added the surname Doyle. You have to understand, everyone was in on it. Subconsciously, we all fed the conspiracy.'

'That may make you feel better, but it started with you.'

'I don't feel better. I certainly don't expect to justify to you what I cannot justify to myself; I'm simply telling you what happened. I promised myself that if the man with the limp was ever found, I'd come clean. But he never was.'

'Fortunately for you.'

'I followed the story, all this time, through every stage of Romano's mad search. He disappeared, he was never found.'

'Someone found him. Someone tied him up in chains, threw him into an open pit and let him slowly drown in rising sewage on the day of Jonny's death or sometime soon afterwards.'

Peter Boateng remained steadfast. 'If you say so. But it had nothing to do with Jonny's death. Deep down, everyone knew the evil drug dealer didn't exist. Why would they kill a man that didn't exist?'

He poured them both another glass of red wine. Jessie needed to order before she drank too much on an empty stomach. She chose snails, followed by roast lamb and flageolet beans. She believed Boateng was a kid who'd told a lie and the lie ran away with itself. Even so, it was possible that the mob had wound themselves up into such a frenzy that when they saw the man who resembled Peter Boateng's description, they turned on him with enough ferocity to kill him. Maybe he pleaded his innocence, tried to tell the mob who he really was, but they were beyond reason. Maybe, after everything he had done, what Malcolm Hoare received in the basement of Marshall Street Baths — if it was Malcolm Hoare — was not revenge or retribution but poetic justice.

'I can see you don't agree with me, but I've spent a lot of time trying to rationalise what happened that day and the days that followed. The reason why the idea of "Ian" took hold was because his very presence made us all feel less guilty. Jonny's friends, his teachers, the pool staff, the lifeguard, his parents — everyone got away with the small part they played in Jonny's death. Even Jonny himself. They didn't go looking for him, Detective. They just wanted someone to blame. If they'd found him, he would have been able to defend himself, prove his innocence — no one wanted that.'

'When the mob rules, anything can happen. Remember the *News of the World*'s "Name and Shame" campaign? An innocent man was hounded out of his home. It happens. Sometimes it gets out of hand.'

He drowned. It was an accident.

Peter didn't say anything. Jessie's food arrived. She prised out each rubbery snail, dipped it in the melted garlic butter, and put it in her mouth.

'I've always wondered,' said Peter Boateng, 'who the man with the limp was.'

'I can't tell you,' said Jessie chewing.

'Can't, or won't?' he asked.

Jessie didn't reply.

'There was something about him that just gave me the creeps. He had the look of the hunted.' The lawyer shook his head. 'The haunted.'

Jessie had seen those hollow eyes stare back at her from a mug shot. Empty eyes, with no guile or guilt or look of remorse. Soulless eyes that would sneer at forgiveness.

'Sometimes,' Peter continued, 'when work is really stressful, I have dreams about him — well, not him, but those hollow eyes.' From nowhere, tears filled his own eyes. He wiped them away. 'It's really smoky in here,' he said.

'Never underestimate the power of your conscience.'

'You've got to believe me, he wasn't killed because of what I said.'

'Let's hope not, Mr Boateng, or that brass plaque may soon be spelling another name.'

He folded his arms defensively in front

of his chest and tried to sound more in control, less frightened. 'What do you think is going to happen?'

'You tell me,' said Jessie. 'You're the lawyer.'

He had no answer to give her, and she had nothing more to give him. He put some money down on the table and stood nervously. 'You will let me know,' he said, 'when you do identify him?'

'Why? Would you sleep easier?'

Jessie knew she had touched a nerve, because Peter's skin took on a chalky appearance. Whatever part the younger Peter Boateng had played, he hadn't played it intentionally.

'I don't know for sure,' she said, suddenly wanting to ease his misery, 'but I believe his name was Malcolm Hoare.'

Peter Boateng landed back on the wooden chair heavily.

'He was a thief,' she said, trying to reassure him, to quell the look of panic on his face. 'But then he upped the ante and kid—'

'—napped a young girl called Nancy Scott-Somers on February 23rd, 1976 from Farm Street in Mayfair.'

Jessie stared at him. Peter stared back.

'How do you know that?' she whispered.

'It can't be Malcolm Hoare — you've

got it wrong. He was big and blond and . . . he was big and —'

'How the hell do you know about Malcolm Hoare?' demanded Jessie.

'Edmonds, my mentor — you've seen his name on the plaque — it was his case, his first fucking case. I spent my articles studying the fucking thing. It can't be *that* Malcolm Hoare.'

They walked through the empty London streets together, aimlessly, like a couple on a romantic walk. But their walk was not aimless. And their object was not romance. Jessie had every intention of extracting as much information as she could out of the man before someone told him to keep his mouth shut.

'So tell me, what happened when Nancy took the stand?'

'She had identified Malcolm Hoare, so had the nanny. Edmonds had no choice but to go for the jugular.'

'She was ten.'

'Eleven, by the time it came to trial.'

Jessie was rapidly rethinking the concept of conscience.

'We have a duty to defend our clients to the best of our ability,' said Boateng. 'Edmonds is one able defence lawyer.'

She'd heard it all before, and it still disgusted her. 'If you can afford it.'

'It was the prosecution who handed what should have been an open-and-shut case to Edmonds. They produced the missing nanny, all weepy and nervous. After the little girl was taken the nanny ran off because she felt so guilty and was, understandably, scared of the Scott-Somers. It may be true that Edmonds was rough on the girl, but he had to discredit her identification of Hoare. She'd been snatched from behind, covered in a cloth bag, and always kept in the dark, down a narrow, empty well. How could she have got a proper look at him?'

'And no one thought she'd been put through enough?' Jessie was beginning to realise why the case had made the young Emma Cook turn to Child Protection for a career, and why Paul Cook died an uneasy man.

'It was a different era,' he claimed defensively. 'Anyway, Nancy couldn't take it. She started to have trouble breathing, so the judge let her out for a few moments to calm down.'

And he should have been disrobed too, thought Jessie angrily.

'Somehow, Nancy and the nanny ended up in the same antechamber. The stupid

French girl started blabbering about how sorry she was, that it was all her fault, that she'd made it all up. Everyone heard the commotion. "Made what up?" asked Edmonds, naturally. The question didn't require an answer. Edmonds argued successfully that the case had been compromised, that the two central witnesses had been caught colluding —'

'She was a ten-year-old girl!'

'— and the case should be dismissed. The prosecution was weak, they let Malcolm Hoare walk.'

'Why wasn't there a retrial?'

'I don't know. It was before the CPS existed, so it was up to the police to decide what went to trial. Perhaps someone in the Force decided that the girl had been through enough.'

Paul Cook, probably. Which meant no closure for the Scott-Somers. They were failed by the police and the justice system and were left having to explain the inexplicable to an already traumatised little girl.

'What a mess,' said Jessie.

'It was all the nanny's fault. She blew it. She should never have approached Nancy like that.'

Jessie and Peter Boateng walked as far as

her flat. The lights were off; Bill was out again. She felt bad about how little she'd seen her brother in the last few days. Police work was like that. There was never a convenient time for murder, revenge, betrayal, suicide, abduction. Maybe Jones was right. Maybe this was only a half-life. She spent all her time with one foot over the threshold of life and death.

Tired and feeling depressed, she opened the door. It seemed only fair to let the barrister wait for his taxi inside. She didn't notice the noise of a motorbike backfiring as the front door closed, she didn't notice the handbag in the hallway, and she didn't have the energy to go through the package that Burrows had left for her in the sitting room. After what seemed like an age of small talk, the taxi arrived and Peter Boateng stepped back into the stairwell.

'Of course, if it is Malcolm Hoare, then it couldn't possibly have anything to do with me.'

'Whoever Malcolm Hoare had been, he wasn't that person any longer. Malcolm Hoare disappeared the day he walked out of court. Thirteen years later, and changed beyond all recognition, he winds up dead in the basement of a swimming pool. Either someone found him and, thinking he was your evil drug dealer and child-killer, sought retribution. *Or,* someone found him, thought he was your evil drug dealer and child-killer, forced him to reveal the person he *really* was and sought retribution for the kidnap of Nancy Scott-Somers. I don't have an exact time of death; all I have is a watch that stopped on a certain day. A day that meant a lot to whoever killed him. Mr and Mrs Romano, possibly — it was the day their son drowned. Or the Scott-Somers: it was the day all their lives were ruined. Two very different families, I agree, but both hang off your pointed finger. Sorry, Mr Boateng, I don't think you should look forward to a good night's sleep for a little while yet.'

He stepped back, wounded, then turned and disappeared down the stairs. Jessie closed the door, stumbled down the hallway and literally fell into bed. That night she, at least, slept like the dead. The restful dead.

Chapter 16

In the morning Jessie woke with a much clearer head. She walked through to the sitting room to retrieve the information from Burrows, but couldn't see it. She found it on the kitchen table with a note from Bill. Jessie reached for the cafetiere and waited for her soldiers to arrive. By nine, Niaz, Burrows and Jessie sat on the floor of her living room peering over the contents of two battered jiffy bags that held the secrets of the Nancy Scott-Somers kidnapping. With a stroke of genius, Burrows had signed out the evidence bag collected during the case. These were stored separately from the files themselves and Moore had not had the good sense to put in a request herself. Jessie was still within her orders. She had not gone anywhere near the family. The thinning jiffy bags didn't contain much, but what they did could end the quest for proof that the man in the morgue, the man they had pulled out of a disused pit, was indeed the man who had kidnapped the Scott-Somers' daughter.

Inside the polythene bag were Nancy's clothes. There was also a picture of her wearing them. For the first time Jessie looked into the child's eyes. Angelic was right. She had huge blue eyes and bouncing blonde curls, her mouth was a perfect rosebud, her cheeks round and freckled. A picture-perfect little girl holding an innocuous daily newspaper. Except Jessie knew that the photo was proof of life and what it captured was a nightmare. Of course the little girl could identify her captor — who else had taken the photo? Looking large and grotesque next to the dainty floral dress and red-leather buckled shoes were Malcolm's trainers. His not-so-lucky shoes. As well as evidence from the tread, forensic scientists had matched dirt from Nancy's clothes with dirt from the shoes. The same dirt was found in the disused farm building that housed the partially filled well down which Nancy had been hidden. Photos of the scene showed a wooden structure with beams and a corrugated iron roof. On the beam that passed directly above the well hung the skeleton of a cat, its four limbs pointing down to the black hole beneath.

In the final zip-lock bag was the one piece of written evidence in the whole case. A hand-delivered, unaddressed envelope containing neatly typed instructions for the drop. The money was to be taken to a green-field site in Essex, the exact grid reference was to follow. Nancy would be waiting in one corner of the field; all Mr Scott-Somers had to do was leave the money in the opposite corner and walk clockwise around the perimeter until he reached his daughter. The kidnapper had added a warning. The field was 128 metres above sea level with a 360-degree view of the surrounding, flat, arable land. Any sign of police, back-up or intervention of any kind, and neither Scott-Somers nor his daughter would make it out of the field alive. Jessie assumed that the grid reference had subsequently been relayed over the phone. She also had to assume that Mr Scott-Somers followed Hoare's instructions to the letter. He got his daughter and himself out of that field alive.

All the evidence had been dusted for prints. None had been found. Jessie returned to the only piece of written evidence and began to wonder whether science, not faith, could show her the way, expose the truth and shed some much-needed light on this dark and sorry tale.

Niaz drove Jessie back to Lisson Grove while Burrows paid a visit to the forensic lab. Now that she had him alone, she wanted to know what Niaz had discovered about the elusive Scott-Somers family.

'They are very reclusive, with the exception of the younger daughter Charlotte, who frequently makes the society pages. Rumours abound of a family curse.'

'Based on what?'

'The origins of their enormous wealth.' Niaz explained that the Scott-Somers had made it rich by buying tracts of bombed-out London after the Second World War and, so the story went, bulldozing the bodies into the rubble without ceremony in order to turn a quick profit. According to Niaz, it was a much debated subject, fuelled by Miss Charlotte's penchant for spiritualists, charms, crystals and spells, and interviews with the press in which she claimed to have been told by mediums that a lot of angry, displaced people were bearing down on her.

'Do you believe in all that?' asked Jessie.

'I do not believe in curses, but neither do I underestimate the power of them. The idea of a curse is simply a fixation in an already unsettled mind. But with enough telling and retelling, the sense of the curse can grow strong enough to plague all who are told. At that point it becomes self-prophesying.'

'Especially if some medium tells you you're surrounded by angry dead people.'

'Spiritualism can be a reassuring substitute for the vacancies in people's lives. Perhaps Charlotte Scott-Somers feels she is missing something.'

A childhood, by the sounds of it, thought Jessie. 'Exactly. They play on people's loss and confusion. No one goes to a medium because all their relatives are well and happy and life is good. You go looking for answers. It's etched on the faces of all the people who go in and out of the room. They will cling to anything. There should be a law against it. What's the difference between the old travelling salesman and his elixir of life and the spiritualist? Very little. I don't think there's anything reassuring about that.'

'Why did you go?' asked Niaz.

Jessie crossed her arms defensively and looked out of the car window.

'We weren't talking about me.'
'Were we not?'

. . . It was a year after her mother died. She was desperate. Jessie hadn't received a single sign. No unexplained incident that she could cling to for proof of life eternal. No dream. No sleepy whispered message. Just the endless dull thud when she woke and realised it was all true. Someone had taken her mother away. A friend had given her the number. A friend she could no longer remember the name of. She made an appointment. Three times she went to the address. Three times she chickened out. She saw all the other people. Loss is as powerful as bad body odour. The fourth time, she went in. It was so obvious afterwards what had happened. She was in her mid-twenties. She was lost. She was unmarried. She probably had no kids. She was a professional but she wore a piece of jewellery that didn't fit the time or her age. Clearly she'd lost her mother. Add on twenty odd years — unlikely to be a motorbike crash, so statistically you're looking at cancer. *Your mother says she's glad to have her hair back.* Wham. Bam. Jessie reeled. She was furious with the pious woman who sat opposite her, she was furious with herself and she was furious with her mother who'd refused treatment and died quickly, but with a full head of hair . . .

'Your mother died, didn't she?' asked Niaz gently.

See, thought Jessie, watching the flyposters whip through her line of vision. Even Niaz could see it.

'We're nearly there,' she said. 'You'd better tell me about Mrs Romano.'

Mrs Romano had been reported missing, just once, by the daughter of her mother's sister. At least someone in Mrs Romano's family had given her a moment's thought. Originally she came from York. It was probable she'd been cut off when she moved south and married an Italian. As Niaz said poignantly, 'You know what people can be like.' Jessie didn't doubt Niaz knew exactly what people could be like every day of the week. The police had been given very little to go on and the search soon dried up because there were no suspicious circumstances, Mrs Romano wasn't a minor and, most importantly, she had left of her own free will. Unsurprisingly, it never got as far as the Met. Until there was a national missing person's register, people were going to remain lost, MIA, or, like the headless woman found in the ditch near Jessie's home, unclaimed.

Niaz parked the car. 'Are we going to question him about this now?'

'Indirectly. I'm more interested in his notebooks. When he was trying to force them on us, it was like the scene in *Green Card* where Depardieu tries to force that elaborately created photo album on the immigration officer as proof . . .' Jessie saw Niaz's look of incomprehension. 'I always thought it was a carefully constructed alibi, and now I'm sure he's hiding something. Ian Doyle, aka Malcolm Hoare, couldn't have got very far that day; someone must have found him. All those police and paramedics probably scared him into the basement. What if someone went looking for him, some of that angry mob who later set up a vigil outside the baths, or the Romanos themselves? We need to find the inconsistencies, but I don't want Romano to know we are suspicious, so let's keep the information about his wife's cousin to ourselves.'

They walked up to the now-familiar door. Jessie knocked, but there was no answer. She looked at her watch and decided to wait. They asked a couple of passers-by whether they knew where Mr Romano was, but it was all the same around there: everyone was deaf, dumb and blind when it came to dealing with the police. An hour slowly passed. The only sign of Mr Romano was the pile of mess in the kitchen, which seemed to have grown since their last visit. It wasn't particularly odd to find someone out during the middle of the day, but something about Romano's absence and the filthy kitchen made Jessie feel a little uneasy.

'Perhaps you should go back to the station and start tracing Mrs Romano's cousin. Can you drop me back at the flat? I'm going to stay on the Scott-Somers case.'

'I cannot imagine anyone from that family going to Marshall Street Baths,' said Niaz. 'They have their own swimming pools. Several, in fact.'

'Exactly. They have the sort of money people in the revenge business are after, and people in the revenge business get everywhere — for as long as it takes.'

Niaz looked back through Romano's window. 'Do you think people in the revenge business might know people in the security business?'

'Two vendettas,' said Jessie, following his gaze.

'One victim.'

'There is never only one victim, Niaz.'

'I'd like to speak to Dr Turnball, please?'

'Who may I say is calling?'

'Detective Inspector Driver, West End Central CID,' said Jessie, pulling her legs up under her and dragging a notebook across the bed. She took a pen from behind her ear.

'May I say what it is in regard to?'

'Nancy and Charlotte Scott-Somers.'

The secretary sounded confused. 'Are they patients of the doctor?'

'I think so.'

'If you'd just like to hold on, I'll see if he's free. He is very busy,' she said, politely alerting Jessie to the possibility that the doctor would not take her call. But he did. Within seconds.

'I'm hoping this isn't bad news,' said Dr Turnball.

'No, I'm simply trying to locate Nancy Scott-Somers.'

'Excuse me one moment.' Jessie heard the receiver being placed on a hard surface. An instant later a door closed. Jessie hoped this was a good sign. He retrieved the phone.

'Why are you trying to find her?'

'Well, it's a bit complicated.'

'Most things are with that family,' said the doctor. 'Try me, I'm something of an expert, albeit a reluctant one.'

'We have found a body which I believe to be Malcolm Hoare.'

'Well, well, after all these years, he finally turns up. How did he die? Somewhere alone, I hope.'

'Yes, somewhere alone.'

'And what has this got to do with Nancy?'

'He was tied up, in chains, his hands held high above his head, then dropped into a hole. Sound familiar?'

'Good God — you think this is a revenge killing, after all this time?'

'Actually, he's been dead fourteen years.'

'Even so, it sounds a little tenuous.'

'He died on February 23rd — still sound tenuous?'

'Detective Inspector Driver, I can entirely see why that would arouse your suspicions, but there is something you should know about Nancy: she had the heart of an angel, really, she was the sweetest child. I swear to you, that girl couldn't kill a man. Especially not that man — he was huge.'

Until that moment, Jessie hadn't actually

imagined *Nancy* killing him. She'd been stuck on the idea of vengeful parents. In her mind's eye, Nancy remained the traumatised ten-year-old, unable to conceive of revenge, let alone haul a grown man up on to a hook, or lower a lid that took four policemen to lift. But of course Nancy wouldn't have been ten at the time. She'd have been twenty-three. And Malcolm Hoare was no longer a great bear of a man, able to snatch his prey at will. He'd wasted away to nothing and his gammy leg would have made him an easy target. Even angels fall.

'Undoubtedly, he ruined her life,' the doctor continued, 'but she remained decent to the core. She pretended to be happy for her family's sake, but I know she never stopped wetting her bed or having nightmares. It was always the same bad dream: she was dying, alone, surrounded by dead cats. That's what terrified her most — dying alone. You have to believe me, she simply couldn't kill a person.'

'So you looked after her for a long time.'

'I helped when I could. Once a nanny telephoned me in the middle of the night; they thought Nancy was having an epileptic fit. When I arrived a few minutes later, her eyes were wide open, her body was rigid and she was screaming. I'll never forget the feel of her skin — she was as cold as a cadaver and slick with sweat. It was a dream from which we could not wake her. I'd seen it in babies before, but never a fourteen-year-old.'

'Where were her parents?'

'Where they usually were: away on business.'

'And Charlotte?'

'Allowed to watch, as usual. Detective, if I could give any piece of helpful advice, it would be this: keep away from that family. You could go mad watching them behave in a way that is inconceivable to you or I. Those two little girls didn't have a hope in hell.'

'I met Charlotte,' said Jessie. 'Very attractive, though I gather this was not always the case.'

'It depends on what you are judging a child by,' he said sourly. 'She was a pocket battleship and, as far as I was concerned, just as attractive as her sister. Unfortunately, no one bothered getting to know her. Perhaps if they had, she wouldn't have resorted to such extreme measures.'

'Meaning?'

'She's had more than a little help from a surgeon, I believe. Uncanny, don't you think, how much she now resembles Nancy?'

'So she emulated her sister?'

'She revered and resented her in equal measures. Who could blame her? She saw Nancy as the reason no one loved her. But it wasn't her fault that she resented her sister. They all fluttered around Nancy. Perfection can be a curse. Charlotte was very bright — brighter than Nancy, but sadly no one picked up on that. No one except Nancy, that is. Whatever Charlotte may have thought, Nancy adored her little sister. Adored her. I'm afraid Charlotte didn't feel the same way. I take it the family couldn't tell you where she was?'

'They told me she was skiing.'

'Most unlikely,' said the doctor. 'Nancy was severely overweight by the time she was twelve and clinically obese at eighteen. They wouldn't listen to me; they thought it was a disorder, binge eating — anorexia in reverse. I think she was bulking up to protect herself. It didn't work; the larger she got, the smaller she seemed to become and the more terrified.'

'Do you know where she might be?'

'I don't. I wish I did.'

'Aren't you still in contact with her? As a doctor.'

'I am a paediatrician, not a GP,' he said by way of explanation. 'I wanted to save her. I wanted to save them both. But I couldn't. The court case was too much for Nancy, it was disgraceful what they made her do. And all the while Charlotte sat on the sidelines and looked on while the world watched her sister. It didn't matter that Nancy hated it. It didn't matter that Nancy hadn't asked for it. Once again Nancy was the focus of attention. It would have been so much easier if the police had never found Malcolm Hoare. Mr Scott-Somers just wanted Nancy back, he didn't give a monkey's about the money. That's about the only thing I admire him for.'

'So, not an admirable man?'

'Maybe an admirable man, but not an admirable parent. He was very distant from the girls, especially after the court case collapsed and Nancy started to put on weight. I can see that any parent would blame themselves, but shying away from the children wasn't the answer. And I'm not sure why Mrs Scott-Somers had to go with him on *every* business trip. After Clemy disappeared, there was such a high turnover of staff that I rarely saw the same one twice. There was no constant in those girls' lives.'

'Clemy?'

'Sorry, Clementine Colbert — the nanny. She'd been with them for three years or more before the kidnapping, that's why it was so hard to understand. She would never have left Nancy on the street alone to go looking for Charlotte. With the collapse of the trial went the truth, but I for one always believed Charlotte when she said the nanny lost them and a man took Nancy, despite what her parents thought. For one thing, if Charlotte had run off, how could she have reported the kidnapping?'

Jessie couldn't answer that question because she had none of the information, none of the facts, none of the witness statements, none of interviews. All of it remained closed to her unless the seal of the kidnapper's demands could open them, and she wouldn't know that until Burrows returned from the lab. Until then, everything had to be done on the QT. She thanked the doctor and replaced the phone. Tomorrow she'd return to the station and work a normal day following up the Romano story. No one must know of her suspicions. She didn't want to give the Scott-Somers the chance to build up their barricades.

Jessie heard the key in the lock and Bill

stomping down the hallway. The telly in the sitting room went on. Jessie put her papers away and went to join him.

'Hey, Jess! Come and watch — Amanda's got the lead story!'

'Who?'

'Amanda! We've met up a couple of times.'

'You're a dark horse, Bill Driver. And a weird one at that.'

'Quick, she's on.'

'Let me get a glass of wine first,' said Jessie, retreating to the kitchen.

Jessie's home phone started to ring.

'Leave it!' shouted Bill.

Jessie poured out the wine as the pager in her jacket pocket beeped to life. She ignored that as well.

'Quick, you're missing it! Jesus, she looks great.'

'Hang on, I just want to turn my mobile off,' she replied, fearing the persistent caller, whoever it was. She scooped it out of her bag, walked back into the sitting room and saw what Bill was riveted to. Amanda Hornby, all leggy and blonde, standing outside an elegant townhouse. Jessie cocked her head to one side.

'. . . That's right, the family are refusing to comment and as yet no one has been able to track down the missing heiress.'

Jessie's phone twitched in her hand. Her brain was operating a few seconds behind Greenwich Mean Time. She glanced down.

'. . . So now the big question is: was the body found in Marshall Street Baths that of Malcolm Hoare? And, if so, has he been doing some haunting . . . ?'

DCI Moore. Private line.

'Isn't that your case?' said Bill, leaning back over the sofa.

'Oh my God,' said Jessie, staring back at the TV screen. 'What the hell have you done?'

'. . . Leading the case is DI Jessie Driver, pictured here a few days ago leaving a London hotel in the early hours of the morning with the musician P. J. Dean. No stranger to the spotlight, Driver first made the headlines when . . .'

'I'm going to fucking kill you,' said Jessie, seething.

'. . . I am reliably informed by someone close to this very individual detective that she is using a retired exorcist to help her determine who the remains in the Marshall Street Baths belong to . . .'

Bill looked pleadingly at Jessie. 'She's just doing her job.'

'I mean you, you fucking idiot! Someone

close! *Close,* Bill! Who the fuck do you think that is!' Her landline started to ring again. So did her mobile. 'Have you got a mobile yet?'

'. . . strange goings on have beset development plans for this historic building . . .'

Bill scrambled in his pocket and threw her a small blue Nokia phone. Jessie dialled a number from memory.

'You brought her back here, didn't you?'

Bill ran his hands through his hair.

'Didn't you!'

Eventually the call went through.

'Are you watching this?' Jessie continued to stare at Amanda Hornby's pert mouth spouting shit about her life. 'I'm finished if you can't pull something miraculous out of the bag.'

'How much time have you got?'

Jessie's doorbell rang.

'None.'

Chapter 17

'I didn't leak the story,' said Jessie as soon as the lift doors opened. Well, not intentionally, anyhow.

'Then what was it doing splashed all over Channel Five news?' asked Moore in an arch voice.

'I dread to think,' said Jessie, which was at least an honest response. 'It wasn't in my interest for the story to go public because I didn't know all the facts.'

'I ordered you not to go looking for the facts.'

'We're talking about a murder.'

'You *think* we are.'

Jessie pulled a face. 'You should have more faith in me.'

'That works both ways, Detective. When I said this came from the top, I meant from the top. The Deputy Commissioner is in there. He had a taxiing plane return to the gate in order to get here this evening. This is serious. Mr Scott-Somers gave a lot of money to the government during his lifetime and his friends are still prepared to go to the aid of his very wealthy widow.'

'And that buys the Scott-Somers their get-out-of-jail card?'

'No. But it should buy them the guarantee of not being dragged through the press again.'

'They weren't dragged through the first time; I've looked. It was sat on then, it's being sat on now.'

'They are very private people.'

'Private or afraid?'

'I am hoping you can tell me. In fact, I would say your career depends on it.'

Jessie could not bring herself to tell Moore that she didn't have absolute confirmation that the dead man was Malcolm Hoare. But her silence spoke volumes.

Moore shook her head with disappointment. 'Then I cannot support you. My hands are tied, Jessie,' she said.

'Please, unpick the knot. I need to buy a little time.'

'How long?'

Burrows' mate at the Forensic Science Service hadn't been able to say. This procedure usually took months, not days —

and certainly not hours, which was all they had.

'Not long,' she prayed.

They were all there. Their weapons were loaded, raised and pointing at her. Jessie faced the firing squad alone with only one hope of reprieve and she didn't know how far away it was.

The Deputy Commissioner's office was a spacious room with two leather sofas, two armchairs and a low oblong glass coffee table. Refreshments stood neatly in the centre of the table: a flask of coffee and a decanter of whisky. Whisky seemed to be the preferred option that evening. Also in attendance were Mrs Scott-Somers, her daughter Charlotte, their respective lawyers and *their* assistants, and a man in a suit whom she did not recognise. It turned out he was a lawsuit specialist employed by the Metropolitan Police in crises like this. Presently he was here in a mediating role. If that were true, thought Jessie, shouldn't he have heard her side of the story prior to entering the room?

Christina Scott-Somers was thin like her daughter. Whereas on Charlotte it looked vulnerable, on Christina it looked pinched. The angles on her face were sharp, her eyebrows were plucked into a razor-thin arch and her chin was set a fraction higher than was comfortable. Condescension seethed out of every pore. She wore her ebony hair swept back in a chignon held fast with an ivory pin. Her wardrobe was cool, understated wealth. A black cashmere jersey, dark grey slacks and patent leather pumps. Her only jewels were a large engagement ring and a pearl choker. Mrs Scott-Somers looked every inch the respectable, grieving widow, though Jessie suspected that anything resembling sympathy would be knocked away with a single barbed comment. Jessie tried an apology instead, but that too was swiftly brushed aside. Mrs Scott-Somers didn't want an apology, she wanted an explanation. And so the tap dance began.

'Mrs Scott-Somers, when your daughter was kidnapped —'

'Not me. I wasn't kidnapped.'

Pacing the back of the room, looking miniscule in knee-high boots and a floral print dress, was Charlotte. She had one of the Deputy Commissioner's heavy-base lead-crystal tumblers in her hand. It looked too big for someone so slight. Jessie was reminded of a child again, picking up an adult object and lurching under the weight of it.

'Just for the record,' she said, before raising the glass to her lips.

'Please, Charlotte, for once, let's not make this about you.'

Jessie remembered Dr Turnball's words: if Charlotte was guilty of attention seeking, surely it was because this had never been about her. Jessie turned back to Mrs Scott-Somers. 'Malcolm Hoare was very careful not to leave any fingerprints on the ransom letter, but he didn't think twice before licking the envelope.' *Someone* had licked the envelope — Burrows' forensics man had been able to confirm that much. 'In 1976 the police lacked the technology to extract DNA from the gum on the back of an envelope . . .' She paused for effect. 'We now have that technology.' Of course, having the technology and finding a technician willing to set aside everything else to rush through a series of tests that would normally take weeks were two different things. Once again Jessie prayed for the text message to wing its way to her across the ether.

'Indeed, Detective. I too have watched *CSI*, but what has this breakthrough in forensic science got to do with my family?'

The tap dance continued.

'A match between that sample of DNA and the body we found in the Marshall Street Baths would prove that the dead man was Malcolm Hoare.'

'So?'

'He never paid for his crime.'

'A matter for the police force to obsess over, Detective. My husband was never interested in catching the man, he only wanted Nancy home.'

Jessie found the sweetness in her voice sickly. She wasn't the only one. Charlotte reached out for the decanter. 'His precious little princess,' she said in a barely audible whisper. Everyone else pretended not to notice.

'It didn't matter to him that the person responsible walked out of court a free man?' asked Jessie incredulously.

'What mattered was that Nancy was alive, Detective. Nothing more.'

'Alive. But not the same.'

Mrs Scott-Somers stood in disgust. 'I am not prepared to sit here and listen to these veiled accusations. You will be hearing from my lawyers.'

'Nancy's feet were bound,' said Jessie, standing too. 'Her hands were tied, pulled over her head and attached by a rope to a beam. Her feet only just touched the floor of the well.'

Mrs Scott-Somers quivered with fury. 'There is no need for this,' she spat through clenched teeth.

Jessie remained very calm. 'Not so easy to forget, is it?'

'Of course we haven't forgotten. How do you forget something like that?'

'You don't,' said Jessie.

'Well, of course you don't. Come on, Charlotte, we're going.'

'The man in the baths was tied up in exactly the same way, Mrs Scott-Somers. Exactly the same way. On exactly the same date.'

'I can see what you are trying to do.' The widow visibly composed herself. The condescending tone returned to her voice, enabling her to remain far removed from any event that was not to her liking. 'Nancy came home, our prayers were answered, and that was the end of it as far as we were concerned.'

'Was it? Really? Perhaps Nancy wasn't able to brush it under the carpet as easily as you and your late husband were.'

'You are on very thin ice, Detective,' she sneered. The lawyers hovered.

'*I'm* on thin ice? You're the one with all the lawyers.'

'That's *enough,* Driver,' said Moore.

'Why do you feel you need all this protection? I only want to talk to Nancy.'

'Driver!'

'It's Nancy I am trying to protect,' said Mrs Scott-Somers.

A mean little laugh escaped Charlotte's lips.

'My daughter has nothing to do with this. I don't care if it is that man. As a matter of fact, I'll be glad if it is.'

'Mrs Scott-Somers —' warned the lawyer.

The phone buzzed in Jessie's pocket. She glanced at the display and saw all that she needed to know.

'Well it *is* that man. The DNA confirms it. Now you are going to have to answer some questions.'

Jessie re-read Burrows' message while the lawyers made frantic phone calls to other lawyers, inching their final bill ever skyward. It was a positive match. There was no longer any doubt: fourteen years ago someone had killed Malcolm Hoare on the anniversary of the kidnapping using a method that imitated the way Nancy had been held captive. At last her case wasn't looking so tenuous.

★ ★ ★

Moore took the opportunity to have a quiet conversation with the Deputy Commissioner. Jessie watched him retrieve his cap and nod once, curtly, in her direction. She couldn't read the nod. Friend or foe? Goodwill or trap?

Moore whispered in her ear: 'Ask the questions, keep it to a minimum — just get enough to cross Nancy off the list.'

'And what if I can't cross her off the list?'

'You don't really think Nancy Scott-Somers went into a place like that and killed a man with her bare hands, do you? There's a swimming pool in the basement of their house, Jessie. And it's hardly likely she'd have taken a job at the baths! So, go gently. It's your neck on the line.'

'I think I got that.'

Jessie faced Mrs Scott-Somers on the sofa and asked the only question she'd ever wanted to ask her: 'Where is Nancy?'

Jessie watched Mrs Scott-Somers struggle with the words. They stuck in her throat like burrs. Not to be extracted without causing pain.

Charlotte leaned over the back of the sofa. 'Malcolm Hoare is haunting that pool, isn't he?'

This was not the answer Jessie was looking for. She attempted to ignore Charlotte, as everyone else did.

'We all saw the news,' Charlotte continued. 'Strange things have been happening, and you've been talking to an exorcist.' It sounded so damaging coming from her. Moore coughed nervously.

'I spoke to a retired vicar on matters that do not concern this case. A propos of nothing, he thinks the term "exorcist" is objectionable,' said Jessie firmly. 'Now, if we could return to the question of Nancy's whereabouts . . . ?'

'I've seen spiritualists, they all say I'm quite psychic. I hear ghosts sometimes, footsteps at night — clairaudience, it's called.'

They also tell you you're surrounded by a lot of angry dead people, thought Jessie. Poor Charlotte. They would have seen her coming. The walking wounded, so easily swayed. Her imagination took over where their suggestions left off.

'Charlotte, those people aren't to be trusted —'

'Enough of this nonsense!' said Mrs Scott-Somers loudly. She continued in a quieter voice: 'I don't know where Nancy is. She left home some time ago. We miss her very much and we are looking forward to her return.'

Jessie watched Charlotte turn away and lean against the office wall.

'When will that be, Mrs Scott-Somers?'

'I don't know.'

'When did she leave home?'

Charlotte was eyeing her mother. 'When she was too fat to stay hidden in the house.'

'How long ago? A few months, a few years? Fourteen years, by any chance?'

'Mrs Scott-Somers is here because she wants to help. Any more threatening questions, and she will leave,' said one of the lawyers.

'It's ironic, really,' continued Charlotte, unabashed, 'in that the Scott-Somers are renowned for their large houses.'

'How long ago, Mrs Scott-Somers?'

'Some people just can't control what they eat.'

Jessie looked at Charlotte again. 'You're right. It is an addiction —' she glanced down at the recently refilled tumbler — 'like any other.'

'I fail to see what Nancy's eating habits have got to do with anything,' exclaimed Mrs Scott-Somers.

'I'm sure it has a great deal to do with

everything,' said Jessie, deflected again.

'Meaning?'

'Meaning: children often eat to protect themselves. They see safety in size.'

'Your point is?'

'Nancy kept on eating. Why? Because she kept on being afraid. She couldn't forget what happened, could she? And you, with the help of your daughter here, are procrastinating. So, for the last time: where is Nancy and when did she leave home?'

. . . Some time after turning sixteen, Nancy started walking out of the house during the day and not returning for hours. She wouldn't tell anyone where she was going, and she wouldn't tell anyone when she was home. The child psychiatrist believed these wanderings were a direct result of the claustrophobic surveillance Nancy had undergone since the kidnapping. They were told that locking her in at this stage might prove fatal. She had already shown suicidal tendencies, signs of depression and food addiction, had fitful sleep and problems with bed-wetting. It was a good indicator, therefore, that she felt confident enough to get out of the house and the family was advised to let her go. When she returned, the doctor told Mr and Mrs Scott-Somers to welcome her back with open arms; the phase would soon pass. It didn't pass. Gradually the hours turned into days. Sometimes weeks. Then months would go by before Nancy returned and eventually years . . .

'The last time we saw her was on the eve of Charlotte's eighteenth — 1985.'

Jessie was staggered. 'You haven't seen her for nineteen years?'

Mrs Scott-Somers shook her head. 'I thought she would come back for my husband's funeral, but . . .' She cleared her throat.

'Do you speak to her?'

'No.'

'And you haven't seen her since —'

'No. Are you enjoying rubbing my nose in it?'

'Actually, that's not strictly true . . .'

'Charlotte, please —'

'She rolled up one year, right in the middle of Christmas dinner. The size of a house and as bald as a baby. She knelt down at Daddy's feet and cried. Fucking mad, right? But once again, we killed the fatted calf then heaved the gargantuan up the stairs. In the morning she was gone. I would have thought it was another dream, but the Christmas cake was missing, so I guess it wasn't.' Again Charlotte drained her glass. She had honed her act of arched indifference. It was close to flawless, but not perfect. Perfect indifference did not require alcohol as a prop.

'When was that?'

'The following Christmas,' said Mrs Scott-Somers. 'She only stayed for one night.'

DCI Moore stepped forward. 'This is very serious, Mrs Scott-Somers. How do you know she is even alive?'

'The money,' replied Mrs Scott-Somers. 'Every month it goes out of the account we set up for her.'

'How much?' asked Jessie.

'That is none of your business.'

'I'm afraid it is,' said Jessie. 'There are many unscrupulous groups of people who target the vulnerable, especially if they have a lot of money. Is it a lot of money?'

'Twenty thousand.'

'A year?'

'A month.'

Jessie's eyes widened. 'And do you know for sure she collects it?'

Mrs Scott-Somers shook her head. She started to weep. Another lawyer stepped forward and offered her a handkerchief. Jessie wondered how much he'd get of Daddy's money for that small gesture.

'There are literally hundreds of organisations and religious cults in this country who fund themselves by obtaining money from people unable to defend themselves against brainwashing. Nancy was obviously at risk.'

Charlotte slid into one of the large leather chairs and was immediately dwarfed by it.

Mrs Scott-Somers, on the other hand, was at last rising to the bait. 'Now what are you accusing me of? That doctor said to keep the doors unlocked, he insisted we let her go,' she said defensively. 'That was the way to get her back.'

Perhaps Nancy was yet another Scott-Somers to make a pact with the devil, thought Jessie. Perhaps someone offered murder as a way to put an end to the nightmares, an end to all the things that had conspired to make a young woman dream of death. The sweet seduction of revenge. But it came at a price. And all the money in the world couldn't cover the cost.

'She might not be able to get back.'

Finally the veneer cracked. 'You think

this is my fault! I didn't do this! That fucking man did this! It's his fault! He ruined my life! I'm glad he's dead. Do you hear me? The day Malcolm Hoare walked out of court was the day my husband died. It killed him. He ruined everything.'

'Christ, Mother, don't you get it? We were ruined long before.' Charlotte was slurring her words, she had drunk too much to hear her mother correctly. Mrs Scott-Somers hadn't said *their* lives, she'd said *my* life. *That fucking man ruined my life.* And not the day he took Nancy, but the day he walked free. Jessie studied the woman and wondered what it was that Malcolm Hoare had done to her?

Angry at her own outburst, the widow snatched up her handbag and stalked out of the office, her chin, once again, raised slightly higher than was comfortable. A lawyer pulled Charlotte Scott-Somers out of the chair; she had rubbed her eye so viciously that her smudged make-up made her look bruised.

Jessie and Moore watched them go. Together they began clearing up the used glasses.

'What do you want to do, Driver?'

Jessie suppressed a yawn. 'Trace the

money. It will lead to Nancy, or whoever is bribing her — or, worse, whoever is masquerading as her.'

'Do you think she's still alive?'

'Somewhere, yes. But I get the feeling she's not in a good way, not in a good way at all.'

'And what do you make of the family?' asked Moore.

Jessie knocked back a slug of whisky. Not in a good way at all. 'Cursed,' she replied.

It was one o'clock in the morning by the time Jessie got dropped off at home. A small group of people were milling around the entrance to her flat. Journalists. She'd forgotten that Amanda Hornby knew where she lived. She swore loudly.

'Do you want me to come with you?' asked the young police driver.

She took out her keys. 'It's okay, I'll run for it.'

'For what it's worth, DI Driver, you have our full support. All of us feel the same.'

It was worth a lot. More than she could say. She mouthed words of thanks and dived out of the car. A couple of the journalists turned at the sound of the closing door. By the time she was across the road, they were all looking at her and the questions began:

'Are the Scott-Somers going to sue?'

'Is it true you've been suspended?'

'Will P.J. stand by you?'

Jessie lowered her head and pushed her way through, her mind focused on one thing: the gate that took her on to private property. She reached out. Someone jostled her. An elbow. A microphone. The gate felt cold. Relieved, she pushed it. It didn't move. The journalists crowded in behind her. She pushed again, beginning to panic slightly.

'Is it Malcolm Hoare?'

'Did Nancy kill him?'

'Are the family cursed?'

'Are you cursed?'

They'd jammed the gate with gaffer tape. She tried to turn round, but there were too many of them. She tried to signal for the driver, but he'd already pulled away. Determined not to cry out for help, she lifted a leg and put her foot on top of the gate.

'Come on, Jessie, give us something?'

'How long you been lovers?'

'Where is he?'

'Is it true Charlotte Scott-Somers has undergone laser surgery to look more like a little girl?'

Someone pulled on her leather jacket. She fell backwards. She pushed someone away. Someone pushed back. *Do not react. Do not react. Do not react.* Someone pushed her again. She swung round.

'This is HARASSMENT!' shouted a male voice. The domineering figure of a finely spoken, bespoke-suited, six-foot black man pushed his way through the journalists. 'Not to mention criminal damage against private property. If you are not out of here in three seconds, DI Driver will press charges on all of you for gross misconduct, assaulting a police officer, the aforementioned criminal damage, and anything else I can throw at you . . .'

Jessie watched them move away.

'Have you got one of those plastic bag things?' he whispered.

Shaken, Jessie pulled an evidence ziplock out of her bag and held it open while Boateng cut the tape with a small penknife, then placed it into the bag without touching it. He took the bag from her, sealed it and held it up to the journalists.

'Exhibit number one,' he called out to them as he pushed open the gate and escorted Jessie inside.

She was shaking. 'Bastards taped the gate shut.'

'It's one of their favourite tricks: corner the hunted and close in. Lose the gate, or it'll happen again.'

'Fucking hell,' said Jessie, because she couldn't think of anything else to say.

'I have some interesting information for you that I didn't want to leave over the phone.'

'Don't freak me out even more,' she said, keen to put distance between herself and those people on the street.

'Be careful who you speak to and on what line.'

Jessie blocked her ears. 'I'm not listening. This is not my life!'

'It is now. I'm trying to help.'

'Why?'

'Because you're up against something much bigger than that problem out there.'

Peter Boateng handed Jessie a drink. 'I don't suppose you have a cigarette as well, do you?'

'I wouldn't have if you'd asked me a week ago,' he said, pulling out a package with the fatal warning written boldly across it.

'I seem to have that effect on people,' said Jessie.

He returned with an ashtray. It didn't

bother Jessie that he was making himself at home. She knew she was out of her league and, relieved, she handed over the reins. Just for an hour or so. Until the whisky and cigarettes had done their work.

Finally Peter Boateng sat down opposite her. 'The Scott-Somers will do everything in their considerable power to protect themselves from you and your case, and if that means discrediting you through underhand means —' he glanced out of the window — 'then that's what they'll do.'

'Did they kill Malcolm Hoare?'

'Their overwhelming desire for privacy pre-dates Malcolm Hoare's death, but that doesn't mean the two aren't connected.'

'What are they hiding?'

'I don't know. What I do know is that Tobias Charles Edmonds was hired to defend Malcolm Hoare by Nancy's own father — Nicholas Scott-Somers himself. It took a while for Edmonds to disclose that information. You can't use it, because it's covered under client–lawyer privilege, but I thought you should know.'

Jessie was shaking her head. 'Why would he do that?'

'He wanted to control the court case. Legally, Malcolm Hoare was entitled to representation; Scott-Somers couldn't get around that. What he didn't want was some nosy little bugger going over affairs that did not concern the case.'

'Affairs?'

'Business affairs, family affairs — I don't know. Edmonds wasn't privy to any of that, he had to stay within the remit of the case. What Scott-Somers did not account for was the abysmal way the prosecution was put together, presumably because they got lazy — the smoking gun and all that, or Edmonds' own ambition. When they passed him a sitting duck, it would have been professional suicide not to shoot it.'

'And shoot he did.'

'He argued for a mistrial on a whim, assuming they'd settle for a re-trial, but won an acquittal. Go figure. Edmonds never heard from Scott-Somers again. Understandably.'

The day Malcolm Hoare walked out of court was the day my husband died. No wonder the court case killed him, no wonder he blamed himself. No wonder he withdrew from his children. He'd put himself first and in doing so ruined his precious daughter's life. He, more than anyone, had a reason to see Malcolm Hoare dead. He wasn't going to risk another trial; he had friends in high places, a word in a judge's ear and Hoare is acquitted. Scott-Somers had more control dealing with him out of court. But Hoare gave them the slip, went on a diet and dyed his hair and for thirteen years escaped retribution, until someone found him cowering in a deserted boiler room . . .

'What was so important to Scott-Somers that he would ruin his daughter's life?'

Boateng shrugged. 'His own?'

'You're genetically wired to save your children before yourself.'

'Women may be. I'm not sure I can vouch for men.'

Jessie stood up and walked to the window. The journalists had gone. It was late and Bill had still not come home. Not dared to, more like.

'I'd better be going.'

'Listen, thanks for coming over and rescuing me. You didn't have to tell me any of that.'

'I guess I feel I owe him something. As you said, it might have been my words that got him killed. I looked at his background notes, I wanted to find something that would ease my conscience, if it turns out I was responsible. When he was first taken into care he was forced to steal by older boys. They shunned and bullied him when his limp slowed him down and got him caught. They annihilated him before he'd reached double figures. He was a miserable creature, but he wasn't evil. He didn't mess with Nancy.'

'He'd had sex with a minor before.'

'I looked at that. He was just sixteen, the girl was two days away from turning fifteen, they got caught having sex in their care home. It was her mostly absent father that started the rape allegation, which never went anywhere, but legally Malcolm had had sex with a minor. It was a shitty deal that left him a marked man. He only started getting into real trouble after that. With that on his rap sheet, it's not surprising. The rest you know. What I'm trying to say, in my convoluted manner, is this: he didn't deserve to die like that. That's why I would like to help you.'

'There's one more thing you may be able to help me with . . .'

'Anything.'

'If you didn't buy the drugs off Malcolm, where did you get them?'

Peter Boateng's eyes narrowed. His skin creased. He looked at the door he was holding ajar. Anything but that, it seemed.

'Why don't you shut the door?' said Jessie, pressing gently.

Reluctantly he did so.

'Who got the drugs?'

'Jonny,' he said finally.

'Jonny Romano was bringing drugs into school?'

'Yes.'

'Oh, come on. Where did he get them from?'

The question hung in the air. The lawyer battled with himself right there in front of her.

'He stole them,' he said at last.

The next question was inevitable. Peter Boateng didn't even wait for Jessie to ask it.

'I don't know,' he said, crossing his arms in front of him.

Jessie pointed back to the sitting room.

'It's late, Detective.'

'You should have told me this earlier.'

'Really, I never knew. I never wanted to know.'

'Why didn't you want to know?'

'The Romano family weren't known for their integrity and honesty.'

'Funny that — Mr Romano said the same about your family.'

'He hated us because we were black.

End of story. The Italians, now there's a good reason to keep out of their way. If there is one difference between my old life and my new one, it's that, back then, knowing too much was never a good thing.'

'How much did Jonny get his hands on?'

'Enough to sell the surplus to some of the older boys for a pound a pop.'

'He was selling it?'

'It made him popular. We were the geeks, remember. Being clever isn't cool.'

'How long had this been going on for?'

'I don't know.'

It was Jessie's turn to fold her arms.

'Six months, maybe less.'

'What did he do with the money?'

'What every normal kid does with money. We bought records, played on the slot machines. It wasn't a huge amount, he was selling the stuff very cheaply.'

'Where was he getting it from?' Jessie asked again.

'I can't tell you what I don't know.'

'Then tell me what you think.'

He rubbed his hand across his cheek, then shook his head.

'Peter, you've been thinking about the events at Marshall Street Baths for almost half your life, you must have come up with some explanation, even if it *is* theoretical.'

'Really, I don't know,' he insisted.

'I've got all night,' said Jessie.

A stony silence ensued. Finally Peter Boateng spoke. His words demonstrated what a deliberate wordsmith and fine lawyer he'd become.

'I don't know who Jonny could steal drugs off who wouldn't have killed him if they'd found out.'

Jessie nodded. She was beginning to understand the man.

'Can I go now?'

'Sure.'

'Do you mind if I use the loo before I go?'

Jessie nodded. She returned to the sitting room semi-exhausted, semi-elated, armed with more information from Peter Boateng than she needed.

Her home phone broke the silence. She looked at caller ID and was surprised to see the one number she least expected but most wanted.

'Hey,' said P.J.'s familiar voice.

'Hey.'

'Been in the wars?'

'A bloody battle.'

'Casualties?'

'Wounded, but there are glimmers of life.'

There was a pause. P.J.'s mobile crackled.

'I'm so sorry,' he said.

'Me too.'

'It got out of hand.'

Jessie nodded at her reflection in the dark glass.

'Can I use the phone? Oh, sorry —' said Peter Boateng, walking over to her.

'Who's that?'

It was two thirty in the morning. She didn't want to complicate matters.

'My brother is still staying with me,' she said into the phone, but looking at Peter.

'Your brother?'

'Bill. I told you about him.'

'The one who lives in Africa?'

'Yeah.'

'The one who has been staying with you for a while?'

Jessie wanted to change the subject. So far she hadn't actually lied.

'The one you had dinner with the other night?'

Peter tapped Jessie on the shoulder and silently signalled to her that he was leaving.

'Half brother, is he?'

She gave him a thumbs-up. He was astute, Peter Boateng, she had to give him that. He took her hand and squeezed it. Jessie smiled gratefully.

'Been in Africa long, has he, this brother of yours?' asked P.J.

Jessie watched the front door close. 'A few years.'

'Got under his *skin*, has it?'

Jessie suddenly focused on the window again.

'Oh, hello, suddenly not looking so relaxed.'

'Where are you?' she asked, peering at the street below.

'You could have just told me —'

'I can explain.'

'Don't tell me, Jessie: another *fucking* suspect?'

Jessie shook her head. In denial, yes; in the hope that he would see, yes; but also as a mark of horror, that he could use such vicious words against her so soon after he'd apologised. She was still shaking her head when the taillights of the motorbike disappeared and a shaft of light fanned out over the street below then slid back as Peter Boateng pulled the door close behind him. Jessie watched as he turned his collar up round his neck and walked quickly away in the opposite direction. Who the hell was

directing this pantomime?
You, Jessie.

She didn't think she would sleep, but she curled up under the duvet and closed her eyes, slowly her breathing regulated and her body sunk heavily into the mattress. Within a few seconds she was dreaming. A young girl was sitting in a wood clearing. A bear with a man's face and a withered leg was circling her, but the little girl could do nothing about it; she was tied to a post with heavy cold chains. Even as she watched the scene unfold, she knew that she was the little girl. Just beyond the edge of the clearing, a woman walked among the tree trunks. At first it looked like an angel, dressed in white, but as she came nearer, Jessie recognised her. She was tall and slim and had short dark hair, large hazel eyes and pale skin. The bear was getting more and more aggressive, getting nearer but never reaching her. She tried to call for help, but her mouth felt as if it was filled with glue, all she could manage was a muffled moan. The woman couldn't hear her; she was just standing there, with her back to her, while the bear took swipes with his claws. She tried to call again, over and over.

'Mmmmm.'

'Jessie, wake up.'

'Mmmmmmm!'

Bill shook her gently. 'Wake up, Jessie, it's just a dream.'

'MMMM —'

'Jessie!'

She opened her eyes. 'Mummy!' Bill pulled her towards his chest and rocked her gently backwards and forwards. Jessie sobbed painfully, her throat aching with tension. 'It wasn't her,' said Jessie.

'It's just a dream.'

'She can't hear me,' she said.

'It's all right, it's over.'

'I see a woman, I think it's Mum, I get closer, but it's never her. Why isn't it ever her?'

'Who is it?' asked her brother.

'It's me.'

Bill stroked her head. 'Because you are her, Jess. That's why we don't miss her as much as you do — we still have her, because we have you.'

Jessie stared up at him.

'Isn't that what life after death is?' he said. 'Sometimes you look so like her that I forget she's dead, but you never get to see it.'

'I don't look in the mirror much,' said Jessie, realising as she said it, it was true.

'You should, you're a great-looking girl.'

'Once I caught sight of her inside a shop. I ran in. She wasn't there, naturally — we'd buried her the year before. When I went back on to the street I realised there were mirrors in the window display. I'd seen myself.'

'She wasn't afraid of dying, Jessie.'

'How do you know?'

'We talked about it.'

'Wasn't she sad she'd miss out on watching us grow up?'

'She thought she'd still be able to.'

'That's bollocks, Bill. She isn't watching us.'

'How do you know?'

'Because I'd have heard from her by now.'

'The Africans I treat go through very lengthy rituals to make sure the dead person's spirit goes on a one-way journey to the other side. They don't want their ancestors popping back over. They think that calling up the dead is as stupid as it is evil. Be glad Mum isn't wandering around picking up your wet towels and straightening out your knicker drawer.'

Jessie felt a faint smile cross her lips.

'You've got me into terrible trouble,' she said, her head still resting on his chest.

'I'm sorry,' he said.

'Maybe it doesn't matter,' she said, leaving the dream behind her. 'I got further this evening than I would have without the story breaking.'

'She swears she didn't get the information from here.'

Jessie looked up at her brother. 'Do you believe her?'

'I don't know. I really liked her.'

'But you're going back to Africa anyway. Aren't you?'

He shrugged. 'For the first time in a long while, I'd entertained the thought of staying here. Hanging out with you guys, seeing Colin and Kate's new baby born. But if she shafted you, it would change things. Do you think she could have got that information from anywhere other than the notes you left here?'

She wasn't going to lie to him. 'No.'

'She was here when you told me all about everything that had been going on at the baths, the day you were sick.'

'Fucking hell, Bill, I shouldn't have told you!'

'Sorry. It isn't often you get things off your chest like that, I didn't want to stop you. I didn't know she'd be listening, but then she ran off to work even though she'd said she had the day off. I didn't think at the time. Who's the mug?'

Jessie squeezed his shoulder. 'I might be wrong. She must have other contacts in CID.'

'You're a terrible liar, Jess, but thank you for trying.' He ruffled her hair. 'Are you feeling better?'

Jessie could see the wood clearing in her mind's eye. 'Much. Thanks.'

'Any more bad dreams, you come and get me.' He kissed her goodnight.

'Will do. Thanks. And, Bill, I'm sorry about Amanda.'

'Don't worry about it. Plenty more fish in the sea — isn't that what we all keep telling ourselves?'

Jessie sighed heavily. 'Fat lot of good it does us.'

'They were saying a lot about you and that guy on the news.'

'They don't know anything.'

'You're not pregnant, are you?'

Jessie laughed in surprise.

'Well, you were sick, and then . . .'

'No, that's not it.'

'Doesn't he want to see you again?'

'It would be easier if that were the case. Actually, that might be the case now. Either way, it's a mess.'

'So he did want to see you, this P. J. Dean?'

God, it sounded strange coming out of her brother's mouth like that.

'I resisted, Bill, for a while. But he's persistent, I'll give him that. And so convincing; he makes me think that it could actually work between us, that it's possible to go out with a man who the entire world knows. But it isn't.'

'Why isn't it?'

Jessie rubbed the fog out of her eyes. She couldn't keep things from Bill as well as she could keep them from herself. 'Because I'm terrified that I'll never find anything better.'

'That's good, isn't it?'

'Not if you're a fling, it isn't.'

Bill nodded. 'Ah.'

'Anyway, the last few times we've spoken it's ended up in a horrific row, the likes of which I've never had with anyone.'

'It's because you like him, Jess.'

'Me and every fourteen-year-old girl in the country. It's hopeless.'

'It's risky, sure. But life is risk. Africa teaches you that. It's also a privilege. Don't blow it because you're scared of what might happen. No one knows what's going to happen. That's the miracle of life.'

'It's fucked up now, Bill, it's too late.'

'If you can't talk to him, write to him. At least then you'll know you did what you could. People rarely regret the things they do, only the things they don't.'

A terrible feeling of regret . . . That wasn't always the case.

'I'll think about it.'

'Write the letter, even if you don't send it. It will clear things up in your own head. Trust me, I've been writing letters I don't send for years.'

'Who to?'

Bill smiled. He didn't have to answer her question, Jessie already knew.

Chapter 18

Vision Inc was the low-rent porn shop near Marshall Street Baths where Mr Romano had worked. Of course Jonny's friends would have known where it was, they were sixteen-year-old boys. Jessie wasn't sure what Mr Romano's involvement with the outfit was; maybe he was just a security guard with a little habit of his own, or maybe he was the mafia don, capable of murder, who had frightened Peter Boateng into conjuring up an evil drug dealer in the shape of Malcolm Hoare. Somehow Jessie doubted it. She believed the Romano story to be more tragic and more costly than either. Mr Romano had needed money to afford his son the chance of a better life, so he'd decided to do a little moonlighting in the speed trade. What was supposed to save his son, killed him. Jonny must have found the drugs, taken them to school, as Peter had said, and handed them out to his mates. It was only small amounts, Mr Romano probably didn't even notice until one day the amphetamine caused Jonny to have a seizure. Had it not been for the fact it occurred in a pool, and had it not been for the fact that Don Firth had been told by the teachers to ignore the rowdy Italian boy, the seizure would have left Jonny unscathed and maybe even a little wiser. But fate had other ideas.

Peter Boateng had been afraid of Mr Romano; fear made his story of Ian Doyle all the more convincing. Mr Romano was afraid of himself; it was fear that made him believe. Even so, deep down Mr Romano must have always felt that he killed his own son. The son he loved, took pride in, worked for, broke the law for.

Jessie knocked on the black door for what she thought would be the last time, then waited for the grieving father and abandoned husband to admit them to Flat G and play his final role. That of the guilty man. She didn't have to wait long.

The door opened of its own accord, the latch ripped from the frame. Jessie stared at the mess. Pictures hung at precarious angles along the wall, others lay smashed on the floor. Jessie stepped over the glass. All the drawers in the kitchen had been pulled out, cutlery and crockery covered the ground in an aluminium patchwork. The fridge door swung on one hinge, all the compartment trays marked with a spider's web of cracked plastic; milk from a burst carton tapped out a strange tune as it dripped on to the plastic floor. Jessie knew before she pushed open the door of Jonny's room that this was no violent burglary. The room was a mess, but it was in exactly the same mess it had been in for fourteen years. She radioed for assistance.

The first police officer to arrive at the flat was a young, spotty lad, who had a look of concern in his eyes that was not reassuring. Lisson Grove was his beat. He knew Romano well.

'I arrested him two nights ago for drunk and disorderly behaviour out by the allotments. He was shouting and screaming at no one. He slept it off in a cell and in the morning I discharged him. I know about his loss, see. I know it's been hard for him. Maybe I should have read the situation differently.'

'Have you seen him since?'

The officer shook his head. 'It's 'cause of that body in the baths, isn't it? It's making him relive it all, brings it all back. Poor bloke, enough to send anyone round the twist.' They were in the small sitting room. The pine dresser had been pulled from the wall, Mr Romano's notebooks lay sprawled over the carpet. Jessie picked one up, and flicked through it. *Take them,* he had said. *It's all there, everything you want to know about that evil man.* She had dismissed his words. At the time she couldn't face reading the ramblings of an increasingly deranged mind. At the time, she couldn't take on more grief. Jessie looked up when she heard Burrows and Niaz out in the corridor.

'I'm in here,' she called. Jessie told them everything Peter Boateng had told her. A call to a mate in the narcotics department had confirmed that the Italians had run the drug trade in the late eighties. Since then the Albanians had taken over.

Niaz and Burrows took in the mess with their eyes, then looked at Jessie.

'Do you still think Mr Romano is protecting his wife?' asked Burrows.

'No. He's just like Mr Scott-Somers: he's been protecting himself all along.'

'But criminals are the only people who leave no paper trail,' he offered.

'You're forgetting the dead, Burrows,' said Jessie. 'Peter Boateng suspected that some fate had befallen Mrs Romano, he hinted at it when Niaz and I first went to see him. The question is, what did Romano do with her once he'd killed her?'

'How do you know for sure that he killed her? She didn't go missing for two years. Their divorce was through, he didn't have a reason to kill her.'

'He did if she'd worked out that Doyle didn't exist. He did if she'd worked out where her son had got the drugs from. He did if she was threatening to tell. Peter Boateng was right when he said keeping Doyle alive meant no one having to face up to their own responsibilities. It was easier for Romano to blame the mythical drug dealer than admit his role in his son's death. Everyone was convinced.'

'Except his wife,' said Niaz.

'When he could no longer convince her, he killed her. In a terrible way, Mr Romano's life only became significant after Jonny drowned. The sympathy, the social standing, the support — it all came because of his loss. A guilty man would lose all that. He is very afraid right now, very afraid and very dangerous. We need to find him before someone else gets hurt.'

'I'll put an APB out for him,' said Niaz, reaching for his radio. 'What do you want to do about Mrs Romano?'

'We should get forensics down here. Blood leaves stains that are invisible to the human eye.'

'Not to the human conscience,' offered Niaz. 'We know what that sort of pressure did to Don Firth, and he didn't murder the boy. Imagine what sort of state Romano's mind must be in by now.'

'He's on the edge of an abyss, looking down,' said Jessie. She should have seen it earlier.

'You think he's going to fall?' asked Burrows.

'Worse, I think he may take someone with him.' Jessie looked over the spidery writing in the book, then at the bold angry capital letters, then back to the illegible scribbles. She had been right about one thing: these were undoubtedly the scrawlings of a deranged mind. A message she was not qualified to decipher.

She dialled a number on her mobile and smiled when she heard Father Forrester's soft voice accept the call.

'Ah, Jessie, I was just thinking about you.'

'Without corroboration, Father, I cannot accept that as evidence.'

Father Forrester chuckled. Glass marbles. 'I've been to see your friend. The dreams are a common thing among retired CID officers. The brain is a muscle like any other; adrenaline will get an athlete through a race, but when the run is completed the pain that could not be felt before rears up. No one can suppress pain for ever.'

Jessie stared at Romano's illegible scrawlings.

Father Forrester continued: 'It can be like a tiny leak. No one knows about the dripping pipe until the roof caves in.'

'Father Eric, I'd like to ask you for another favour . . .' She told him the address of the flat in the Lisson Grove Estate and outlined the task in hand.

'What happened to this Romano fellow?'

Jessie looked around the room again. 'His roof just caved in.'

'He said he liked to think of his ex-wife in Spain, that she liked the food or something,' said Burrows, reading back over his notebook. 'We should get on to Interpol.'

'I remember — the stuff about tomatoes, she liked tomatoes,' said Jessie.

'He grows them,' said the young police officer. Everyone turned to look at him. 'He showed them to me. He hands them out when he's got a good crop.'

'This is down on the allotment?'

'Yeah.'

'Where you arrested him?'

'That's right. I've even helped him carry his stuff down there — what do you call it? He makes it himself to go on the garden . . .'

'Compost?' ventured Jessie.

'Yeah, that's it — compost.'

Jessie turned back to her officers, her fear reflected in their expressions.

'He said she liked the feel of the sun on her bones,' said Niaz. 'Do you remember?'

'What do you want me to do, boss?' asked Burrows.

Jessie felt deeply disturbed by the inevitable conclusion they were all drawing to. 'This is so sad,' she said. She wanted the woman who had buried her son to be slicing vine tomatoes in the sunshine, sipping sherry and enjoying a little of life. But in her heart she knew that wasn't the case.

'Dig up his allotment. Start with the tomatoes.'

'We'll need a court order,' said Burrows.

'Then get one.'

Jessie felt heavy hearted as she walked up the stairs to her office. She had been right about Mr Romano all along, his grief had become his alibi, but that only depressed her more. Outside the canteen she toyed with the idea of eating, but found she had no stomach for it. A piece of well-thumbed newspaper fluttered as the canteen door swung closed on its hinge. The movement caught Jessie's eye. She walked towards the noticeboards. She expected an embarrassing ghost story. She found one, in full-colour copy. P.J. was photographed in the back of a stretch limo. He had a leggy blonde on either side. Models both, if the pose they struck for the intruding lens was anything to go by. P.J. had his hand up one of the girl's skirts. They were girls, too. No more than eighteen. Jessie felt a lump in her throat and before she knew it, she'd ripped the page off the wall and thrown it in the bin. It missed. In her pocket she felt for the recently sealed envelope, the letter her brother had suggested she write, and scrunched it into a ball.

The next person to come out of the canteen was Mark. They looked at each other; he glanced at the clipping on the floor, then back at Jessie. He'd aged in a week. She wasn't sure who looked worse. Slowly he bent down and picked up the offending article. He screwed it up and dropped it in the bin. Jessie was mute. As he walked past her, he squeezed her arm.

'His loss,' he said.

Jessie shook her head. 'I don't want your pity,' she said quietly.

'What do you want?'

'Your support.'

Mark nodded once. 'Ditto.' He moved away.

'I'm sorry about your —' He held up his hand to silence her. She understood the gesture. It was too early for words of sympathy to cause anything other than more pain. Jessie bit down on her lip as she watched his hunched shoulders walk away.

Outside her office was a young WPC whom Jessie liked.

'I can't —' Jessie began, but the lump in her throat was making it difficult to talk.

'There's a woman in your office who needs to see you.'

Jessie shook her head. 'I can't —'

'She says it's very important. Her name is Clementine Colbert. She was the woman who —'

'It's okay,' said Jessie, finding her voice. 'I know who she is.' She held up her hand. 'Just give me a few minutes.'

The WPC retreated. 'I'll get you some tea.'

Tea, the panacea WPCs were taught to give to victims, thought Jessie. You didn't need psychic powers to spot one. She leant back against the wall and summoned the strength to go on.

The Scott-Somers' nanny had aged well. Like most Parisian women, she was immaculately dressed, with shiny, neatly cropped hair, and a silk scarf peeking out between the stiff collars of her white shirt.

'I am a lawyer now,' she said. 'International law. I only took the job with the Scott-Somers to perfect my English . . .' Clementine Colbert paused. 'I stayed too long.'

'How long were you having an affair with Mr Scott-Somers?' asked Jessie.

The Frenchwoman's eyes rose to meet hers. 'Who told you?'

'No one.'

'I loved him,' she said in plain English. 'I was not a silly little girl with a crush on her boss, it was not like that. There was a real connection.'

'Isn't there always?' said Jessie, more angry than she had a right to be.

'I did not come here to justify our relationship. I came here to help you find Nancy and to explain.'

'Why did you run away?'

'I was making a phone call to Nico— Mr Scott-Somers when Nancy was taken. It was completely my fault and I was so scared about that, I fled. When little Charlotte arrived home without us, she told the staff that I had lost her and a man who looked like a bear had taken Nancy. They didn't believe her, of course. She was always running off; it was just her way of making people notice her. She was not as attractive as her sister, who always got much more attention. Mrs Scott-Somers was not a very maternal woman. Anyway, no one believed Charlotte; perhaps Mr Scott-Somers did little to change the view that she had run from me. Everyone thought I had gone away because I was scared of the family, you see, that way it took the attention off me.'

'And in doing so put a hefty charge on some very small shoulders,' said Jessie.

'No one was thinking straight.'

'Clearly.'

Once again Clementine raised her chin defiantly. 'Your opinion of me matters very little. I simply want to do my duty.'

A little late, thought Jessie, but she didn't say anything.

'He told me I must not come back. He

was angry, of course. With me, with himself. I thought when things had passed, when the man was in jail, eventually we could . . .' Wishing for it hadn't made it happen, she couldn't change the past. 'But, as you know, they found me, the prosecution. I was subpoenaed, I had to go even though I had promised I wouldn't. I meant what I said to Nancy that day in court: I *was* sorry. I *would* have done anything to make it up to *her*. My English was good enough to know what I was saying — they twisted my words, I did not know about the law then. I do now. That case should never have been thrown out of court. I don't know who that lawyer was, but he pulled the wool over everyone's eyes that day.'

'He was paid for by Mr Scott-Somers.'

Clementine Colbert looked genuinely surprised.

'It took me a little while to figure out that he was trying to protect himself. Not his family. Certainly not Nancy. Expensive divorce, and all that,' continued Jessie.

Mr Scott-Somers' mistress was completely serene when she spoke again. 'No, it was *me* he was trying to protect. You don't have to believe me, but what we had was real. What could we do after that terrible day in court? Nancy was ruined, she had terrible nightmares, wet her bed, became completely withdrawn, and poor little Charlotte was completely subsumed by it. All because we had been too timid to do anything about our relationship earlier. There is no right time for these things, is there?'

Jessie wasn't feeling in a sympathetic mood.

'I went home to Paris, I studied hard, I got a job, I worked at getting over him.'

'Successfully?'

The woman opposite her did not respond, she glanced at her empty wedding finger, then looked Jessie firmly in the eye.

'I came back for his funeral. I decided to stay on in London. It is easier to grieve alone. When I saw the news, I came here. I don't care what they are saying. Nancy could not have killed anyone.'

'How can you be so sure? You haven't seen her since she was eleven.'

'Nicholas and I promised never to see each other again. And we fulfilled that promise, though now I cannot understand why. No one benefited from the punishment we imposed upon ourselves. If I could just go back to that one day . . .'

Again the futility of her words was not lost on Jessie. 'We wrote when things got unbearable. A letter can breathe life into you, if you let it. This is why I know things about the family. I know that Nancy had suicidal tendencies. She wanted to kill herself, but she couldn't. Like me, she believed, you see. She believed in God — why wouldn't she? She'd been told she was an angel enough times. So you see, she couldn't kill anyone.'

'What about Mr Scott-Somers? After all, Malcolm Hoare ruined his life, your life, his daughters' lives . . .'

'No, Detective Inspector, we did that.'

Jessie escorted the missing piece of the puzzle to the exit. 'What was so important, Madame Colbert, that you had to ring Mr Scott-Somers that day?'

Jessie watched the shudder pass through the woman's petite frame and immediately regretted asking.

'I was pregnant,' she said, nodding, as if she still could not believe it. 'I miscarried in the seventh month. They told me they found nothing wrong with our son.' She gave Jessie a challenging look. 'The wrath of God, you think?' Jessie said nothing. 'I miss them both,' said the

Frenchwoman. 'All the time.'

The press were camped behind temporary barriers outside the Scott-Somers' house. The family — what was left of it — were holed up inside their gilded cage. Amanda Hornby had opened the floodgates, the protective fence was down and Mr Scott-Somers wasn't alive any more to exert his personal kind of pressure. Those in power might be loyal to their benefactors, but this was a question of murder. Every aspect of the Scott-Somers' life, from disgruntled ex-employees to tailors to the bevy of ex-husbands that Charlotte had accrued and discarded, were speculating, cogitating and agitating. As Niaz and Jessie approached, the swarm of leather jackets and long lenses turned their way and the battering of questions started.

'Who killed Malcolm Hoare?' 'Is he haunting Marshall Street Baths?' 'Where's Nancy?' 'Is she haunting Marshall Street Baths?' 'Where's the exorcist?' 'Did they get him bumped off?' 'What about the explosion?'

Jessie turned away and ran up the steps. The door opened.

'Hey, Jess, did you and P.J. have a lover's

tiff?' The door closed.

They stood in the cool marble vestibule and for the briefest of moments Jessie felt the reassuring warmth of Niaz's hand on her back. Strength, thought Jessie, comes from the least likely of places. Terence Vane showed her into a plant-infested 'breakfast' room. It had a glass ceiling that was wound open by a long metal rod. Coffee was being served. The women drank it strong and black. Mrs Scott-Somers half-turned towards Jessie and spoke over her shoulder.

'See you've met our friendly press corps?' she said, a strange smirk in her voice. BBC News 24 was playing on a television mounted on the wall. Jessie's own photograph was floating ominously over the muted newsreader's lapel. Next came a picture of P. J. Dean and his murdered wife Verity Shore. She knew the shot; it was from *Hello!* Yet another of those 'confirmation of our love' pieces. Jessie didn't need to hear the voice-over, she knew well enough what was being said. It would be the Ritz photograph next; followed, no doubt, by P.J. in the limo. The story was on a loop, but she was not enjoying the ride. She turned to face Mrs Scott-Somers.

'We have traced the money,' she said.

Nancy's mother stiffened. Her sister appeared to stop breathing.

'She gives every penny to charity,' Jessie announced.

'What?' Mrs Scott-Somers was completely thrown.

'Quarter of a million pounds a year!' said Charlotte incredulously.

'It is donated to a number of charities which vary in profile and size.'

'What does she live on?' asked Mrs Scott-Somers.

'Perhaps she has a job and lives off the earnings, though I should add she isn't a registered tax payer.'

'She's dead,' said Charlotte.

'No, she isn't dead.'

'She must be. Nancy isn't capable of getting a job.'

Jessie thought she detected a note of envy in Charlotte's voice. Was the idea of a small, unencumbered, independent life the one jewel that the heiress could not afford?

'The list of recipients changed quite recently, and only Nancy could instruct those changes.'

Charlotte was shaking her head. 'I dreamt about it, Detective. She was alone, in the dark, surrounded by dead cats.'

'That was your sister's childhood nightmare. Not yours,' said Mrs Scott-Somers impatiently.

Jessie watched Charlotte pick up the phone. 'Terence, Bloody Mary please.'

'For pity's sake, it isn't even noon.'

Charlotte ignored her mother. 'Things go missing — I don't care if you believe me or not — little items of no monetary value. A photo of me disappeared for a whole year, then suddenly, there it was, back in the same place. What spirit would take those things if it weren't Nancy?'

'I wouldn't put it past you to hide these things yourself, Charlotte.'

'So you concede that things do go missing?'

'Witness, Detective, the selective hearing. We've had more weirdoes with crystals pass through this house than Stonehenge. The other day I caught her with a ouija board trying to talk to my husband. Our priest was furious. He said you invite the devil in when you play with his toys.'

For once Jessie agreed with Mrs Scott-Somers.

'Let's keep to the matter at hand. Can you assure me, Detective, that Nancy hasn't been taken in by a religious cult?'

'Until we find her, I cannot completely rule that out, but sects tend to appropriate their "disciples'" money, and we've found no evidence of that yet.'

'I was beginning to think the Moonies had her.'

'No, Mrs Scott-Somers, it appears your daughter stays away of her own free will.'

Mrs Scott-Somers' eyes narrowed imperceptibly. 'So how do we get the money back?'

'You can't,' said Jessie. 'We're checking every single recipient, in case of fraud, but so far the charities that received the most substantial donations are legitimate.'

'That money was intended for Nancy.'

'Perhaps she didn't want it. Money is a burden, like her angelic looks — surely you can understand why she would have given it away?'

Mrs Scott-Somers looked confused.

'For the same reason she put on weight,' explained Jessie.

Mrs Scott-Somers was still perplexed. So Jessie spelt it out: 'If you were snatched off the street because you were pretty, blonde and rich, what wouldn't you want to be any more?'

Charlotte stared at her own reflection in one of the mirrors that adorned the walls of the breakfast room. 'Pretty, blonde and rich,' she said quietly.

'I took her to every decent dietician in Europe. They informed me my daughter had an eating disorder: binge-eating. I told her it would kill her if she went on, but nothing worked.'

'She didn't want it to work,' said Jessie.

'Why? It wasn't Nancy's fault she was kidnapped,' said Mrs Scott-Somers angrily.

'I wonder if anyone told her that.'

'Of course we did. We all knew whose fault it was —Malcolm Hoare's. And that bloody nanny, for letting it happen. Then she reappears and does it all over again in court.' There was so much bitterness in Mrs Scott-Somers' voice, so much anger. Had she known all along that she was a cuckold? Was she aware that her marriage, her lifestyle, her very existence had only continued as it had because of her daughter's kidnapping? Was she in the unenviable position of having to feel grateful towards Malcolm Hoare?

'We loved her,' said Charlotte, turning away from the mirror.

'You would like the one person who ruined everything.'

'At least she cared.'

'She was *paid* to care, Charlotte.'

'You're wrong, Mother. She did care and you know it, that's why you never let any of the other nannies stay longer than a month.'

'If you loved her so much, why did you run away from her and cause all this trouble?'

There were a few seconds of silence as Mrs Scott-Somers' words sunk in.

'I knew you blamed me.'

'Charlotte didn't run away,' interrupted Jessie.

'Yes she did,' said Mrs Scott-Somers, no hint of conciliation in her voice.

'No, her crime was that she'd run away before. When she arrived home and said the nanny had lost them, all you heard was "run-away".' Like Jonny Romano, she had cried wolf too many times. 'Charlotte wasn't to blame.'

'I should have stayed with her,' said Charlotte.

'Malcolm Hoare was a huge man, there was nothing you could have done.'

'I could have protected her.'

Jessie wanted to reach out to her. 'It's not your fault. You were only nine years old.'

'I didn't stop him. I didn't shout for

help. I could've got Clemy out of the phone-box.'

Mrs Scott-Somers hurled herself out of the plush sofa. 'You don't know what you're talking about. Your father hated the way you lied.'

Charlotte continued to stare at Jessie. 'Everyone loved Nancy, do you see?'

Jessie nodded. She saw. If Nancy went away, maybe someone would take a little notice of Charlotte. But it wasn't to be. Nancy came back and even more attention was lavished upon her.

'It didn't matter what I did, I could never compare to my sister. Even when she was fat and ugly, and I was the pretty one, it was always Nancy. I started to punish her for it. I made her wet her bed, I told her Malcolm was waiting down the corridor.'

'You always were a hideous child!'

Charlotte turned to her mother. 'Can't imagine who I take after.'

'I'm glad your father isn't alive to hear this.'

'I'm pretty certain he's glad he isn't alive either. We weren't enough for him, Mother. All he wanted was Nancy back. But he never got her back, did he? DI Driver is right: she was never the same.

Didn't matter how good you looked or how many business trips you went on with him, or how many A-grades I got, we couldn't make him happy, because Nancy wasn't happy.'

Jessie looked to Mrs Scott-Somers to correct her daughter; that wasn't why Mr Scott-Somers had withdrawn from his family, and it wasn't why he couldn't be reached. Mr Scott-Somers had made his own pact with the devil and his name was Tobias Charles Edmonds. The lawyer who enabled Malcolm Hoare to walk free. He destroyed both his children, ruined his wife, broke the heart of the woman he'd loved and probably believed he'd killed their unborn child. He had much more to mourn than Charlotte could possibly imagine.

'The very last time she came back, she said she was coming home, that it was all over and she was going to be fine again. She said she was sorry about everything she'd put *me* through.' Charlotte shook her head in disbelief. 'I didn't believe her. She'd been back before and said the same things. I told her we didn't want her. I told her she was an embarrassment, that we didn't love her and we never talked about her. I told her that, as far as we were concerned, she *was* dead.' Charlotte looked pleadingly at Jessie. 'You have to understand, I wanted to tell her to stay, I wanted to tell her I missed her, but I couldn't. She'd left before, she'd leave again. I couldn't take that chance, so I made her go.'

'When was this?'

'I can't remember.'

'I think you can,' pressed Jessie.

'Why didn't you tell me? When were all these times she came back? Why didn't you come and get us?'

A weariness filled Charlotte's voice. 'You weren't here. You never were.'

'It's very important you remember when this last time was,' said Jessie.

'Yes. When was it?' demanded her mother.

'I told you, I can't remember.'

'You can help me find her,' said Jessie.

'I'm not helping you find her. You want to prosecute her for Malcolm's murder. Don't, for fuck's sake, pretend that you give a shit. Nancy didn't kill him, she would never have gone to a swimming pool — she was fat! You think she'd take her clothes off in public? She couldn't at home! She's got nothing to do with this!'

'I'm sorry, but I think she has.'

'You don't understand, do you? What everyone saw in my sister was real. She was an angel. I should know. I did everything in my power to hurt her, and she never, ever did anything back. She couldn't kill a man. She wouldn't.'

Charlotte was the third, and least likely, person to vouch for Nancy's innocence.

There was a sharp rap on the door and Terence entered, carrying a tray. He knew his mistress well. On the tray was a large jug of Bloody Mary and one glass.

Chapter 19

The SOCOs encircled the small plot of land. Jessie glanced down at the neat row of beds. A mixture of Mediterranean vegetables were being painstakingly grown in grey, wet London under sheets of corrugated plastic. They had been there a long time. Thick green algae grew along each trough. Mr Romano's description was out on the wire as a man possibly armed and highly dangerous, both to himself and others. Burrows handed Jessie the approved court order, she signed it and handed it back. The first spade went into the tilled earth.

'What happened at the Scott-Somers' place?' he asked.

'Some time after Christmas 1987 Nancy told her sister she was coming home, but now Charlotte is claiming she cannot remember the date. Which is highly unlikely — Nancy has only been home three times in nearly twenty years.'

'Why do you think she is lying?' asked Niaz.

Because, thought Jessie, after a lifetime of not doing so, Charlotte was trying to protect her sister. 'She feels guilty. And she shouldn't, none of this was her fault. So, we have two avenues. First: the charities. Somewhere in that long list is a clue; it's who Nancy is now and who she was back then. They've changed over the years, there must be a pattern, something. It's a puzzle for which you, Niaz, have the perfect brain.'

Niaz bowed slightly. 'I was certainly very speedy on the Rubik's cube.'

'Burrows, you go back to the council. Her name doesn't appear on any of the council lists, so she wasn't there as a qualified instructor because she'd need to have given proof of her identity. Maybe her sister was right and she didn't go to the baths to swim, maybe she went for another reason. Start looking at the casual workers, cleaners, assistant carers, volunteers — the sort of people who could stay in the shadows if they wanted.' Jessie heard the roots of a young tomato plant snap as it was pulled from its resting place. 'The sort of people who wouldn't be noticed if they went missing.'

The first bone they found was part of a finger. The dig stopped and Sally Grimes was called in. The next bone was a portion of the tibia, the shinbone. There was not a morsel of flesh on it. According to the pathologist, not only had it been in the ground for over ten years, it had been sawn down to size by a domestic handsaw, the type sold in any DIY store.

'Take samples of the soil,' said Jessie, as several sections of a rib were uncovered. 'There should still be traces of blood.'

Sally turned a bone over in her hand. 'I'm not so sure,' she said.

'I'm not suggesting he killed her here. He probably did that in the flat and brought her down bit by bit in compost bags. When bodies decompose in the soil don't they leave a trace element of deposits?'

'If there's flesh on the bones they do.'

Jessie frowned at the pathologist. 'Why wouldn't there have been flesh on the bone?'

'That's your job, but my guess is that these bones were clean when they got here. The depth of discolouration means the soil was attacking the calcium very quickly. No wonder he had good tomatoes.'

'That's disgusting.'

'Not as disgusting as what he did to get the bones clean.'

'Which is?'

'I'm not sure you're going to believe this.'

Jessie swallowed nervously. These were the nightmares of the future.

A SOCO passed Sally another handful of Mrs Romano's remains. All about the same size: four inches in length. She examined each one in turn. 'Every segment of bone is showing signs of heat stress.'

Jessie waited.

'I think he cut up his wife into manageable bits and cooked her.'

She left a note and a fridge full of food. I haven't seen her since. Jessie recalled the recently destroyed refrigerator in Romano's kitchen. *Everything I've eaten since has tasted bad. Except my tomatoes. They remind me of her.* A chilling image moved across Jessie's mind. Romano, sitting in the kitchen, forcing forkfuls of gristle into his mouth.

'I think Mr Romano ate his wife.'

Jessie responded to Sally's look of disbelief.

'Hear me out. His wife found out what

he'd done. He didn't want to go back to being vilified, the scummy man in the porn shop. They had a fight. A domestic row is hardly going to raise eyebrows in that neighbourhood. He would have had to do something with the body.'

'Maybe, but what makes you think he ate her?'

'Intuition,' said Jessie.

'Can't prove intuition.'

Jessie smiled wryly to herself. 'I know.'

'Well, I'll keep an eye out for teeth marks, but I can't promise anything,' said Sally.

Black humour. Whisky. P. J. Dean. Gnomes. Whatever got you through the day. Or night.

'By the way, what had he done that was worth murdering his wife for?' asked the pathologist.

He drowned. It was an accident. 'Killed their son.'

'Dr Grimes,' a voice called, 'I think we've found the skull.'

'Do you want to come?' said Sally.

'No, you go.'

Jessie looked out over the sad rectangles of land, some little more than a dumping ground for shopping trolleys and ancient washing machines, others cared for, worked over by gardeners who took pride in their plot. It wasn't always about where you came from, it was what your attitude to it was. Did you want to leave the world a better place or destroy it? Did we come back over and over again until we got it right, only then free to move on to a higher plane? Was this hell, here on earth?

'He hit her over the head from behind and smashed her skull,' said Sally. 'Death would have been instantaneous; she wouldn't have known what happened.'

If it was over in that instant, maybe. But what if it wasn't? What if the souls of those people who'd died in horrific and unjust situations did get stuck, as Father Forrester believed? What if they moved between us, unseen, angry and confused, until someone could help them let go? What would Mrs Romano have made of her husband cutting her up into edible pieces and cooking her? Jessie felt a damp, cold wind snake through her leather jacket and under her skin.

'Find every bone,' Jessie instructed the SOCO team. 'Mrs Romano deserves a proper burial, alongside her son.'

Feeling shell-shocked, Jessie returned to

477

the station with Burrows and Niaz to continue the search for Nancy and the hunt for Mr Romano. All exits out of the country were being watched. Moving targets were easier to find. But Mr Romano was wounded to the core, and wounded targets were desperate. Desperate meant dangerous. Nancy may have stayed hidden for years, but her danger was to herself. Finding her was going to require a miracle.

She was just on the verge of returning to the Scott-Somers house to grill Charlotte when Burrows walked through her door holding a photocopied letter of recommendation addressed to the head of social services. Jessie read it quickly. The letter was a character reference for a twenty-year-old woman called Rose Williams. According to the letter, she was efficient, kind and bright, and brought a caring approach to all her work. She helped out at her local dog's home and had a volunteer assistant carer's place at a shelter, where she had demonstrated exceptional ability in working with people who had special needs. Rose Williams was a saint. Certainly according to her referee: Dr Christopher Turnball of St Audley Street Surgery, Mayfair.

'One of Nancy's middle names is Rose,' said Jessie, excited.

'And if that were not proof enough, her paternal grandmother's name was Williams,' said Burrows.

'He lied to me,' said Jessie. 'Dr Turnball said he didn't remember Nancy having any connection with Marshall Street Baths.'

'The council didn't specify which of the baths under their jurisdiction they were going to send her to. So, technically, he didn't.'

'Rose Williams,' said Jessie frowning. 'Why does that name ring a bell?'

'I don't know, but she worked there for three years. Right up until the drowning incident.'

I've worked here all my life. 'Don's scrapbook, where is it?'

'Niaz has it.'

'Where is he?'

'Working on the charities.'

'Let's go.' Jessie stood. 'Good work, Burrows. You've done brilliantly.'

'It was your idea, boss.'

Niaz was hunched over a computer. It looked like he had been there for some time. Information about each of the charities Nancy Scott-Somers supported had been meticulously entered on to a spread-sheet Niaz had designed himself. There were over two thousand so far, and further details were still coming through on the fax machine. The recipient organisations had been altered over the years to meet the changing misfortunes of the neglected. Niaz looked up from a stack of pages. His hands were smudged with print.

'Children's charities are clearly domi-nant. A number of animal charities benefit too, but only on a small scale. She's given a lot of money away.'

'She had a lot to give,' said Burrows.

'What are the animal charities?'

Niaz handed over a master list. It was colour coded. 'The animal charities are in green.' There was money for guide dogs, the Battersea Dog's Home, the RSPCA, mistreated horses, neglected farm animals and beleaguered cats.

'Can you find out if any of them have re-ceived funds continually?'

Niaz nodded, pressed a few keys and waited a nano-second for the response.

'NSPCC, Oxfam, the Red Cross, the Home for Beleaguered Cats.'

'Cats,' said Jessie. 'How much?'

'In total, £216,000.'

'Lucky cats,' said Burrows.

'Nancy had a thing about cats. Remember the photograph of the place where she was held? The skeleton of a cat was hanging from a beam right above her head. Have you got the paperwork on these donations?'

'Hang on,' said Niaz. He pressed some more buttons, turned to a stack of grey folders and pulled a numbered one out. Burrows and Jessie looked at each other.

'Who are the registered directors?' asked Jessie.

Niaz skimmed the page in front of him, stopped, frowned, then brought the folder closer to his face as if he couldn't believe the words. 'The doctor.'

'What?'

'Dr Christopher Turnball.'

'Anyone else?' Jessie asked quickly.

'No, just a company secretary.'

'Called?' asked Burrows.

'Rose Williams,' said Jessie, answering for Niaz.

'Correct.'

'Got an address?'

Niaz passed the open folder over to Jessie.

She felt a bubble of delight rise up in her. 'We found her! We found Nancy.'

'I don't understand,' said Niaz.

'I'm not sure I do either,' said Burrows. 'Why has she been sending her own money to herself?'

'Burrows, show Niaz Dr Turnball's letter.'

'You think the *doctor* has been nicking her money?'

'No. The amount is negligible.'

'You think £216,000 is negligible?'

'It is if you break it down to £250 a week. She had no other source of income — she worked for free; getting a job or claiming benefit would mean filling in paperwork, supplying proof of identity — so that £250 would have paid for rent, bills, food, transport. Let's not forget, she could have had a hundred times that amount every month.'

Niaz finished reading the letter of recommendation. 'He is still protecting the little girl he once took care of.'

'Protecting, or perverting the course of justice? Nancy sends the money to herself so that she can remain incognito. Murder is a good reason to stay hidden.'

'I do not believe a doctor would do such a thing.'

'Niaz, you're too naïve.' Jessie replayed the conversation with Dr Turnball in her mind. 'He seemed so bloody sincere, charmingly warning me off — and all the time he knew exactly why I was calling him. If Nancy killed Hoare and the doctor knew, he could be in serious trouble.'

Burrows held her back. 'Mr Romano is still missing. He could have killed Malcolm Hoare to prevent him protesting his innocence, the way he killed his wife to prevent her revealing where Jonny got the drugs.'

'Mr Romano didn't kill Malcolm Hoare. That was a revenge killing. Why else would he have been tied up in exactly the same way Nancy was?'

'But we don't know yet if they met,' protested Burrows. 'And look how much they'd changed — even if they had met they would never have recognised each other. They could have seen each other every week for the three years that Nancy worked there and never worked out who the other was.'

Jessie looked at him. 'Of course. Burrows, you're a genius.'

'I am?'

Jessie grabbed the scrapbook lying innocuously on Niaz's desk. 'It's been under my nose since the day we went into those baths,' she said, flicking speedily through it. 'Rose Williams . . . I knew I'd come across the name somewhere before. Father

Forrester was wrong about one thing, this never had anything to do with a girl called Ann.'

'Anna — I thought he said Anna, as in Anna Maria Klein?'

'Actually, he said Ann. I assumed he meant Anna because Anna Maria Klein was missing. But really this was about a woman who called herself Rose. Look —' Glued to the fuzzy mauve paper was a newspaper cutting. They all looked at the feather-light document and weighed up its meaning. A sponsored swim had been organised to raise money for a minibus. There were young crash victims with legs and arms missing; a thalidomide victim with shrunken limbs; elderly people propped up in wheelchairs; stroke victims . . . Jessie knew the backdrop of the photograph well. It was the foyer of Marshall Street Baths. Standing at the back, turned towards the well-built, handsome lifeguard was a large, smiling lady. She had soft curly hair and laughing eyes. Her round face was hidden behind her fat hands, which were held up in a gesture of applause. A mask of pride. The only other person half-concealed from the photographer's eye was a skinny man with slicked-back black hair. He too stood at the back, and even though half his face was obscured by another man's shoulder, he too was smiling. Malcolm Hoare. A kidnapper who had once been described as a bear, standing alongside his victim, no longer the little angel.

'Don told me about this before the explosion. I've stared at this photograph for hours, but I didn't see it.' Everyone was smiling. They'd raised the money. Achieved a common goal. 'I wasn't looking for friends, all laughing together on the back row. Look — their names are typed out below: "Michael Firth, Rose Williams, and all the other helpers".'

'That's Don Firth,' said Burrows, incredulous.

'Yes, this is who he was three weeks before Jonny Romano drowned. Before he dropped Michael and became Don. The life and soul of Marshall Street Baths. And these are the people Nancy and Malcolm had become. Judging from this photograph, neither of them had any inkling who the other was.'

'They're both hiding from the camera.'

'Of course. They knew themselves, they knew who they were hiding from — the whole bloody world.'

'What do you think changed?'

'I don't know. Let's assume the group met on the same day as the school swimming trips, because Boateng mentioned seeing him there every Tuesday. Three weeks after this celebration, Jonny Romano drowned. It was February 23rd, a significant date for both of them. Who knows what might have come out during a conversation brought on by the tragedy of an innocent boy's death or an angry mob's hounding.'

'If Malcolm Hoare had been there that day, wouldn't someone have recognised him from Peter Boateng's description of Ian Doyle?'

'They were looking for a drug dealer, not a fund-raising disabled man. And remember, Boateng left out the limp.'

'Boateng thought he was a pervert, staring at them.'

'Or maybe he was simply a loner, as he'd always been,' said Jessie. 'Either way, something good must have happened in both their lives,' she added, looking again at the group photo. 'They're smiling. Despite themselves. Niaz, go and fetch the doctor. Burrows, you and I are going to find Nancy.'

The house in South London could not

be reached by car. They had to go on foot, past a grim one-storey pub and along an alleyway that showed the tell-tale signs of marginal living. This was such an undesirable place it wasn't even used as a rat-run. It cut through to nowhere. At first it was hard to tell which of the four two-storey residences were inhabited, such was their derelict state. 'House' was too generous a term for what stood before them. A room atop a room. The first window was boarded up, the next had curtains pulled against the light — somewhat ineffectually, for they were thin and hung loosely off the rail. Jessie initially dismissed them as drug dens or squats, and began moving towards the fourth, but then she saw something moving in the rubbish dump that had grown up in front of the door. She recoiled, the memory of the rats too fresh in her mind. A scrawny black cat darted towards the third door and disappeared through a cat entry that had no flap.

'She's in there,' said Jessie.

Already she could smell it: rotting flesh.

Burrows knocked on the door. There was no answer.

'Can you break the door down?' asked Jessie.

'We don't have to.' Trying the handle,

he'd found the front door was unlocked. He pointed out a wooden symbol nailed to the door frame. 'A mezuzah,' said Burrows. 'It's used in the Jewish faith to bless a house.'

It was dark inside the narrow hall. Jessie tried the light switch. Nothing happened. From the narrow strip of bald carpet that rose up the staircase, a phalanx of skeletal cats stared back at them. The stuff of nightmares. Past. Present. And Future. Predestined as Mary and Father Forrester thought, or self-prophesying, as Niaz believed, Jessie didn't know. What she did know was that Nancy was here, alone, in the dark, surrounded by cats and that she was very afraid. On the wall hung the bleeding, anguished figure of Christ nailed to the cross. *Father, why hast Thou forsaken me?*

They saw the first dead cat in the doorway at the end of the hall. Jessie wondered whether it was fear of the deceased cat that kept the others on the staircase, or fear of what lay beyond it. Another mezuzah was stuck to the door frame. Above it was an Arabic inscription. 'It's a quote from the Koran about the wrath of God.' He looked at Jessie. 'I studied all the major religions before deciding that Christianity was the one for me.'

'I don't think religion can save her now,' said Jessie.

'Don't be so sure.'

The dead cat suddenly moved, making Jessie jump. A rat ran out from underneath it, leaving it lying hideously flat. Jessie swallowed back her saliva. 'We need to get pest control down here now,' she whispered, then took a deep breath and stepped over the deflated carcass.

'Nancy?' she said, her voice trembling only slightly as she stepped into the dim, stagnant air.

The thin, ill-hung curtains let in a sickly and uneven light. Jessie put her hand over her nose and mouth. It was ineffectual. The smell was noxious and all pervading. Partially turned away from her, in the middle of the room, was an old, misshapen armchair piled high with blankets. All around it were plastic bags spilling their used contents on to the floor. Family-size Coke bottles, empty processed food packets and biscuit tins. Jessie saw a loaf of bread, stiff with mould. Burrows pulled back part of the curtain. In the weak light Jessie saw the outline of the chair's contents take on the form of a person. A grotesquely overweight person. Jessie stepped closer. Nothing moved except flies and dust motes in the shaft of light now dissecting the gloomy room. It fell across the curve of a broad sloping shoulder, a lumpy mound of chest and stomach, the stump of a leg and a cracked, shoeless heel. It passed over the rubbish-strewn floor and up the opposite wall. There it illuminated the statue of the Virgin Mary holding the baby Jesus.

Jessie walked around the chair to see what the Virgin Mary's glazed gaze was fixed upon. Nancy Scott-Somers; a little girl lost inside thirty stone of flesh. She was wearing a huge sleeveless dress that dropped almost to the floor. The thick, lumpy skin of her arms flopped over the edge of the armrests and hung like stretched-out pizza dough. They fell away from her body as if offering up a prayer to Mary. Roped between each broad, mottled finger on her left hand was a Rosary. Unblinking, Nancy stared back at the Blessed Mother, her bottom eyelids pulled down by the weight of her jowls to reveal the yellowing whites of her eyes. A filament of drool had slipped out of the side of her partially open mouth and dried. Around her neck was a gold chain with a cross, a

Star of David and an Ohm. Nancy Scott-Somers was taking no chances.

Unable to detect any sign of life in the thirty-stone body, Jessie reached forward to close Nancy's eyes, then withdrew her hand, surprised.

'Is she dead?' asked Burrows from the window.

'She's warm.'

Jessie reached under Nancy's flabby chin and tried to feel for a pulse. Nothing. She raised one of the thick wrists and pressed two fingers down hard into the flesh.

'I've found a pulse, but it's very faint.'

'Is she conscious?'

Jessie took the slim black torch out of her bag and twisted it until a bright white beam shot forward into Nancy's face. Her head jerked to the left. 'Yes.'

I told her she'd kill herself if she didn't stop eating.

'Burrows, we need medical assistance here. Fast.'

Nancy let out a guttural moan of protest.

'Don't keep her alive for your own satisfaction.'

Jessie looked up. 'Excuse me?'

'I think she has suffered enough. What would a prison sentence do now?'

'Look at her, she's already in prison.'

Someone in here needs forgiveness. 'She needs help.'

'Forgiveness isn't yours to give, boss.'

'I know that.'

'Then leave her be.'

'No.'

'Boss —'

'Get the paramedics down here, insist on a bike so they can come right to the door. She needs oxygen.'

'She's been through enough,' he pleaded.

'Now, Burrows. She's holding on by a thread.'

'So let her go.'

'No,' she said again. Not yet, not like this.

The paramedic's report was bleak.

'It's all that weight on her lungs — they can't cope. Basically, she'll suffocate if we don't insert a tube and link her up to a respirator. Then we need to deal with getting her out of that chair. She's been sitting in her own urine and faeces for God knows how long, hence the smell. Infected sores. The sweat gets trapped and the skin begins to rot.'

'How will you move her?' asked Jessie, cutting him off, minimising the details.

'By winch.'

'No,' said Burrows. 'She's dying. Save

her that humiliation at least.'

'There's a chance we can save her,' said the paramedic, pulling breathing apparatus out of the bike's side-box.

'It isn't for us mere mortals to save her any more,' protested Burrows.

'But we do what we can,' said the paramedic, carrying the life-saving equipment into the house.

Jessie watched from the doorway as the emergency nurse knelt down at Nancy's side. Burrows didn't believe Nancy could be saved, not by anyone in this life, but if the Marshall Street Baths and the Scott-Somers case had taught Jessie anything, it was that belief in the afterlife was inconsequential. The afterlife was exactly that. After life. While we were here, living this one, it had to be faced full on. Nancy had been living in limbo for too long. At first afraid to live and now too afraid to die. One look at the religious artefacts had confirmed what the nanny, Clementine Colbert, had said: Nancy believed. Hell was all too real a prospect for a person who had committed the number one sin on God's not-to-do list. Jessie turned away as Nancy was intubated.

'I don't know what you expect to get out

of this,' said Burrows in disgust.

'Time,' replied Jessie.

'For what?'

'To talk.'

'She can't talk. Thanks to you, she has a pipe down her throat forcing oxygen into her lungs,' said Burrows angrily.

'But she can listen,' said Jessie, walking back into the house.

'Nancy,' said Jessie. 'We haven't got long, do you understand? Blink once for yes. Twice for no.'

Nancy blinked once.

'My name is Detective Inspector Jessie Driver and I believe you killed Malcolm Hoare. Is that correct?'

Nancy blinked once.

'Is this necessary, boss?' interrupted Burrows, looking crossly at Jessie.

Nancy blinked once.

'I said, is this necessary?'

Nancy blinked once, again. The quiet undead. Jessie continued.

'In 1986 you applied for a job as a volunteer assistant carer. Thanks to some creative writing from Dr Turnball, you got that job and you were excellent at it. Kind, considerate and caring. Everyone who has ever met you confirms these characteristics. You began to lose weight. You grew your hair back but dyed it darker to be on the safe side. You never wanted your identity to be found out. At the baths you met a man who'd suffered from childhood polio that had left him with a limp. A limp that got progressively worse with age. He was older than you, but that didn't seem to matter. There was a pain common to you both, and over the weekly visits to the pool, you became friends. You may not have had a friend like this for years.'

Nancy blinked once.

Jessie walked over to the shelf. Alongside the Virgin Mary was an assortment of things quite out of place with their surroundings. A silver photo frame; in it a young, dark-haired little girl smiled back mischievously. Charlotte, before she lost herself in becoming Nancy and Nancy lost herself in becoming no one.

'Your sister thinks you're a poltergeist,' said Jessie, picking up a set of keys. 'They never did lock you out, did they?'

Nancy closed her eyes for a while.

'You went back to tell Charlotte that you were coming home because you'd met someone. You had found happiness at last. But Charlotte didn't believe you; you'd promised to come home before, and you'd reneged every time. She only said those hurtful things to you to protect herself. She would never admit how much she needed you back. She believes you didn't return because of what she said to you that night. I think the real reason you never came back was because something went horribly wrong at Marshall Street Baths . . .'

Nancy blinked once.

'Jonny Romano drowned. A mob chased your friend into the boiler room. He protested his innocence and, under siege, he told them who he really was: Malcolm Hoare. Your nemesis. You heard his plea and, in a fit of rage, you killed him.'

Nancy blinked twice.

Jessie felt the Virgin Mary's gaze shift.

Nancy blinked twice again, slowly moving her head from side to side as a tear escaped over her sagging eyelid and ran down her heavy cheek.

'You planned it then? You lured him down there?'

Nancy continued to protest silently. Jessie looked to Burrows for guidance.

'But you knew who he was?' Burrows asked.

Nancy blinked once.

'Did he tell you of his own free will?'

Nancy fixed her sights on Burrows and blinked again.

'Did he go down to the basement with you, of his own free will?' he asked.

Nancy blinked once. Another tear rinsed another clean track over her soiled cheek.

Jessie was still frowning. Why would Malcolm Hoare go into the derelict basement? Why would she . . . ? Burrows placed the newspaper cutting into Jessie's hand. His fingers closed over hers, his thumb stroking the back of her hand. It was a soft, gentle motion. It wasn't a friendly gesture. It was a romantic gesture.

'Do you see?' he said quietly.

Jessie looked from Burrows to the newspaper cutting. Malcolm and Nancy standing at the back, laughing, half-hidden behind their hands — not just looking away from the camera, but looking at each other. Friend or foe? Or lover?

One glaring fact had troubled Jessie from the beginning: Malcolm Hoare had not committed a single crime since he'd walked out of court a free man. Peter Boateng had read Hoare's file looking for the sign of the devil, but all he had found was another disappointed man. Had the breakdown of a little girl shown

Malcolm the error of his ways? Did he believe he'd been given a chance to change? Had her ruin been his redemption?

'You loved him?'

Nancy blinked once. She had found something in that redeemed man to love.

'And he loved you too?'

Nancy didn't move. The respirator continued to suck in air with a sharp, regular hiss. Finally, she closed her eyes. They stayed closed for a full minute. When they opened again, Jessie saw in them the full horror of regret. If Nancy's ruin had been Malcolm Hoare's redemption, then his redemption had been her ruin. She was trapped here, grotesquely overweight, because she had loved him.

'What did you think re-enacting your kidnapping was going to do? Purge yourselves?' asked Jessie.

Nancy hung her head.

Jessie could see the whole tragedy unfurl.

. . . They chose the date specifically. February 23rd, the day on which all their misery hinged. Nancy needed to atone for loving the man she believed had ripped her family apart. He needed to purge himself of the sins he'd committed against the woman he now loved. They saw it as an act of cleansing. A baptism of sorts. Mad? Possibly. But they were desperate to be free. Delivered. He would suffer as she had suffered, and together they would be reborn. Innocent. Able to love without regret. To live. To forgive. Nancy knew about the derelict basement, she worked in the building. She was able to locate the keys, find the chains. The ash-pit would be the well. The steel girder, the beam. They said prayers. They kissed. She bound his feet, chained him up and lowered him into the pit so his toes barely touched the ground. She promised to return once a day to give him food and water, as he had done for her as a ten-year-old. But something went horribly wrong at Marshall Street Baths that day . . .

'You left him in the boiler room, entirely unaware of the other tragedy that was taking place upstairs?'
Nancy blinked once.
Jessie knew the rest.

Jonny Romano drowned in an epileptic fit brought on by ingesting his father's ill-gotten drugs. Mr Romano, at that point believing Peter Boateng's story about an evil drug pusher, immediately began searching the baths and asking everyone if they'd seen the man Peter described. He had recorded their answers in his book: *Fat Lady, too upset to talk*. Mr Romano hadn't found Malcolm, nor had he found Ian. The drug dealer was no more than he'd ever been: a figment of the imagination.

'They locked the doors of the baths while the investigation into Jonny's death was underway?'

Nancy blinked once.

'You were part of the vigil outside?'

Nancy blinked once.

She must have stood in the rain for three days and three nights. Knowing Malcolm was tied up inside, but too ashamed to tell anyone. It wouldn't have killed him. Unless . . .

Friend or foe? Goodwill or trap?

'Did you know about the flooding?'

Nancy blinked twice, again and again, the tears seeping out of her. Jessie believed her. Nancy would have been frantic but paralysed. Desperate but embarrassed. She could not have known about the rats and what they'd do to Malcolm as the water rose inch by inch, filling the empty pit while the man she loved twisted and turned. She couldn't have known about the sewage pipes backing up with the rainwater and drawing into the disused boiler room all that filthy effluent. Neither of them could have known that an act of salvation would end in a slow and vile death that neither could escape from. Nancy had saved Malcolm once in court, again when they'd met in Marshall Street Baths, but she couldn't save him a third time. She'd tied him up, she'd left him there. It didn't matter to her that he had been a willing participant. As far as Nancy was concerned, she had his blood on her hands.

'Murder requires intent to kill, Nancy. You didn't murder him.'

She continued to weep.

'There was no malice aforethought; you couldn't have foreseen the events that led to his drowning. It wouldn't even hold up as manslaughter.'

That wasn't necessarily true, Jessie knew. It was Nancy's word against a dead man's. But Nancy was dying, and even the most cold-hearted killers repent to some degree at the end. God may not be all-seeing, but death was.

'That makes it accidental,' continued Jessie. 'A tragic accident,' she said softly.

Nancy's teeth trembled against the plastic tube.

He drowned. It was an accident.

'He drowned,' said Jessie. 'It was an accident.'

The paramedic slipped a needle into the back of Nancy's hand and taped it there. Saline solution and a mild sedative. He feared she was going into shock. Jessie stared out of the window while he worked. She'd sent Burrows off to fetch Charlotte with instructions to tell her everything they knew, including the truth about the nanny and Mr Scott-Somers. It would be up to Charlotte to decide what she wanted Nancy to know. There wasn't a lot of time. Nancy wasn't leaving that chair alive. Jessie didn't want her to die confused, angry or scared. The little girl hadn't had a lot of peace in her life, she deserved a peaceful passing. But Nancy seemed more distressed than before. She was agitated and pulling at the tube. Then she began to cough uncontrollably.

'I think she wants the tube to come out,' said the paramedic. 'She wants to talk.'

Jessie returned to her side. 'Can you put a mask on her?'

'I can, but I don't know how long her lungs will be able to take the pressure.

Even with the extra oxygen.'

'How long?'

He shrugged. 'Hours.'

Jessie turned to the enormous woman, enveloped in her own self-loathing. 'Do you understand what he is saying, Nancy?'

Nancy blinked once.

Jessie hoped Burrows would hurry.

The tube came out and Nancy began to talk. Syllable by syllable. Word by word. It was arduous and painful to watch as she struggled to get the words out and keep death and her tears at bay. 'He . . . Thin . . . ks . . . I . . . A . . . ban . . . don . . . ed . . . him.'

'No, Nancy,' said Jessie, replacing the mask on her pale, pasty face. 'He knows you didn't abandon him.'

Nancy's face creased in pain.

'I promise you.'

Nancy shook her head a fraction.

'Yes, I can. The sewage system requires only a centimetre of rain to fall before it begins to back up. The boiler room is two floors underground. It started raining at two thirty on the afternoon of 23rd February — I know because I checked with the Met Office. It was torrential for the first hour or so, then rained steadily on

503

and off for three days. You'd know that because you were standing in it. But the first centimetre fell within the first four to six hours. You left the building at twenty to four, according to Mr Romano's meticulous notes. Malcolm wasn't expecting you back for twenty-four hours and, Nancy, he would have drowned long before that. It wasn't a trap. You were his friend. He knew that.'

The radio on the paramedic's bike crackled loudly. An indecipherable message skimmed over the airwaves. The nurse hung up the drip and ran out to answer a distress call. Jessie stayed in the house, to answer another.

'A good friend, too, I think.' Jessie crouched down next to Nancy. When she spoke again it was in a quieter voice. 'Don Firth says the baths are haunted. He says that someone didn't like to be disturbed down in the basement. Someone strong enough to stop people going down there, strong enough to stop developers signing their name on the dotted line, strong enough maybe to shield the person who would be blamed if his body were ever discovered.'

Nancy pointed at Jessie.

'We found him by accident. Exactly

where you had left him, in the dry pit at the back of the boiler room, the one that wasn't under the flood water, the one with the heavy lid that you somehow managed to shift.'

Jessie knew also that Nancy had tried to resuscitate him, because she'd seen the bruises, but she figured those details were unnecessary.

The paramedic returned. 'False alarm,' he said. 'Radio's playing up.'

Jessie winked at Nancy, then looked up. 'Your sister is here. Can I let her come in?'

Nancy pulled the mask away and smiled at last. The paramedic pointed to the drip. 'The sedative is working,' he murmured. Jessie didn't think it was the sedative. She had seen that same look in the eyes of a girl who died under a train. *I'm okay. I don't hurt any more.* Death's approach brought with it the promise of imminent peace. It was nearly over. Just one more thing.

Jessie watched Charlotte with admiration. She was sober, for a start. She didn't balk at the filth surrounding her sister, or her sister's appearance. She'd brought candles. The first thing she did was light them all, scooping up the rubbish as she went. When she was finished, she brushed Nancy's hair. Jessie saw the blond roots coming through behind the darker, dyed hair. Like Malcolm, thought Jessie, Nancy's true colour was at last beginning to show through. When Charlotte was finished she curled up at Nancy's feet like a miniature piece of porcelain at the base of the Sphinx. She reached up and took Nancy's hand. Finally she started to talk. Jessie didn't need to hear the story retold. She knew it by heart. She went out on to the street inhaling the cold air with relief. What she'd said to Nancy was true: Don did think the baths were haunted, and he wasn't alone. And it was also true that the water would have risen too fast for Malcolm to expect a rescue. If he needed forgiveness, it was more likely from himself, not Nancy. Jessie stared back at the crumbling façade and wondered whether for fourteen years Malcolm Hoare had been doing what everyone else had failed to do: protect Nancy.

In her pocket the phone vibrated.

'We've found Mr Romano,' said the breathless voice of the young officer from Lisson Grove Estate.

'Where is he?' she asked.

'On the roof of his building. He's threatening to jump.'

'Is he serious?'

Forty-three 999 calls from an estate where the police were seen as the enemy said he was. She told Burrows to stay, and ran for the car.

With sirens blazing, Jessie weaved perilously in and out of traffic, her faith in the flashing blue lights absolute. She pulled up alongside a growing crowd of spectators. People had come to see the Italian fall. Jessie alerted the local officer to her presence. He looked terrified.

'If he jumps, it'll be all my fault —'

'Don't worry, he'll be talked down. The unit is trained for this.'

The young officer looked forlornly at Jessie.

'What?'

'The unit are four hours away.'

'So who's that guy?' asked Jessie, nodding in the direction of the man entering the maintenance door to the building.

'PC Jack Shayer, but he has a nickname . . .'

'I'm afraid to ask.'

'Jumping Jack. You want them down

quick, call for Jumping Jack, he has them down in a —'

'Flash.'

'You get my drift.'

'If that's you being subtle, I'd hate to see you being indiscreet,' said Jessie, starting to run.

The officer ran alongside her, flat-footed and panting. 'Please, DI Driver, I don't want Mr Romano's death on my conscience. That sort of thing can ruin a person's life.'

This was something Jessie knew. 'Don't worry. I can handle him.'

'He's been shouting and screaming at someone like he was down the allotment.'

Jessie reached the staircase. Father Forrester was waiting for her, Romano's notebooks cradled in his arms.

'Be careful up there. The man may not know his own strength.'

'Have you read them?' she shouted, taking two steps at a time.

'All of them,' the priest called back.

'And you think Mr Romano is hearing voices?'

'Yes. And right now, they're telling him to jump.'

Jessie stopped for a second. She looked back at the beat officer. 'Clear this area —

just in case this doesn't work.'

Jessie caught Jumping Jack Flash at the roof door. He would not hear of allowing her out there in his place, but told her that she could accompany him in his rescue mission. Jessie couldn't fault his enthusiasm for his job. She followed him out on to the flat asphalt roof, and listened as he quietly called Romano's name. Mr Romano didn't respond. He didn't even turn round when they approached him.

'Mr Romano, whatever the problem is, jumping isn't the solution,' said Jumping Jack Flash, at which point Jessie decided she too might jump. So she took over.

'Mr . . . Doyle,' she said calmly. 'We've been looking for you for some time.'

'Who?' exclaimed the officer.

Mr Romano slowly turned round. His naturally olive skin had paled to a ghoulish white. He obviously hadn't eaten or slept for several days. His clothes hung loosely off him, dirty and crumpled; his dark wavy hair hung in greasy tendrils over his shirt collar; his face was gaunt and skeletal, his eyes dusted with a dark shadow that traced the edge of his eye sockets. He looked as though he was already dead. Jumping Jack stepped back. Mr Romano seemed a man possessed. Such was the transformation that for a second Jessie forgot that Doyle had never existed, as she looked into the eyes of the man that the children had described. The bogey man. Boo Radley. The evil drug dealer who had killed their golden boy.

'I'm a very bad man,' said Mr Romano.

'Why have you come back, Mr Doyle?'

'I never went away. You just couldn't see me. Poor Romano, in front of his very eyes and he never knew. They're so stupid, the Italians. All that macho crap.'

It was only the mention of his nationality that made Jessie realise even Mr Romano's accent had gone. 'He said he saw you.'

The man who looked like Ian Doyle's Identikit smiled ghoulishly and tapped his head. 'But he could never stop me.'

'Mrs Romano — did she try to stop you?'

Mr Romano trembled at the sound of his wife's name.

'She knew.'

'What did she know?'

'Fuck off, bitch!'

'Mr Romano —' warned the gallant officer before Jessie had a chance to shut him up.

'I'M NOT MR ROMANO!' he shouted,

lunging at the officer and sending him crashing to the floor. 'Mr Romano wouldn't do that! He wouldn't do that! He loved his son.'

Jessie grabbed the Italian by the arm as he pulled it back to launch another blow at the snivelling policeman. She forced him into a half-nelson, but he was stronger than he looked and threw her off. Only a low wall now separated her from the bone-shattering concrete eighty feet below. As the suicide specialist got up on all fours and shouted for help, Mr Romano turned and kicked him hard in the belly.

'Squealing pig!'

As he lined up a second kick at the man's kidneys, Jessie propelled herself off the ground and began to run in his direction. Mr Romano glanced at the moving object and tried to redirect the force of his kick, but he was caught off-balance. Jessie threw herself at him with all her weight, landing on top of him with such force that his head seemed to bounce off the asphalt. The fire-exit door opened and Father Forrester and Sister Beatrice emerged, each holding a cross. Jessie was so startled that she took her eyes off Romano. He didn't need a second chance. He grabbed her round the neck and forced her back. Hard.

As he pushed her down, he got to his knees, then stood up. He now had both hands around Jessie's neck. She could feel the cartilage in her oesophagus cracking.

'Our Father, who art in Heaven . . . give us this day our daily bread. And forgive us our trespasses, as we forgive those who trespass against us. And lead us not into temptation . . .'

Jessie was beginning to choke and black shadows were appearing on her peripheral vision.

Another voice joined in, mingling with the others. Her head was swimming. 'O God, forasmuch as without thee we are not able to please thee, mercifully grant that thy Holy Spirit may in all things direct and rule our hearts; through Jesus Christ our Lord . . . Amen.'

She thought she felt something wet and warm fall on her head. Stop fucking praying and do something, she cried out silently as she pulled in vain at Mr Romano's strong fingers. She was weakening fast.

Jessie hit the ground before she realised the hands she'd been struggling against had released her. When she looked up, all she saw was Mr Romano running for the edge of the roof. He leapt high over the small wall and vanished into thin air. Father Forrester and Sister Beatrice ran to the edge and looked down.

It took Jessie's lungs a few moments to realise that they had air in them again. She drew in painful, heaving gasps as her system fought to absorb the oxygen, then staggered to her feet and stumbled forward. Father Forrester held his arm out for her. Leaning heavily on him, she peered over the wall. Beneath her a ring of firemen stood on the tarmac playing area. Faded green, white and red lines crisscrossed one another, forming geometric shapes beneath their feet. Like kindergarten children preparing themselves for a game of ring-a-ring-of-roses, their arms were stretched out to one another. They were holding a thick, dark grey blanket, in the middle of which lay Mr Romano, curled up like a baby.

They sat in a nearby café and ordered tea. Jessie sipped the hot drink and felt her bruised throat struggle with each swallow. It felt like the first symptoms of flu. She touched her neck gingerly with her fingertips. She now had plasters dotted all over her forearms, a face that looked like she'd stepped too close to a seventies sun-lamp, and now the mark of Mr Romano's fingers embedded in her neck. And she'd still not had time to get a proper haircut.

'I suspected he was hearing voices, but it didn't occur to me it was Doyle's voice he heard. That was brilliant deduction on your part. How did you work it out?' asked Father Forrester.

'Inspiration. Notebooks,' said Jessie with difficulty. 'Writing was,' she swallowed, 'different.'

'Inspiration or divine intervention?' said the ever-smiling Sister Beatrice.

Jessie shook her head.

'It would have taken a cataclysmic event to split his personality like that,' said Father Forrester.

He was right. Killing his son had not caused Mr Romano's personality to split, it was killing his wife that brought about the seismic shift. Doyle had taken the blame for the first crime, so Doyle could take the blame for the second. Once again Mr Romano's guilt got buried and Doyle became the guilty one. And as the blunt object came down on Mrs Romano's head, Mr Romano became Ian Doyle.

The nun continued: 'His actions have made him especially susceptible to demonic attacks.'

Jessie shook her head again, remembering the prayers and the sprinkled water. 'You thought . . . exorcism would . . . cure him?' she croaked.

Sister Beatrice chuckled. 'Good heavens, no. Your Mr Romano is as mad as a fish. We didn't think a person of restricted growth and an arthritically riddled old man made up much of an opponent. He certainly had you in a good grip, though. So we decided we'd put on a little performance. The "Holy water" you might have felt was Father Forrester's tea. It did the trick — he let go.'

'So convincing, he . . .' Jessie made a diving motion.

'Now, perhaps that was divine intervention,' said the nun.

Jessie frowned. 'That he . . . ?' She repeated the diving motion.

'No, that there were eight well-built firemen ready to catch him.'

Jessie's phone rang. It was the hospital doctor attending the unconscious Mr Romano. He'd come round with no apparent memory of his leap of death, his assault on a police officer, or that he'd answered to the name of Ian Doyle. Mr Romano had returned, the injured man searching for justice for his dead son. It was Doyle's turn to sleep, until a doctor with the right qualifications could entreat him to reappear.

Jessie's phone rang again. She clutched her throat, shook her head and passed it to Father Forrester. She couldn't talk any more. It was Burrows. Nancy was asking for a priest. A priest answered the call.

Nancy died a few moments before sunrise on what would turn out to be a glorious day. Charlotte was with her, Father Forrester blessed her and Dr Turnball was summoned to ensure that she did not suffer. Peace had come to her at last. Jessie walked Charlotte back to the car.

'It was beautiful really,' said Charlotte. 'Thank you for finding her.'

Jessie nodded, accepting the thanks.

'She was lucid, almost up to the end,' said Charlotte. 'I can't believe I thought she was a poltergeist.' She looked seriously at Jessie. 'She'll cross over now, won't she? Father Forrester granted her absolution . . .'

Jessie squeezed her arm. She still couldn't answer questions like that.

'She was talking to Malcolm at the end,

as if he was right there. She said she'd always forgiven him, that she wanted him to come with her. She even thanked him for protecting her, for keeping her secret — I don't know where she would have got an idea like that.'

Jessie said nothing. People were getting used to her silence.

'Like I said, she was confused by then. Still, she asked Father Forrester to forgive him too.' She stopped walking. 'Do you think that's the key to all relationships — forgiveness?'

Jessie looked back at Charlotte, her throat tightening. She nodded.

'Do you think I can forgive my mother for leaving me?'

Jessie blinked once.

Epilogue

When Jessie could speak again, she went to visit Don in hospital. He was tucking into breakfast and talking animatedly to a man in a dressing gown when Jessie walked into the busy ward. Don had colour in his cheeks, he'd put on weight and he was smiling. He waved at Jessie and introduced her to his new friend. She stayed long enough to assure herself that in his heart Don was strong and in his mind, he was well. On leaving, she pulled the nurse to one side and asked him what Don's new medication was.

'Medication?' he repeated, shaking his head. 'He isn't on any. He's been right as rain for a few days now and we've seen no reason to put him back on. The symptoms of stress and exhaustion often mimic mental illness. He probably just needed a good rest, some regular feeding, and a change of scene.'

'Probably,' repeated Jessie, looking back at Don. A free man.

He smiled at her.

She smiled back.

In the mortuary Jessie was handed the results of the routine autopsy. She glanced down at the death certificate. At 05.58 Dr Turnball had pronounced Ann Eugenie Valeria Rose Scott-Somers dead, of natural causes. She read the name again.

'There's been a mistake,' she said to the man at the desk. 'She wasn't called Ann. Her name was Nancy.'

'Checked it off the birth certificate myself,' said the clerk. 'She might have been called Nancy, but she was christened Ann, so she dies Ann. They'll probably put Nancy on the gravestone in inverted commas — that's what they do with nicknames or abbreviations. I assure you, there has been no mistake.'

Jessie set off in the direction of the station. It was another blissful day, crisp blue sky and bright sunshine that dazzled her eyes every time she stepped out of the shadow of a building. She wasn't sure what to think any more. Was there a benevolent old man sitting on a throne somewhere above us? She didn't think so. Was there something in the energy of the individual, some forcefield that a sensitive person is able to read and feel? Possibly. Could that forcefield remain after our death? Perhaps.

Her walk took her to the end of Dufour's Place. She looked left and saw the cul-de-sac that led to the entrance of the grand old building. The developers were circling, planning consent was imminent, soon it would make way for modern housing, cafés and offices, holding within them a secret. A huge swimming pool consisting of 286 hand-laid Italian marble tiles that hadn't leaked a drop of water since the day it was built. Jessie walked the length of the truncated street. Parked at the end of the road was a car displaying a disabled sticker; on the back seat was a well-worn brown trilby. Jessie glanced sideways; the door to the baths was open.

The miniature nun leant on the back of Mary's chair. They both waved at Jessie as she entered the foyer. Sunshine was streaming through the high windows. The Art Deco tiles gleamed.

'Looks better now that it's been cleansed, doesn't it?' said Mary.

Jessie chose to deliberately misunderstand her. 'The windows certainly look better.'

'My Lord, you're a stubborn one,' said Mary.

'We're on a PR exercise,' said Sister Beatrice. 'The developers don't want future investors thinking this place is haunted. They've got Father Forrester down there in full regalia. Still, the place probably needed a blessing — right, Mary? Turns out it was built on the site of a workhouse, so perhaps it wasn't your Malcolm Hoare causing all the trouble, after all.'

'I couldn't say,' said Jessie.

'Rather like the Bermuda Triangle, though on a far smaller scale.'

Jessie wasn't sure she'd heard right. 'Bermuda Triangle?'

'I don't think the detective is ready for that story, Beatrice.'

'Right now I'm about ready for anything.'

Sister Beatrice took a deep breath. 'That area of the ocean covers the old slave trade route between West Africa and America. At first only the weak ones were thrown overboard, but when the market became saturated entire shiploads of Africans were dumped into the sea. Chained up. Alive.'

Jessie recoiled in horror. The nun continued.

'The ship owners could claim more in insurance per head than live slaves would fetch on the open market. They died violently in their multitudes, after great suffering.'

Mary joined the discussion: 'Most churches are built on places of human sacrifice to counterbalance the negative energy created by the displaced souls.'

'But you can't build a church on water,' offered Jessie.

'Exactly. All that negativity had nowhere to go.'

'And you think that's why all those planes and boats disappeared in the Bermuda Triangle?'

Mary and Beatice nodded. 'Until it was exorcised, yes.'

'By Father Forrester?'

'A man very like him, but more psychic.'

'Father Forrester isn't psychic?'

'He's pretty sensitive, actually,' said Mary. 'But not an actual psychic.'

'He's always looking over my left shoulder,' said Jessie, 'as if he can see someone.'

Mary and Beatrice laughed. 'That's just a sleepy eye. Very off-putting, I know.'

Jessie pretended to laugh with them. She couldn't explain why, but she felt a tinge of disappointment inside. Mary reached up for Jessie's hand. 'I understand your resistance to all of this. But, you know, there are many people who appreciate what you do for them. This is your calling, you do it well.'

Jessie met Mary's eyes. 'Her name was Ann,' she blurted out unexpectedly.

They stood in silence for a long moment. Then Mary nodded, let go of Jessie's hand and turned the chair to the door. 'We ought to be going.' The heat on Jessie's palm slowly dissipated.

'Tell me,' Jessie called after her.

The wheelchair stopped. 'Tell you what?'

'Whatever's on your mind.'

Slowly the chair rotated. 'Jessie, the messages sent from the other side aren't always the ones we want to hear. Because of that they claim not to have been heard. This causes distress on either side.'

'Please.'

Mary studied Jessie. Jessie held her breath. 'Send the letter.'

'What?'

'She wants you to send the letter.'

'What?' Jessie said again. 'Who does? I don't know what you're talking about.'

'Remember what I said, Jessie.'

Jessie marched away from the baths crossly. They lured you in, that was the trouble. They made you want to believe. Burrows was right all along. Belief demanded such an enormous leap of faith because a rational mind would see the gaping holes in any religion. What was it that she wanted, what had she been expecting? Jessie stopped walking. She knew what. A message in a bottle. A message from the big blue. From her mother. She wanted a hand to stroke her forehead, a voice telling her it was all going to be all right. That she was doing okay. She always thought she'd been striving for her brothers' approval; now she wondered if it was in fact her dead mother's approval she'd been striving for.

She found a step and sat on it. Jessie was exhausted. Utterly exhausted, and the day was just beginning.

Jessie ended up walking home. She didn't have the energy to go to work. She didn't have the energy to face Mark's grief, fight over the office, or do the paperwork on the Marshall Street Baths case. She didn't have the energy to be brave about

P.J. She rounded the corner to her street, trudged along the familiar pavement and inserted the key in the entrance. She checked her mail. There was a postcard of a gnome. She smiled as, turning it over, she recognised Jones' writing. Father Forrester had sent him on retreat in Wales. *No beer!* said the postcard. *Send supplies!* Jessie put the postcard in her pocket. Everyone wrote letters. She wasn't falling for that old trick. The corrosive power of suggestion.

Someone knocked on the door. There was a woman standing the other side of the mottled glass. Jessie pulled it open. 'Bernie.' She was stunned to see the woman standing in front of her. P. J. Dean's long-term housekeeper and friend had never liked Jessie, especially after she'd forced out some painful home truths.

'P.J. doesn't know I'm here, I'd like to make this quick.' She reached into her pocket and held out a set of keys. 'These are for you. It's over there —'

Jessie stepped out into the raised porch. Parked a little way off to her left was a pink Triumph Bonneville.

'I don't believe it,' said Jessie.

'Believe it — P.J. bought it for you.'

'I was only joking about the bike. Pink Bonnies don't exist. They only come in one colour — burgundy. I thought he knew it was a joke.'

'He had it custom made. It's been sitting at home for days. P.J. along with it.'

Jessie knew that wasn't true.

Bernie glared at her. 'When are you going to learn that you can't believe what you see in the paper? That photo was taken ages ago. Look, I'm not going to pretend I like this, but I can't watch him be so miserable. I'll do whatever it takes if it means he'll be happy again.'

Jessie started to say something but Bernie stopped her.

'I'm not doing this for you. Put him out of his misery, either way.'

'This hasn't been that easy for me, you know.'

'But I don't care about you.' Bernie turned to leave.

'Can I give you a lift home?' said Jessie.

'No thanks, my son is with me.' Jessie noticed the car next to the bike. A tall young man emerged on to the street. Jessie smiled at him; he waved back. The family resemblance was strong.

'He looks well,' said Jessie.

Bernie didn't reply. Halfway back to the waiting car, she turned. 'P.J. could do with a holiday. Somewhere hot. Somewhere he can relax and be anonymous for a week. He has a good friend with a house in Barbados. It's empty at the moment. There's a direct flight leaving this afternoon. The housekeeper has the keys.'

Jessie nodded.

'Goodbye, Detective.'

'Bernie —'

She held up her hand. 'It's wasted on me. Save it for P.J.'

Jessie ran back up the stairs and into her flat.

'Have you gone mad and bought a new bike?' asked Bill.

'Where the hell is my spare helmet? I left my other one at work.'

Jessie picked up the phone and dialled a number.

'Driver, why aren't you at work?'

'DCI Moore,' said Jessie, 'I was wondering if I could have the day off? I'll be in tomorrow.'

'No you won't.'

'What?'

'You are long overdue some time off. Take it — you need it.'

Jessie began to feel nervous. 'Forget it, I'll come in now.'

'I insist, Driver.'

'If I'm being squeezed —'

'It's nothing like that. You need a holiday. That's what I wanted to see you about. You need to let yourself heal — you've only just started talking again. I've had words with Mark and I think there'll be a considerable improvement when you return. His mother took a long time to die, Jessie. He's been coping with a lot.'

'What about the Klein case?'

'Powell has been charged — unlawful sex; Sarah Klein is out on bail; Anna Maria is under constant supervision — she's pregnant.'

To Jessie, this was the saddest news of all. 'You know what, I think you're right, guv. I do need a holiday.'

'Good. Go somewhere hot, where you can relax — that's an order from above.'

Jessie put down the phone and turned to her brother.

'I'll help you pack.'

'I can't be bothered to pack. I'm just going to grab my toothbrush and my passport.'

Jessie pulled open the dressing-table drawer, but her passport was not in its usual place. She searched through her backpack, but it wasn't there either.

'Damn.'

'Perhaps you took it to work?' offered Bill.

'No. Never.'

Jessie started pulling her bedside table drawers open.

'Shit, I can't believe this is happening! For once I'm attempting to do spontaneity and spontaneity is laughing in my face.'

'Try the bookshelves, I'll look in the sitting room. Don't worry, we'll find it. If not, you can borrow mine.'

'That isn't even remotely funny.'

'The picture was taken a long time ago, and with your hair like that —'

Jessie held up two fingers. She went through every drawer in her room. Her passport had gone. She stood in the middle of the disarray and looked around the room, thinking hard. Her focus kept returning to the same object: her mother's jewellery box. It was sitting on a bookshelf, staring down at her. She pulled a chair across the room and climbed on it to reach the inlaid wooden box. Then she sat on the bed and slowly lifted the lid. Her passport lay neatly in the top compartment, next to the one item of jewellery she kept in there: her mother's engagement ring. She must have put her passport in there for safekeeping, though she couldn't remember doing so.

As she lifted out the small red booklet, she saw the white envelope underneath. Her heart contracted. *I'm okay,* said a voice. *I don't hurt any more.* The girl's name was Harriet and she had jumped in front of a train. Jessie had heeded a dying girl's wish, she had not handed over the letter. Instead she had thrust it deep inside her trouser pocket and, when she'd arrived home drunk that evening after dinner with Bill, she must have put it away in her mother's jewellery box — though, again, she couldn't remember doing so.

Jessie picked the envelope up and turned it over in her hands. The writing was spindly and uneven, but it was bold in sentiment. The dead girl's letter was addressed to God.

Jessie left the house with her passport, her toothbrush, a set of keys to a pink motorbike and a letter. When she reached Heathrow, she had one other thing with her.

'Hang on a second,' said Jessie, stopping at the post box before the final departure gate. 'I have to post a letter.'

'Something important?' asked P.J.

'Very.' Jessie watched the little white envelope flutter down inside the Perspex box and land with a thousand other good wishes and final thoughts.

She re-joined P.J. He took her hand and did not let go until they were belted into their seats and handed a glass of champagne. She drank two in quick succession and was already feeling the effects when minutes later the engines roared and they were pushed into the back of their seats. P.J. took her hand again as the plane rose over London, banked left and broke through the cloud cover that had gathered through the day. The enormity of the sky engulfed her. Limitless. Illogical. Magic.

'What are you thinking about?' asked P.J.

She faced him with a smile. 'I was wondering how a lowlife like you managed to get such good seats at short notice?'

He winked at her. 'One of the perks of the job. I have friends in high places.'

Jessie turned back to the window and looked out at an unforeseeable future.

'You're not alone,' she said, feeling a rush as another plane, on another path, sped off to another destination.

About the Author

Gay Longworth was born in 1970, graduated from university, and trained as an oil trader. Eventually, her love for writing wouldn't be ignored, and she left the job and moved to Cornwall, England, to write. *The Unquiet Dead* is her second novel to be published in the United States, following *Dead Alone*. She is now a full-time writer in London, where she lives with her husband and daughter.

For more information about current and upcoming titles, please call or write, without obligation, to:

Publisher
Thorndike Press
295 Kennedy Memorial Drive
Waterville, ME   04901
Tel. (800) 223-1244

Or visit our Web site at:
www.gale.com/thorndike
www.gale.com/wheeler

OR

Chivers Large Print
published by BBC Audiobooks Ltd
St James House, The Square
Lower Bristol Road
Bath BA2 3SB
England
Tel. +44(0) 800 136919
email: bbcaudiobooks@bbc.co.uk
www.bbcaudiobooks.co.uk

All our Large Print titles are designed for easy reading, and all our books are made to last.